THE
HUNGRY
SEASON

THE HUNGRY SEASON

T. GREENWOOD

KENSINGTON BOOKS
http://www.kensingtonbooks.com

KENSINGTON BOOKS are published by

Kensington Publishing Corp.
119 West 40th Street
New York, NY 10018

All Kensington titles, imprints, and distributed lines are available at special quantity discounts for bulk purchases for sales promotion, premiums, fundraising, educational, or institutional use.

Special book excerpts or customized printings can also be created to fit specific needs. For details, write or phone the office of the Kensington Special Sales Manager: Kensington Publishing Corp., 119 West 40th Street, New York, NY 10018. Attn. Special Sales Department. Phone: 1-800-221-2647.

Kensington and the K logo Reg. U.S. Pat. & TM Off.

ISBN-13: 978-0-7582-2878-9
ISBN-10: 0-7582-2878-3

First Kensington Trade Paperback Printing: February 2010
10 9 8 7 6 5 4 3 2 1

Printed in the United States of America

For my beautiful family

Hunger cannot be ignored . . .
You cannot live without hunger.
Hunger begins your exchange with the world.

—From *Hunger: An Unnatural History*
by **SHARMAN APT RUSSELL**

ACKNOWLEDGMENTS

Thank you first to Beya Thayer, who helped me survive that NaNoWriMo November and get through to the *first* end. To Vas Pournaras, Maria Mechelis, and Alexis Katchuk for helping me get the details right. To Henry Dunow, Peter Senftleben, and everyone at Kensington for their continued and tireless championing of my work. And to my family, who sacrificed so much so that this family's story could be told.

In addition to the books mentioned in my notes, I am indebted to Todd Tucker for his book, *The Great Starvation Experiment,* and to Sam Shepard for his powerful and haunting play, *Fool for Love*.

Lastly, I am tremendously grateful to the Maryland State Arts Council for their financial support of this project.

BEFORE.

Once. Not that long ago, Sam believed that they would always be happy. That they had found the secret, stumbled upon it by accident perhaps. Or maybe they had done something to earn it. Regardless, they had found what had managed to elude everyone else: all those miserable bickering families, the ones they saw and pitied (the couples who love each other but not their children, the ones who love their children but not each other). *Happiness.* They had this. He was full of it, smug with it, bloated and busting at the seams with it. He basked in it, in the cool softness of it, thanked his lucky stars for it. But what he didn't understand (or couldn't, not then) is that everything is precarious. That even the sweetest breezes can change directions, that not even the moon is constant.

Here they are before:

Early summer evening when everything was still possible, Mena was in the kitchen of the rented cottage, washing lettuce from their summer garden. Sam could see her from where he sat in a wooden chair in the yard. The light from the window made a frame around her. She was standing at the sink, running water over the green leaves, her hands working. She caught his eye, smiled. Held his gaze until he blew her a kiss. Through the open screen door, he could smell dinner. Something Greek; there would be olives in a chipped porcelain bowl from the cupboard. Soft cheese. Warm bread. Franny would save the olive pits on a wet paper towel, bury them in the garden with her small fingers, hoping to grow an olive tree by morning.

Finn was down at the water's edge, ankle deep in the lake, his naked chest white in the half-light. He had a red plastic bucket for the polliwogs. He was soundless in this task. Single-minded and intent. In the morning, Sam would go into town and get him a fishbowl. Most of them would die, but one or two might grow legs, eyes bulging. Franny was swinging in the tire swing that hung from the giant maple tree near the edge of the woods. She leaned backward, and her long curls spilled onto the ground. She had also abandoned her clothes in this rare June heat. They were six. It was twilight, and everything was possible.

Sam was thinking, of course, about the words that might capture this. Words were the way that he tethered the world, kept it close. Mena didn't understand this need to articulate a moment, all moments. To convey *moonlight, water, hair kissing the ground*. She didn't understand this inclination, this necessity, to render everything in prose. *Just eat,* she said. But Sam could not just eat. First, he needed to classify: *casseri, calamata, ouso.*

They sat at the rickety picnic table Mena had covered with a batik cloth that smelled of mothballs, of cedar. She lit the tea lights with a pack of matches she pulled from her back pocket. When she bent over to light them, he could see the soft swell of her breasts pushing against the edges of her tank top.

No peeking. She smiled.

Aidani, he thought, skin like wine, contained but threatening to spill.

Olives! she said, and Franny came running. Sam intercepted, picking her up and swinging her around until they were both dizzy.

Daddy, she said. The best word of all.

Finn joined them reluctantly, holding the bucket with both hands, plastic handle and skinny arms straining with the weight of lake water and tadpoles. The water sloshed onto the grass at his feet, and it took all his strength to set the bucket down on the table next to the moussaka.

Mena: *tsk, tsk,* and she lifted the bucket, examining its contents before lowering it gently to the ground. Inside, the tadpoles swam blindly in dark water, bumping into the edges.

They ate. Red tomatoes, purple eggplant, black pepper and lamb. They drank wine; Franny and Finn had their own small glasses, jelly jars, which they clanked together so hard you'd think everything would shatter.

Their voices, tinkling like glass, were the only ones here. It was the beginning of the summer, dusk, and the lake was theirs. They had been coming here, to Gormlaith, every summer since even before the twins were born. This is where Sam grew up. Home. Nestled in the northeastern corner of Vermont, on the opposite side of the earth from where they spent the rest of the year, it was a secret summer place. Undiscovered, for now. Theirs.

After dinner, the wine was gone. Finn had abandoned the polliwogs in favor of fireflies that flickered intermittently, teasing, in the hedges surrounding the house. Mena brought him a glass jar, the lid riddled with nail holes. He caught them easily with his clumsy little hands; they were more sluggish than you would think. Sam remembered this from his own childhood: the easy capture, the thickness of wings and the flickers of light. Finn was like Sam; he understood the need to contain things.

Franny twirled on tippy-toes, her bare feet barely touching the grass, her arms outstretched. Her ribs made a small protective cage around her heart, which Sam imagined he could see beating through her translucent skin, that miraculously transparent flesh of childhood that reveals every pulse and the very movement of blood. She spun and spun and spun and then collapsed on the grass, laughing, examining the twirling sky above her.

Mena sat down next to Sam in the other Adirondack chair,

facing the water. Franny came to her, still naked, but cold now that the sun had set. Mena offered Franny a sip of her hot Greek coffee—*vari glykos,* very sweet—before placing the cup where it wouldn't spill. She pulled Franny into her lap, enclosed her with her arms. Sam watched as Mena's fingers wound in and out of Franny's curls, listened as Mena hummed along with the music that wound *its* fingers through the night. Chet Baker crooned. Bullfrogs croaked and groaned. Crickets complained.

There must be a word for this, he thought. It was on the tip of his tongue. He struggled, but it wouldn't come. A sort of panic buzzed as he reached for it. Without the word, he was almost certain he would lose this. The lid would open, the fireflies escape. The bucket would spill, and the polliwogs would swim through the grass.

Finally, it came. *Storgē,* he remembered. Mena once gave him the Greek words for love. Whispered them each, her breath hot in his ear: *agapē, erōs, philia, storgē.* A gift. *Storgē.* And so, for now, everything was safe.

AFTER.

Mena watches Sam as he considers the winding expanse of road in front of them. He has been driving since New York. He doesn't say so, but he doesn't like it when she drives. When she drove, she could see his jaw muscles flexing, the way they worked and worked, even if he was feigning sleep. And so she stopped offering to take over the wheel. She'd rather look out the window anyway, read or nap. It was Sam's idea to come here.

It's been nearly three hundred miles, and no one has said a word. Finn is in the backseat with headphones on, the music so loud she can hear it, like jingling bells. It can't be good for his ears, but she bites her tongue. She doesn't want to take his music from him; it's one of the few things they haven't confiscated in the last couple of months. She watches him in the rearview mirror; his eyes are vacant. Not even sad anymore, just empty. Next to her, Sam is concentrating on the road. He's been stiff like this, focused, since they left Manhattan. But they're far, far from all that gridlock now. He could relax a little. Theirs is the only car on the road.

They could have gotten here more quickly if they hadn't had to stop in New York, but as soon as Monty found out that they were coming back east (driving back no less), he'd insisted they take this more circuitous route. Mena knew it wasn't a good idea to stop, for a lot of reasons. She worried about New York, about all the places Finn might run. But Monty was per-

sistent, and Sam felt guilty, and so they drove the long way. Luckily the stay was uneventful, in terms of Finn, and Monty put
them up at the Four Seasons (which, Mena had to admit, was a
welcome change after the series of Motel 6's they'd occupied
each night since they left San Diego). That night he took them
all out for dinner at the Union Square Café (also a welcome
change from the Burger Kings and Wendys along the way). All
of this just an effort to coax Sam into spilling his plans for the
next book.

"Don't want to jinx it?" Monty asked when Sam quietly
pushed his duck confit around his plate. "Mum's the word, huh?"

Only Mena knew that Sam was not being evasive or elusive, but that he simply had no plans to reveal. He was under
contract for the next book, and the deadline was just six months
away, but as far as she could tell, Sam hadn't started it. He still
disappeared into his office every day, but Mena knew that while
he might be typing in there, he certainly wasn't writing.

Not that long ago, Sam and Monty would spend hours
over multicourse dinners talking about his fictional characters
as if they were real people. Gossiping like schoolgirls about
people who existed only in Sam's mind. Mena used to love to
listen to them chattering on and on. For twenty years Monty
had been Sam's agent. Twenty years of friendship. You'd think
he'd realize something wasn't right.

"Vermont will be good for you," Monty said, spearing a
bloody chunk of meat with his knife and popping it into his
mouth. "You renting that same place?"

"I bought it," Sam said.

"Bought it?"

Sam nodded.

"How much a place up there cost you? Two, three hundred
bucks?" Monty chuckled.

"Something like that," Sam said. In fact, Sam had spent his

entire advance for this novel on the little cottage, financed the rest.

Monty smiled his big warm smile. "What're *you* gonna do stuck in the woods up there, Finny?"

"Probably lose my fucking mind," Finn said.

"Mouth," Sam said, grimacing.

Finn's arms were crossed over his chest; he hadn't eaten a bite. He was peering across the restaurant, but when Mena followed his gaze, she saw only the empty bar. The doors to the kitchen. She couldn't help but imagine him casing the place, looking for the glowing EXIT signs, plotting his escape. Sam seemed oblivious, his thoughts elsewhere. Mena noticed a vein throbbing at his temple, noticed the gray hairs sprouting there too. She looked down at her salad, the heirloom tomatoes arranged like a painting on her plate.

"You got any neighbors up there?" Monty asked. "Some moose maybe? A few cows?"

Sam poked at his duck.

"Didn't you hear?" Mena asked, laughing just a little too loudly. "McNally finally put it on the map. Since then it's been swarming with tourists. A real hot spot."

Finn snorted.

"It really is beautiful," Mena said, and smiled, suddenly feeling bad for Monty, who was trying so hard. She reached for his hand across the table. "You and Lauren should come up and visit. You *should*. Get out of the city, breathe some fresh air." She tried to imagine Lauren Harrison in her Chanel suits and pointy shoes navigating her way up the winding driveway to the cottage. Mena has always liked Monty (with his boyish enthusiasm and boyish looks and boyish manners), but Lauren has a way of making her feel uncomfortable. She is so polished, she almost shines. The thought of her in that musty cottage was ridiculous.

"Maybe we will." Monty smiled, nodding his head. "See the sights."

In the hotel that night, Mena stayed awake, waiting for something bad to happen. But both Finn and Sam fell asleep as soon as their heads touched the downy pillows, and she watched them until the sun filtered through the butter-colored curtains.

"We're almost here," Mena says, gently touching Sam's leg. He turns to her, startled, his face slowly softening, as if he has been woken from a dream. "Isn't Hudson's just up the road?" she says. The last stop in civilization before the lake.

They pull into the dirt lot in front of the store. Sam turns off the ignition and rolls his head from side to side, stretching. Mena resists the urge to reach over and knead out the crick that she knew would come if he kept driving like that, sitting upright, not using the headrest.

"About time," Finn says, pulling the headphones from his ears and tossing his iPod onto the seat. "I need to take a piss."

Mena feels her chest tighten. "Okay, but come right back. I'm just going in to get some milk. Coffee. I'll come back into town tomorrow for real food."

Finn gets out of the car, stretching his long legs. He has grown four inches since last summer. He's already over six feet tall, and not even seventeen yet. At night, in his sleep, he moans as his bones expand. The sound makes Mena cringe. In Amarillo, he'd been moaning so loudly in the motel room that Sam had gotten up, delirious, convinced that a wounded animal had found its way in.

"Hurry back," Mena says again, this time more reprimand than plea, as Finn disappears around the side of the gas station with the restroom key attached to a large wooden paddle. He rolls his eyes at her, and she winces.

Sam has gotten out of the car too and is battling with the

vending machine, hitting the side of it with his palm, muttering under his breath.

"Need more change?" Mena asks, reaching into her pocket.

"Nah. Forget it," he says.

Mena touches him on the shoulder. She can't stop touching him, even though he barely responds anymore. "Sure?"

He nods and walks back to the car, stretching his arm over his head, cracking his back. She watches as his pants slip a few inches. All of his clothes are too big for him lately. She would have been smart to pick up a few pairs of his favorite khakis at Brooks Brothers before they left California. Once they get to Gormlaith she'll have to do all of their shopping online. She wonders if they can even get Internet access at the lake.

When she comes out of the convenience store with an overpriced gallon of milk, a block of cheddar cheese, a dozen eggs, and a six-pack of beer, Finn is rounding the corner. She adjusts the grocery bag on her hip like a baby, leans into him, and kisses his cheek. She can smell the smoke on his clothes, on his breath, but she doesn't say anything. She is simply grateful that he is still here.

"Ready?" She musters a smile.

"Do I have a choice?" he asks, and gets into the car, plugging up his ears again with music.

It's not the way Finn remembers it. He's even convinced for a
minute that they're fucking with him, that this is some sort
of joke. He looks to his father for the punch line, but he's already disappeared inside the cottage with some of their suitcases.
It's not the same place; it can't be. True, they haven't come here
since he and Franny were twelve or so, but he's not crazy. He
knows this place like his own goddamn dick. For one thing,
the tree in the front yard is way smaller than the one in his
memory. He distinctly remembers his father having to use a
ladder to hang the tire swing on the tree's one thick limb that
jutted out over the front yard. But looking at it now, he's pretty
sure he could just jump up and grab a hold of it if he wanted
to. And the cottage itself seems like a doll's house, like a playhouse. Like something at fucking Disneyland.

He gets out of the car and starts walking down the hill toward the water. It must have rained earlier; the grass is slick.
He almost loses his footing as he makes his way down the hill,
glancing around quickly to make sure nobody saw him almost
wipe out, and then realizes that there's nobody here to see him
anyway.

Butt Fuck Nowhere. That's where he'd told Misty they were
going when she asked. They were making out in the parking
lot at the beach. Misty had gotten a hold of some X, and he
could feel every single inch of his skin. He wanted to lick things.

He wanted his tongue on everything: the leather seats of her father's car, her skin, the sand.

"Will you miss me?" she had asked, twirling her tongue around in his ear.

He'd nodded, touching each of her eyelids with the tip of his tongue, tasting the mascara and tears that were brimming in the corners of her eyes. This made him want to go taste the ocean. He wanted to go to the water and take the whole thing into his mouth, swallow it in big gulps. He wanted everything inside of him: Misty, the ocean, the night.

"I guess," he'd said, smirking. "A little bit."

The lake also looks smaller, a miniature version of what he remembers. Compared to the Pacific, still bodies of water like this are pathetic. He picks up a rock and chucks it into the lake, watches as it disturbs the ridiculous peace of the water's surface. He looks across the lake at the opposite shore. There are a handful of houses, all of them empty still. Beyond that are trees and still more trees. A small mountain jutting up into the hazy sky. What have they done to him? What has he done to deserve this?

Of course he knows exactly what he's done. And when he thinks about that night now, even *he* thinks it was stupid. The trip to Tijuana, and coming back across the border so loaded he could barely walk. They'd gone down there to celebrate Misty getting into Brown. She was a year ahead of him at school, second in her class. She'd gotten into every goddamn school she'd applied to, but Brown was her top choice. And he was an asshole that night, jealous a little, maybe, of Misty getting exactly what she wanted (she always got exactly what she wanted). Jealous of the way she was dancing while every guy at that dirty bar was watching her. He was wasted, but he remembers the flash of her skin, the belly ring, the way her sweaty hair clung to her face and neck. But he shouldn't have left her there alone. God, it *was* stupid.

Where's Misty? his father had asked, shaking him by the shoulders inside the brightly lit cubicle at the border station until he felt almost carsick. *Where's Misty?*

It took six hours before he was sober, six hours before they found her. Her parents were mad as hell; they'd never liked him before and now this. But *Misty* had forgiven him. And wasn't that all that really mattered? Nothing bad had even happened. Everybody was down in TJ that night. Half the kids from their school did the same thing almost every weekend. When Finn left, Misty just found another girl from Country Day. They'd crossed back over the border and went to the beach. A fucking bonfire in Mission Beach. No big deal. It wasn't his fault she didn't go straight home. Later, when he told her what his parents were making him do, she'd apologized to *him*. Said it was her fault that he was getting banished for the whole summer before his senior year. Their last summer together before she went off to college.

Of course he knows that TJ wasn't the last straw. That came afterward. He's never really known when to stop. Even he has to admit that. But still, he is pissed at his father. At his mother. He knows that Misty won't wait for him; why the hell should she? He's got to figure out a way out of here, a way to get back to her. He looks up at the cottage, at the scraggly lawn, at the woods behind the house that, for all he knows, stretch all the way to fucking Canada. Where the hell can he go? He picks up a handful of rocks and hurls them into the quiet water, watching the stones come crashing down like rain.

Sam wrote his first novel when he was twenty-one years old. He can still remember what it felt like the day he sat down to write. He remembers the massive oak monstrosity from Goodwill that served as both his kitchen table and his desk. The blue electric typewriter he'd bought at a pawnshop for five bucks and some change. His father had just died. Sam was living alone with a family of gray mice in an apartment in downtown Burlington, the one above the French bakery. There was a poster of a giant fried egg that the last tenant had left behind, hanging from thumbtacks in a bright yellow kitchen. Every morning he bought a chocolate croissant and a cup of coffee from the pretty redheaded girl who worked in the bakery. It was the winter of his senior year at UVM, and outside the wind coming off Lake Champlain felt like knives. After his father died, he'd stopped going to classes and started to write. He didn't plan on getting famous; he just wanted to bring his father back.

But strangely, as he wrote, it wasn't his father who appeared on the page; all that crazy love and grief and horror conjured, instead, a girl. When she first appeared, he'd been thinking about his father's hands. About the gray work gloves he wore when he was splitting wood. He'd been thinking about the sound of the ax splitting through the thick trunks. He'd been thinking about the way his father would run his hand over the top of his head, leaving a dusty layer of sawdust in his hair. But the words that came out (*pine, autumn, chill*) captured, instead, a girl in a red wool coat standing in a field of fallen leaves. He knew he was meant to be a writer when he left his father and followed her, when she offered him her soft hand and he took it.

What he didn't expect was everything that happened afterward. He didn't expect when he finally showed up to English class again that spring with the manuscript (a cardboard shirt box filled with smudgy onionskin papers) that his professor at the university would give it to his friend's son, Monty Harrison, who had just started up a literary agency in New York, and that three days later Monty would drive all the way up to Burlington in his beat-up Karmann Ghia to tell him that he'd written something brilliant. That this novel would make them both famous. He also didn't expect that Monty, who was only a handful of years older than Sam himself, would proceed to pull off what finally amounted to a series of small miracles: a book contract with a reputable house, a sizable advance, and the one thing that would change everything: a film deal with an independent film producer in Los Angeles who knew a girl who would be perfect to play the lead. She was nineteen, a student at CalArts who came from somewhere in Arizona. *Phoenix, Flagstaff?* No matter, she was Greek, a knockout, and her name was Mena.

Mena. The first time Sam saw Mena was on the film set, inside a crappy warehouse in Studio City. But when he saw her, it was as if she had crawled out of the pages of the book. Mena, with her gypsy hips and oil spill hair. She was wearing a pair of brown motorcycle boots and faded Levi's held up by a belt with a massive pewter Alice in Wonderland buckle. When she offered him her hand, he couldn't stop himself from turning it over and over in his palm, examining it. He had written this skin. This smell of trees. She was his words manifested in lovely skin and hair and breath. And when she leaned into him and said, "Come with me?" he understood that, just as he had pursued the woman in the woods, he would follow Mena anywhere. Within a couple of months, he'd relocated to Los Angeles, leaving Vermont and school and his old life behind.

He watches her now, as she unpacks the groceries, as she blows the dust off the cupboard shelves. Her hair still spills down her back, liquid, but in the last year he has watched as tiny gray hairs sprouted up, asserting themselves with their wiry defiance. He has watched lines etch themselves into the corners of her eyes. He has watched sorrow take its toll on her. Looking at her now no longer fills him with desire but remorse.

"You want the loft again?" she asks. "For your office?"

He nods.

"Why don't you go set it up," she says. "I'll make dinner."

Her eyes are so wide now. She always looks on the verge of tears. At first it made his heart ache; now, it makes him want to retreat. He can barely stand to look at her, at those pleading eyes asking him for something he doesn't have.

He leaves her and goes to the main room. The furniture is covered with tarps. The windows are greasy. There is an upright piano here now, painted bright blue and sitting in the middle of the room like something abandoned. It wasn't here the last time. The dining table is still there, the long wooden expanse of a top and its wobbly legs. They used to put matchbooks under them to keep it still, opting to eat outside most nights. Everything smells like dust. He remembers the way it used to feel to come here, the excitement of uncovering the furniture, the sense of anticipation. He used to love to sweep the dusty floor, tear the cobwebs down, collect handfuls of dead flies from the windowsills. The windows, swollen shut all winter, always seemed to thank him as he lifted their sashes. He remembers the thrill of two tiny sets of footprints leading from the dusty floor all the way to the back door.

He climbs the ladder to the loft. Years ago, he had the blue electric typewriter that he would lug up with him every summer. He still has the typewriter, but has opted now, reluctantly, for a laptop. It was a gift from Mena. After two years, he still resists its streamlined body. Its silent keys. As he climbs up, he misses the old typewriter, both the burden and the sense of possibility. He will miss the rhythmic clickety-clack. He will miss the noises.

It isn't the same. He must have been crazy to think it would be. The faded red velvet chair and small wooden desk are still there, but the view out the window is not as he remembers it. The first time he brought Mena here, she was pregnant with the twins. He remembers her sleeping on the mattress he'd also hauled up here, while he wrote. He remembers the words and the way they felt: *swollen, sunshine, repose.* He remembers the way the light caught on the water through the small round window over the desk. Later, when the twins were small, he would watch them below through the window—the choreography of a mother and her children: *bloody noses, pinched fingers, tiny toads* and *perfect stones.* But now, as he looks through the dirty window at the still water, he only thinks: *lost, gone, was.*

Outside the sun is starting to melt over Franklin Mountain in the distance, like pale fire.

"Where's Finn?" Mena hollers up, and he hears that new panic in her voice that's been creeping in lately. A tremble, a breaking. And the worst part is, he doesn't think there's a damn thing he can do to make it go away.

"He's just down by the water," he says. "Throwing rocks."

Mena wishes she had the ingredients to make a real dinner, but she only has the things she bought at Hudson's and some nonperishables she brought from California. She finds a jar of organic spaghetti sauce and some whole wheat pasta in a box. But she doesn't even have an onion, garlic. The dusty tin of oregano she finds in the cupboard has lost its potency.

She can't see Finn from the kitchen, and this makes her nervous. She feels the same way she did when he and Franny were little. In San Diego, she never let them go outside alone. Not after that string of abductions: little kids snatched right out of their own front yards—the one girl who was abducted when her mother went inside for sunscreen. Mena would bring whatever she was doing outside with her as they played in the sprinkler or in their playhouse: her reading, her knitting, the bills. If she had to go inside for something, they came with her. After the twins were born, the world became dangerous; it seemed that there was always someone waiting, lurking, ready to steal your life out from under you. Mena used to be afraid of how other people might harm her children. She was worried, then, about strangers.

One of the reasons she first loved the lake was because it was the one place where that insidious anxiety would disappear. She, like Sam, had grown up fearless, free. In Flagstaff, she played in the woods alone, took long bike rides without bothering to tell her mother where she was going or when she'd be home. Coming to the lake was like returning to the world of her childhood. At first, the twins were skeptical of this new freedom. Mena remembers the first time Franny took a bike ride by herself, looking back over her shoulder, wary, as she pedaled away from the cottage. And then the furious and joyful way she disappeared down the winding dirt road that led around the lake.

As the water heats in the large pot, Mena goes to the main room where the smudged windows look out over the water. She can see Finn at the shore. He's smoking a cigarette. She doesn't know when he started being so brazen. He probably figures he's got nothing left to lose. In a way, she can understand this. The smoke from his cigarette curls up into the air as the sun sets. She watches him, his slouchy stance, his hair a mop of white blond curls. *Finny. My little boy.* She wants to believe it was a good idea to come here.

When she hears the oil crackling in the pan, she leaves the window and returns to the kitchen. Sam has brought in the box she packed with the spices and staples she knew she would never be able to find here: *Attiki honey, Kalas sea salt, mastiha.* In the morning she will go into town. There's a Shop'n Save in Quimby, but they probably won't have the ingredients she needs: *Vine leaves, filo, anthotiro cheese.* She'll need to order those items. The Athenaeum probably has a computer—there must be someone, somewhere, who can ship her *tarama.* Suddenly she feels disconnected from the entire world. Did she feel this way when they came here before?

She cracks the fistful of pasta in half so that it will fit in the small pot of boiling water. She can't find the colander; she'll need to use the lid to drain the water. She pours the sauce over the pasta and dumps everything into a giant bowl. She feels awful about this dinner. No salad, no *bread.* God, she hopes Sam packed a bottle of wine. Remembering the six-pack of beer from

Hudson's, she goes to the refrigerator and grabs one. It is cold and good.

She clears the long wooden table that separates the kitchen from the living room, grabs four plates from a box and unwraps them from their Bubble Wrap. She circles the table, setting. She digs through another box for four forks, four knives, four spoons. Napkins. Glasses. She arranges the table and then steps back. And then, that choking feeling, the suffocation that comes every single time she forgets. It's been seven months; how can she keep making this same mistake?

She glances quickly up to the loft where Sam is shuffling around and then out the window at Finn, who is making his way back to the cottage, his hands shoved into his pockets, kicking at the ground. She hurries to the table before anyone can see, and pulls the extra setting from the table. She sits down at the vacant place and closes her eyes, imagines Franny and swallows hard, past the terrible swelling in her throat.

"Dinner!" she says, brushing at the tears in her eyes.

Finn says he's not hungry, and he knows this hurts her. He finds himself doing things to hurt her all the time lately. It feels good, and then it feels like shit. He leaves them sitting at the table with not just one, but two empty spaces.

They told him that he could pick whichever bedroom he wanted. This concession was supposed to make up for them dragging his ass all the way across the country for the summer. *Well, thanks,* he thinks. *That makes up for everything.* He thought about taking his parents' room, leaving them with the one that he and Franny used to share, but he knew that this was a cruelty that not even he was capable of. And so he drags his duffel bag into the room at the back of the cottage, the one with the small window and the awful peeling fake wood paneling. The last time they were here, he and Franny had peeled one whole panel off, written their names on the battered wall behind it with a Sharpie.

The last time they were here. God, he was still just a little kid then. Twelve seems so far away now. He remembers that at the beginning of that summer he'd fallen off his bike in Jimmy Goldstein's driveway, and that his knees were raw. Every time he bent them, the scabs cracked open. He hadn't been able to go surfing afterward, because the salt water made his knees feel like they were on fire. He'd been so happy to get to the lake that summer that he ripped off his clothes as soon as they got out of the car, ran down the path to the dock and threw himself into the water. It had stung too, but only from the cold.

In the house in San Diego, in the house they left behind, Franny and Finn each had their own room. Finn's room was painted a midnight blue, one entire wall papered with a topographical map of Southern California. He'd used those little pushpin flags to mark every beach he'd surfed: from Encinitas to Baja. Someday he'd go to Costa Rica, Australia, Brazil. Both bedrooms had a view of the beach, though Finn's was actually a little better. They each had a twin bed. Franny's was unadorned (none of the stuffed animals or frilly pillows you'd expect of a typical teenage girl), but it was always made. Finn's, on the other hand, was a catchall, a chaotic mess of blankets and books and whatever else hadn't fallen to the floor. The sheets on Finn's bed were the same ones he'd had since he was little, patterned with cowboys and Indians, threadbare but so soft they were mildly pornographic. The Patagonia blanket was also time-worn—something one of Finn's father's fans from the Northwest had sent.

Finn's walls at home were riddled with thumbtack holes. He never bothered to try to put up posters in the same spot when he took the old ones down. He was restless in that room, the holes a testament to his inability to settle on anything, not even a picture on the wall. He must have had a thousand CDs, most of them stacked up in teetering piles on his bureau. His musical taste was also fickle. He was the kind of kid who could never name his favorite color, his favorite food, his favorite anything. Franny, on the other hand, was resolute. She had chosen red as her favorite crayon from the time she knew the names of the colors. She'd picked it and stuck with it. It was the same thing with favorite food (sushi), music (Tchaikovsky, Billie Holiday, Coldplay) and old movie stars (Audrey Hepburn and Gregory Peck). When she decided on ballet at six years old, their father had installed a barre along one long wall. Franny's room was an exercise in certainty while Finn's was a wasteland of abandoned interests.

Their mother said that when they were babies, they would start out at opposite ends of their shared crib every night, but by morning they would be nose to toe, like two little slugs curled into each other. When they were little, Finn never woke up without Franny's breath being the first thing he smelled. Before coffee, before bacon, there was always the musty sleepy smell of Franny. Of course, they eventually got too old for that, but sometimes Finn missed the way it felt waking up next to his sister. Sometimes he'd wake up and knock on their shared wall just to make sure she was still there, on the other side. His four quiet taps echoed by four more; she always answered back.

He lifts the heavy moth-eaten quilt off the bare mattress and grabs the new package of sheets that his mother has left on a wicker chair by the window. He rips open the package, which are crisp and unyielding. He makes the bed and curls up inside the covers. He can hear the clanking of glasses and silverware, the distant sound of the radio. Quietly, he reaches for himself, closes his eyes and thinks about Misty. About Heidi Klum. About the girl he saw at the gas station somewhere around Little Rock. Afterward, he's spent and hungry.

"We saved you some." Mena smiles and motions for him to sit at the table with them. "Come sit."

He sits down and shovels the pasta into his mouth without speaking. She's the best cook; even lame old spaghetti tastes amazing. But he doesn't tell her this. He just eats until his stomach feels full and then drinks a glass of milk in one big gulp. He's got a bag of weed hidden inside his tennis shoe, and he wonders if he'll be able to smoke some after they go to bed.

"So here we are," his father says, forcing a smile.

"Yup," Finn says. "Back in Butt Fuck Nowhere, U. S. of A."

"Mouth," his father says.

"Does anybody want dessert?" Mena asks. Her eyes are brimming with tears. "There are still some blood oranges in the cooler."

Later, with the window cracked open, Finn rolls a joint and listens to the sound of the paper crackling, feels the sweet smoke fill his lungs. He closes his eyes, holds his breath. He can barely sleep without dope anymore. He doesn't remember the last time he slept through a whole night without smoking. And even when he does, he almost always wakes up after only a few hours, sweating and panicked.

Tonight when sleep finally comes, he dreams about surfing. He's at the Cove in La Jolla, by himself, about a hundred yards out, just sitting on his board, waiting. He can hear the seals at the Children's Pool, barking. *Hey,* she says. *Here comes a big one.* He looks left and then right, sees Franny paddling out to him. *Ready?* she asks, and then the wave comes.

*T*he dream is always the same: a table. The curvature of a tar-
nished spoon in her hand as Dale sips from a white bowl of
thick soup. There is wine, both red and white, glasses reflecting the light
that emanates from a thick candle dripping wax onto the rough wooden
table. There are faces illuminated by the candlelight, laughter, and
music, scratchy from an old record in the background. He is sitting next
to her (he is always sitting next to her) and the heat of his presence
flickers like the heat of the candle. The soup is the best soup she has
ever tasted. She cannot get enough; she wants to lift the bowl to her
face like a child and drink and drink and drink. There is bread too,
crusty sourdough, creamy butter smoothed across its surface. She dips
the bread into the soup and puts it to her lips. "Is it good?" he asks,
and for the first time she turns away from the feast to look at him. He
is smiling, though his eyebrows are raised, waiting for her answer. She looks
at the other faces, and they are waiting for her approval too. The woman.
The boy. Even the girl, whose face is merely a shadow. A shadow of a
shadow. "Is it good?" he repeats, and covers her free hand with his own.
She feels his warm skin touching hers. She nods and whispers, "Yes."
All of the faces smile. "It's delicious."

Dale Edwards awakens from the dream as she always does,
hot and buzzing. She sits up in bed and squints at her clock. It
is only seven. She can hear her mother in the kitchen, smell
her cooking. Dale's sense of smell is acute, as if she were an animal, able to discern even the subtle nuances of scent. Today

there will be ham steaks pink as babies, fried eggs and frozen crinkled French fries sprinkled with Old Bay seasoning. Since classes let out in May, Dale has awoken to a rotating variety of pungent breakfast aromas, all underscored by the minty scent of her mother's Kools and weak coffee, heightened by the heat of another Phoenix summer with only a swamp cooler to keep them cool. Her skin is constantly, constantly too hot. Dale had registered for eight o'clock classes every day that spring, managing to avoid the inevitable olfactory by-product of her mother's cooking and the skin-prickling heat of that house, escaping into the cold classrooms at school. But now she has nowhere to go in the mornings, and the smells and the heat are like a daily assault.

Dale gets out of bed, rubs her hand across her cheek. The deep slumber that comes from her mother's pilfered sleeping pills inevitably results in a thick crust of saliva trailing from either corner of her mouth to her chin by morning. It is disgusting, she knows, but still. The dream came the first time she took one of the pills, and now she senses that without them she will likely lose the dream, and this is an idea she cannot bear. And besides, without the pills, she is awake all night, her mind racing. Tripping and stumbling over itself in the heat.

She grabs her glasses from her nightstand and vision is restored, making clear all that was hazy. This room, her childhood room, is unchanged in all these years. Pink canopy bed, white painted furniture. Posters of ponies and unicorns and boys who have long since grown into men. She grew up in this room, lived here all through junior college and then left for a while when she got into ASU. She rented a shabby little apartment on campus, but it was too hard. The money, the worry. Her mother needs her. This is the real reason she stays. Because as much as her mother complains (about the extra laundry, the extra groceries, the extra mess), Dale knows that without her, she might finally fall apart.

She keeps telling herself that it's not her responsibility to keep her mother from going off the deep end, that no twenty-four-year-old woman should be strapped with such a burden. That her needs should come first. And lately, she has so many needs. She can feel the want somewhere at the base of her spine, her whole body yearning for something she can't articulate. It's like an itch she can't locate to scratch.

Dale leaves her computer on all night long; she likes the quiet hum and clicks. If she listens closely, there's a certain pattern to them, some sort of electric lullaby at work. And when she isn't able to sleep, the computer is ready and waiting for her. She should be working on the one class she didn't quite finish last semester. She'd talked her professor into giving her an Incomplete so that she could finish the paper on Mary Shelley's *Frankenstein*. She'd started but quickly became sidetracked. This was a problem she knew she had, and not just at school. She was going into her senior year and all she could think about was her senior thesis. It was the only thing that got her butt out of bed and to school every morning last semester. God, last semester, when everything slowed to a sort of puddly stillness. Thirteen weeks had seemed like thirteen years. Sometimes she thinks she's like a record playing at the wrong speed: first too slow and then too fast. But she knew then and she knows now that she has to finish her junior year in order to get to her senior year, and then she'll be free to work on the only project she really cares about. She knows she should just finish the stupid *Frankenstein* paper and e-mail it off to her professor. Take the D she knows it deserves. But she doesn't care about the Romantics. She only cares about him.

So instead of writing, she searches eBay endlessly for artifacts. The key words are saved in the drop-down menu: *Mason, Samuel; Mason novels, The Hour of Lead, Small Sorrows, The Art of Hunting, Paper Rain*. She navigates the stuff for sale: first editions, signed hardcovers, movie posters, tattered scripts. She can't help herself. She's not sure exactly what she's looking for, but she knows she'll know it when she sees it. This is *research,* she justifies. So far she's been pretty good . . . just a rare signed first edition of his first novel. A review copy of his second. She knows if she's going to follow through with her plans, she's going to need to save her money. The temptation is there though. Just last week she bid $800 on one of his high school notebooks. The photos showed a black and white composition book, edges curled. Sam's name on the cover. The photos of the notebook's inside pages revealed the notes he'd taken during an English class. His doodles in the margins. And she had to have it. She'd sat rigid-backed at her desk, watching as the auction end time approached, waiting until the last two minutes before she entered her modest bid. But when she was instantly outbid, she suddenly felt that familiar urgency, a need so intense it spread to her tongue. She'd gotten up to $800 when her competitor bid $802 in the final seconds and she lost. She started getting dizzy then, realizing she'd been holding her breath the whole time. She has to be careful. She has to control herself.

This morning, she exhausts each search quickly: no new items up for bid. So she moves to the Web site the publisher set up for Sam. It hasn't changed in over two years now, not since his last novel came out. She looks at his serious face, his serious eyes. She clicks on the audio button and listens to Sam's serious voice, the NPR interview she has almost memorized. *Is it good?* he asks. She closes her eyes and listens to the inflections in his voice, wonders at the pauses and spaces between the words. She listens for the sorrow that lurks under the surface. She hears it in his breaths.

There are a zillion reviews but only a handful of news articles that appear when she searches his name on Google. One is an interview, from a decade back, archived on *The New York Times* site. Another is an article Sam wrote for *The New Yorker* about growing up as the child of a single father. This one brings tears to Dale's eyes every time she reads it. The last one she finds is the small article in the *San Diego Union-Tribune,* published last October. This one, too, is unbearable.

While her mother eats, Dale stays inside her room, clicking away at her computer, searching, studying. She thinks of this project as a puzzle, the jigsaw pieces of a life scattered before her, waiting to be assembled. She proposed the thesis to her advisor at the end of the semester, but he was leery. He was leery of all living authors, as if literary value couldn't possibly be determined until after death. It was here that the lie that set this all into motion was born. When she went from 33 to 78 rpm. Inside his messy office, Dale, feeling the same dizzy feeling she felt whenever she got really upset, blurted out, "I have an interview arranged. We've spoken, and he's agreed to talk to me. About his daughter."

The truth was that she hadn't actually spoken to him, but she *had* been writing letters. And he'd written back. His first letter was just a quick note dashed off on a note card. But the one that came later was the letter that lived in her back pocket, the one whose paper was worn as soft as velvet from the constant friction against her jeans. It was the letter she'd read and reread so many times, she knew its contents by heart. Black ink, medium point pen. Careful cursive: *Dear Ms. Edwards, While I am certainly flattered that you have chosen to focus on my work for your project, I think a biography, as you describe it, would be premature at this time. I believe I have much more writing (and living) to do before anyone might find enough biographical information of interest to produce even a slim volume.* Though it frustrated her, she was touched by his modesty; he simply didn't feel worthy of the attention. She kept sending letters, but he didn't write back again. She knew she just needed to meet with him in person. Talk to him face to face, and then he might really open up. The longing traveled up the ladder of her spine and settled into the spot at the nape of her neck, throbbing. She had to go to him.

Now, in her room, she waits for the scent of ham and potatoes and eggs to dissipate. For the telltale shuffle of her mother's house slippers. For the "Come on down!" on *The Price Is Right*. For the whoosh and whir of the swamp cooler. And she looks for the clues in cyberspace that will tell her where to find him.

Sam hasn't started the new novel. It's due in six months, and he can't write. That old ability to conjure, to invoke the imaginary, has disappeared. Every time he tries to work, to imagine, his mind careens with the *real* stories: the only ones that really matter anymore. The truths. Besides, the words don't work anyway. They are too flat; on the computer monitor they are dimensionless, just pixels, without even the frail substance of ink. How do you do justice to something real with words made of air?

And so instead, he remembers. But the memories come in fragments, in twinkling pieces of tissue paper and sequins and colored beads inside a kaleidoscope. Trying to capture one moment, to examine it, is nearly impossible, because it appears but is also reflected again and again, making patterns too intricate and beautiful to deconstruct.

This morning, instead of rising to go to the loft to write, he stays in bed. And as the sun comes up over the lake, as its weak light travels through the paned window on the other side of the room, it glances off his arm, refracting onto Mena's hair and bare shoulders. This sliver, this softly shining shard, reflects a thousand other mornings, each exactly the same as the other: *birdsong, stillness, breath, hair.* How many mornings has he awoken next to Mena? To the identical fragile scent of Ivory soap and that lilac lotion she uses on her hands?

He turns the kaleidoscope's wheel, and the pattern shifts, the scents change and he is lying next to Mena, but a different Mena, hair tethered in a tight rubber band, body curled tightly away from him, the whole room smelling of that sweet smell of breast milk. The sheets are the same, but the space between them is wet with milk; Mena is asleep, but not asleep, that strange fugue state in which new mothers reside. The birdsong, the cooing of doves, or the sounds of seals barking or of waves crashing on sand are still there, but underneath, the tissue paper breaths of Finn and Franny, one sleeping in the crook of Mena's arm, the other in the bassinet next to the bed. He was worried about crushing them, about rolling over, about Mena falling asleep and dropping one of them. But he has watched her (for days now, how many days, weeks now?) as her eyes rest, but her arm remains vigilant, a cradle of bone and skin holding them tight.

Twist, the sun shines through the pale curtains, waking Mena, her eyes (the lashes like a curtain rising), with the look of surprise she always has when she sees him there (as if he might one day just vanish). The warmth in her brown eyes is gratitude. And this is his favorite pattern: both babies (are they babies anymore?) still sleeping in their crib, the space between them closing in, Mena's skin coming close to his, he can feel the warmth of sunlight and her skin radiating. Always, even before the children, she whispers, *morning, morning, morning.*

Twist, this moment is the same, but different, two toddlers, heads full of curls the color of spun sugar, pouncing between them, one curling up under the quick of his arm, the other straddling his back, riding like a pony, Mena's hair spilled across the sheets like ink, *morning, morning, morning.* This pattern, of four instead of two (it is always two or four, never three, never three) is predictable, certain.

Later, alone, stolen time, her hair cool across his arm, they whisper, *morning, morning,* which becomes the moaning of desire, hers, his, indiscernible. Until. The padding of feet in the hallway, two identical fists knocking, she covers his mouth with her hand, giggles, and he closes his eyes, smelling that scent of lilac on her palm against his lips.

Twist, all of them, lying on that great expanse, adrift on a sea alone but together and content, this bed their raft. Legs grown, stretching to the edges, but still, four bodies and the gentle nudging, *Wake up, Daddy. Get up, get up, get up.* And then other mornings when they were alone again in their bed. The kids asleep or making breakfast on their own (he knows the sound of cereal being poured into a bowl, the glug, glug of milk). In this pattern, Mena curls into him like a child herself.

The landscape beyond the window changes: California, Florence that one glorious summer, visits to friends in New York, Portland, Michigan. Hotels and motels and here. *Here* where he is now. It is once again *morning, morning,* but the birds, the doves, he can't remember the word for them anymore. It sounds the same, but it isn't at all the same. *Morning.* If there were a name for this pattern: the tear-stained cheeks of Mena, her black hair matted with the sweat of another migraine nightmare, for the way the sun mocks them both. *Mourning.* There it is. *Birdsong, repose, breath, hair.* These fragments cannot be reassembled or scrutinized; they just spin endlessly, beautifully, full of splintering sorrow in every configuration.

He should be writing, but words can no longer do justice. To all that old bliss. Or to this impossible sadness.

Mena rises as she always does, when the nightmare ends, and she carefully tiptoes out of the bed and out of the room. He pretends that he is asleep. And he will give her another hour, two, before he follows her into the morning.

M ena quietly walks across the cold dusty floors of the cabin at dawn, leaving Sam to sleep. They have been here almost a week now, and she's still getting the headaches she thought would go away when they left the house in San Diego. It is only 5:00 A.M., but she knows that trying to go back to sleep would be futile.

It was Sam's idea to come here. In the morning, after they had gone and picked Finn up at the border station, as he knelt on the cold bathroom tiles, vomiting, Sam sat at the kitchen table with his head in his hands. "We need to get out of here."

"What do you mean?" Mena had asked. She was making muffins, stirring blueberries into the bowl. She watched as they smeared in violet streaks across the clean white batter. She would overfill the muffin tins, making enormous muffins, each a meal in itself.

"It's too much," he had said. "We're suffocating here. All of us."

Mena looked around at the kitchen, at the warm autumn-colored walls that she had painted, at the stained-glass lamp that shone down on the kitchen table. There was a layer of Magic Marker, crayon, glitter glue that had become imbedded in the grains of the wood. This was where the twins did their art projects, where they played Uncle Wiggily and Scrabble and Monopoly. Where they learned how to add and subtract. Where they had made papier-mâché volcanoes and topographical maps. The place where they had been eating together as a family for more than sixteen years. The conversations they'd had in that kitchen rattled around in her mind, loud and loose like pebbles.

She didn't want to go, but he was right. Franny was everywhere. Pervasive. You couldn't turn a corner without finding her. She filled the rooms when she was alive; now that she was gone, she permeated them.

"Where would we go?" Mena asked, her voice breaking.

"Finn is going to get himself in too deep."

Mena nodded, her throat thick, thinking of his red tear-streaked face when they picked him up from the border police. "I'm sorry," he had cried, and he could have been six instead of sixteen. "I'm sorry."

"I made an offer on the cabin," Sam said.

"At the lake?" she asked. They hadn't been to Gormlaith in five years. As the kids got older, it was harder to leave for a whole summer. Finn had his surfing, his friends. Franny had ballet. Mena still dreamed about the lake. About Franny swinging on the tire swing. About Franny floating on her back in the water. About Franny stepping onto a hornet's nest.

"Just for the summer," he said, pulling her into him. It was the first time he had touched her first in weeks.

In the other room, she could hear Finn wretching, spilling. The phone was ringing: Misty's parents again, she was sure.

His face was hopeful. Bright. Sam had smelled like citrus; his hands were rank with the scent of the oranges he'd just squeezed. He touched her face, looking at her, really looking at her, for the first time in a long, long time. She knew that it must pain him, to see Franny's nose. Her mouth. Her chin.

She shook her head. She couldn't imagine going back to Vermont without Franny.

"We can't lose him too," Sam said.

She knew he was right, but still, she'd resisted the idea of the lake. She couldn't imagine that it would be any better anywhere. She worried that at the lake there would be too few distractions. At least here there were things to do, places to go, people in their lives whose main purpose was diversion. She had her catering business, as sporadic and small as it was. She had some semblance of a life. But then, two days after the Tijuana episode, Finn gave them no other choice.

The Monday after that awful weekend, Finn disappeared. He took off for school that morning as usual, backpack slung over his shoulder, skateboard tucked under his arm, but that afternoon, he just didn't come home. Normally, he was in the house to grab his wetsuit and surfboard by 3:00. And then he was making his way down the wooden steps that led from their house to the beach. That day, as the hours slipped by (*3:00, 4:00, 5:00*), Mena tried not to panic, but by the time the sun started to disappear into the water, casting brilliant golden shadows across the empty living room, she could feel the prickly disquiet of his absence turning into paralyzing fear. She could taste it, bilious and sour in her swollen throat.

Misty's parents assured them that he was not with her.

"Misty is home. *Grounded,*" Misty's mother said. "She has been punished for *her* behavior the other night."

Mena felt scolded, ashamed.

Sam dialed the police, and as he waited to speak to someone about filing a missing person report, he paced back and forth across the kitchen floor.

The hours continued to pass. *7:00, 8:00, 9:00.*

"I'm going to look for him," he said.

All night long, Sam drove aimlessly around the city, looking for Finn—as if he might just be standing somewhere at the side of the road. Mena stayed at the house, in case he came home, sitting at the edge of the couch, a kitchen chair, her hands gripping anything (counters, tabletops, the walls) to keep from falling.

When Sam pulled into the driveway, the sun was already starting to fill the house with light. He opened the front door, pushing Finn ahead of him.

"Apologize to your mother," Sam had said, pushing him toward her.

Finn shook his hair out of his face, defiant. His pupils were so large, the black obliterated the normal clear blue of his eyes.

"Why?" was all Mena could manage. She had to resist the urge to pull him into her arms, to cradle him as if he were a child still.

"*Apologize,*" Sam said, his jaw set.

"Why did you do this to us?" she cried, as he came toward her. Still, she reached for him, even though she half-expected that her hands would go right through him. That he too was only a ghost.

She wants to think this was a good idea, that taking Finn to the lake would at least get him away from the kids he's been hanging out with lately. She wants to blame San Diego for everything that is happening; she wants to believe that geography alone can save him. But she knows that it has nothing to do with California and everything to do with Franny. And as she wanders around the cabin, she knows that Franny is no less present here than she was at home. She is in the crazy quilt that covers the overstuffed chair on the sunporch (Mena's arms still remember the way she would have to lift her sleeping body and carry her to bed). In the jelly jars they used for glasses (*jellies,* she called them). In the ticking of the clock shaped like a loon (she'd learned to tell time on this clock: *half past a feather, quarter to an eye*). But at least here Franny is still just a little girl. Here she is never older than twelve. God, even Mena has to smile at the thought of Franny at twelve. *Before.*

Finn's cell phone doesn't work here. He's tried it from every room in the house, from the neighbor's dock, even up on the roof. Nothing. He's not even sure if they've gotten the regular phone hooked up yet. Maybe they won't get it connected at all. He wouldn't be surprised. He needs to call Misty. He just wants to hear her voice. Just shoot the shit for a bit. Sometimes, at home, he'd call her in the middle of the night, and they'd watch something stupid on TV together. Listen to each other breathe. Once he even fell asleep with the phone resting on his pillow, the sound of her sleeping on the other line.

He thinks about what she might be doing now, and it makes him crazy. He wonders how long it will be before she finds a new boyfriend. He's not stupid; he knows that if he's not around, somebody else, somebody better, will be.

Misty doesn't live in Ocean Beach like the rest of his friends. He wouldn't have met her at all if his parents hadn't spent every dime they had to get him into Country Day after Franny was gone and he started smoking weed so he could sleep at night. He and Franny had gone to the public schools since kindergarten. They probably thought that sending him to some stuck-up private school would straighten him out. What they didn't realize was that private school kids were actually worse than any of the stoner friends he had in OB. It wasn't private school, but their parents' bankrolls, that kept them out of trouble. At first, he figured Misty was just one of those bratty rich girls who got her rocks off slumming it. There were a lot of girls like that at his school, the über-wealthy chicks who hung out with the scholarship kids and kids like him to either feel cool or pretend that their whole lives weren't dipped in freaking platinum. Misty's parents own a gazillion-dollar place up in La Jolla: obnoxious, pseudo-Mediterranean villa crap. And the first time she brought him to her house (with its Mexican-tiled fountain out front and double winding staircase inside, its *great room*), he knew she was way out of his league.

But she liked him. God knows why. And even though her parents had more money than God, she wasn't like some of those other girls at Country Day. She honestly didn't seem to care too much about it. She thought it was cool that his mom and dad were artists, and that their house was just a nine-hundred-square-foot bungalow in OB. She liked him.

The real test would have been Franny though. Franny was the gauge by which Finn tested just about everything. Franny *got* people. She just did. She knew when somebody was a liar or a cheat or the kind of person who would say one thing to your face and another to their friends.

"She's good," Franny said. "For you." She had said that about Finn's *first* girlfriend, Jessie. Jessie who was smart and funny and could burp the alphabet backward. Jessie who smelled like suntan lotion and Big Red gum.

They were all at the beach, and Jessie had gone to use the restrooms. He waited until Jessie's bathing suit was just a hot pink speck in the distance before he raised his eyebrows and said, "Well?"

Franny was digging in the sand, letting it pour out through her fingers. "She has honest eyes." She nodded approvingly. "And *really* big boobs."

"And that's the most important thing," Finn had said, laughing.

"I like her," Franny said.

With Franny's seal of approval, he'd asked Jessie out again, and again, and soon Jessie was a fixture at their house. And because she and Franny became friends too, sometimes she was even allowed to sleep over. The three of them would stay up all night watching old movies on TV, falling asleep spread out across the living room floor. In the morning, his mother would make mountains of pancakes, and they'd eat until their stomachs hurt.

But then Franny was gone. And he couldn't even look at Jessie anymore. He transferred to Country Day, he met Misty, and that was that. Franny wouldn't have liked her at all. She would have told him to turn the other direction and run away. That he knew for sure.

God, this sucks, he thinks, peering out the window at the lake. There is haze covering everything. It's hanging in the trees like ghosts.

He's been thinking about how he can get back to California. He knows it's probably ridiculous, but there's got to be a way. They can't watch him twenty-four hours a day. This isn't fucking prison. If he had some money, he'd hitchhike into town and get on a bus. He's pretty sure there's a Greyhound that comes through Quimby. But he has no cash. Not a dime. They took away his credit card after he took out the hundred-dollar cash advance to buy weed. Maybe he could hitchhike home to San Diego. Kerouac his way back. Or maybe, instead, he could just kill them with kindness. Show them what a good boy he is. Convince them that he can be trusted. Then maybe they'd realize what a mistake they've made. Let him go *home*.

But he knows this isn't even totally about him, not really. Granted, he's been getting into a lot of trouble lately, smoking too much weed, the whole TJ thing, and then his taking off that night. But his mom and dad are cool. They've always been way more understanding than anybody else's parents. Some of his friends' folks are so uptight. They act like they were never kids. Like they don't remember anymore what it's like to be young. But his mother and father at least always listened to him. If he had a case to make, he was always allowed to make it. At least that's the way it used to be.

They told him this is about the X they found in his pants pocket after his father found him camped out underneath the lifeguard tower that night, about his not coming home, about anything but what was really the problem. *Franny.* Why wouldn't somebody fucking say it? Nobody even says her name anymore. *Franny.* They lost their grip on her, and now they're afraid they're going to lose it on him too. They're cool, but they're afraid. Both of them. Terrified of everything.

There must be a word for this, Sam thinks. For the sound of Mena downstairs when she thinks that no one else is awake. For the quiet careful sounds of her feet moving across the floor. There must be a word for a woman awake and moving in the glow of dawn. Once, a long time ago, he had called it *Tara*. Once, when he was young and his father was newly dead, he had decided that writing was the best way to deal with the overwhelming pain and panic and pathos. The words are what saved him. They helped him identify, classify, protect. He had only to sit down and tap at the typewriter for a few minutes before the letters formed words which formed sentences and paragraphs and chapters which compartmentalized his grief. Transformed it into something real: the blocky letters of the typewriter ribbon's ink making solid all that liquid horror. And soon the words grew fluid again, into the hips and calves and breasts of a woman standing at the edge of a forest in a crimson coat, rubbing her hands together, leaves crackling under her small feet. He'd called her *Tara*. And later, *Mena*.

It used to be that the words came in a seemingly limitless supply. He had simply to sit down, and they poured out: copious, an endlessly replenished stream. He was wrong. He did take things for granted. He took a lot of things for granted.

He can't write. And he and Mena haven't had sex in months.

The last time they tried was the night before they left San Diego. It was three o'clock in the morning before they finished packing. Their backs were sore, their hands tired. But she had moved toward him, her hands reaching to cradle his face. It was the first time he'd seen anything even remotely resembling hope in her eyes for months. It was contagious. "This will be good," she said. "For us. A fresh start."

And then she was slipping out of her clothes, letting her jeans pool around her feet. Pulling the soft white T-shirt smudged with newsprint from packing over her head. He let her undress him; he wasn't even sure how it was that they used to do this. How long had it been? How long had they managed to keep from touching each other? It used to be that they couldn't stop.

As she buried her face in his neck, her hair soft in his face, she reached down into his shorts and touched him. Tentatively.

There must be a word for this, he thought then. There must be a way to describe this old touch, this familiar hand and the softness of fingerprints. But he couldn't find it, nothing.

She tried, whispering her own words on his neck. But after a few minutes, she withdrew her hand from his limp penis as if she'd been burned. "We've got an early morning tomorrow," she said, blinking hard, climbing back into her T-shirt and into the bed.

"I'm sorry," he said. When he crawled in next to her he should have reached over and held her, but he was too ashamed, and so instead he rolled onto his side and shut his eyes.

After breakfast, Mena leaves to go to the grocery store, and Sam surveys the yard from the window. It looks like some godawful jungle out there. Feeling suddenly full of purpose, he goes out to the shed and finds the lawn mower behind a bunch of rusty lawn chairs. He gives it a few good yanks, but it's dead. Finn is pouting in his room, waiting for the good people at

AT&T to come and connect him to the world again. Mena had offered him a phone card at breakfast. "They'll be here between two and five. You can use the phone then."

Sam stands in the knee-high weeds and wonders if one of the neighbors has a mower he can borrow.

Inside the cabin, he hollers down the hall to the bedrooms, "Going for a walk!" But when he pushes Finn's door open, he sees that Finn has fallen asleep again, curled up into a tight ball. His impulse is to go to him, brush the mop of white blond curls out of his eyes. But instead he just stands in the doorway, leaning against the woodwork for support.

When the twins were little, he could never leave them alone when they were sleeping. He would check on them two, sometimes three times a night. "Let them *sleep,*" Mena would say, as he slowly opened their door again. They slept curled around each other, holding hands, little feet tangled. Intertwined the way they probably had been inside Mena's womb. When he couldn't see the blankets rising and falling with their breaths, he would feel a sort of urgent rush of blood in his temples, and he would go to them, press his large flat palms or his ear against their tiny chests until he could confirm first one and then two heartbeats. Sometimes he woke up in the middle of the night in a panic and he would check again.

He starts down the road, sure that Finn will be out for another hour or more. He knows he has trouble sleeping at night. At home, Sam could see the green glow of his desk lamp under the door all through the night. Finn had become nocturnal, staying up all night and then crashing after school and through the weekends.

Most of the camps are still empty. The summer people usually don't come until the Fourth of July, which is still a week away. The blackflies are the primary residents this time of year. When he was a kid, his dad would bring him here to go fishing, back before the lake's peace had been disturbed by sum-

mer folks' powerboats and water-skiers. He'd hated the blackflies that filled his ears and flew up his nose, but he loved being
with his father out on the empty lake. They'd sit there for hours,
with their lines the only interruption in the still surface of the
water. They didn't talk much. There wasn't any need then for
words.

He wonders if Finn would agree to go fishing with him.

He gets to the McInnes camp. Gussy McInnes used to be a
fixture here, sitting on the sunporch watching the world go by.
Today the Athenaeum Bookmobile is parked in the driveway;
he seems to remember someone telling him that her granddaughter lives there now. That she works for the library.

Old Magoo still lives in the next camp over. His boat-sized
Cadillac is in the driveway. He'll have a mower.

"Sammy Mason!" Magoo says, opening the door after Sam
has almost given up. "How are you?"

This simple question, this nicety mumbled a hundred times
a day, is still excruciating.

Sam nods and smiles. "We're up for the summer again, but
the yard's a wreck. You wouldn't have a mower I could borrow,
would you?"

"Oh sure," he says. "It'll give you a workout though. Still
using the old reel mower."

Magoo motions for Sam to follow him to the shed and
gives Sam the manual mower. It looks like some medieval tor-
ture device.

"Thanks," Sam says, shaking Magoo's hand. "I figure I
should be done in a month or so." He smiles.

"Hey, Sam," he says, his face softening. "I just wanted to let
you know I heard about your little girl. And I'm real sorry."

Sam nods again, says nothing. He appreciates the apologies,
but they make him cringe. It makes it sound like it was someone's fault.

Back at the cottage, he starts to mow, pushing the mower

through the weeds and grass. His arms tremble after the first hour, but something about this hard work feels good. His father always used to say the best way to work out a problem was to go chop some wood. Better for your back to hurt than your heart. The sun is hot on his neck. By the time Mena pulls up, he is drenched in sweat, and only a quarter of the front yard has been trimmed.

"I'll make some iced tea," she says. "Come inside?"

"I've still got the side yard to do," he says. He's on a roll now, he doesn't want to stop.

"Sure?" she asks.

"Yeah," he says. He wipes his arm across his forehead, sweat stinging his eyes. "I'll be in soon."

He doesn't know why he can't give her what she wants. What she needs. Not even the simplest things. And he hates himself for it.

A s Mena unloads the groceries, she watches Sam through the window, the smooth muscles of his arms as he hacks through the jungle of goldenrod and ragweed. His last haircut has grown out, and his hair is falling in his eyes. He is so thin. He looks up, sees her in the window, but turns back to his work just as she raises her hand to wave.

She knew she loved him before she even met him.

Her teacher at CalArts (what was it, twenty years ago now?), *Jim,* at a party when he was drunk and she was not, handed her the galley of Sam's first novel. "You have to read this," he had said, his speech blurry, his breath licorice sweet with scotch in her ear. She was standing outside the bathroom door, waiting. He pushed the book into her hands. *"Tara.* The girl. We're making a film, and you'd be perfect. It's going to be huge."

She'd taken the galley home with her that night, home to that awful apartment in Venice she was sharing with three other people (the one with the roaches and the broken dead bolt), and thumbed through the ratty paperback as she tried to fall asleep. She'd never heard of Samuel Mason before. *Some kid from Vermont,* Jim said. *The next Styron. The next Kesey.*

She didn't put the book down until she'd read through to the very last page.

She remembers feeling light-headed, almost like she'd had too much wine. Or not enough food. He'd written her life. It was as if she were some sort of butterfly he'd captured and pinned between the pages of the book. It made her feel scared, and it made her feel safe all at once.

When she finally met him, it barely mattered that he was so sweet and kind. So beautiful and unassuming. He *understood* her, and he hadn't even spoken to her yet.

After shooting that day, they'd driven to the beach together, gotten fish tacos and Coronas with pulpy slices of lime at the place near her apartment. They spent the whole afternoon talking, walking. When he ran his hand down her back and kissed her, it was as if he'd already memorized each vertebrae.

She was nineteen, but she already knew that she would marry him, have children with him, grow into an old woman with him. In the words he'd written, she already had.

How did you know? she'd asked him.

It kills her that he doesn't want her anymore. All the desire has drained from him. He can barely touch her. In the last six months, they've made love only a handful of times, and each time was excruciating.

She tries to be angry with him. It's easier than feeling sorry for him, for herself.

She fills the refrigerator, fills the cupboards, fills the stockpot. By the time Finn emerges from his room and Sam comes inside, she has filled the house with the smell of lemon, garlic, and fish. She hands Sam a glass of iced tea. She kisses the top of Finn's head as he sits down at the table. She kisses him all the time now. She can't stop.

"I'm going to pick up a basketball net this afternoon," Sam says. "The barn is big enough for a half-court."

Finn's eyes brighten, despite the scowl on his face.

"Wanna come into town with me?"

"Whatever," Finn says.

★ ★ ★

While they are gone, Mena climbs the ladder to Sam's office. She knows she shouldn't do this, but there are secrets between them now. All of a sudden, they don't know each other at all anymore. His laptop is turned on, the screen saver floating across the page. She lets her hand bump the mouse, turning the screen from black to white, the Word document open in front of her. The blank page blurs as her eyes fill with tears.

The closest town is Quimby. It's hardly a metropolis, but at least there's a main street there. Sidewalks for Christ's sake. When they used to come to the lake, they would drive into town once a week to go to the Athenaeum, the library, to get books. That building, at least, looks the same.

Finn remembers the kids' room with its battered piano and puppet theater, its tinfoil rocket ship big enough to crawl inside. He used to really dig that rocket ship. He'd never tell anybody, but for a while he really believed he could make it to outer space if he just wished hard enough.

Franny never bothered with the kids' room. While Finn got out books about bugs and reptiles and sports, Franny wandered around upstairs with their father. She read everything she could get her hands on: Faulkner, Wolfe, *Woolf*. At ten, she had already read all three of their father's novels. Finn had tried to read the first one, but he'd gotten bored.

"I'll just be a minute," his father says today. They are parked in front of the library. "You wanna come in? Check your e-mail?"

"Nah," Finn says. Misty's parents had cut off the Internet to the computer in her room, and he'd told her he wouldn't be able to get his e-mail here anyway. Now he's kicking himself. She could have sent him a text message from her phone. There are always ways to communicate. His father leaves him in the car and then comes back, grabs his keys from the ignition and stuffs them in his pocket.

Finn's cell phone's dead. The battery must have gotten drained looking for a signal up at the lake. There's a pay phone next to the library. How long has it been since he's used one of these? He digs around in the center console and finds a roll of quarters they'd gotten for the tolls. He pops half of the quarters into his hand and goes to the phone booth.

He drops the quarters in and dials Misty's cell number. He doesn't want to get stuck talking to one of her parents. The phone rings and rings, and then Misty's husky voice says, "Hey, I'm not here, but I will be soon. Leave a message." She's changed the message. And something about this makes him feel more like he's lost her than anything else so far. He slams the phone down and goes back to the car. He gets in the passenger's seat and is sulking when his father comes back with an armload of books.

They find a backboard, a basketball rim and net at the hardware store. While his father pays the cashier, he wanders around the dusty shelves looking at all the crap and thinks about Sundays at home.

His father knows how to build things. Most of the kids at school, especially at Country Day, had dads who made lots of money (developers and software engineers and plastic surgeons) but they didn't know how to use a hammer or a wrench. His dad could make things, and it made Finn feel sort of cool. They made trips to OB Hardware together almost every Sunday; there was always some sort of project underway at their house. They'd wander around that hardware store, his father picking out the things he would need to build his mother a gardening table or a new bookcase for his office. Afterward they'd go to the Village Kitchen next-door for breakfast and eat biscuits and sausage gravy. These were the mornings when Finn had their dad all to himself. He can still remember what it felt like to want to be alone with his dad on a Sunday; where did that go?

"You ready?" Sam asks.

Finn is standing, looking at spools of chains, links thick and shiny.

"Whatever," he says, and follows him back to the car.

His dad spends the next hour installing the backboard in the rafters of the barn. Finn watches him struggling but doesn't offer to help. And his father doesn't ask. Finn bounces the basketball on the dusty floor of the barn, dribbling and pantomiming layups. The sun is bright now, but it is dark in here. The sun comes to them in slivers through the cracks in the wide wooden door. It smells like dirt in here, like earth and hay.

"There," his father says, looking proudly up at the net. "Wanna play some one-on-one?"

Finn shrugs.

They don't speak as they play.

His dad played ball in high school, and even though he's only six feet, he's quick. Quicker than Finn. But today Finn is making every shot. *Jesus, what's he doing?* Finn grabs the ball and dribbles down the makeshift court, easily faking his father out and then going to the hoop. *He's letting me win.*

"What are you doing?" Finn asks.

"Huh?" his father asks. He hasn't even broken a sweat; he worked up more of a sweat mowing the yard.

Finn rushes toward him again, clumsily, exaggerated, practically handing him the ball.

"Goddamnit," Finn says, stopping. Holding the ball under his arm.

"What's the matter?"

"Nothing," Finn says, chucking the ball at the backboard. It smashes back down to the court and rolls toward a pile of hay in the corner.

As he opens up the door, letting the sunlight spill into the barn, he remembers playing with Franny. She'd never pull this shit. When they played (cards, Scrabble, Xbox), she was hard-core. She'd kick his ass and then kick it again. Does he think he's a fucking baby? Like letting him win some stupid one-on-one game is going to make him feel better?

He walks down the path to the water and stares out at the still gray expanse before him. He can hear the ball echoing inside the cavernous barn, his father's feet shuffling across the floor. Finn is suddenly so hot inside his clothes he can barely stand it. He looks back to the house, knows that his mother is watching from some window, though he doesn't know which one. He pulls off his shirt, drops his shorts, and because he's still so hot, he drops his boxers too and leaps quickly off the dock into the water.

There are no waves here. No ebb and flow. It's as if this water is dead. He is buoyed by nothing but his own sheer will.

"Where you going?" Dale's mother asks. She's sitting on the couch with a full ashtray on the coffee table in front of her, their Siamese, Pookie, curled up on her lap.

"Just over to work. I need to pick up my paycheck."

"Grab some cigarettes on your way back?" her mother asks, pulling the last one from her pack. "There's some money in my purse."

"I may stop at Sarah's for a minute too," Dale lies. She needs to buy time. She hasn't spoken to Sarah in over a year.

"What for?"

Dale shrugs.

Sarah lives down the street from Dale. They grew up together, and she heard she's home from college for the summer. Dale and she don't have anything in common anymore. Sarah is premed at the U of A. She's engaged to some guy she met at school and volunteers at St. Joe's three days a week. The last time she and Dale hung out they ran out of things to talk about pretty quickly. Sarah is nice, but she's not the same girl that Dale grew up with. Looking at her fiddling with her gigantic diamond ring, Dale could barely believe this was the same girl who used to eat her own scabs and gave her instructions, in graphic detail, about how to give a blow job. Sarah knew things that nobody else knew when they were kids: about periods and Schnapps and S and M. Now she seems so *sorority*. So prim and *good*.

Dale's mother thinks that Sarah's stuck-up. She's always thought so. Dale knows it's actually just that she hates Sarah's mother. Her perfect house and her perfect husband and her perfect vacations to their time-share in Puerto Vallarta. Dale misses Sarah, misses the long afternoons they spent sitting by Sarah's pool, drinking her mother's wine coolers and talking about boys. She felt almost normal those days, almost real.

"I'll be back in a couple hours," Dale says, grabbing a five from her mother's wallet.

She found the car on craigslist. Some guy over near school was selling it for $750 OBO. She offered $500, and he bit. She walks the three blocks from her house to the Blockbuster to pick up her check. It's her second to last one; she gave her two-weeks notice during her last shift. It's already over a hundred degrees, and her thighs stick together as she walks. She goes to the bank next-door, cashes her check and takes out another $300 from her savings account. She gets the bus to Tempe, and fingers the crisp bills. She can't sit still in the seat, and she keeps craning her neck to see if it's her stop next.

The house looks just like her house, small and flat and stucco. The yard is the same too, except most of the grass is brown, and there's a FOR RENT sign planted by the sidewalk. The guy, his name is Eric, is out in his driveway, leaning over the engine of the Bug. Her gut tells her this is not a good sign, but when he stands up, she can see he's just been polishing it. The innards shine and shimmer in the heat.

"Hey," he says. His smile is warm, and his face is smudged with grease. Dale likes him right away. "You Dale?"

She nods, feeling shy.

The guy looks like a college student, sort of a hippie. Long hair in a ponytail. No shirt. A tattoo on his chest. He catches her staring, trying to decipher what looks like script.

"Thoreau," he says.

"In wildness is the preservation of the world," she reads aloud. "Cool." She has the impulse to trace the words with her finger. Instead, she pulls the bills from her wallet and hands them to him.

"Thanks. Like the ad says, she's a sixty-four. Last year I replaced the whole brake system, lines, rotors, shoes, pads. Everything. The engine's about five years old, but she runs great."

He opens the door for her and motions for her to sit in the driver's seat, like a guy on a date, pulling a chair out for her. She blushes and sits down inside the car, examining the unfamiliar dash. It is so simple. No frills. Speedometer. Gas gauge. Radio.

"Sorry, the wipers totally don't work. Haven't really needed them here." He laughs. "But you might, so I installed this little device . . . cutting edge of technology . . ." He motions to the shoestrings, attached to the wipers and then threaded through the smaller triangular driver and passenger side windows. "Tug on these and they'll do the trick."

She takes the key from him and looks for the ignition.

"Oh, sorry, it's right here," he says, motioning to a place below the steering wheel, a small chrome receptacle. His hand brushes hers, and it feels like she's been shocked. She puts in the key, depresses the clutch, and starts the car. A billow of smoke blows out behind her. She glances in the rearview mirror anxiously.

"No worries . . . that happens every time you start her up. It's just oil on the engine burning off. I call her *Puff.*" He laughs again and whistles the first bar of "Puff, the Magic Dragon."

He hands her the title and she fills out her information. He tears his part off and then kisses the other half and hands it back to her. This makes her blush again. He closes her door and pats the hood. "Bye, old friend," he says. She grips the wheel and feels her heart beating in her throat.

"Where you headed anyway?" he asks.

She looks at him, at his pale chest and the black ink that crawls across it.

"Vermont," she says.

It was by accident that she found Sam Mason's son's My-Space page. She'd actually been looking for the soundtrack to *The Hour of Lead.* She'd bought the DVD with her employee discount at work. When she hadn't had any luck finding the soundtrack on Amazon, she returned to Google. Out of habit, she tried *Franny Mason, Finn Mason, Mena Mason,* just to see what appeared. First a Web search and then an image search. That's how she'd found the pictures of Franny a month ago, which led her to *her* MySpace page. That's also how she'd found the name of Mena's catering company. That's the great thing about the Internet. It's always changing, expanding. There is new information available about everything, *everyone,* every day. She knew it was just a matter of time before she found what she was looking for.

Of course, she knew they lived in San Diego. It said so at the end of every author bio since his second novel. But it's not like they were about to print an address. San Diego's a big city; he could be anywhere. The letter she'd written had gotten to him via his publisher in New York. (She read once in an interview that he didn't use e-mail. He called himself a *Luddite,* a word that tasted like dense bread on her lips as she tried it.) And the letters that came back had no return address. But then, a new Web page appeared . . . black background, purple font, loud surf music playing in the background. *Male, Sixteen, Last Log-in: June 8, Mood: Pissed Off, Latest Blog Entry: Headed to Butt Fuck Nowhere (AKA Lake Gormlaith, VT) in two days. Hasta.* Next to the entry was a photo of Finn and some girl, arms around each other, leaning against a Buick woody station wagon with a surfboard on top. It was the only entry, the only photo. It was as if it was there just for her.

No wonder Sam hadn't answered the most recent letters she sent to his publisher. He probably hadn't even gotten them. According to Finn's entry, they had left for Vermont nearly two weeks ago. The letters were probably sitting in some pile on an editorial assistant's cluttered desk. She felt such tremendous relief she couldn't believe it. But now it didn't matter. She had found him. She used the Google hybrid map to locate and look at Lake Gormlaith. From what she could tell, it was a pretty small lake. Maybe only twenty or thirty cottages or so littered around it. She zoomed in as close as she could on each of them, wondering which one he was inside.

She gave notice at work that day, found the Bug on craigslist, and started to pack her clothes.

Hasta, she thinks as she pulls out of Thoreau's driveway, rolling down the windows and feeling the hot air on her skin like a kiss.

They have already started getting mail. The flag is up on the mailbox when Sam gets home from dropping off the mower at Magoo's again. He can barely keep up with the yard. In San Diego it was all he could do to coax some crabgrass out of their lawn. This is the second time since they got here that he's had to borrow the mower. He reaches into the mailbox and feels a slight wave of anxiety. He quickly thumbs through the stack: AT&T, a Shop'n Save flier, *Have You Seen Me?* postcard. Nothing important.

Sam hasn't told Mena about the letters. He usually doesn't keep things from her, but the last thing she needed after everything with Franny was to worry about this too. The first one had gone to his publisher, and so it (like all the other fan mail) arrived in his mailbox about three months after its postmark date. It arrived unopened but slightly battered. He'd expected the usual: some oddball writing to find out if he had based the characters on *real* people, because the narrator was *so very much* like him or her that it was eerie. Or, if the author of the missive was a woman, it might be a solicitation for something varying from the romantic to the lurid. (The author photos on the back of books were generous in their renderings of him. The photographers, all of them, had instructed him not to smile, to look contemplative, intellectual, and the airbrushed results had been of a man who was both serious and playful. The dimple

in his right cheek never disappeared, not even when he was trying to look serious. And they'd done a terrific job hiding the
small bump on his nose and the remaining half dozen pock-
marks on his cheeks that served as a reminder of a ridicule-
filled adolescence.) But now, the most recent book (and author
photo) was over three years old and he suspected that if he ever
published another book, they'd have to bring in a team of ex
perts to photograph him. Of course, he was flattered. There had
even been a few times when he'd realized that, had he been so
inclined, he could have slept with some very attractive readers.
(Sometimes they attached photos of themselves—one brunette
included a photo of herself wearing nothing but his second
novel spread open across her quite lovely torso.) But it had
been a long time since he'd gotten one of those sorts of letters,
and so when this letter arrived, he opened it with more anticipation than normal.

The first one had been relatively straightforward. It was
from a student named Dale Edwards at Arizona State who was
writing her Honor's thesis on the novels of Samuel Mason.
She'd read somewhere that his wife was from Flagstaff, and she
was wondering if he might be willing to meet with her the
next time they were in the area. This was the third or fourth
time he'd been contacted by a student, though ultimately he
never actually read any of their theses. It, frankly, scared him to
imagine the kind of people they must be: students who, with
the pick of the greats, chose *his* work to analyze and postulate
about. What was *wrong* with them? He wrote a quick note back
(he always wrote back), and said that certainly, the next time
they were in Arizona, he would get in touch. His response was
followed almost immediately by another letter with a series of
questions for him to answer regarding his work. This one he
ignored, pretending that it had gotten lost in the mountains of
fan mail he hoped she wrongly assumed that he was receiving.
But the third letter persisted.

He didn't want to encourage her, but, again, he was simultaneously flattered and horrified by the prospect of someone's academic career hinging on his work, and so he obliged. He'd written a kind letter thanking her but suggesting a biography might be a bit premature. The letter she wrote back was handwritten—he could barely make it out.

I've received an advance, she wrote.

At first he thought she meant an advanced reader's copy. But there was no book coming out. No new work. He scanned the page, the scribbling. *I have received an advance from a well-known publishing house. To write your biography. I hope you will authorize it.*

"Are you kidding me?" This had to be a joke.

I submitted my thesis to an agent who thought there might be a lot of interest.

He'd laughed at that. He couldn't help it.

Especially now, she wrote. *After Franny.*

And then Mena had pulled into the driveway. He'd taken the letter and stuffed it back into the envelope.

"What's that?" Mena asked. She'd been at the doctor's office again. She'd been getting headaches since September.

"Fan mail," he said.

She probably wrote a half dozen more times over the course of the next few months; he tried to ignore them, but they just kept coming.

Mr. Mason, if you just give me a chance. I'll let you see every chapter. You can approve every single word. Please, she pleaded. He did not respond.

Finally he stopped opening the letters and told his editor to hold any mail until after they got back to San Diego from Vermont. He kept the letters though, and reread them a few times, looking for clues about what her motives might be. She didn't really sound like some sort of parasitic journalist. She sounded like a kid. But still, he had no idea what was sitting on his editor's desk. He'd deal with that when they got home. He didn't want anybody digging into his life. His *work,* fine. But his life? It seemed both ludicrous and cruel.

As he thumbs through the junk mail, he knows it's ridiculous to think she'd have found his address at the lake. He's pretty sure that even Monty doesn't know his address here.

He brings the small, benign stack of mail into the kitchen. Mena is sitting at the table, looking at a recipe in a glossy paged magazine.

"Anything exciting come?" she asks, not looking up at him.

"Not today," he says.

He knows he should have told her, but she'd only worry. She worries about everything lately. He can't protect her from much, but he can protect her from this.

"How does moussaka sound for dinner tonight?" she asks.

"Good." He nods. "It sounds good."

After dinner Mena tells them she is going for a walk. The kitchen is hot and thick with the smell of eggplant and garlic. If she can get some fresh air before the headache starts, maybe it won't start at all.

She slips on her flip-flops and leaves Finn and Sam at the table. They haven't spoken to each other for hours, and she figures they might be forced to if she leaves them alone. She's not sure what happened in the barn, but Finn's been pissy all afternoon.

She decides to walk to the small grassy beach that also functions as the boat access area. She used to bring the kids here when they were really small. At home, they were allowed only at the edges of the ocean. Sam was worried about the riptide, the undertow. But the lake was the perfect place to learn how to swim. At the access area it's shallow for about twenty feet before the drop-off where the bottom of the lake seems to simply fall out. There's also a secret sandbar Franny and Finn discovered when they no longer needed her or their foam noodles anymore. She hadn't known it was there until they both disappeared under the water's surface only to emerge again about a hundred yards out, standing. Franny had waved gleefully back at her, delighted, jumping up and down on the water's surface. She was ten, and her bathing suit was bright orange with a yellow bow.

The headache is just a tickle right now, like the telltale scratch at the back of the throat when you're about to come down with a cold. They start like this, but sometimes she is able to will them away. She concentrates on the slap-slapping of her flip-flops on the dirt road leading away from the cabin.

When she hears the sounds of people at the beach, her heart sinks. She had hoped to have it to herself. Still, she'd rather be here than back in the cottage where the air is too thick to breathe.

She walks to the water's edge and sees a couple with a baby. They have a dog too, a mutt that is jowly and gray. He is paddling in the deep part of the water, his fur slicked back, his face determined as he makes his way from the deep end back to the shore. The woman is sitting on one of the big boulders that make a sort of jetty into the lake. The man is standing in the water, the cuffs of his pants rolled up, holding the fingertips of the baby, lifting her and then lowering her, dipping her toes in and out of the water. They don't notice Mena as she approaches.

The woman is tiny, pale with long black hair. The man is tall, dark-skinned, and his russet hands envelop the child's. The woman watches him, and he croons to the little girl. "There you go, Zu-Zu, is it too cold?" The little girl squeals each time her feet touch the surface of the water. When they all turn around and see her, Mena feels like she's interrupted something.

"Hi," the woman says, smiling at her.

"Hi," Mena says, and then, feeling like she has to explain her sudden appearance, she says, "I'm Mena Mason. We've just bought the Carson place." She motions behind her, toward the cottage.

"*Effie*," the woman says, offering Mena her hand. "This is Devin." She gestures to the man. "And Zu-Zu. It's her first dip in the lake."

"Like Zu-Zu in *It's a Wonderful Life*?" she asks.

"I'm a sucker for Jimmy Stewart," Effie says. "And it was

on the entire time I was in labor. I swear, it's the longest movie ever made." The baby looks up at Mena, and her heart quickens. Her skin is the color of caramels, but her eyes are the same bright blue as Effie's.

"Hi," Zu-Zu says softly in the sweet, high voice of a toddler.

Mena wades into the water and crouches down so that she is at eye level with her. "Hi, Zu-Zu," she says, her throat constricting. "Is this your first swim?" She looks up at Devin then. "She's stunning."

"Thanks," he says.

"How old is she? About eighteen months?"

"You're good!" Effie says.

"Are you here for the summer?" Mena asks.

"No, we live here year-round. The camp with the tree house over there." She gestures down the road.

"Oh, I remember that place," Mena says. "Are you Gussy McInnes's granddaughter?"

Effie nods. "You've been to Gormlaith before?"

"It's been about five years. We used to come here when our kids were little."

"Oh, how nice. How old are they now?" she asks.

The pounding starts at the back of her head with one hard blow, like someone has hit her with a pipe.

"Seventeen," she says. "My son, he'll be seventeen in a few months. A Thanksgiving baby."

"Wait a minute, are you *Samuel* Mason's wife?"

Mena nods. This place is so small.

"We heard a rumor that he was coming," she says. And then, apologizing, "I work at the library. He called about getting a library card."

"Oh," Mena says.

"You know, we would love to have him come speak some time," she says. "I mean, if he does that sort of thing. There's a book club that meets once a month. I'm sure they'd love to discuss one of his novels."

"I'll mention it to him," Mena says, watching as the baby reaches into the water and picks up a flat gray stone, squealing with delight. She holds the stone out to her mother. "Mum—Mum."

Effie accepts the stone and examines it in the light as if she were a gemologist. "It's beautiful, sweetie. I love it. Can I keep it? Can I put it in my pocket?"

She nods. Effie turns to Mena, smiling. "And if you need anything, just let us know." There doesn't seem to be any pity in her voice, but Mena wonders how much they know. Because of Sam, because of his books, people seem to know more than they might otherwise. She pictures the book club ladies at the library clucking on and on about that poor, poor Mason family. She imagines awful casseroles starting to arrive at their doorstep.

"Maybe we can have you over for dinner one night," Effie says. "We don't have a lot of couple friends here at the lake."

She tries to imagine herself and Sam having dinner with them. She struggles to picture the table, the food, the conversation. When did simple things like this, the normal interactions of life, become small miracles? How long has it been since she and Sam have had dinner with another couple? She can barely remember the last time they drank too much wine, the last time they laughed too loudly or stayed up too late. "Let's do that," she says. "Absolutely."

"Great! How about Friday night?" Effie says. She has scooped Zu-Zu up now and is wrapping her in a towel, drying off her small bare feet.

"That sounds good. We'll bring wine."

Back at the cabin, the headache has retreated. She imagines her migraines like animals that reside in her skull. For tonight anyway, this one has curled up in the recesses. When she closes her eyes, she can almost hear the sound of it sleeping, breathing, waiting.

Finn is sitting outside, the portable phone in one hand, a cigarette in the other. As he sees her approach, he quickly snubs the cigarette out, nods at her, and goes back to his quiet conversation. Inside, the kitchen table has been cleared, the dishes washed. Sam. He's always been good about this. Her girlfriends used to bitch and complain about how sloppy their husbands were, how they felt like they were always cleaning up after somebody: their kids, their spouses. That all the work they did was so quickly undone. But Sam was thoughtful about this. He mopped the floors, cleaned the grout. Did the laundry.

Suddenly, she is struck with the image of Sam sitting amid a pile of laundry in the living room of the bungalow in San Diego, not long after the babies were born. She remembers watching him for ten or fifteen minutes (he didn't know she was there) as he folded the twins' tiny onesies, their jammies, their impossibly small T-shirts (those soft white long-sleeve T-shirts with the straps that snapped to keep them enclosed). When he caught her watching him struggle to fold a pair of miniature blue jeans, he'd looked up at her as if he were just a helpless man, just a stupid know-nothing new daddy, and God, she'd remembered loving him so much it almost hurt.

"What are you reading?" she asks him.

"The new John Irving," he says, holding the book up for her to see. "Good, but not my favorite."

She smiles and sits down on the bed next to him.

"Finn talking to Misty?"

Sam nods. "Not sure. But he's been on and off the phone for about an hour now."

Mena touches Sam's hand, scared that he might pull it away. He doesn't though, and he leans over, kissing her slowly, precisely on the forehead. She closes her eyes when his lips make contact with her skin.

When he pulls away, she looks at him, wanting to ask him a thousand things, but instead she only says, "Are you tired?" Her heart is pounding.

This is their code, the way he used to find out from her whether or not there was the possibility of sex. It started after the kids were born, when she was so exhausted she could barely imagine the effort of taking off her clothes, let alone making any sort of semblance of love to him. *Are you tired?*

Sam looks hard at her, his eyes apologetic, even before he says the words. "I'm sorry."

"Me too," she says, disappointment cold and sharp in her chest.

She turns away from him then to pull off her clothes, wonders if he is watching her as she bends over. Wonders if he even considers the contours of her body anymore. Wonders if he even thinks about her breasts, her hips, her thighs.

Then she thinks about Zu-Zu, about that strangely familiar ache she felt as she looked at her small hands. No. She couldn't possibly want another baby. Not now. It's too late for that. Her body is just confused, she thinks, wanting to fill a hole that can't be filled. Like water seeking its own level. That's all.

"I met a nice couple at the access area. Gussy McInnes's granddaughter and her husband. They've invited us to dinner on Friday," she says.

Sam has picked up his book again. He peers over the top of it at her as she climbs into bed. "Friday?"

"You have other plans?" she asks. She feels herself getting nasty. Angry. She hates this, but it happens every time he rejects her. "You don't have to come, but I plan to go." And then she rolls over, turning her back to him again. She squeezes her eyes shut, willing the migraine to stay huddled in its cavern, to not come out tonight.

In the morning, Finn decides to take a walk, asks his mother permission. He's trying to be nice, considerate. *Obedient*. But still she looks at him in that awful way she has that tells him she doesn't trust him at all anymore, and that she is disappointed, so very disappointed in every decision he has ever made.

"I'm not going to fucking run, if that's what you're worried about," he says, unable to keep up the farce.

She shakes her head and blushes then, and it makes him feel a little bit sorry for what he's said, but mostly just sorry for her.

He lets the screen door slam behind him as he stomps out of the cottage. It is overcast out, on the verge of rain. He doesn't even know where he thought he might walk to. The only road, besides the one back to Quimby, just makes a circle around the lake. So instead, he goes straight to the barn and picks up the basketball his father left behind yesterday.

He had finally gotten a hold of Misty on her cell phone last night. She was at Fashion Valley Mall with a bunch of people, including Sadie Silverman, who has always hated him. He could hear her in the background, *Mist, come on. Let's go.*

"Listen, Finn, now's not a good time. I'm at the mall; I can barely hear you. These guys are being so obnoxious."

"Who?" he asked, feeling bilious. Suspicious.

"The same old same olds. You know."

"Justin?"

"What? I can't hear you," and then muffled, "Christ, cut it out!" Laughter.

"I need to give you my number here," he said.

"Huh?"

"The number at the cottage, at the lake. My cell doesn't work here. You got a pen?"

He heard her rifling, pictured the big floppy backpack she carries to school, his name etched in ballpoint pen on the small pocket next to the Maroon 5 pin.

"I don't have one, Finny. Can you call me back later?"

"Fine," he had said.

But when he tried her later, he kept getting her voice mail. He left three messages, each one progressively more agitated. Finally he just called and hung up. Called and hung up. He could almost hear Sadie's grating nasal voice, "What is he, some sort of sicko stalker or something?" But he wasn't a fucking stalker. He was Misty's fucking boyfriend. At least he used to be.

He dribbles the ball and then chucks it as hard as he can. It rattles against the backboard and comes crashing down again, rolling toward the door. Outside it is starting to rain. He can hear it on the roof of the barn. So much for the fucking walk.

"You're not very good at that."

He turns toward the door, startled. There's a girl standing in the doorway of the barn. Her hair is wet, plastered to her head, and she is holding his basketball.

"Give it," he says.

She clutches the ball to her chest. "I'll give it to you if you tell me why you're so pissed off," she says.

"Who says I'm pissed off?"

"Well, my mom says that most people throw tantrums for two reasons. Sometimes they're really pissed off, but most of the time it's just for attention. Since you thought you were alone out here, I'm betting on the first one."

The girl is smiling, examining the basketball now. She looks younger than him. Maybe fifteen or so. She's short and skinny, knobby knees. She's wearing a wife beater, plaid boxer shorts, and black low-top Converse, no socks.

"What's your name?" she asks.

"Finn," he says.

She walks over to where he's standing and hands him his ball back. "I'm Alice."

He takes the ball, dribbles it, sort of half-assed, and is suddenly self-conscious.

"What's your girlfriend's name?" she hollers after him.

"What?"

"The girl who just dumped you? What's her name?"

He stops dribbling and makes an easy shot from the foul line his father painted with fluorescent orange paint on the wooden floor. He catches the ball on its descent and tucks it under his arm.

"You smoke weed?" he asks.

They walk together in the rain through the woods behind the house. He remembers playing in these woods with Franny. Franny had created an entire imaginary world for them there. It's where they could disappear for hours on end every summer. Their parents never even came looking for them. They built forts and hunted for treasures in the place where people dumped their old appliances. But today when they get to the spot, there's not much there but a rusted-out car he's pretty sure was there the last time he came and an old washing machine.

He sits down on a stump and pulls the Baggie and rolling papers out of his pocket. Alice stands next to him, shielding him from the rain that has lessened to a weak drizzle now. He lights the joint, takes a puff, and offers it to her, holding the sweet smoke in his lungs as long as he can bear. He loves the smell of the rain and the pot smoke.

"Where do you live?" he asks her.

"Not far from here. We're locals. Me and my mom."

From the way she says this, he knows better than to ask where her dad is.

"My dad's an asshole. He's in jail."

"TMI," Finn says.

"Huh?" she asks, taking a puff on the joint, coughing.

"Too much information." God, where is this chick from?

"Sorry. My mom says I'm an open book," she says. She coughs again, covers her mouth with her hand. "Sorry."

"This your first time?" Finn says.

"Open. Book." She nods, hands him back the joint, and pops a piece of bubble gum in her mouth.

After a while, they start to get cold. It's raining harder now, and Finn is hungry. "My mom's probably making dinner. You want to come over?"

"Nah," she says. "Maybe next time."

"Okay." Finn shrugs, and Alice takes off, running through the rain ahead of him, turning around to wave at him as she runs down the road.

Sam has never had this problem before, not once. Not the first time when he and his high school girlfriend, Catherine, groped and clawed and finally, finally made love in the back of his pickup parked under the stars on the first day of summer. Not ever with Anna or Paige, the girls he dated in college. Not with the others, the ones he didn't love but who offered themselves up to him in a way that made his indifference to anything but their bodies irrelevant. Not with Mena. Never with Mena. Not even when they were trying desperately to get pregnant and sex, for the first time, had a higher purpose.

The twins did not come easily.

They got married a year after they met, in Flagstaff in a field of wild sunflowers behind her mother's house. By then the film was finished with production, and they were both finished with Los Angeles. Mena had dropped out of CalArts by then; she was ready to just get on with her life, she said. She wanted to be an actress, but she also wanted to be a wife. A mother. Sam suggested they move to Mexico. He thought that with the money he'd made selling the film rights and the advance he'd gotten for his second novel, they might be able to live forever on some beach in Baja. Raise little suntanned babies. He could write and she could go to LA for auditions whenever the spirit moved her. Mena's mother was sick though, just diagnosed with MS, and she didn't want to be that far away from her. And so the compromise was San Diego. They bought the bungalow perched on Sunset Cliffs with cash. He finished the second novel in that house, pounding out the words at the dining room table where he could be close to Mena, who was experimenting in the kitchen. He remembers that time in a hazy way, as if filtered through a thick marine layer.

Mena was still acting a little then, but mostly just at the smaller fringe theaters in San Diego, and she had decided to start up a catering business to fill in the gaps. He would spend all morning at the typewriter, sometimes not even bothering to get dressed, and she'd bring him plates toppling with the rejects: overstuffed mushrooms, miniature triangles of spanikopita, melon balls wrapped in prosciutto. At noon, they'd retreat to the bedroom where they spent entire afternoons making love, trying to make a baby. Exhausted, hopeful, they would emerge again just as the sun was softening over the horizon. Sam would go back to work, and Mena would take off for whatever event she was catering.

Never, not in all that time, did he have this problem.

But despite his vigor and their persistence, after two years without any luck, Mena was defeated. Desperate. They were both still so young, but there was an urgency about Mena. She had such intense desires. This was something Sam loved about her.

"What's wrong with me?" she had asked.

The idea that there might be something wrong with either one of them had not really crossed Sam's mind. He'd chalked it up to bad timing, to bad luck. But now he quickly realized that this actually might be his fault; that maybe *he* was the reason why she wasn't getting pregnant. It made him feel terrible. He quickly scheduled an appointment with a fertility specialist. They endured the usual tests: his embarrassing, hers painful. And, to his relief, his sperm count was just fine, and they believed that everything might be solved by giving Mena some chalky white pills. Magic pills. There was hope again, and about three months after she started taking the Clomid, she was pregnant with not one, but two babies.

They'd fallen into bed after she came to him with the positive pregnancy test and made love for the first time in two years without an agenda. Not once, not then and not later, did he have this problem.

He drives into town and finds a computer at the Athenaeum that is tucked away where no one can see what he's doing. He doesn't even know what to look for. He rarely uses the Internet. *Performance enhancing pills*, he types. It makes it sound like he's some sort of athlete. Is this cheating? Is it legal? He Googles Viagra and finds 63,600,044 sites. He's pretty sure he's going to need a prescription. A doctor. More embarrassing tests.

But he needs to do this for her. For them.

Mena wakes up on Thursday morning with a headache, but she gets up anyway and makes breakfast for Sam and Finn: homemade oatmeal with bananas and real maple syrup. Fresh carrot juice. She drinks coffee. She concentrates on the news coming from the little radio Sam brought home for her a few days ago. But by the time they have devoured the food and retreated to their separate corners of the cottage, the distant rumbles in her head have become seismic.

She tries to ignore the migraine, will it away. She takes a Motrin and walks to the boat access area. She slips off her shoes and rolls up her cuffs. The water is clean and cold. She watches a pair of loons make their way across the water. Still, despite the quiet calm of the water, the headache persists. She's ready to vomit from the pain by the time she gets back to the cabin.

"I'm going to lie down," she says to Sam. "I took the phone off the hook." She is standing at the foot of the ladder, looking up at him in the loft. He is clicking away at his laptop.

"Okay," he says.

He's not listening. This may be a good sign, she thinks. When he's writing, really writing, he can't hear anything. She cracks open Finn's door, but he's not there. The surfboard he insisted on dragging across the country leans against the wall. The world's biggest security blanket.

"Where's Finn?" she asks, trying not to sound panicked.

Tap, tap, click, tap.

"Bike ride," he says without stopping. "I told him to be back in time for lunch."

She squeezes her eyes shut, sees Franny riding, wobbly, on the pink one-speed beach cruiser Sam bought her. Thinks of the white plastic basket and snap-on flowers. She remembers Franny's tan feet, her long fingers and toes. Mena remembers those monkey feet in her lap as she painted her toenails bright pink for her.

Her vision blurs and she stumbles down the hall to the bedroom. She's in too much pain to worry about Finn. She clicks the light switch off, pulls down the blinds. It is coming now, in waves of pain. She lies down in the bed, pulls the covers up over her head. The sheets are cool against her skin, and she tries to imagine that she is in the ocean, swimming in the salty sting of water. Each time a wave of pain comes, she lets her body be carried by it, lets it wash over her.

She remembers doing the same thing when the twins were born. They came a month early. They were supposed to be Christmas babies, but an hour after they finished Thanksgiving dinner, as she was picking turkey meat off the bones to save for soup and stew and sandwiches, her water broke. She remembers the empty turkey carcass, the cranberries splattered on the wall behind the stove, and the warm liquid pooling around her feet. The pain had come then too, and outside, the tide was crashing against the shore. As Sam drove her to the hospital in Coronado, across that endless bridge, she'd concentrated on the ebb and flow. She'd insisted that she could do this alone, that she didn't want medicine. No drugs. And so at the hospital, she'd closed her eyes and pretended that she was only swimming, only caught up in the ocean's arms. She fell into the pain, let it enclose her.

Franny.

Finn came first: six pounds plump and screaming. Franny

followed three minutes later and three pounds lighter: blue and silent. The neonatal nurses whisked Franny away, and there were several awful moments as they sucked the mucous from her lungs, rubbed life into her, when Mena wondered if they would lose her. She was so small, not much bigger than a Cornish game hen, a good-sized London broil. Mena remembers imagining Finn in the womb, greedily sucking the nutrients from her body: iron, calcium, blood and marrow. She imagined him licking his fingers, the faint sheen of grease on his lip. From the beginning, there was barely enough left over for Franny; she came into this world starving.

As soon as the nurse finally put Franny to her breast, she bit her, as if she were trying to devour her. Her hands, as small as dried apricots, grabbing at her skin, her milky eyes wide.

"Slow down, sweet pea," she had said, wincing as Franny finally latched on, her gummy grip like a vice. "There's plenty for both of you. It's okay."

Mena would spend the next sixteen years making sure that Franny was never hungry again, that she and Finn were both fed. Nourished. Full.

Franny.

Mena's body rocks with this imagined ocean. With the pain of her headache. With the pain of everything that she keeps captive inside that cavern in the back of her brain.

Dale Edwards read her first Samuel Mason novel when she was thirteen years old. Her parents were driving a rented RV up the coast of California for their summer vacation, and she found the book stuffed into a cupboard in the tiny bathroom stall. It was a paperback copy of *Small Sorrows,* and the pages were yellowed and warped. She remembers she looked at the author photo first; funny, she still does that—she won't read a book if the author doesn't look kind. But Samuel did. Look kind. He looked like a good guy, a happy guy, and she fell in love with him a little, in the way that she loved the man who ran the Circle K down the street, the way she loved her eighth-grade social studies teacher. The biographical notes said that he lived with his wife and their twins in San Diego. She imagined their family on a picnic blanket on the beach: Mrs. Mason in a yellow bathing suit, an umbrella shading her as she read a book, and Mr. Mason building sand castles with the twins. She bet the Masons never spent their summer vacations stuffed like anchovies in a metal box on wheels.

She didn't know it then, but her parents were on the verge of a divorce, and this ridiculous vacation was her mother's attempt to give fifteen years of a pretty miserable marriage one last shot. Her mother couldn't accept failure, and certainly not a failure of this magnitude. Her father, who was an unwilling participant in most things having to do with their family, agreed to the trip on the condition that he would not have to drive. He must have figured that this would make her mother relinquish the idea; she hated driving and so spent most of her time within walking distance of their one-story house on the west side of Phoenix. But she was hell-bent on making this trip happen, making this marriage work, and so while he sulked, reading the newspaper in the passenger seat, she drove. Perched like a nervous bird behind that giant wheel, she was determined.

They were driving from Phoenix to San Diego, and then the plan was to drive that beastly RV up the coast all the way to the redwood forest. Dale thrilled at the idea that they would be driving right through the very place where Samuel Mason lived. As she curled up in the compartment above the cab, reading the novel, head resting on a fuzzy pink pillow she brought from home, she fantasized that she might escape at a rest stop, look Samuel Mason up in the phone book, and that he'd invite her to join his family for dinner.

Dale did know her parents didn't love each other anymore. She didn't want it to be true, but it was. It was one of those facts she put in a small, quiet corner of her mind. But it was like putting an animal inside a box, which she supposed would probably work better with a smaller animal. A turtle, for instance, would probably sit in a box all day long without trying to escape. But this was no turtle. This was like trying to stuff an elephant into a shoe box and expecting it to keep quiet.

A few months before her mother announced that they would be spending three weeks in an RV together, Dale had been snooping around in her mother's closet. It wasn't really snooping, because she was actually looking for something. There was a stupid seventies dance at school, and she remembered that her mother had a pair of clogs that she could wear with the thrift-store bell bottoms she'd found. When she was little she had clomped around the kitchen in those clogs, banging a pot with a metal spoon, until her father yanked them off her feet and threw the pot in the sink.

Her mother's closet was not like a regular closet, not like the ones at her friend Marissa's house where you slide open the doors and everything is hanging nicely where you can see it—with drawers and hat boxes and shoes lined up on racks on the floor. A "walk-in" closet, her mother called this. "A damn mess," is what her father said. This closet was like a cave, a catacomb of forgotten things. Her mother's actual wearable wardrobe had dwindled in the last couple of years. The clothes that hung inside were relics of a thinner time.

The closet was dark too. Dale had to bring in a flashlight in order to see. Inside, she dropped to her knees and crawled along the floor, over twenty pairs of old shoes and fallen dresses, when the yellow beam of her flashlight illuminated something she'd never seen before. It was a prissy sort of box. *Decoupage.* That's what those paper roses glued on were called. Like the plaque she made for her father for Father's Day in the third grade, the one that said, GONE FISHIN' with a picture of a rainbow trout she had clipped carefully from an old issue of *Field and Stream.* The plaque that her father promised he'd hang up, the one he put on top of the fridge where it sat until, she's pretty sure, her mother finally threw it away.

She knew she shouldn't, but she couldn't resist lifting the lid. She half expected that she might find hidden treasures inside: jewels, pearls, cash. Her mother's stash. But it was simply filled with a stack of five-subject notebooks. Probably her mother's community college notes; she'd been taking classes since Dale was three years old, and still hadn't gotten her degree. Indeed, when she opened the first notebook, she saw her mother's curlicue handwriting. But it wasn't sociology or child development notes inside.

I hate him, it said. *He's a goddamn cheating bastard.* There were lists of women's names, frantic barely legible notes citing dates and places. Suspicions.

And so as much as she wanted to believe that this trip might restore her family, she also knew that even though they would be together for the next three weeks, hurling along the asphalt ribbon that teetered along the edge of the world, her father was already gone. And her mother knew it.

So each night, as her mother drove steadily on, the smell of 7-Eleven coffee wafting up to where she lay above their heads, Dale climbed inside the pages of Samuel Mason's book and tried not to listen to the silence growing louder between her parents below. Sam's novel saved Dale's life. She wonders now what would have become of her if she hadn't found that tattered copy of his novel that day in the RV. She wonders what would have happened to her if she had found something else abandoned in the john instead: *Anne Rice, V. C. Andrews, Jackie Collins,* God forbid.

They didn't make it to northern California; they didn't even make it past San Diego. While Dale and her mother were sleeping, the RV parked in a grocery store parking lot, her father packed a bag and disappeared, leaving only a credit card behind, tucked into the driver's side sun visor. As her mother pulled out of the parking lot that morning, the air thick with fog and smelling of salt, Dale tried to picture him walking across that dark asphalt expanse, rolling his suitcase behind him.

"Motherfucker," her mother said, pulling out into oncoming traffic. Her face was red, her thick tanned arms trembling as she drove back out to where the freeway started.

"Where did he go?" Dale asked.

Her mother had looked at her then like she was an idiot. "You think I know? How would I know?"

"Are we just going to leave him?" Dale had asked, trying not to cry.

"He left us, Dale. And don't you ever forget that."

The drive back to Phoenix only took five hours. The RV's air-conditioning broke in Yuma. It was 106 degrees, and Dale remembers that she was worried her mother might have a heart attack. She was sweating and breathing hard, trembling as she sped across the desert. She must have been going a hundred miles an hour.

"Ma?" Dale said.

"Can we not talk about your father?" her mother had said, not taking her eyes off the road.

"Do you want to hear a story?"

"What?"

"Do you want me to read to you?" And suddenly Dale was overwhelmed by a memory of her mother sitting next to her bed when she had the chicken pox. She stayed with her all night, applying thick pink lotion to her skin, reading books to her to take her mind off the itching.

Her mother softened, and still staring straight ahead, nodded.

And so Dale read, Sam's words liquid in her mouth like medicine. For five straight hours, in the unbearable heat, she read the novel to her mother. When they pulled into the driveway in front of their house, her mother put her head down on the steering wheel and cried.

"It'll be okay, Ma," she said, touching her back, which was soaking wet with sweat.

"I know," she said.

Her father came back and got his stuff a week later, moved in with his girlfriend in Scottsdale. Dale went to the library and took out every one of Sam's novels, and at night, she and her mother would sit in the backyard, listening to the cicadas, eating Del Taco, drinking Diet Cokes, and Dale would read aloud to her. Two years later her father left Phoenix, and they never heard from him again.

Finn follows Alice as she rides her bicycle up the winding hill. She wants to show him something. Her blond braid is swinging across her back as she stands on the pedals, struggling against the incline. He knows he's supposed to be back at the cottage by noon. At least they are starting to give him a little room to breathe; they must know there's nowhere he can go But the freedom has limits. Strict ones. Be back by noon for lunch. Home before dark. In bed (with lights out) by ten.

Alice doesn't seem to have any rules. Her mother works at the Miss Quimby Diner every day except for Monday, and Alice is mostly on her own. And her mother *trusts* her. Then again, she's probably a good kid.

"So do you live at the beach?" Alice asks when they get to the top of the hill.

"Yeah."

"That must be so cool. I've never been to California."

"It's all right," he says.

"You must hate it here," she says.

"Nah," he says. "I used to come here when I was little. And it's just for the summer."

"Follow me," she says, getting off her bike. He gets off his bike too and leans it against a tree. She takes his hand and pulls him toward what seems to be the entrance to a path in the woods that border the road.

"Where are we going?" he asks, aware of her hand squeezing his.

"Don't worry about it," she says, and pulls him along.

They trudge through the forest, which is thick and smells good. Woodsy. Alice pushes aside branches that obstruct their path, holding them for him as he follows close behind.

"It's not much farther," she says.

Finn looks at his watch: *11:15*. He wonders if there's any way he's going to be able to make it back to the cottage by noon. He promised his father he'd be back for lunch. It was part of the deal.

Finally, they get to a clearing. The sun is so bright it's almost blinding. There is a huge field, so impossibly green it might not be real. There are wildflowers everywhere: *pink phlox, purple violets, yellow euphorbia, red trillium*. He miraculously recollects the names his father used to recite when his family took long walks together in the mornings after breakfast. Some of the names reminded him of nursery rhymes: *lady's slippers, Dutchman's-breeches, jack-in-the-pulpit*. Franny liked to collect the flowers and press them between the pages of the heaviest books in the bookcase. There are flower petals carpeting huge expanses of the field, like snow in the summertime. And around the entire field are weeping willows, bowing.

"Wow," Finn says.

"Nobody knows about this place, except for me," Alice says. "And now you."

Finn sits down on the ground, surveys the scene in front of him.

"I come here when I'm stressed out," Alice says, sitting down next to him.

He nods.

Alice sighs. "You probably should know my daddy's up for parole in August. My mom's a wreck. If you meet her and she's kind of weird, that's why." She plucks a long blade of grass from the ground and slips it between her fingers.

Finn looks at Alice's skinned knees, at her sneakers, which are dirty and riddled with holes.

"My mom's a mess too," he says.

"Really? Isn't your dad some famous writer or something? It must be awesome to be in a family like that."

Finn shields his eyes from the sun. "My sister died last fall." As the words come out, he imagines them like birds. Big ugly crows, flapping their wings, hovering in the air between them. "And since then everything's gone to shit."

Alice nods, looks past him at the endless field of Crayola colors: *magenta, cornflower blue.*

Then she cups her hands together, presses the blade of grass to her lips, and blows. The sound that comes out is loud and shrill. Like sadness, like moaning.

"That's a cool trick," he says, and she shows him how to do it.

At 11:45 he says, "Hey, I gotta get back home."

"Okay." She shrugs. "Let's go."

He writes and then deletes. Writes and deletes. There are words and then nothing but pure, white space. It's the technological equivalent of a wastebasket overflowing with balled up pieces of paper. He smirks, thinking how many trees he must be saving. The books he has taken out of the library are stacked precariously at the edge of his desk. He has read them like a child, flipping open to random pages, unable to sit and concentrate on any single book long enough for it to make real sense. But he knows the answer is somewhere in these pages, in the pages he has not yet written. In the words that won't come.

This is what he has learned so far:

A healthy, properly nourished human being can live for sixty days without food.

Fasting can bring euphoria, heighten the senses.

Hindus fast. Moslems fast. Jews, Mormons, all sorts of Christians fast. People of all faiths feel closer to God when they are deprived of food.

People fast to change the world: English suffragettes, Irish nationalists. Bobby Sands, Francis Hughes, Raymond McCreesh and Patsy O'Hara. The body can become the battleground for political struggle. Mahatma Gandhi. One's own life the means of negotiation.

Kafka's *A Hunger Artist* inspired a flux of public fasts in 1920s Europe: starvation performances, the body a circus.

There are litanies of medieval women who fasted for prolonged periods of time, refusing sustenance other than twigs, herbs and the Eucharist. This denial was considered a miracle, and the women were deemed saints.

Despite all this, hunger is rarely voluntary. The number of people dying of malnutrition, of poverty related starvation, in the world at any moment is unknown.

In many cultures hunger is cyclical: a balance between satiety and starvation, the knowledge that before feast there must be famine, a hungry season before the rains and the harvest.

Sam does not know what to do with this information. It swirls in his head like numbers used to when he took calculus his first year of college. It is both connected to the world and completely disengaged. When he closes his eyes, he pictures a man. It is winter in Minnesota, in 1944. He is one of the men who volunteered to undergo a controlled experiment. To be systematically starved and refed so that the US government might understand how to revive all of the people who had been deprived of the most basic of human needs. He is tall, already thin, and he can feel the winter in his bones.

Sam stares at the blank screen, at the blinking cursor. He types a sentence, two, three, conjuring winter, evoking snow. But the words are too thin, as fragile and brittle as bones. He hits the backspace button and puts his head in his hands.

Mena and Sam walk toward Effie and Devin's camp on Friday night, and the loons are cackling on the lake. Mena can see them preparing to lift off from the water, their wings spread wide, their beaks set, certain. She feels her own chin rise up, determined. "This will be nice," she says.

Sam is inspecting the label on the bottle of wine.

"What does he do again?" Sam asks.

"I think he's an artist. Assemblages. Like Joseph Cornell. Remember the exhibit we saw at MOCA?"

Sam nods.

"What are we having for dinner?" he asks.

"Does it matter?" Mena asks, and then bites her tongue. "Let's just try to enjoy their company. It's been so long since we've done anything like this."

When they get to the camp, Effie is outside and Zu-Zu is toddling around on the large front lawn. Effie stands up and comes to them. She is wearing a long sundress, and her hair is pulled back in a loose ponytail. "Hi!" she says. She embraces Mena, kisses her cheek, and Mena is surprised by this easy affection. She envies her grace, the breeziness of her. She smells like cinnamon. "I'm so glad you came! And you must be Sam," Effie says, reaching out her hand.

"Nice to meet you," Sam says.

"I'm a big, big fan."

Sam looks at her, momentarily bewildered.

"I've read *The Hour of Lead* about fifty times. *English major,*" she says, by way of explanation.

Effie gestures to the camp. "Devin's cooking dinner. I'm pretty useless in the kitchen." She smiles and lifts up Zu-Zu, who is tugging at her skirt. "Have a seat. I'll open the wine," she says, and disappears inside with Zu-Zu on her hip.

Later, inside, as the manicotti cooks, Devin shows them his work, the assemblages displayed on shelves, which cover an entire wall. The boxes, most not much bigger than a shoe box, are handmade, wooden, and inside each one is a different miniature world made of things like sand, glass, butterfly wings and colored paper. Mena looks at Devin's big hands and wonders how they could possibly do such delicate work.

"These are beautiful," she says, peering into one box; suspended, magically, in thin air is one black curl, tied with a tiny yellow ribbon. The tiny engraved silver plaque on the box says, ZU-ZU'S FIRST HAIRCUT. Another one, labeled NOVEMBER 28, has a tiny blue robin's egg with the smallest crack.

"The day Zu-Zu was born," Devin says.

She tries to imagine what she would put inside a box like this. What the plaque would say. What objects could make the museum of her family's life.

They eat outside at a picnic table. Mena keeps accepting the wine they offer her, feeling the warm happiness of forgetting. Of losing herself in the flush and buzz. After Devin clears the plates away, they sit in chairs facing the water and drink more wine.

Sam is playing peekaboo with Zu-Zu. Mena watches his face light up each time she squeals. Zu-Zu comes over to him, pulls his nose and runs away, laughing with one of those full belly laughs that makes Mena weak in the knees. Devin and Effie sit together on the grass; she fits snuggly into his lap, like a Russian nesting doll. Mena watches him kiss the top of her head. It makes her ache.

"We'd really, really love to have you come to one of the book club meetings at the library," Effie says. "I know it's pretty small-time compared to what you're probably used to."

"Why not?" Sam says. His spirits seem high tonight, Mena thinks. "Just let me know when."

Effie claps her hands together. "That's great! Thank you so much. There might even be a small stipend. It would probably be small enough to be insulting actually, but I can at least promise you some lively conversation."

"Sounds like fun," Sam says.

"Are you working on anything new?" she asks.

Sam nods.

"I'm sorry. I'm so nosy."

"It's okay," he says. "I'm only beginning, really. It's just a bunch of images in my head right now. Just ideas."

They eat as the sun goes down. They drink. Mena drinks and drinks. When it is time to go, she stands up and feels wobbly with the wine. Thick and buzzing.

"Next time, you guys come to our place. Mena is an amazing cook," Sam says. "Do you like Greek food? Maybe *pastitsio*."

And then Sam is steering her toward the road, waving good-bye to Zu-Zu. Mena looks at them, this family, at all that promise. They stand together, a portrait that reminds her of everything she's lost.

She's had too much to drink. She is trying not to cry until after they are out of sight of the house. She is aware of everything: the pebbles under her feet, the indigo sky streaked with clouds. She is aware of Sam's palm pressing on her lower back, holding her up. They walk in silence all the way back to the cottage. She will not cry. She will not fall apart. Luckily, Sam doesn't let go. He must know that if he does, she might simply not be able to stand up on her own.

She remembers this feeling, this falling feeling. She remembers the way her body defied her. The way she crumpled, the way she collapsed. The feeling like those dreams where you are plummeting, but unlike the dream, she kept falling and falling. He'd been there then too. Holding her up.

Inside the cottage, Sam helps her get undressed, lays her down. He sits down on the edge of the bed.

"Sam," she says, her voice catching in her throat like a burr. She reaches for him and when he takes her hand, she pulls it, gently, pleading without speaking for him to come to her. To lie with her. "Please," she says. "God, please just come to me."

Sam looks at her, his face full of pity.

She tastes bile in her throat, the wine sour as it rises. And then all that sadness turns to anger, to rage. She sits up and starts to hit him, softly at first and then harder and harder as his body refuses to yield to her hands. She pounds his chest, his back, his legs.

"Goddamn you! You bastard. You goddamned bastard!" she yells.

He glances at their open door. "Shhh," he says.

And this makes her angrier.

She hits and hits and hits until she is drenched in sweat, until he grabs her wrists and stops her. After a while, he lets her go and she lets her numb arms fall to her sides. Then she lies back down, curling into herself, weeping. But he doesn't touch her. Not even a soft hand on her shoulder. But he also doesn't move from the bed.

They stay like this for a long time. Long enough for her ragged breaths to grow slower, more even. For the hiccuping sobs to subside.

Finally, she says softly, "Remember?"

Mena tries to think of the moment she had wanted to share,

but suddenly the memories are all fragmented, each recollection a tiny bit of paper, confetti tossed up into the air, falling all around her. Coating her eyelashes, her shoulders, her hair.

She reaches for him then again, still trying to hold on to something, but he is standing. Leaving. And when he closes the door behind him, she starts to fall again, and this time there's nothing at all left to hold on to.

Sam Mason has saved Dale's life more than once. Thank God, he was there for her after the whole Fitz business. She could always count on him. She has even started to wonder if everything that happened with Fitz wasn't just a necessary step on the winding path toward Sam.

It was during Thanksgiving break after Fitz went to Eugene that she found out about Sam's daughter. This was long before she had decided on her thesis, long before the daily Internet searches had become a habit. She actually was just poking around online, looking for a Christmas gift for her mother, when she came across the article on Yahoo! News. She had clicked on the link about Britney Spears and wound up on the Entertainment page where three headlines down was the one about Franny. She could have just as easily missed it entirely. She didn't give a damn about Britney Spears, had no idea why she'd even bothered with the article.

Novelist Samuel Mason's Daughter Dies Unexpectedly, it read.

She felt her heart start to pound hard in her chest, like someone banging against a wall with their fists. She quickly scanned the article, but there were no details, no explanations. It simply said that she had died in the family's home over the weekend. That she was sixteen years old.

In the photo accompanying the article, she was standing next to her father on the beach. She was a good head shorter than

Sam, thin and smiling. His arm enclosed her, and he was looking down at her, his profile offering only a half smile.

This was before she found Franny's personal site, the other
pictures. This was the first time she saw her face. Dale saved the
photo to her desktop and opened it in Photoshop, zooming in
to get a better look. The girl, his daughter, was wearing a sheer
yellow sundress. Her long curly blond hair hung in messy ringlets
to her waist. She was barefoot, standing on tippy-toes. When
Dale zoomed in, she could see white tan lines from flip-flops
on her feet. Dale studied Sam, studied the way he was looking
at Franny. The way his arm held her close. *Mine,* it seemed to
say. *My daughter.* In this picture, in this moment, there was no
one else in the world besides the two of them.

She felt tears starting to well up in her eyes and then they
were coming down her cheeks in hot trails.

She zoomed closer and closer and closer until they were
both pixilated beyond recognition. Until they were just tiny
little dots. Dots within dots on the screen.

"Dinner's almost ready!" her mother hollered up to her. She
could smell the turkey, the green beans and crunchy onions,
the mincemeat pie. As always, it would just be the two of them,
but her mother insisted on a full Thanksgiving feast. In a week
there would still be leftover mashed potatoes congealed in a
Tupperware bin that they'd have to throw out along with the
dried up and picked over carcass of the bird.

"In a minute," Dale hollered back.

Then she grabbed the first three of Sam's books from the
shelf next to her bed, quickly finding the dedication pages. *For
my father.* That was the first one. *For Mena,* of course, the second. *For Finn and Franny, my moon and stars.* She traced Franny's
name with her finger. She read somewhere once that Mena
and Sam named their children after characters in their favorite
books: Mena's was *Huck Finn.* Sam's was *Franny and Zooey.* Afterward, Dale read all of Salinger's Glass family stories and novels.

She wished her own name had such significance. Dale was named Dale because her father liked Dale Earnhardt, and because he had wanted a boy.

She took the books and shoved them in the bag she'd started to pack and then she opened the desk drawer and reached in for the old serrated hunting knife her dad gave her for her tenth birthday. She'd wanted a bicycle, a pink one with a banana seat and a basket. Instead he'd offered her this, and she'd burst into tears. It was his grandfather's, and then his. And now it was hers. She thought about leaving it behind, like all the other artifacts of her father's failures, but she also knew she would be on the road alone and even she had to admit it might come in handy.

For the first time since Fitz left, Dale felt alive again. She knew how messed up she felt after Fitz was gone, but nothing could possibly compare with how Sam must be feeling. She knew then and there that she needed to do something, something big that would save him in the way that he had, continually, managed to save her. She'd sat down that night after her shift ended at Blockbuster and started writing. She wrote for six hours straight, until her wrists and neck and back ached.

She thinks of Franny now as she tethers the pages of her manuscript together with a bunch of rubber bands. And when she stuffs the Phoenix Suns T-shirt and sweatpants she wears almost every day into her backpack, she sees the corner of the sheer yellow sundress she bought at Lane Bryant. She pulls it out by the hem and holds it against her body. It's almost exactly the same as the one Franny was wearing. Bigger, of course, but still, when she closes her eyes, she's standing on the beach. She rises up on tippy-toes. Her feet are tan, and Sam Mason is holding on to her. Proud. Looking down at her, smiling. *Mine.*

Alice suggests that they hang out at her house while her mom is at work.

"The castle," she says as she holds the screen door open for him. The screen is ripped, and one of the hinges holding it onto the door frame has come loose. The paint is cracked and peeling.

Her house is not right on the water like a lot of the other cottages and camps here; it's deeper in the woods, and the shade from the trees makes it dark inside. It's small, only two tiny bedrooms. The walls are paneled with wood, and the kitchen has avocado-colored appliances and an orange countertop.

He thinks about Misty's house, about the cold stone floors, the pristine stainless and marble kitchen. Her family has a Mexican maid who is only about their age, which always made Finn feel weird.

Alice leads him down the hall to her room and opens the door with great fanfare. "Ta-da!"

"Holy shit," he says.

Inside, everything is purple: the shag rug, the walls, the ceiling. The curtains, the bedspread, the painted wooden furniture. There is a violet-colored telephone sitting on her nightstand beneath a lamp with a lavender shade. There are purple pencils in a purple pencil cup. A plum-colored teddy bear perched on a purple pillowcase.

She shrugs her shoulders. "I told my mom I liked purple when I was like seven. And now, it's turned into this crazy thing. I used to really like it, but now it's starting to drive me sort of nuts. Every time she finds something purple, she brings it home to me. Candles, baskets, light switch covers," she says, pointing to the wall.

"Why don't you tell her you're over it?"

"I don't want to hurt her feelings." She shrugs.

"It's crazy in here." Finn laughs, picking up a purple picture frame. "Is this your mom?"

"Yeah," she says. "Her name's Maggie. She's really awesome."

Finn looks around and thinks about his father. Why are parents like that anyway? Franny started ballet when they were about six. All of a sudden, she was taking classes two days a week, private lessons on the weekends. Their father put the barre in her room, and sent her away to ballet camp for a week that following June. But the difference was, Franny stuck with it. When Finn decided maybe he should have a hobby, his father should have realized it would last about five minutes. His fourth-grade best friend, Roger, was really into stamp collecting then, and so Finn told his father he wanted to collect stamps too. His dad took him to a philately shop, bought him albums, glassine envelopes, a magnifying glass. He got him a subscription to *The Philatelic Exporter*. But it didn't take long before Finn decided that stamp collecting was about as exciting as picking his nose but without any of the payoff, and his father sulked for about a week when he told him he wasn't really into it anymore. Luckily, when he decided to start surfing, the only investment they had to make was on a board. Finn refused lessons in fear of what his father might do.

"You hungry?" she asks, going to her cupboard and pulling out stuff to make sandwiches.

"What's that?" he asks.

"You've never had Fluff?" She looks at him in disbelief.
"What's Fluff?"

"Oh, my *Gawd,* you are in for the treat of your life."

Mena buys all of their groceries at Whole Foods or from the Greek specialty market in Clairemont. He wonders what she'd think of him eating something that looks like liquid marshmallows.

Alice hums while she spreads the Fluff on one piece of bread and peanut butter on the other. "Your very first Fluffernutter!" she says, licking her finger and handing it to him.

He takes a bite, and it does taste awesome.

"You'll find nothing but fine cuisine here in the Northeast Kingdom. Tomorrow I'll introduce you to my specialty: tuna pea wiggle."

"You're wacked." Finn smiles and finishes the sandwich. He imagines these would taste really, really good if he were stoned.

"I know where there are some pot plants," Alice says, plopping into a Barcalounger that faces a console TV. "I found them by accident when I was out taking a walk one day."

"Where are they?" Finn asks.

"Behind your house, actually," she says. "Not far from your barn."

"How do you know they're pot plants?" he asks.

"Just 'cause I don't smoke it doesn't mean I don't know what it looks like." She laughs. "And my dad had a Bob Marley T-shirt with a picture of a leaf on it. My mom uses it to clean the toilet."

"Will your dad come here?" he asks. "After he gets out?"

Alice looks at him, bites her lip and goes back into the kitchen. "You want another one?"

"Sure," he says. "Listen, I'm sorry."

"S'okay."

Alice is unlike anybody Finn has ever met. He can imagine

what Sadie and Misty would say about her. They could be mean, especially to kids who didn't have money like they did. Hell, Sadie made comments about him all the time. He didn't have the right shoes, the right jacket, the right baseball cap. They would have called her white trash. Even thinking about their cruelty makes him feel bad for her.

He follows her back to his house, and they sneak behind the barn to get to an overgrown path that leads to a wide open field. It only takes a few minutes to get there. You might not notice right away; it would be difficult for the untrained eye to discern these plants among the other weeds and grasses. But this was *weed* weed . . . about a half acre of marijuana.

"Holy shit!" he says.

"No kidding," she says and smiles.

"What are we going to do?"

"That's up to you," she says. "It's your backyard."

Sam is at the doctor's office, under the pretense of getting a suspicious mole checked. This is what he tells Mena when she asks. This is what he tells himself, looking at the same brown spot that's resided on his forearm, unchanged, for a decade. He is still not sure, even as he fills out the form, which asks for the nature of the visit, if he will be able to talk to the doctor about what's really happening (or not happening) with him. He leaves the space blank and sits in the uncomfortable chair waiting for the nurse to call him in. There are three other men here. He can't decide whether this makes him feel more or less comfortable with the situation. The waiting room is small, the office inside his old elementary school. He went to fourth and fifth grade in this building. He can see the blackened marks and holes in the wooden floor where the school desks had once been bolted down. There is a water fountain mounted on the wall at hip level. The nurse's station used to be the school secretary's desk. He wonders if the examination room will still have a chalkboard, cursive letters written on a green border at the top.

"Come on in, Sam," says the nurse. He feels found out already.

The nurse takes his blood pressure, his temperature, weighs him—165 pounds. God, he's lost 15 pounds. When did that happen? "Okey dokey, Dr. Benjamin will be right in. Why don't you undress down to your boxers. Put this on if you like." She hands him a paper gown. "It ties in the back." When she leaves, he watches her walk away. Her hips are more narrow than Mena's, almost boyish. But she's cute. Long eyelashes and dimples in both of her cheeks. Still, nothing. Not even when he tries to think about her naked. Tries to conjure up some old naughty nurse fantasy cliché.

"In for a checkup?" the doctor says, not looking up from his clipboard.

"Sort of," Sam says.

"Well, let's take a look here."

The doctor is young, maybe thirty. He is good looking in a Ken doll sort of way. Tan and angular. As if he's just popped out of a plastic mold. He looks more Southern California than rural Vermont.

"You're just here for the summer?" he asks Sam, pressing the cold stethoscope to his chest.

"I think so. But we're thinking about staying on." He's not sure why he just told the doctor this. He hasn't even talked to Mena about that possibility, or thought it through much himself.

"Heart sounds good. Now take a deep breath . . . good."

He checks his reflexes, his eyes, his ears. Asks all the usual questions. And then he says, "Do you have any questions? Any concerns? Any reason why this couldn't wait for your regular GP at home?"

Sam looks at the window that faces the parking lot. He's pretty sure this is the classroom he had in the fourth grade. Miss Higgins.

"I'm having difficulty," he says. His heart is starting to race. At least if he's going to have some sort of cardiac event, he's in a good place.

"Difficulty with?"

"With my wife," he says. He didn't mean to say that. "I mean, with, oh shit."

"Enough said." Dr. Benjamin nods. "Let's see what we can do to help remedy that."

He steps back and looks at Sam, his brow furrowed. "How long have you been experiencing problems?"

"Since last fall," he says.

He glances at the chart; Sam thinks he is avoiding making eye contact with him. Is this so bad it's even embarrassing for a doctor? "I see you're not on any prescription medication. Are you using any other drugs?"

"You mean *illegal* drugs?"

"Yes. Marijuana? Cocaine?"

"No." Sam shakes his head. "I have a couple of glasses of wine with dinner. A few beers on the weekends."

"Okay. How about herbal supplements, vitamins?"

"No." Sam shakes his head again.

"Alrighty then, I think we should take a closer look at things. Many times there is a physical explanation for this. And there are a variety of treatments possible."

"My daughter died," Sam says. Again, this is not something he intended to say. It truly is as if he no longer has any control over his words.

"Oh," the doctor says as he snaps his rubber glove on. "When did this happen?"

"Last fall," Sam says, wincing involuntarily.

"Have you suffered from depression in the past? Since . . ."

"No," Sam says.

"Depression, anxiety, both can sometimes cause erectile dysfunction. The treatment for impotence would entail treating the depression, or anxiety, you might be feeling."

"Can you just prescribe some Viagra?" Sam asks, exasperated, already regretting all of this.

"I would recommend that you schedule an appointment with a psychiatrist. There's a terrific doctor in St. Johnsbury who is taking new patients. Perhaps you and your wife could seek counseling together. If, after evaluating things, she determines that Viagra might be helpful in your situation, then she will be able to prescribe it for you."

Sam stands up from the table where he has been sitting. The tissue paper crackles loudly beneath him. "I shouldn't have come," he says, reaching for his pants, which he left on the chair by the door. When he picks them up, loose changes drops to the floor. Pennies, quarters, nickels rolling across the warped wood.

"I know this must be difficult for you," the doctor says, his chiseled jaw set. His brow furrowed in concern.

"That's an understatement," Sam says, feeling irritable now. What does this asshole know about anything? He's not even wearing a wedding ring.

"Listen, if you want to try something nonpharmaceutical, there is an herbal alternative that some people claim to have had success with. It's called yohimbine; it comes from the bark of a West African tree. You might be able to find some at the natural food store. But I must warn you, I wouldn't recommend this particular route. It's been known to cause an increase in heart rate, in anxiety, and if you're already suffering from anxiety, it might exacerbate your problems. Also, it sometimes is used for weight loss, and you frankly can't afford to lose any weight. Just please consider getting therapy first. Be smart about this."

Sam gets back into the car and heads straight for the natural food store. He finds the bottle of yohimbine next to the natural weight loss supplements. He picks up one bottle and then a second. He buys some lilac lotion for Mena and some beeswax candles. He lets himself imagine for a minute that he might seduce her. That he's found everything he needs to love his wife again at the health food store.

Mena doesn't tell Sam about the auditions. She saw the sign posted at the grocery store the first time she went into town, and she hasn't stopped thinking about it since. The Quimby Players are putting on a production of *Fool for Love,* by Sam Shepard. She has always loved this play. She and Sam saw it once in Los Angeles when they were dating and again a few years ago in San Diego at the Fritz. She remembers thinking both times that if she were ever to act again, she would love to play the role of May. For some reason, the play stuck with her. Every time they made the trek across the desert to visit her mom in Flagstaff, there was a town somewhere between San Diego and Gila Bend she imagined as the place where Eddie and May's drama might really be playing out. She even started to think of them as real people. "Oh look, there's May's laundry on the line," she'd say, gesturing out the window as the desolate desert seemed to stand immobile outside the abandoned motel. When a blue Chevy truck was parked out front, "Looks like May's got company."

This was the first time she really understood Sam's tenderness toward his characters. His protectiveness and concern. When she saw the audition sign hanging next to the ads for babysitting services and used cars and lost dogs, she felt a sort of excitement she barely remembered anymore. She had quickly jotted down the place and date, stuffing the note back into her purse. *Quimby Town Hall, 7:00 P.M. Tuesday, June 29th.*

All day she debates with herself. She hasn't acted in ages. After she had the twins, she did one staged reading of a play in San Diego, a favor to a playwright friend. Then there were those awful corporate training videos she agreed to after the brief success of Sam's film faded. She was perfect for the sexual harassment prevention videos, the pimple-faced director had assured her. The money was pretty good too, though for a couple of years afterward she'd get strange looks from people on the street who must have recognized her as the office whistle-blower. But being on a stage again: that was something else entirely. She wasn't even sure she knew how to act anymore. But now, the audition date had come and she hadn't stopped thinking about it.

She is going mad inside the house all day, trying to pretend that this is all about saving Finn. That her marriage isn't crumbling. Maybe this is exactly what she needs. It's only an audition anyway; she's probably being presumptuous assuming that she'd be offered the role. She's a little too old for May. There's probably some lovely drama student at the high school, a girl who looks older than her age, who is dying to add this role to her résumé.

"I'm going into town for a few hours," she says to Sam. He is upstairs in the loft, typing again.

"Tonight?" he asks.

"Yeah. Why? Did you have plans?"

"No," he says. He sounds dejected. Disappointed.

"You sure?"

He's been acting funny all afternoon.

"What did the doctor say?" she had asked when he came back after his appointment. He'd been gone for hours. By the time he got home she'd had time to imagine the worst-case scenario:

melanoma, metastasized. She has become the queen of the worst-case scenario. "Anything to worry about?"

"Nothing, everything's fine. Oh, I also stopped by the health food store and got you some of that lilac lotion you like."

He had looked nervous. Like he was hiding something. Mena is good at reading people's faces, and he was reading like a kid who's done something wrong. She's all too familiar with that look.

"You sure?" she asked again.

"I'm fine."

"Okay then, there's leftover moussaka in the fridge from last night. Make sure Finn has some salad with it. And water. No soda."

"What are you doing in town?" he asks, but she is already out the door.

In the car, she rehearses the monologue she has prepared. It's the same one she used to use in all of her auditions. It is amazing how easily the lines came back to her, the words engraved somewhere in her distant memory. It's the piece from *Who's Afraid of Virginia Woolf?* the first play that made her cry. She and Sam were trying to have a baby when they went to see it at the Old Globe, and Honey's hysterical pregnancy, the loss of something that wasn't even real, was so vivid to her then. Everyone thought Honey was crazy, but Mena knew exactly how she felt.

She looks in the rearview mirror as she parks in the dirt lot behind the Town Hall. Her face looks older. She can't remember the last time she really looked in the mirror. She's worn the same makeup for so long, she barely needs a mirror to put on the brown kohl eyeliner, the mascara, the smudge of blush. Her eyes look sad, turned down at the corners. There are lines now at their edges. She blinks hard and clears her throat.

Inside the Town Hall there are about twenty people milling about. They all seem to know each other. She finds herself quickly sizing up the competition, an old habit from back in the days when she was always auditioning for something. One woman is about six feet tall with dirty blond hair pulled back into a ponytail. She's rail thin, and her face reminds Mena of a horse. The woman she is talking to is her polar opposite: short, round, with a black bob and moon face. There are several men sitting together in folding chairs, chuckling and drinking coffee. Most of them are older, probably auditioning for the part of the Old Man. There are a couple of high school girls giggling in a corner, skinny girls in sweatpants and sneakers, messy ponytails. A young woman in glasses, sipping coffee from a ratty plastic travel mug. A guy about her age, reading a newspaper: black hair, the scruff of a new beard. And a woman she is pretty sure is in charge of things, bustling about with a stack of scripts and a clipboard.

"Do I need to sign up somewhere?" Mena asks the woman who approaches her.

"Yep, just put your name here," she says, gesturing to the sign-up sheet. "You here for the summer?"

Mena nods. "We just bought a place up at Lake Gormlaith."

"*New York?*"

"Excuse me?"

"Are you from New York?"

"No," she says.

"Oh, most summer folks up here are from New York."

Mena is uncomfortable. Maybe she should just turn around and go home. "I'm Mena," she says instead, smiling and offering her hand.

"Lisa," she says. "I'm directing the show. Do you have a monologue?"

"I do." Mena nods nervously, reaching into her purse for the tattered script. Just in case she couldn't conjure up the lines from memory.

"What we'll do is let you do your monologue, and then if

we decide to have you stay for callbacks, we'll ask you to read for the specific part. You know there's only one female character in this play?"

Mena nods, feeling deflated.

They audition for the Old Man role first. She finds herself assessing each of the actors: too tentative, too quiet, too loud, too over the top. She figures it will be the man she saw smoking a cigarette on her way in. He's got a great gravelly voice, kind eyes. They'll need to work with him on his projection though.

Next they audition for Eddie. There's a kid, maybe twenty, who is painfully flamboyant. He ends his monologue from *Rent* with a deep bow. A few guys mumble through their parts and then the guy with the newspaper stands up.

"I'm Jake Rogers, and my monologue is from Shepard's *Buried Child*." His voice is quiet, a little unsure. But as he speaks, he seems to gather confidence. By the time he has finished, Mena looks at Lisa and sees that she is grinning. This guy is good. Really, really good. Even for a community theater. He sits back down when he's done and picks up his paper.

They audition for the role of Martin, a small part, and then for May.

Mena is the last to go for the women. The others—the tall one, the short one, the high school girls—are not as bad as Mena had anticipated. The woman with the long face does a piece from *Streetcar* that could have been a train wreck but was actually pretty moving. Mena stands up and feels her knees quaking. It's just a silly community theater audition, she reminds herself as she walks to the front of the hall.

"I'm Mena Mason, and I'll be doing a monologue from *Who's Afraid of Virginia Woolf?*"

Lisa nods, signaling for her to begin. And then, as the first lines come, she loses herself. The words are like magic, transporting her. She is Martha, drunk and angry and frustrated. She is desperate and fierce. She thinks about what happened between her and Sam the other night. She recollects that wasted rage. When she is finished, her heart is beating so hard she's sure that everyone will hear it. That it will give her away.

Lisa asks everyone to hold on for a few minutes as she and the assistant director, a kid who is probably home from college for the summer, make the first round of cuts.

Mena goes outside for some fresh air. It is dark outside, the porch light the only illumination. "That was great," the short woman with the black bob says. "You act before?"

"A little bit." Mena smiles. "Your piece was lovely too."

"They should pick you for May and Jake Rogers as Eddie, but they don't really like to cast summer people. The locals get mad if they don't recognize the actors."

"Oh," Mena says.

"Good luck." The woman smiles warmly. "You do really deserve the part. Don't take it personal if you don't get it."

It seems like forever before Lisa calls them back in. "We'd like Oscar, Frank and Larry to stay. Jim, Kyle and Jake. Hanna, Ashley and Mena. The rest of you, we need a crew. Stage manager, props, costumes, that kind of thing. If that's not your thing, we're doing *Oklahoma!* again this fall, and we'd love to have you back."

"I'll stage manage," the girl with glasses says.

Mena feels an old rush of excitement as she stands up to read lines, first with Jim (a lanky guy with cowboy boots) and then with Jake Rogers. She thinks she's doing well, but she is incredibly nervous—as if getting this role suddenly matters more than anything in the entire world.

"Okay, everybody," Lisa says after about an hour of mixing and matching of actors. "I've got your numbers. We should have our decision by tomorrow night. Rehearsals start on Tuesday and run for six weeks. The show opens August sixth and runs three weekends."

In the car on the way home, Mena sings. She used to do this when the kids were small, drive them around at night to try to get them to sleep. Especially Finn. He was so restless. She'd drive from their house to the freeway, north on the 5 to La Jolla, and then back again. Usually she could get through the entire sound track of *Grease* or *Godspell* or *The Music Man* before Finn fell asleep. Franny was easier. Always so much easier.

When she pulls the car into the driveway, she sees the light on in the loft. The lights in Finn's room are out. She opens the door quietly; if Sam is working she doesn't want to disturb him.

"You back?" he asks.

"Uh-huh," she says.

She should tell him, share this with him. She remembers the way it used to be when she came home from an audition, buzzing the way she is right now, hopeful. They'd stay up half the night sometimes talking about what would happen if she got the big part in the new Scorsese film, whether or not he might be able to go with her to whatever location they would be shooting at. Before the kids were born, there was always the possibility of something big happening. At any moment, their lives might become enormous.

But she can't tell him. They have an unspoken agreement between them now. They are not allowed to get their hopes up anymore. It's too hard when things don't work out. The disappointment is too much to bear. They've made the mistake of optimism before. The error of wishful thinking. And so she says, "I'm exhausted. I'll leave a light on. Good night."

Finn doesn't know anything about growing weed. In San Diego, Misty could always get them hooked up. He actually met her when he was looking for pot. It was Christmastime last year, only about six months ago. It was at a party somebody was having up in Mission Beach; he'd gotten a ride up there in the hopes of scoring a dime bag for Christmas. He'd started smoking pot to help him sleep at night, but now he liked the sort of peace and quiet it brought to his brain during the day too. The forgetting. The possibility of having to endure their first Christmas without Franny straight was not an idea he had wanted to entertain. When he walked into the party, he recognized Misty from school right away. He couldn't figure out who she could possibly know here. The crowd was all surfers and burnouts.

"What are you doing here?" he had asked her.

"Same thing you are." She shrugged. "My friend *Mary Jane* invited me."

She said she knew a guy who knew a guy, and a few minutes after disappearing into a bedroom at the back of the house with Finn's money, she came out with a small bag of weed and two beers.

"Let's get out of here," she said, looking around as if there might be some reason to stay, and then took his hand. They walked to the boardwalk and sat down on the seawall.

She was pretty high on X that night, and she just wanted to

kiss. For hours and hours they kissed. He remembers the way the boats in the bay were lit up, like floating Christmas trees. She lit a joint, inhaled and then kissed him: blowing the smoke into his mouth as she did. And then there was that warm happiness, that lovely distraction. He could have stayed like that forever, the sand cold on his feet, her hair warm in his hands.

He loves Christmas at the beach. A lot of people might think it would be weird to be somewhere so warm during the holidays. That Christmas couldn't be Christmas without snow. But it's all he's ever known. White lights in all the shops. The giant tree decorated with beach balls by the pier. The Christmas parade down Newport Avenue: Cub Scouts and bagpipers, the Geriatric Surf Club, the hot rods and Harleys. Sometimes it would be cold enough to need a sweater, and they'd get hot chocolate from the Lighthouse, the ice-cream shop near the end of the street. Christmas in San Diego was Franny's favorite time of year too.

After Franny started taking ballet, Mena would take them to see *The Nutcracker* at the San Diego Ballet every year. Finn used to bitch and complain, *ballet* for Christ's sake, but Mena insisted that they all dress up and go. And it actually was kind of great. Before the performance, they'd have dinner at Mr. A's. It was the one time every year that they went somewhere fancy for dinner. Mr. A's was at the top of one of the buildings near downtown. From up there you could see all of San Diego: the bay, Balboa Park, even Coronado. And the best part was that the airplanes landing at Lindbergh Field flew so close, you could almost see the people inside. His father always got the duck, and his mother always got salmon. Franny ordered lobster tails. Every single time. God, they were such creatures of habit. Finn ordered something different every year. After dinner, they would go to the ballet, which, though Finn would never admit it, was always sort of magical. Franny watched the ballet on the edge of her seat, her eyes reflecting the lights. Rapt.

"I want to be Clara," she said. Determined. Certain. And then, when she was twelve, she got the role. The youngest Clara ever cast.

That year Finn and his parents went alone to Mr. A's, and it felt strange without Franny there. It was never just the three of them anywhere. Without Franny, it was like they didn't know what to say. How to act. Finn ordered the lobster that year, but he didn't like it very much. He had them package it up for him; he figured he would give it to Franny later.

Watching her dance was not like anything he'd ever seen. They'd been going to *The Nutcracker* for ages, but this year was different. He felt the way Franny must have felt: transfixed. Mesmerized. He sat at the edge of his seat the entire time, and at the end, when the cast came out to take their bows, he felt his throat swell up. Embarrassed, he had to squeeze his eyes shut for a second so he wouldn't cry.

Afterward, they'd piled into the car together, the entire back of the station wagon full of flowers that people had given to Franny. His parents and Franny were buzzing and laughing. Franny kept talking about how she had messed up during the party scene. She could never, ever accept a compliment, not even when she was a kid. Finn didn't speak the whole way back to the house. It's hard to say what he was feeling that night, but now he thinks it might have been the night he realized that Franny was different than he was. That while he was just a regular twelve-year-old kid, Franny was *extra*ordinary. He was so proud of her he could barely stand it; his skin felt stretched tight. But he also felt like she was slipping away. He'd handed her the tinfoil swan with the lobster tails inside, but she said she was too excited to eat. He knows now, that if he'd been smarter, he would have realized that this was the night they started to lose her.

After his mother takes off into town and his father goes up to the loft to work, Finn decides to sneak out to look at the plants. He hollers up to his dad, "'Night!" and goes to his room. He turns on his stereo to mask the sounds of his escape. He has discovered that his window opens easily and almost noiselessly; it's not painted shut like some of the others in the house. And the screen pops out easily too. So in just a few seconds, he's standing outside. He could run! He could run all the way into town, start hitchhiking back to California. He could be hundreds of miles away before his parents even woke up. But what the hell would he do when he got there? He has friends, but all his friends still live with their folks. Misty's parents aren't about to let him crash there. He isn't even sure if Misty would *want* him to come back. The last time he talked to her, she'd sighed a lot. He'd been the one doing all the talking. And finally, she'd said, "Hey, I gotta go. My mom's home."

It's chilly out tonight, but the moon is full and bright. A few more of the camps across the lake are lit up. He imagines that by the Fourth of July this weekend every camp will be full of people. He is careful to walk around the cabin, out of his father's line of sight, should he happen to look out the window. Finn shoves his hands in his pockets, looks back one more time and then starts walking toward the field.

It's dark, with only the moon to illuminate his way. He thinks he should have brought a flashlight with him. He remembers the lighter he has in his pocket and, as soon as he's out of sight of the house, he clicks it. It hisses and then lights up. He gets to the field quickly and finds the first plant.

He holds the lighter up to the plant. He has no idea how this green plant becomes the stuff he smokes. He'll need to do some research. Some reading up. That ought to be a challenge here.

Franny's favorite book when they were kids was *The Secret Garden.* He thinks about this as he makes his way back to the house: Franny curled up in their father's lap on the couch as he read to her. Finn would sit on the floor, pretending to be absorbed in his LEGOs or Transformers. But he was listening too. He remembers lying in bed at night trying to imagine finding a secret door hidden by ivy behind their house. Franny would like this. He wishes he could tell her what he's found.

Sam doesn't feel anything at first. After Mena leaves he takes two of the capsules with a glass of wine and waits. Finn is listening to music in his room. He can hear it wafting up to him in the loft. It reminds Sam of California. *Sublime,* he thinks. When he's sure that Finn is in for the night, he starts looking for something to help things along.

He's got no pornography here. No Internet. No magazines. He'd tried this before, a few months back when they were still in California, one night when the house was empty. He'd browsed the Internet for hours. He'd looked at tame stuff: supermodels, bikini models, even artists' models. When that didn't work, he'd looked at hardcore stuff too: women with other women, women with objects, women with animals (though that was the result of an accidental click of the mouse). He remembers how it made him sweat, as if he were twelve and stumbling upon one of his father's *Playboys*. How it made him blush. But despite his efforts, there was simply nothing. He felt nothing. He had turned the computer off finally, his skin raw from rubbing. His eyes wet.

He picks a book off the shelf. *Anaïs Nin.* The old standby. He'd found a tattered copy of *A Spy in the House of Love* at a yard sale when he was a teenager. There were many nights when he went to bed curled up with Sabina. He could remember the quiet anxiety of turning the lock on his bedroom door in case his father came checking on him. He could remember the head-lights from the dirt road cutting through his room in sharp white flashes. He can almost remember the way it felt to be sixteen. Alive. And tonight, as he scans the paragraphs, he does feel something familiar. A relic of some other time. A tingle. An ache. A whisper of desire. *Desire,* his old friend. He closes his eyes and concentrates.

As he reads, his heart is pounding hard in his chest, his mind is reeling. He can't stay focused on anything long enough. Not the words on the page, not on his own flesh in his hands. Nothing. God, this is fucking misery. It's as if someone has flipped a switch, turned everything that was once electric inside him off. And in this awful darkness, he can't find the breaker to re-store things. He's stumbling around without a flashlight in an unfamiliar house. Everything is treacherous.

When he hears the screen door open, he sits up, trembling. He shoves the book back on the shelf. Straightens himself up. His heart is pounding hard in his chest.

"You home?" he asks.

"Uh-huh."

He wonders when they both started keeping secrets. He used to hate secrecy. He promised Mena early on that with him there was nothing to discover. That he would always tell her the truth. But this was before there were things that could hurt between them. Before there was a need to keep things to him-self. She does it too, this concealing. It's as if they are both con-stantly, constantly protecting each other from harm. Tonight, he doesn't know where Mena has been. He doesn't even feel like he has a right to ask. The rules are different now. Every-thing has changed.

He hears Mena getting ready for bed: the running of water, the brushing of teeth, all of the lights getting clicked off down-stairs. He hears her feet padding down the hallway toward their room. He imagines her undressing, her skin, exposed in its entirety for a moment before she pulls her nightgown over her head. He imagines the way she used to wait for him.

He makes his way down the ladder with only a small light in the hallway to guide him. But when he crawls into bed next to her, she is already asleep. He considers waking her, thinks about giving it a shot. His body is still trilling with the pills, though he's not sure if there's any connection between this feeling and that other one. Besides, her body is curled away from him: a fiddlehead fern, spiraling inward. Every night she makes a protective shell of her body, at the edges of the bed, and she doesn't unfurl until morning, and then she sneaks out of bed when she thinks he is still sleeping.

She has left the light on his side of the bed on: at least she is still considerate. He almost always reads himself to sleep these days. The book is his signal to her that he is preoccupied, otherwise engaged. Sometimes he'll read until his eyes are crossing, falling asleep with a book across his chest.

He worries that she has finally given up on him.

He looks at her, in her pale blue nightgown, at the gentle curve of her body. He remembers tracing her edges, memorizing the slope of shoulders, waist, hips. He used to love when she slept turned away from him. It used to mean that she wanted him to press his body against hers, to feel the front of him against that glorious expanse of her back. But now it only means, *Leave me alone. This is too much for me.*

When he touches her, it feels illicit.

He remembers once as a child when his father drove him all the way to Philadelphia to the Rodin Museum. He was maybe seven, old enough to know better, but one of the sculptures had moved him so much, he couldn't resist. He had reached out and touched the cold marble, just for a second before withdrawing his hand as if burned. The security guard scolded him, and he'd felt ashamed. He couldn't explain that the impulse, to touch that beauty, was too strong to resist. Instead, he'd nodded, mumbled his apologies.

He touches her.

He allows his hand to follow the path her spine makes, the curvature of bone beneath fabric and skin. And when his fingers reach the place at the bottom of the trail of bones, her body reacts. Just a shiver. He could have imagined it, this response. But there it is again: a twitch of skin, a tremble. He nods and nods. She is not dead. They are not dead.

Mena got the call from Lisa as she was making sandwiches for their picnic. Effie and Devin had offered them their rowboat when Sam mentioned that they used to go to the island on the Fourth of July. What Mena didn't expect is that he would take them up on it. The idea of a family picnic seemed almost laughable these days. Of course, they used to take the kids out when they were younger. Have picnics. Spend the afternoon exploring. Mena would pack enormous lunches: sandwiches, homemade potato chips, individual berry cobblers made with blueberries they'd picked, a large thermos of sun tea. On the Fourth of July they would go out to the island and stay until the sun set, until the sky was exploding with lights, the air above them cracking, the shells hissing as they hit the water.

"You didn't tell us you were a professional actress," Lisa said.

"Oh, I'm not a professional. Not anymore." Mena felt disappointment swelling up inside her, certain they had already cast someone else. "I let my Equity contract expire more than ten years ago."

"I know. I checked. I hope you don't mind. Our stage manager, Anne, saw *The Hour of Lead* recently, coincidentally, and recognized you," Lisa said. "And so . . . on that note . . . we'd love to have you play May. Are you still available?"

"Yes," Mena said, blood rushing hot to her cheeks. "Absolutely. Thank you so much."

"I haven't spoken to the others yet, so please don't say anything, but we plan to offer the role of the Old Man to Hank James, Kyle Smith will play Martin, and Eddie will be played by Jake Rogers. He's the second guy you read with. The one with the beard."

"I remember," Mena said. "Thank you again."

"Rehearsals start next Tuesday. At seven o'clock. Have a terrific holiday."

Mena finishes making the sandwiches: chicken pesto *panninis*. The bread is still warm; she baked it at five o'clock this morning. She found a patch of basil growing on the side of the house, probably from a previous tenant of the cottage. She puts everything in a picnic basket: sandwiches, fresh fruit from the Quimby Farmers' Market, and a bottle of wine. She digs around in the cupboard for paper cups. Napkins.

On the way out to the island, Sam is talkative. Finn is not.

"Remember when you used to swim the last quarter mile to the island?" Sam asks, digging the oars into the water. "You think you could still do that?"

Finn and Franny both became good swimmers. They almost always dove off the boat as they approached the island, racing each other to the shore. It made Mena nervous, but they were strong, strong swimmers. Little fish.

It's one of those rare clear-sky days at the lake. No clouds, and the sun is almost oppressive. Mena can feel it beating on the back of her neck. She wishes she had brought a hat for shade.

"How long are we going to be out here?" Finn asks, swatting at a mosquito that has landed on his arm.

"I don't know. Maybe three, four weeks," Sam says. "Hope you brought a change of clothes."

"Ha. Ha," Finn says. "We'll be back by tonight, right? For the fireworks?"

"You don't want to stay? Like we used to?"

Finn shakes his head.

They glide through the water toward the island. Mena watches Sam's thin arms, the muscles flexing and retracting as he moves the oars. He is wearing the boat shoes Mena bought him the first summer they came to Gormlaith. She spent a lot of money on them; they are still in perfect condition.

When they get to the center of the lake, Sam lifts the oars into the boat and pulls a pair of binoculars out of his backpack. He peers through them for a second. The sun is so hot.

"I think I see a pair of loons," he says. "They've got a baby."

Mena takes a deep breath. "I'm going to be in a play."

"What's that?" Sam asks, peering into the distance at the three loons.

"A play. *Fool for Love*. The Quimby Players are putting on a production of it. I'm going to be May. That's where I was the other night. I didn't want to tell you about the audition in case I didn't get the part. But I did." Mena feels nervous. "Get the part."

Sam is quiet. He puts the binoculars back in the bag and picks up the oars. They creak in the oarlocks.

"Sam?"

"Huh?"

"What do you think?" she asks. "You know how much I've always wanted to do this show," Mena says, feeling defensive, already defeated.

"That's great," Sam says, but she knows what he's going to say next before he says it. "So I guess you'll be gone a lot now. Most nights?"

"Well, rehearsals are four nights a week. And Saturday afternoons."

Sam nods, keeps rowing.

Mena feels herself getting angry.

"I'll make sure that there's still dinner every night, if that's what you're worried about," she says. "You're up in the loft doing whatever it is you're doing every night anyway."

"Writing," Sam says. "I'm up there writing."

"Sure," she says. Her eyes sting.

Mena looks at Finn. He is staring down into the water. He dips his hand in, watches the light catching in his fingers when he pulls it back out. He is quiet. But still, Mena can't stop. "It's not like I'm *abandoning* you two. I'm alone in the house at night anyway. Finn's locked in his room or off God knows where. And you're, you're . . ." She sighs.

"So, basically you're checking out," Finn says quietly.

"What?" she asks, feeling her heart pounding in her throat.

"Nothing. Forget it."

"*What*, Finn?" she asks.

"This was a stupid idea," he says.

"*I'm* checking out? Christ. *Fine*. Just forget it. I won't do it. I'll stay home." It's too late, she's ruined everything. This happens all the time lately. She goes too far. When did she lose control of her words?

On the island, Mena gets out of the boat, almost tripping on a slippery rock. She slams the picnic basket down and stomps off. She's not hungry anymore. While Sam and Finn devour the meal, she walks as far away from them as she can get. But it's an island. She's surrounded by water, stuck here with them. And she realizes this is what she's been feeling for a long time. Like she's stuck on some terrible island. Deserted but not alone. And one of these days one of them is going to try to swim away. She just hadn't planned before that it might be her. Maybe Finn was right. But so what if he was?

This island is completely undeveloped, too small for a house, too remote for visitors. The island used to be nameless but in recent years it was named after a dead child. A stillborn baby that belonged to someone who spent their summers at Gormlaith. The decision to give the island the baby's name was unanimous; the Vermont Board of Libraries accepted their petition without hesitation. As she wanders through the brush, the brambles scratching her bare legs, her face, her hands, she starts to cry. She wants to feel sympathy for that family, for their loss, but now she only feels anger. They stole the island. They named it. Made it their own. The island's namesake never breathed this air. Never stepped foot on this grass. Never swam off this island's shore. Franny. This was always Franny's island. And Franny lived here, still lives here.

Mena finds a willow tree that has been split down the middle (a lightning strike most likely) and sits down next to it. And she lets herself, just for a moment, remember. Franny. Another Fourth of July, before:

"Mommy," Franny said, holding out the sparkler to her. It crackled and sparked, the light illuminating Franny's face. "Make a wish."

"It's not my birthday, honey," she said.

"No, but it's America's birthday. Make a wish for America." Her eyes were as blue and as wide as water. She was seven years old.

Mena closed her eyes, concentrated, and then made a wish. But she was selfish. The wish was not for America at all, but for herself: *keep them safe.*

Today, they stay on the island for only an hour or so. Finn and Sam are both pouting when she finds them sitting among the wreckage of her carefully prepared picnic.

"Let's just go home," Sam says finally, looking defeated.

"It's not home," mumbles Finn.

Mena sweeps the debris into a plastic bag, and they all climb back into the boat again. No one says a word the entire way back to the cabin. When they get back, she considers calling Lisa and telling her that she can't take the part. She even dials the number, which she has scratched on a piece of paper. But then when Finn slams the front door and Sam disappears up the ladder to the loft, she puts the phone back on the cradle. She needs this.

It is the Fourth of July, and someone is shooting a shotgun off into the air down the street. Her mother is watching TV, and Dale is peeling off her Blockbuster shirt for the last time. *Independence Day,* she thinks. She can't leave until Friday, because she needs to pick up her last paycheck, but she still feels liberated. She stands naked in her room, looking at herself in the mirror. She can feel every fiber of the pink carpet under her feet. She smiles until her cheeks hurt.

After she got out of work she went next door at the strip mall to the beauty parlor and got her hair cut. She usually cuts her own hair, trims her bangs once a month or so. Cuts off the dead ends. And so when the beautician asked her what she wanted to do with her hair, she had no idea.

"You tell me," she said. She was feeling brave. Adventurous.

"Well, you've got a real pretty face," she said. "But I think the bangs are hiding your eyes. And they just make your face look rounder. I think we should do something to get them off your face, thin you out a bit. Show those pretty brown eyes. What do you say?"

She'd taken off her glasses while the woman washed her hair and left them off as she started to cut.

"What's the occasion?" the woman asked. "You got a date?"

"No," she said. "I'm going on a trip."

"Oh, how nice! A little summer vacation? I always try to

get to Palm Springs for a week in the summer. Sometimes the girls at work and I go down to Rocky Point. You been to Rocky Point?"

Her nails felt good on Dale's scalp. She watched her fuzzy reflection in the mirror and waited until the beautician had pulled the plastic apron from around her neck before she put her glasses back on.

She looked different without bangs. Naked. She tugged self-consciously at the hair that now came only to her chin.

"A bob will help lengthen your neck, make you look taller."

She felt the bare back of her neck with her hand and shivered a little. It was like her nerves were exposed, raw. Like she was feeling something for the very first time. It felt great.

"I love it," she said. And she tipped her twenty dollars on the way out.

"Have a good trip!" the beautician said, waving as Dale pulled out in the Bug, checking her new look in the tiny rearview mirror.

"What have you done?" her mother asked.

"Do you like it?"

"Oh, honey," she said, consoling, as if Dale should be upset.

"I like it," Dale said, pulling away. "It elongates my neck." As she said this, she felt herself stretching, thought of that Tenniel drawing of Alice in Wonderland.

"Well, at least it will grow out quickly," her mother said. And she walked behind her, pulling what was left of Dale's hair behind her head in a stubby ponytail. "I just like your hair back so much, like when you were a little girl."

"Well, I'm not a little girl."

Her mother has no idea that she's leaving.

Dale hears a series of pops and cracks, fireworks. She grabs a glass and pours herself a big tumbler of Chardonnay from the box in the fridge. She looks toward the living room and then gets another tumbler from the cupboard.

"Hey, Ma, come watch the fireworks with me?"

Her mother is half asleep on the couch. Pookie is curled up on top of her.

"Go without me," her mother says. "*CSI*'s on. . . . It's a good one."

Alone on the back patio, Dale watches the intermittent flashes of light. Hears more shotguns exploding. She drinks her glass of wine and then the other one. And she touches the back of her neck with her hand, tickles that exposed skin and smiles.

Alice has the Internet at her house, but it's only dial-up, and the connection is as slow as Moses. Finn whistles, taps his fingers impatiently on the computer desk as he waits for the page to load. Her mom is working again, and they are in her mom's bedroom where the computer is. It's smaller than Alice's room. And nothing in here is purple. The picture on Maggie's desktop is of Alice making a goofy face.

"God, you're impatient. I thought surfers were supposed to be all *chill,*" Alice says, trying on the word like a little girl trying on her mother's heels.

Earlier she had scoured the kitchen for something for them to eat. Usually their fridge is filled with leftover food her mother has brought home from the diner, but today there's nothing. "I'm hungry. What are you looking for anyway?" she asks.

"I need to know when these damn things can be harvested. They're not doing me any good right now."

He has almost no pot left. Last night he rolled a joint out of the twigs and seeds left in the Baggie and climbed up onto the roof of the cottage to watch the pissant display of fireworks over the lake. It hadn't gotten him stoned, and the fireworks, if you could even call them that, were done in about ten minutes. In San Diego, they could see *three* different displays from their house: the ones off the pier, the ones in Mission Bay, and the

SeaWorld fireworks. They didn't even have to leave their deck. His parents used to throw huge parties for the Fourth. All of their parents' friends got loaded; one year one of his dad's friends set his chest hair on fire trying to set off a Roman candle. Finn and Franny were always allowed to hang out with the grownups during the Fourth parties, even when they were little. Finn has memories of sitting underneath the dining room table watching everybody's feet. When they got older, they snuck beers from the ice chests and hung out on the beach, three hundred and sixty degrees of lights over their heads. Sometimes he and Franny would paddle out on their boards and watch the fireworks from the water. On a still night, you couldn't tell which way was up and which way was down from the lights reflecting off the water.

He wonders if there's any way Misty could mail him some weed. He's never going to make it through the summer without it, unless he plans to never sleep again. He wouldn't even know about where to find any in Quimby. There were a couple of shady looking kids hanging out by the Cumberland Farms the last time he was in town, but he's pretty sure he might get more than he's asking for approaching a bunch of rednecks. Most of the locals aren't nearly as friendly as Alice, it seems. There's one neighbor down the road who comes out of his house and glares at them whenever the woody drives past. He's got a dog too, and it chases their car every single time they drive by. Finn keeps hoping it will run under the wheels one of these days. Fucking bastard and his fucking inbred pitbull.

He prints out the pages he needs: how to take care of the plants, their life cycle, how to harvest the crop. It looks like he's going to have to wait until at least late August before he can get anything smokeable. They'll be back in California by then.

"You know anybody who sells?" he asks Alice.

"Sells what?" she asks.

Sometimes he forgets that she's only fifteen. She looks a lot older, and she's smarter than most fifteen-year-olds too. But she's so naïve. *Country*, Misty and her friends might say. *Innocent*, he thinks.

"P-O-T."

"My friend Ruby's brother smokes." She shrugs. "He's kind of an asshole though."

They ride their bikes all the way into Quimby, and lo and behold Alice signals for them to pull into the Cumberland Farms parking lot.

They get off their bikes, and a kid in a dark denim jacket says, "What the hell you want?" to Alice.

"Don't give me any grief, Muppet," she says. "I'm here for a corn dog and a slushie. My friend's the one who needs something."

"Hey, California," he says, nodding at Finn.

How does everybody here know his story? This place gives him the creeps.

Within three minutes, Alice has her corn dog, a slushie and a candy bar, and Finn has enough grass to get through another couple of weeks.

They ride home fast; it feels good to make his legs work hard. His lungs feel like shit though; he needs to quit smoking cigarettes. They leave the bikes at Alice's house and take a walk to the secret garden.

"Want a Kit Kat?" she asks, offering him one of the sticks from her bar. "I love these. My dad always used to use them to bribe me when I was little. I'll do anything for a Kit Kat."

At the garden, Finn pulls the folded up instructions out of his back pocket. "We've got to weed. And we've got to get rid of the males."

"Just tell me what to do," Alice says. Her lips are red from the slushie. It makes Finn smile.

There must be a word for this. This being alone but together. Sam retreats to the loft after dinner, listening to the quiet sounds of Finn and Mena below. No voices, just the shuffling of feet, the opening and closing of doors. The music from Finn's room, the clink clank of dishes, the cadence of pots and pans and running water in the kitchen. Mena has her first rehearsal tonight, but she said she would be home by ten.

He pulls the bottle of capsules out of the drawer, pops two in his mouth and swallows them dry. He can feel them as they make their way down his throat, to his chest, and finally when they dislodge and make their way to his gut. He will try again, he thinks. He just needs to keep trying.

He pulls a book out of the pile on his desk, thumbing through the pages he's marked with Post-its.

During World War II, at the University of Minnesota, a physiology professor named Ancel Keys solicited volunteers in an experiment in starvation. The experiment, involving thirty-six men, was aimed at determining the physical and psychological effects of starvation and how the people who had suffered from starvation during the war might be brought back to health. The men who joined were, for the most part, conscientious objectors, pacifists (Mennonites, Brethrens and Quakers) committed to nonviolence but eager to make a contribution in the efforts at postwar rehabilitation of the war's victims. And so in November of 1944, these thirty-six men all volunteered to be starved. This was their contribution to their country. Their patriotic gesture.

He imagines the way these men must have felt on that cold November afternoon, walking into the university's lab, where they would systematically be fed and then deprived.

Sam closes his eyes tightly and sees the young man he is beginning to recognize: the worn wool cap over pale red hair, the spray of freckles across his nose, the wire-rimmed glasses that are perched there. He sees him rub his hands together and blow into them for warmth. He sees him smile and nod at another young man who is also standing at the building door, waiting.

Sam looks closer.

The man is not really a man but rather a grown boy, maybe twenty years old. He has a girlfriend at home in Boston. A mother with sad eyes and bad dreams. His father died last year. An accident at the mill where he worked.

Sam imagines what the young man must be feeling as a sharp gust of wind whips across the campus green and cuts through his threadbare coat. As he looks at the brick building where, for the entire upcoming year, he and the other volunteers will feel nothing but hunger.

As Mena pulls up to the Town Hall on Tuesday night, she is still trembling. On the way here, that stupid dog that lives down the road from them came after her car and she nearly went off the road trying to avoid it. She's rattled from the near-accident, and nervous about being here. She thinks about turning back, leaves the car running even after she's parked.

It's a beautiful night though, so clear that the sky is almost bright even after the sun is gone. She sits in her car, fumbling around in her purse, stalling. When she looks up again, there is a man at her window.

Startled, she thinks about the time she almost got carjacked in Chula Vista. It had started like this too. It takes a second to remember where she is and roll down the window.

"You must be *May*," the man says, extending his hand for a shake.

"Hi," she says, smiling.

"Old Man. But you can call me Hank. Pleased to make your acquaintance."

"Mena," she says, and shakes his hand.

He opens the door for her and she gets out. Now there's no going back. Inside there's a card table set up with an urn of coffee and a box of Dunkin' Donuts. "Oh, should I have brought something?" Mena asks Hank.

"We take turns," he says. "My grandson works over to the Shop'n Save, so I'm usually good for a deli platter or two."

"You're from Quimby then?" she asks.

"Third generation." He smiles. "I'm guessing you're not from up here."

"No, but we just bought a place at Lake Gormlaith. The Carson place? We used to come here in the summers when our children were small."

"Flatlanders," he says, shaking his head knowingly, teasing her.

She thinks of the rocky cliffs their little bungalow is perched on and smiles. "My husband grew up here. Samuel Mason?"

"I know Sammy Mason!" he says, slapping the top of the table with his hand. "The only celebrity to come outta Quimby."

Mena laughs.

"You want a donut?" he asks. "I already ate all the jelly ones, but I think there might be some chocolate left over."

Lisa and the girl who is stage managing the show, Anne, are sitting on the stage, their legs dangling over the edge. Jake Rogers and the kid they cast as Martin are sitting in a pair of folding metal chairs at the foot of the stage. She takes a seat next to the kid. He can't be that much older than Finn.

"Hi," she whispers. "I'm Mena."

"Kyle," he says softly. "You remember Jake?"

Mena nods, and Jake leans over Kyle to shake her hand. She notices Jake's fingers are long and thin, square nails. His skin is rough and warm.

They start rehearsal with an icebreaker. Lisa has them put the chairs in a circle, and she asks each of them to fill out a brief questionnaire about themselves. *Name, Age, Sex. Where are you from? What do you want to be when you grow up? Do you have any scars? If so, how did you get them? What do you love? What do you hate?* Lisa gives them each a fresh pencil and a clipboard.

When they are finished, she has them all introduce themselves. Mena is first.

She takes a deep breath, confused again for a moment about where she is. She remembers that awful place she and Sam went, the place the doctors recommended after Franny died. That group met in a church basement. *Caring Friends.* That's what it was called. A whole room full of people who had lost their children. The stories were exhausting, horrific. As if their own grief wasn't enough to handle. It was too much. After the first night they never went back.

"My name is Mena Mason. I grew up in Flagstaff, Arizona, but I've lived in San Diego for the last twenty or so years. Right now, I am living with my family up at Lake Gormlaith. I'm forty years old . . . though I guess I'm probably supposed to lie about that, right?" She laughs nervously. "What do I want to be when I grow up? I used to think that I wanted to be an actress. Then I became a mom. And a caterer. Now, I think I might like to be an actress again." She smiles. Everyone is looking at her. "I have a scar from a car accident I had when I was little. We hit a school bus, and I . . ." She points to the place on her cheek. "It's hard to see now. But I know it's there." She looks at Lisa "These are just physical scars you want, right, not emotional?" and immediately regrets this.

"That's up to you," Lisa says.

"Well, I suppose I have a lot of those," she says. Her throat aches. "Actually just one big one, and it's pretty new. So, anyway." She takes another big breath. "I love my mother, Greek food . . . I'm one hundred percent Greek, second generation American on both sides. . . . I love cooking, the beach. I love collecting sea glass. I love my family." She feels her throat constrict. "And I hate pitbulls. Sorry if any of you have one but, God, there's this awful dog that chases my car every time I drive past his house. I almost ran him over on my way here."

"Thanks," Lisa says, and squeezes her hand.

"Jake, you're next."

Jake smiles. He's shaved his beard. He looks younger without it. His cheeks have that sort of flush red that usually comes with childhood, with winter weather.

"I'm Jake Rogers. I moved to Quimby from DC about six years ago when I got divorced. I'm thirty-seven years old. I wanted to be a fireman when I grew up, but now I make violins for a living. Potato, potahto."

Everyone laughs.

He looks down and taps at his chest. "I have a scar from a surgery I had when I was an infant . . . a hole in my heart. I love music, all kinds, but especially violin. Go figure. I love playing football with my brothers on Thanksgiving. I love snow. I love the cold." He looks down at his clipboard, reading. "I love traveling to places no one usually wants to go. I've been to Iceland. To eastern Europe. To the far northern provinces of Canada." He looks at Mena. "I *love* Greek food."

Mena blushes and then feels embarrassed for blushing. He didn't mean anything by that; what is wrong with her?

"And I hate liars. Oh, and mayonnaise."

After everyone has finished, Lisa hands out a fresh questionnaire with the same set of questions. "Now I want you to fill this out for your character. And when we go around the circle, I want you to become your character and introduce yourself."

This part is easy. As they go around the circle, going in the opposite direction this time, Mena feels herself becoming May. Losing everything that is Mena. It all falls away like a discarded dress. By the time it is her turn to speak, Mena is already long gone.

Dale finds a motel just past Albuquerque that is only thirty-nine dollars a night for a single room. She's been gone the entire length of her shift at Blockbuster as well as an extra hour, and she imagines her mother is probably just now starting to wonder where she is. She knows that her mother will not be alarmed, not at first. Sometimes Dale doesn't come straight home from work. Most Fridays, she goes to the Domino's that's right across from the Blockbuster and waits for an extra large pizza with pepperoni and cheese sticks to be made. Then she walks home, balancing the hot cardboard boxes in her hands, a couple of complimentary DVD rentals from work teetering on top. Her mother may, at this very minute, be standing in the kitchen, staring at the innards of the refrigerator, contemplating what to drink, as she waits for Dale to come home.

Dale knows her mother's first response to her tardiness will be anger. She's come to expect these Friday night dates. Even when Dale moved out that one semester, she was with her mom on Friday nights. She knows it will take at least another hour before the anger dissipates and she begins to become concerned. She'll call Dale on her cell then, and when Dale doesn't pick up, she'll call the Blockbuster, maybe even the Domino's. It will take at least two hours before real worry sets in and her mother has to take a couple of Xanax to calm down. There will be a tall aluminum tumbler filled with wine and ice to wash down the pills. There will be an open freezer door. Spoonfuls of coffee ice cream and handfuls of the Raisinets she buys in giant plastic vats from Sam's Club. And soon the Xanax will take over, calming, soothing. But with the absence of fear, her mother's anger will return, blooming like a wilted flower that's been placed in a fresh vase of water. She'll start leaving messages on Dale's cell then, threatening to call the police if she doesn't hear back in five minutes. There will be another tumbler of wine and then she'll start to cry. She'll tug at her hair and cry, big tearless sobs, pacing around the house, turning the TV off and on. She won't go looking for her, not yet; it will take another Xanax and another tumbler of pink Zinfandel before she gets in the car and starts to drive up and down the streets, with the windows rolled down, shouting Dale's name. Dale knows this, because this is exactly what happened that night with Fitz last fall. Exactly. But that night Dale wasn't in New Mexico. She was in Phoenix, and that night she had finally come home, shown up just as her mother was pulling back into the driveway after a futile search of Glendale's nearly identical streets. And that night she needed her mother almost as much as her mother needed her. As they made their way together through the front door, theirs was a collective sigh of relief. Shared tears. And they'd sat together in the backyard under a starless sky and ate an entire party-sized bag of Cool Ranch Doritos and drank a whole liter of Coke, grateful to have each other. She squeezes her eyes shut, wills her mother away. She's got at least an hour more before the tumbler comes out of the cupboard.

She parks in front of her motel room and starts to unload the Bug. She's afraid to leave anything in the car; it only locks on the passenger's side. Everything she loves is inside this car. By the time she's brought in her backpack and the box of books she squeezed into the tiny trunk under the hood, she's sweating. This is the kind of heat that feels like a spank, like a sharp slap against bare skin. A hand intent upon inflicting pain. Dale shakes her head, as if she can shake this memory away too.

Fitz. Goddamned Fitz. It's funny, she thinks, how he still manages to invade her consciousness like this. Most people don't have any say what happens in their dreams, but they're in charge of their waking thoughts. For Dale, everything's flip-flopped. Thanks to Ambien, she's got control of what happens when she closes her eyes. But the memories that pop in and out of her head during the day are unpredictable and arbitrary. She'll be walking around the grocery store and he'll round the corner, not really, but she'll catch a glimpse of his hair, his elbow, the back of his neck. Then, just like that, she's transported back to that studio apartment where she let him do things to her that no one should ever do. It's those times all of a sudden her record slows down to a crawl, the needle deep and sluggish in the grooves, the sound a sort of moaning.

Fitz. It started with a crush, one of those silly obsessions she'd had since she was a kid that she knew would never amount to anything. She'd had a hundred crushes, a thousand unrequited loves from middle school on. But they never came to fruition. She could fantasize all she wanted, but it didn't matter. The boys never noticed her at all, and if she ever got up the courage to approach them, it inevitably ended with simple dismissal or downright cold-hearted rejection. But Fitz was different.

He sat next to her in her Women's Lit class fall semester last year, one of only two guys in the whole class and the only straight one as far as she could tell. She loved the way he smelled, like clove cigarettes and dirt. Like a garden. Just smelling him made her insides knot up, moisture to seep between her legs. He wasn't the kind of guy she would ever have spoken to first. He was intimidating: too good looking, too smart. And so when he offered her a ride home after class (she was making her way to the bus stop and he said, *Hey, I'll drop you at home if you'd like, my car's right here*), she couldn't believe he was speaking to her.

She remembers there was a lot of crap on the passenger seat, books and papers and some trash. He had to clear it off for her, but he was unapologetic for the mess. She would have been mortified for him to see her own mess (and she certainly had her own mess), but he was unconcerned. "Sit here," he said, patting the threadbare seat.

When they pulled into her driveway, she half expected he'd come to a rolling stop and open the door for her to jump out. But instead he leaned over her, reaching for the handle of the passenger door, and stopped short, and his hand grazed her left breast as the door opened. Then his breath was hot in her ear. "I want to fuck you," he whispered. At home that night she searched the place where his hand had made contact with her, as if there might be some lingering evidence of his touch.

She didn't have class with him again until the following week. It was a graduate level class, and it only met once a week for three hours. By the time the week was over, by the time those excruciating three hours were over, she could barely take the anticipation anymore. This time, he pulled her by the hand as they left the classroom. They drove silently to his apartment, which was at the edge of campus, and then they were, suddenly, at the threshold. She thought about her mother then; she'd told her she was going out to a movie with a friend after class. Dale had known all along what she was doing.

He didn't even bother turning on the lights; through the windows the halogen streetlights made everything in the tiny apartment bluish. Hazy. The sink in the kitchenette was full of dishes; there was clutter everywhere. She tripped over a box that was on the floor next to the bed, which was in the middle of the main room.

That night, the first night, it was over fast. He simply laid her on the bed, pinning her hands with his, kissing her neck with hard, wet kisses, and then he was yanking at her panties and unzipping his fly, not even bothering to take off his jeans.

The zipper was cold on her bare thigh. And then he was doing what he'd said he wanted to do, the legs of the wooden bed scraping on the floor with each thrust. And then there was wetness and the stink of earth and the glowing tip of his cigarette. His penis limp and bathed in blue light.

For two months she told her mother she was going to a movie on Thursday nights, and instead went to his apartment, where he liked to hit her ass, to splay her. Each week, he added something new to the repertoire (pinching, biting, covering her mouth but not her eyes): something that made her a little more embarrassed, a little more shy each time. And this turned him on. He seemed to be falling in love with her.

They never talked about it.

She wanted to tell him she loved him too, but the timing was never right, and then one Thursday night he wasn't in class. And then the next week he wasn't either and someone said he dropped out of school and moved to Eugene with his girlfriend and her little girl.

That Friday night after work she decided instead of going home that she'd go to his house and see if it was true. She couldn't believe he would just take off, that he would leave her after all they'd been through.

The closest bus stop was about four blocks from his apartment. It wasn't a well-lit neighborhood, and she was nervous being there alone. But still, she made her way to the apartment building and knocked on the door. The lights weren't on, but she swore she could hear somebody moving inside. She knocked again and again. When she stopped knocking, whoever was in there stopped moving. And so she leaned her forehead against the door and kept knocking until she felt the skin of her knuckles starting to crack. Until blood was running down the white door. Until a neighbor started screaming out their window, "Nobody lives there, psycho! Go the fuck home."

She didn't get home until after midnight, and her mother's

car wasn't in the driveway. She was starting to feel that hot dizzy feeling she got sometimes, when her mother's headlights swept across the pavement. Her mother's speech was thick, like she was talking with a mouth full of cotton balls, and everything was blurry. But her mother didn't ask her a single question. She just sprayed some Bactine on her cuts and filled a Ziploc bag with ice. Later, when her mom passed out on the couch, Dale tried to touch herself in her own bed. Face down, pajamas yanked down over her naked ass. With her other hand, she tried to hit herself, tried to pretend her hands were his. The tears made her pillow so wet, that when she gave up and rolled over, she had to flip her pillow over in order to sleep.

She glances at the digital clock on the nightstand next to the bed in her motel room. She knows she doesn't have any choice but to call and let her mother know what she's done. But her stomach is roiling, furious. The last thing she ate was a double cheeseburger at ten o'clock this morning. She feels jittery and weak. And, though she knows better, she closes the door and starts to walk toward the IHOP she saw down the street.

Later, full and strangely content, she walks back to her room, but it's still so damn hot. There are fifteen messages on the cell phone, which she left on the nightstand.

"Mama?" she says.

The voice that answers is as thick as this heat. "Dale, where the hell are you?"

It's as though the heat is not in the air at all, but that it's inside her. Inescapable. Cradling the phone between her chin and shoulder, she runs cool water in the bathtub and turns the air conditioner to high. Then she tells her mother the only thing that can make this all right. "I'm looking for Daddy," she says.

She stays on the phone until she knows her mother has passed out, and then sinks into the bathtub.

Sam has no idea what to expect from the book club meeting that Effie has arranged. She has told him very little about what to expect: ten members, only two of them men. They have spent the last two weeks reading *Small Sorrows,* his third novel. He's not sure why they didn't pick something more recent. He supposes it's because it was his best-selling novel after *The Hour of Lead.* Its success was thrilling but undeserved, he thought. It's a good book, but not the best. He remembers how confident he felt when he sat down to write it though. After the film and the success of his first and second books, he'd felt suddenly unstoppable. Of course, he wouldn't have admitted to anyone, not even to Mena, but the success of his second novel had helped to eradicate his fears that *The Hour of Lead* had been a fluke. By the time he set out to write *Small Sorrows,* he wasn't smug exactly, but confident. In his voice. In his ability to tell a cohesive narrative, to captivate his audience. To find the perfect words.

When he thinks about that novel, there's a little part of him that is ashamed. It was cheap in a way, dashed off in less than six months. He'd barely edited it. The idea of reading aloud from it (Effie had asked if he'd be willing to read the prologue to the group) made him feel embarrassed. The heart of the book is true, but it's a mess. Sloppy.

He stands looking at himself in the mirror in the bathroom. The paint behind the mirror is chipped, and so there are entire pieces of his reflection that are missing: left earlobe, right shoulder. A spot below his left eye. He's fragmented.

God, he looks old, he thinks. Five years ago, when they were last here, he remembers looking in the same mirror and thinking he hadn't changed so much from the first time they'd come to Gormlaith. He was unworried then about the slow toll that his age seemed to be taking. But he was thirty-nine then. Something happened to him when he hit forty.

Thankfully, he inherited his father's full head of hair, though the color is definitely much more salt than pepper now, silvery at the temples. And his face looks so damned tired, just exhausted. He pokes at the plum-colored shadow beneath his one intact eye. His face is also thinner than it used to be. He grabs the copy of *Small Sorrows* he dug up for the event and studies the picture on the jacket. "Arrogant bastard," he hisses at the photo of his younger self. This was the guy, the twenty-eight-year-old guy who used to pull Mena by the hand into the bathroom while the twins were napping and remove her clothes without saying a single word. This was the guy who would drop to his knees and make love to his wife with his tongue, and then with his entire body as they showered together. This was the guy who slept with his wife (who slept with his wife!) at least three times a week, even with one-year-old twins. "Cocky sonuvabitch," he says, and slams his old face on the bathroom counter.

He runs his fingers through his hair and buttons his clean white shirt. He brushes his teeth and remembers how his old self would let the taste of Mena linger on his tongue all day: as he sat on the cliffs overlooking the beach, as he shopped for diapers at Rite Aid, as he wrote. He kept the salty tang of her there all day as a reminder of his hunger, their hunger.

He has no idea what to expect from the group, but he knows exactly what they expect from him. And so he puts on his author face, the confident, yet friendly, approachable, author face. He flips open the book and practices reading the first few lines: *Here are my hands. Look at them closely, and remember the knots. The rough skin and certainty of knuckle and fist. Not so differ ent from yours. Not weathered any more or less than your hands. Look at them. It begins and ends here.*

Sam has not asked Mena if she'd like to go to the book club meeting tonight, and so she assumes that he doesn't want her there. During the book tour for his second novel, *Benders,* he brought her with him. His publishing company sent him on a fifteen-city tour, all across the country. What she remembers about those months were the red-eye flights, her head resting on Sam's shoulder, the small dim hotel rooms and their cold sheets, the taxi rides and the awkward new celebrity of Sam's. Everywhere they went there was someone who adored him. He always looked vaguely startled by their fawning, and then uncomfortable, apologetic. She remembers how his modesty made her feel even more proud of him. She always sat near the back during his readings, not wanting to distract him. But somehow, whenever he read, he always located her and focused on her each time his eyes left the page. This was one of the many things that convinced her that every word he wrote was meant for her.

When he was writing, he would read her each chapter he wrote as he finished it. He wouldn't proceed unless she was there to hear what he'd written. Sometimes, she fell asleep at night to his soft reading; he was testing the words, tasting the words, trying them out on her. He started *Small Sorrows* when she was pregnant with the twins. He whispered each word against the stretched skin of her belly. His fourth and fifth novels were also like little secrets they shared. As the kids ran and played outside, they sat at the kitchen table over coffee or warm bowls of bread pudding or wine and she listened to his stories unfold. It hurts her that he hasn't read anything to her for more than a year. It hurts her that he doesn't want her there, at the library tonight.

"What time do you have rehearsal tonight? Should I drop you off?" Sam asks as he emerges from the bathroom. He's been in there for a while now; she could hear the medicine cabinet closing and opening. The water running.

"It's Monday. The theater's dark, no rehearsals," she says. "What time is the meeting?"

He glances at his watch, has to turn it to see the watch face. It's loose on his wrist.

"Seven?"

"Great!" She smiles. "Are you nervous?"

He shakes his head, looks at the book in his hand.

She remembers when he received the artwork for *Small Sorrows*. She remembers how well the black-and-white photo of the child floating on her back in a still lake captured the mood of the book. It still brings a lump to her throat when she sees it.

"Who's that handsome guy?" She smiles, gesturing to the photo on the back.

He looks at her then, really looks at her, and she worries she's said something wrong. But his face is warm, his eyes soft. He looks at the picture again and laughs. "Remember?" he asks.

She nods, shakes her head and laughs.

She thinks of a thousand things then: a meal at home in San Diego with Monty to celebrate the National Book Award nomination for *The Art of Hunting* (lobster raviolis and a bottle of Chianti), Finn riding his skateboard down the driveway that night, swerving back and forth like a dancer, the tinkling of the wind chimes on the back deck, the smell of hibiscus. She thinks about Franny twirling on the deck in that orange bathing suit, while the grown-ups drank and laughed and toasted Sam's brilliant career. She remembers creamy sauce spilled on the tablecloth, the broken street lamp, the way Finn would be there one instant and gone the next when he rode into one of the black holes created by the absence of light. She remembers Franny falling asleep on the rusty old chaise, and she remembers the sound of dishes and glasses being cleared, the crashing of waves, and Sam's hands. God, later, Sam's hands on her face. How she'd said, *You'll never forget me? When you're accepting your Nobel Prize?* Sam's hands on her face, on her waist, on her breast, on her thighs as he said, *No, I have you memorized.*

She waves as he gets in the car to go into town for the book club meeting. She stands at the door and watches as that beast of a car backs out of the drive, as the headlights disappear into the black abyss of this starless night.

After his dad takes off for his reading, and his mom is busy in the kitchen kneading dough for the *psomi,* Finn sneaks out of his room and into the night. He knows the way to the garden by feel now, like a sleepwalker navigating his midnight kitchen in search of a snack. The air is cool and wet; he pulls the hood of his sweatshirt up over his head and crams his hands in the pockets. He feels the Baggie of weed inside, measures, calculating with his fingertips exactly how long it will be before it runs out. Muppet's connection got busted. He's got nothing. Finn figures his stash will maybe last another week or so. If he's careful. His sneakers are wet by the time he gets to the garden, the grass already slick with dew.

He finds the stump that he's come to think of as his own personal smoking throne, and notices about a half dozen new toadstools growing on the bark. He plucks one off, and a familiar pain stabs at his chest. *Shit.* He's been here before. He and Franny, a long time ago. How could he have forgotten this?

A summer years ago. Back when they were maybe seven or eight years old. *Eight.* It was the summer after second grade. He remembers, because it was the same summer he lost both of his front teeth. Every time he opened his mouth to talk, he whistled. It was also the first summer they were allowed to play outside by themselves. They discovered the junk pile in the woods first. They spent hours, days, playing among the wreckage. They had so much freedom then. He should have enjoyed it while it lasted.

One afternoon, it had been raining and they were stuck inside the cabin all day. When the sun finally came out, they'd practically bolted out the door. "Be back by dinner!" their mother had yelled after them.

They made their way through the woods to their normal spot, the place where all the junk was, and then Franny said she was bored and wanted to go exploring. Finn had shrugged his shoulders and followed her. That's the way it worked with Franny; you just followed her lead. Everybody did.

They'd found the tree almost immediately. And back then it was alive, the craziest tree he'd ever seen. It was the perfect climbing tree, with a dozen limbs twisting and turning upward, a canopy of thick green leaves. The trunk itself was massive and gnarled, riddled with all sorts of holes, like little caves. Finn shimmied up to the top and looked down at Franny through the canopy of green.

"It's a fairy's castle," Franny said, nodding. *"Look."*

Curious, Finn climbed back down, scratching his arms and legs as he descended. Franny knelt down on the damp ground, pointing to a place at the base of the tree and, sure enough, there was an arched entrance. A doorway. Finn could almost imagine the gossamer wings shimmering in the moonlight, hear the tick-ticking of their flight.

"Let's leave a note," she said.

"Okay." Finn shrugged.

Franny found a piece of birch bark nearby and pulled a Magic Marker from the backpack she always carried with her. It had her spy notebook, her art supplies, and snacks. When she was finished, she rolled the bark into a tiny scroll and tied it with a piece of yarn she retrieved from a pocket in the backpack.

"What does it say?" Finn had asked.

"I can't tell you," she said, standing up. The knees of her jeans were soaked through.

"Why won't you let me read it?" he had asked then, angry that she was keeping it a secret.

"It's written in a language only fairies understand," she had said matter-of-factly. And with that, she had bent down and stuffed the scroll into the small crevice in the tree. Finn thought about it, wondered what the words were, imagined tiny hands unrolling the scroll. Imagined the words being spoken by tiny clicking tongues.

"Let me see it," he said.

"No, you have to wait. It won't look like anything to you, because you don't know fairy language."

Finn felt the same way he felt whenever Franny made up the rules. Franny was always the one who knew the secret languages, always the one who cast the spells. He suddenly wanted to see what she'd written on the scroll more than anything in the entire world.

"That's stupid," Finn said. "You only know how to write in English."

She stood with her hands on her hips and shook her head.

Anger welled up inside him like a storm. "Fairies aren't even real," he spat, and knew the second the words came out of his mouth that he'd made a mistake.

Franny's eyes welled up, and she shook her head. "I'm going home. Don't follow me. And if you touch it, you'll mess everything up. They won't come. They might even leave the tree. They can't live in a place where people don't believe in them. It makes them sick. It makes them *die*," she said.

Finn remembered Tinker Bell then; he remembered the way they had sat on the floor of the living room in their sleeping bags watching *Peter Pan,* the way Franny had wept as Tinker Bell's light flickered, clapped her hands furiously to keep her alive. He felt awful, like somebody punched him in the stomach. He was always messing things up. Even then.

And sure enough, the next day, the scroll was still there. The fairies had not retrieved it.

"I didn't read it," he had said. "I swear."

"It doesn't matter," she had said, kneeling down next to the knotted stump. "They're gone now."

He'd seen the sorrow in her shoulders, heavy in her the way she hung her head.

"I'm sorry," he'd said. And he was. "I didn't mean to."

He sits down on the stump now, looks up at the sky, and starts to roll a joint. He wonders what happened to the tree, and he thinks about all the times he let Franny down. That wasn't the first time, and it certainly wasn't the last. He licks the sweet edge of the paper and then lights the joint. When it's gone, and he feels that warm quiet of his high descend, he pulls another piece of rolling paper from the pack. It is as thin as a whisper. He's got a pencil in his pocket, and he scratches the words, in the only language he knows, onto the tiny fragile square. *I'm sorry*. And then he rolls it into a tight little scroll and stuffs it into the fairy's doorway.

Sam enters the library and is struck, once again, by how very little has changed since he was a kid. His father would bring him to the Athenaeum on the weekends from the time he was a little boy until he was in high school. They'd have breakfast first at the Miss Quimby Diner (red flannel hash, fried eggs and homemade toast for both) and his father would bring his leftover coffee with him to the library. In the main room, his father would spread out the newspapers on the long wooden tables in the room with the fireplaces while Sam wandered the stacks of books. He dreamed about those labyrinthine stacks still, the knotty pine shelves and musty scent of the old encyclopedias. He never cared for the children's room with its noise and colors and papier-mâché sculptures. Instead he preferred the quiet alcoves and dark corners of the upstairs. The card catalogues and books with thick creamy paper, the smell of ink settled into the pages. Later, when he came home from college, he and his father continued this tradition. He remembered the smell of the fire in the fireplace, the stain of newsprint on his father's hands.

And later, he brought his own kids here. Finn would disappear into the basement, and Sam and Franny would wander the stacks together. When she was very small, they would play hide-and-seek in the library, quietly so they didn't get caught. And then when she was old enough to read, she'd carry as many books as her arms could hold to the room with the cozy couches. They'd sit together, her feet curled up underneath her or her head buried into the crook of his arm.

Effie greets him at the giant double doors to the library. It is after hours, but there is a faint glow of pale peach-colored light coming from inside.

"I'm early," he says, by way of apology, glancing at his watch even though he knows he's not due for another fifteen minutes. He's always been like this, too eager. Never late, not even punctual, but chronically early.

"Oh, that's fine. Just fine. I hope this is okay," she says, ushering him into the library and gesturing toward the reading room.

Effie has arranged a semicircle of folding chairs around the fireplace and put an overstuffed wingback chair in front of the hearth. "It looks like *Masterpiece Theatre,*" he says.

Effie laughs.

He can see that some of the book club members have already taken their seats. There is one woman rifling through her purse and another clutching a library copy of *Small Sorrows.* There is also an elderly man with a handlebar mustache dressed in overalls reading *The Wall Street Journal.* The other seats are still empty.

"Can I get you something? Tea? Coffee? Water?"

"Coffee would be great," he says, though he knows better. He'll be up all night. But the coffee that's bubbling in a pot near the circulation desk smells good.

"I used to come here," he says. "When I was growing up. My kids used to come too. But Finn . . . I don't think he's seen the inside of a library in years." He doesn't know why he's sharing this with her.

He thinks about the way the pages felt as he smoothed the books open on the table next to his father. The purity of those moments alone with his dad. He is overwhelmed by a sense of something lost. So many things lost. His father. Franny. The emptiness that is ever present, a permanent ache. But this is new, this feeling that he has let something else slip. Finn. Mena. It's like dropping a china plate: first alarm, then regret, then just a sense of everything being shattered.

"What made you think of writing about a missing girl?" the woman sitting closest to him asks. She is wearing a thick, heady perfume. She leans in close for his answer, and he can hear the hum of her hearing aid.

"It started with a dream," he says, speaking up so she can hear him. "When my children were still small. I had a dream where I was walking through the woods at night and suddenly arrived at the edge of a murky pond. In the water, I saw a child, floating in her nightgown. I woke up and knew that I needed to find out what had happened to her. How she came to be there."

What he doesn't tell them, the eager readers thumbing furiously through their copies of his novel, is that in the dream he'd seen the child's face, and it belonged to Franny. That he thought if he wrote the words they might act as some sort of magic spell, an incantation, an inoculation against the unthinkable. What he doesn't say is that he knew, long before it happened, that they were destined to lose her.

M ena doesn't need a recipe for this; making bread is simply something her hands know how to do. It is intuitive. Like reading, like riding a bicycle, like comforting an infant with the sway of your body and the hush of your words. It's something that once you learn, becomes a part of you. Intrinsic.

She watches her hands, wonders at the way they turn all of the separate ingredients into a living, breathing thing. This is how she thinks of bread, as something alive. The loaves she has already prepared inhale and exhale beneath dish towels on the counter. She watches her hands turn the oil, the honey, the cool milk into the flour and yeast and salt.

These are her mother's hands.

She remembers waking up before sunrise as a child and finding her mother in their small kitchen, coaxing life into dough. Mena would sit on an old dentist stool dragged from her father's workshop. She would spin it around and around until it was high enough to see over the counter. She and her mother never spoke those mornings. Sometimes, she would even fall back to sleep, her head resting on the counter, dusty with flour, while her mother kneaded and pounded and then waited for the dough to rise. Her mother's hands: long fingers, olive skin, the gold key-patterned ring, identical, but smaller, than the one her father wore. The dough would sometimes imbed itself into the grooves. Into the *meandros,* that continuous wandering pattern that wound its way around her slim finger.

Sam had bought a set of rings nearly identical to her parents' after he proposed. He found them in an antique shop in Ocean Beach. The pattern was supposed to symbolize unity, infinity. Mena thinks of her mother when her father was sick, in those terrible last days, the way she would twirl it around with the thumb of the same hand, working her thumb against her palm, the band spinning around and around her finger. She remembers how at her father's funeral, her mother held the back of her hand to her face, running the ring across her cheek again and again, comforting herself as she might a child. And later, after the MS crippled her hands and she could no longer make bread, the way the ring blistered her fingers. And still, she refused to remove it.

Mena looks at her hands, at her mother's hands, watches them as they push and prod and persuade. She studies the grooves of her own ring, that continuous, uninterrupted yet circuitous path. And she thinks of Sam, so unlike her own father. Her father with his temper and rages. With the way he took and took and took from her mother and never once gave back. Her father with his violence and dismissal. And yet, her mother felt bound. Tethered. Even after his death. She remembers her mother's defending him even after he no longer needed her defense. *You remember how he would carry you on his shoulders,* paidi mou? *All through the kitchen, you banging your head on the ceiling? Remember the music? Remember the way we all stomped our feet?* And it was true, Mena could remember when her father came home hours after the workday had ended, how he would sing, "Tick-tock! Tick-tock! Papa's home from the clock shop!" lifting her up onto his shoulders and marching her about the kitchen. There was a smell to him she always assumed was whatever he'd been drinking at Joe's Place, the bar next to his shop, but later understood to be the smell of another woman's perfume. She even went to Dillard's once in high school, desperate to find that smell, to locate a bottle filled with the tincture that she could offer to her mother as evidence that she deserved better. That she should leave him. But she hadn't been able to locate that scent and left the store feeling dizzy and nauseous. Sickened by the citrus and sweetness and musk.

Mena kneads and kneads and thinks of Sam, who is so even-keeled and predictable, reliable and faithful. She feels guilty even thinking about how far away she feels from him now. How much she wishes he would drink too much, throw open the door, yell. Blame someone, blame her. How much she would welcome a slap across the face. Something, anything to prove that he is alive. *Anger. Joy. Sorrow.* It's all gone now, and he is like the husks of the cicadas that littered her backyard as a child. Transparent and hollow. Fragile.

She works the dough into the wooden butcher block, pressing her palms into it as it resists. She looks to the loaves, swaddled in their gingham cloths, watches as they grow. They have taken on a life of their own.

D ale is driving toward Memphis, and the heat, like an apparition, hovers over the pavement in front of her. The heat is unbearable; her thighs stick to the vinyl seats of the Bug, adhered by sweat. She shifts, rolls down the window, puts her hand out and touches the hot air, suffocating and oppressive, clinging and cloying outside. The jug of water at her feet is already hot. The candy bars she stashed in the glove box have melted. She has only been on the road for a couple of hours this morning, but already she is wondering again if she might be making a terrible mistake. She is nearing Little Rock, and she thinks of stopping there, finding a motel for the night, and then turning back home. When she left Oklahoma City this morning, she felt such a tremendous sense of purpose, such conviction, and so she is surprised to find herself feeling this deflated.

Piece of shit five-hundred-dollar car. What did she expect? The brakes, despite what Thoreau said, are iffy, the windshield wipers don't work (not even with the shoe strings), and she can see the pavement running under her feet through the rusted hole in the baseboard. She's starting to wonder if it will survive the trip. The radio in the car is broken, but at least the tape player works, and she's got a shoe box full of audio books she bought when her last student loan check came in. She'd used what was left after tuition to buy that first-edition, signed copy of *The Hour of Lead* on eBay and audio tapes of the rest of Sam's novels. There are eight altogether. She figures she might get across the country, all the way to Vermont even, before she gets through them all. Of course it isn't him reading them, but she thinks that the actor who read *The Hour of Lead* sounds a little bit like him, with that voice like fallen leaves. When she thinks of Vermont, she dreams of cool pine trees and chill waters of a deep lake. His words pull her into a world that doesn't stink of gasoline, of diesel, of grease. Where the Circle Ks and Home Depots and IHOPS are flattened into the pristine green of unoccupied land. She wants this almost as much as she wants to get to him. Almost.

There are no other cars on this stretch of highway, only the occasional semi that whizzes past her, making the Bug tremble and list toward the center line. She reaches into the box on the passenger seat and grabs the first one (she figures she'll go in order) and pops it into the player. There is a pause, and then the story begins, the gravelly voice of the actor speaking softly, *This is the hour of lead. I remember, because I am the one who lived.* She closes her eyes, just for a moment, and feels his words quiver against her. By the time she opens her eyes again, her resolve is restored. She grips the steering wheel, flashes a bright smile at herself in the small rearview mirror, and pushes the accelerator.

She's thinking of a conversation she had with her mother once about her own visit to Memphis, trying to get to Graceland, back before Dale was born. She and a girlfriend from high school drove all the way there, only for her to get sick on some bad catfish in Arkansas along the way. Her girlfriend went on without her, and while her friend toured Elvis's mansion, she spent the entire day clinging to the motel toilet. She said bad catfish was worse than mayonnaise left out in the sun all day. Graceland is one of her mother's many, many unfulfilled dreams. Dale figures she can take the time to stop—it is on the way— and pick up some sort of trinket to send home. A bobblehead Elvis, maybe. A Graceland thimble for her mother's collection.

She can't get the Bug to go over fifty-five mph though, so

it's taking her forever. She stays in the far right lane and envies the more swiftly moving traffic that passes by her. It's still hotter than hell, and she thinks maybe she should stop somewhere to buy a cooler to keep her sodas and candy bars cold. Just past Little Rock, she goes to a gas station and gets pointed in the direction of the nearest Walmart.

The car is hot. She is hot. Outside the air is as thick as corn syrup and smells like tar. She wonders about leaving all of her prized possessions inside a car that won't lock. She's been able to avoid this so far by going to full-service gas stations and eating at drive-thrus. She's got a pretty big bladder and has only had to stop once or twice to pee. Both times she asked the friendly looking cashiers if they might just keep an eye on her car while she ran into the restroom.

She decides she'll risk it; she's not sure how much longer she can survive without something cold to drink, and she doesn't want to have to keep stopping just to get fresh sodas. She grabs her backpack and stuffs in the important papers she has with her, the signed first edition of *The Hour of Lead,* and the photos she's printed off the Internet. Her laptop. She closes the door to the car and half walks half runs to the sliding doors, feeling the hot pavement through the thin rubber soles of her flip-flops. When she gets to the store, there's a little kid sitting on one of those coin-operated fire truck rides and he's screeching at the top of his lungs, "Fire! Fire!" She smiles at him, and he keeps screaming. "Fire!" He's really into this, she thinks. And then his mother, who's talking on her cell, looks up and says into the phone, "Holy shit, there's a car on fire at the Walmart!"

Dale turns toward the parking lot and sees a big puff of smoke coming from the area where she left the car. And then she quickly realizes that there are flames leaping out from the engine of the Bug.

"Oh, my God!" she screams, and then starts running back to the car. She stands there for a minute, looking around her, feeling helpless. "Help!" she screams, and wonders why she didn't have the sense to tell the woman with the phone to call 9-1-1.

It feels like forever that she's standing there watching the Bug's rear end become engulfed in flames. She wonders if she should run into the Walmart and get a fire extinguisher. And then, like a miracle, there's a guy running from the store toward the car with a fire extinguisher, and he pushes her out of the way. "I got it," he says.

When the fire is extinguished and the Bug covered with foam, the man, who reminds her a little of the guy who sold her the car, shakes his head as if to scold her. "Piece of shit German car."

She nods, feels her bottom lip quivering, trying hard not to cry.

"These things always catch on fire. Probably the cap to the fuel filter broke, so frickin' hot, wouldn't take much, just a little spark. Oil all over the engine, s'like a frickin' rag soaked in gasoline." He pats her back. "Lady, looks like your car's shit the bed."

She can't hold it in any longer. She starts to cry, big embarrassing sobs. She sits down on the hot pavement, feels it searing the backs of her thighs, and she cries until her throat hurts. She's sure she's making more of a spectacle of herself than a burning car in the middle of a Walmart parking lot.

When she hasn't got any tears left, she looks up and sees the guy's still there. He's leaning against the Bug, smoking a cigarette. He has the shadow of a beard, a small hole in the hem of his T-shirt. "Here comes the fire department." He chuckles. "Just in time."

The tow truck driver takes one look at it and says, "Piece of shit German car."

She nods again, ashamed. She's standing with her suitcase and her shoe box of Books on Tape and the other box of stuff from the trunk and the afghan her grandmother made her. The guy who put the fire out has hung around. He said his name was Troy, and he'd wait with her until the tow truck came. "You think it can be fixed?" she asks.

The tow guy, who has a meaty red face and sweat stains like saucers, shrugs. "Ain't nothing that can't be fixed. Anything can be fixed. Just a matter of how long it's gonna take. And if you got insurance or not. Usually fire's covered under your comprehensive."

"I do," she says. "Have insurance."

"Then it's just a question of how much time you got, I guess."

She swallows past a lump in her throat. "I'm trying to get to Vermont. I was hoping to be there by the end of the week."

He laughs a big hearty laugh. "Listen," he says. "I'll bring this to my brother's shop. Depending how busy he is, I figure it's probably gonna take at least three or four days to fix whatever damage you got inside the engine. If you want the body fixed too, you might be looking at a week or more."

She starts to feel hot and buzzing, and she's worried she might pass out.

The other guy, Troy, says, "I know a place you can rent by the week, real cheap. Unless you think you wanna take a bus the rest of the way? Greyhounds go all the way up there?"

Dale tries to shake away the vertigo, concentrating on the feeling of her two feet firmly planted on the very hot ground beneath her. "I need to have a car."

"Alrighty then," Troy says. "You stay until it's ready. Problem solved."

He'd seen it coming, but it still felt awful. After Misty hadn't answered her phone for a whole week, Finn wrote her a postcard. It had a photo of a big red barn and cows in a field on the front. *Dear Misty,* he scrawled. He didn't want to say anything he'd regret. *What's up? Haven't heard from you and thought I'd drop you a note from the land of BFN. Weather is rainy. Wish you were here, all that shit. Miss you,* he started and quickly crossed it out. *XO, Finn.*

"Listen," she said softly, a few days later.

He took the phone out of the cabin as far as he could and still get reception, sat down on the wood pile by the barn, and waited.

"I've been thinking that maybe it would be a good idea if we, before I leave for school . . ." Her voice trailed off.

"If we what, Misty?" he said, peeling a piece of bark from one of the birch logs. It was like stripping off a layer of sunburned skin.

He could tell she just wanted to get off the phone. She sighed. "You know, maybe we should just focus on our *friendship.*"

He didn't say anything. He couldn't have gotten words past the thick knot in his throat if he'd wanted to.

"I mean, I'm leaving for college in like a month, and you're all the way up there. I don't even know if I'm going to get to see you before I leave." He could picture her, sitting on the edge of her bed, painting her toenails, talking but not really talk-ing, like a ventriloquist's dummy . . . saying all the things she was supposed to say, just waiting to get off the phone and get back to her life.

Finn jumped down off the log pile. "Whatever, Misty. You do what you've got to do." He couldn't stop himself. "Or *who*."

"What the hell is that supposed to mean?"

"I don't know, why don't you tell me?" Finn had no idea if she'd cheated on him, but he didn't want her to get away with this so easily. He wanted her to feel even a sliver of what he was feeling, which was a whole lot of crap.

And then she was crying. This, he didn't expect. And it made him feel good and bad in equal measures.

"Mist?" he said.

"I'm sorry," she said. "It's just that I missed you so much, and I've been so confused. And everything with you is always so, I don't know, fucking *heavy*. You've got this cloud over you, Finn, and it's dark. Pete's just so *easy*. And he's going to Brown too. I'm sorry, Finny. I didn't mean to hurt you. At all."

Pete. His supposed *friend,* Pete. Here he'd been worried this whole time about that asshole Justin. "Did you sleep with him?" Finn asked. "Because if you did, you're a fucking slut. And good riddance. Have fun at Brown, Misty. Have a great fucking life."

He hung up the phone before she could answer. He didn't want to know the answer. Not really. He and Misty had fooled around, a lot, but they were always so messed up on X or stoned that it never went any further than kissing. The idea of her sleeping with someone made his whole body ache. The idea of her sleeping with Pete made his eyes burn.

He'd hung up the phone and dialed Alice's number. She could help take his mind off shit.

"Hey," he said, his hands shaking.

"Hi, Finn! What's up?

★ ★ ★

"It smells so good in your house," she says.

His mom has gone to rehearsals already, and he figures his dad won't even notice that he has company. He's been up in the loft since after dinner, shuffling through papers, clacking away at his laptop. Before his mom left, she made baklava. The whole house smells like it. But his room smells like incense, that Nag Champa shit he burns to keep his room from smelling like pot.

"This room smells like feet." She grimaces.

"Thanks," he says. "I've been working on my dirty hippie smell."

"Your room is so cool," she says, scanning the walls, which are bare except for a few posters he's put up. The Clash. The Ramones. A Victoria's Secret ad. He feels his ears getting hot.

"She's all right," she says, nodding. "Kinda trampy though, don't you think?"

He nods. Feels his skin growing hot. He thinks about Misty, about the way her thong would show whenever she bent over, peeking out over the waistband of her hundred-dollar Lucky jeans. Expensive clothes on such a cheap fucking whore.

"And this is where the magic happens, must be," Alice says, plopping down on the bed.

"The magic?"

"Geez, Louise, you never seen *Cribs*? I thought *I* was the hick."

"Oh," he says. He's suddenly wondering if he should have brought her here at all.

"That your surfboard?" she asks, gesturing to his long board, which is tilted awkwardly in the corner. He insisted on bringing it with him despite his mother's obvious irritation, *because* of his mother's obvious irritation. They had strapped it to the roof of the station wagon with bungee cords.

"One of them. I've got a short board at home too. This is my old one. The one I learned on. As soon as I get back to California, I'm going to buy a new one. I know a guy in PB who makes custom sticks."

"That's cool," she says. She's lying on his bed now, looking at the ceiling.

"I've got stars on my ceiling too," she says. "My dad put them there when I was really little. But he screwed them up. They aren't even in constellations. They're just a big mess."

"My sister did these," he says. Finn remembers putting the stars on the ceiling with Franny. He had wanted to just put them up, but Franny had insisted on using the map included in the package. He remembers her directing him: *Ursula Major, Big Dipper, Cassiopeia.* Now when he falls asleep at night he lies on his stomach, face down. He can't stand to look up into that ordered sky.

"I wish I had a sister," Alice says.

He nods.

Finn feels like a dumb ass just standing there, so he lies down next to her on the narrow bed. He looks up at the ceiling, at the stars, the yellow plastic barely discernible from the white ceiling. He feels the edge of her hand touching his, and he opens up his palm, slowly turning it to meet hers. Their fingers lace together tightly, and he squeezes his eyes shut.

"Truth or dare," she says.

"What?"

"Truth or dare, you know, the *game?* Here, I'll do it first. Ask me."

"Truth," he says. "Tell me a secret."

Alice closes her eyes. He turns his head and looks at her. Her hair is spilled all over his sheets. She's pretty, he thinks. For a kid.

"My daddy's in jail for beating the shit out of my mom. I'm pretty sure that when he gets out he's going to come after us."

"Jesus," Finn says.

Alice opens her eyes and turns to face him too. "Now your turn. Truth or dare?" He thinks about it. He looks at her; her eyes are wide and expectant. He wishes he could say *Truth.* He wishes he could tell it. He wishes he even knew what it was. And so he says, instead, not ready, not able, or both, "Dare."

M ena has made a giant pan of baklava, which she sets down at the table next to the coffee inside the Town Hall. The ingredients she'd asked Sam to order online had finally arrived (the eggplant paste, the quince preserves, the boxes of bucatini). She'd had to wait until she had orange blossom honey before she could make baklava. She wouldn't make it without the special honey. Mena peels the plastic wrap off the pan, which is still warm.

"Hi," Jake says.

She looks up and smiles. "Hi."

"Did you make this?" he asks.

"I did," she says. "It's still warm. Do you want a piece?"

"Absolutely. I'm totally starving. I got caught up in the shop tonight and forgot to eat dinner."

"Well, this isn't much of a dinner," she says, slipping a flaky triangle onto a napkin and handing it to him.

He eats half of the piece in one bite, wiping his mouth with the back of his hand. "Mmmm. This is delicious."

She feels heat rise up somewhere through the center of her body. She knows she shouldn't feel this way, she isn't supposed to feel this way, but still she allows that heat to spread, enjoys the way it extends, like a hot river down her arms and legs, up into her face.

"You missed a little," she says, gesturing to a small crumble of walnut in the corner of his mouth.

He wipes at it with the napkin, misses.

"Here," she says, and dabs at the crumb with her own napkin.

"Thanks," he says, and smiles at her. But his smile lasts too long, and suddenly all that hot liquid freezes. She thinks of Sam. What is she doing? God, is she flirting with this guy?

"I made baklava!" she says in her mother's voice, which booms through the small room.

"Oh yum!" Anne says, and suddenly everyone is swarming around the table.

Lisa has them rehearsing the first scene of the play. Mena loves how the play opens with an argument, with violence. Shepard wastes no time. And May is there, in the thick of it, as soon as the curtain rises. Well, if there were a curtain. For now, there's just some strike tape marking off where the stage will be.

" 'You smell,' " she says to Jake. Jake has the cowboy hat that Anne brought in cocked forward on his head. He looks up at her from underneath its wasted rim.

" 'I been drivin' for days,' " he says. And she imagines him, Jake, *Eddie,* driving across the desert to find her, the heat vapors playing tricks on his eyes. He's right. He's come so far. But still, he smells. She smelled it when he came through the motel door. When she pulled his hand to her face to check. His fingers.

" 'Horses,' " Eddie says, his lip rising up on one side. Is he mocking her?

" *'Pussy,'* " she spits.

Still, he won't admit it. He can't ever admit it. She imagines the Countess, the rich bitch he's been screwing.

" 'I'm goin',' " he says, adjusts his hat and makes his way to the makeshift door.

" 'Don't go!!!' " she screams, surprised by her own voice, by the absolute desperation of it. By the keening. She moves to the bed, just a cot for now, and throws herself onto it, writhing, moaning, clutching the lumpy feather pillow.

And then he's back. He always comes back. She feels the relief well up inside her almost as big as the anger was.

" 'What am I gonna do?' " Eddie asks, and as he does so, he bends down to her where she is crouched on the dusty floor like an animal. She is an animal, a wounded beast.

He forces her chin up with his hand, making her look into his eyes, and she watches the flecks of gold swim among all that green. *Goddamned Eddie.*

" 'You're gonna erase me.' "

And as the words come out, she pictures herself, the Cheshire cat, slowly fading into a background of desert sand, of desert sky. But there is no smile to leave behind, and so she simply disappears.

"You guys are so, so, so good," Anne says when they break. "It's like you were meant for these roles. Lisa doesn't even have to direct you. This play is going to be awesome. They did it at my school last fall and it wasn't anywhere near as good as this."

They are standing out on the porch of the Town Hall, which faces a cemetery on the opposite side of the street.

Mena is feeling exhilarated. Antsy. Every inch of her is tingling. She keeps rubbing her arms, as if the sensation she's feeling in all of her nerve endings is as simple as being cold.

"You chilly?" Jake asks. "I've got a sweater in my car."

"No, I'm fine. Thanks though."

"Five more minutes," Anne says, tapping her watch. And then she disappears back into the building.

Jake pulls a pack of cigarettes out of his jeans pocket and smacks it against the palm of his hand. He taps the pack so that a cigarette shoots part of the way out and gestures to her. "Want one?"

She shakes her head.

"Nasty habit. Can you believe it? I didn't start smoking until my wife and I separated. I made it through my entire adolescence, through college without even taking a drag. Now, I probably couldn't quit if I tried."

She nods and looks up at a street lamp, watches some slow-moving moths circle the light.

"Are you having fun?" he asks.

At first she doesn't understand.

"With the play. It's fun, no?"

"Yeah," she says, and rubs her arms three times quickly. "I'm having a good time."

They return to the first scene after the break, trying different things. At one point, Eddie threatens to leave again and she holds on to his legs, clinging, pressing her face into the back of his knees as he drags her across the floor to the door.

Later, as she drives back to the cabin, she turns on the heat in the car, but she still can't stop trembling. And after she gets home, when she starts to get ready for bed, she will feel the places where her skin burned against the wood floor. Touch the raw flesh that by morning will have already started to scab over, to heal.

"Teach me how to surf," Alice says, sitting up suddenly. "What?"

"You picked Dare, and I dare you to teach me how to surf." She jumps off his bed and slips her flip-flops on.

"You can't surf here." He laughs.

"Then why did you bring your surfboard?"

Finn looks at her to see if she's kidding around, but she's dead serious. "You have to have waves to surf. The ocean."

"Why?" she asks.

"Because that's what surfing is. It's riding the waves. The *surf?*" He laughs and lies back down on his bed. It's getting dark out, and the artificial stars are starting to glow.

"Let's try it anyway," she says, and reaches for his hand. She pulls him up off the bed. "Come on! It'll be fun."

Once he's standing up, he realizes she's not going to let this one go.

"All right," he says, and shrugs. "It's your dare."

A huge shit-eating grin spreads across her face. When she does that her eyes get really small. It makes him smile. It's the first time he's smiled all day. All week maybe.

They make their way out of the house as quietly as they can. The light is on in the loft, but it's quiet. He wonders if his dad has fallen asleep up there.

It's a warm night, and for one disorienting minute as they

walk down the winding path to the water, him carrying the surf-board under his arm, he could be at home. He feels a wave of homesickness. Alice walks behind him, holding onto the back of his T-shirt, following his lead. There are only a small row of faintly glowing solar lights illuminating the path.

"Okay," Alice says. "What do I do?"

"I don't know," he says. Smiles. "I've never surfed a lake be-fore."

He's got his board shorts on, and Alice is still wearing her suit from earlier in the day. She pulls off her T-shirt and shorts and chucks her flip-flops onto the grass. "Well, let's try."

He puts the board into the still water, and they both wade in.

"Here," he says. "Lie down on your stomach."

He helps her onto the board. She's so tiny; the board is way too big for her.

"Like this?"

He nods. "I'll swim out next to you."

He shows her how to paddle out. He can barely make her out in the dark, and he's wondering if he should have put the leash on. If they lose the board out here tonight, they might never find it again.

He's grateful for the moon. Once they get out about a hundred yards, he can see her more clearly.

"What next?" she asks. "When do I stand up?"

He laughs, and his laughter echoes on the still lake.

"You can't stand up. You'll sink," he says. "I told you, you need waves. Otherwise, it's just . . . I don't know, *floating.*"

She throws her head back and laughs too. This makes him laugh harder. Soon they are both laughing so hard he almost gets a cramp. Their voices turn into one giant laugh that echoes back to itself. A loon cackles back, which makes them laugh even harder.

"Can I get on there with you?" he asks. "I'm gonna fuck-ing drown."

"Sure," she says. "What do I do?"

He helps her sit up and then he slowly climbs onto the board in front of her.

"It's kind of like riding a horse," she says.

"Is it?"

"Sure, my grandmother has horses. I've been riding since I was a little kid. I actually think my dad was the one who taught me how to ride. I don't really remember that well. But I do remember holding on to him; I remember the way he smelled. Sometimes I'll catch that smell somewhere, probably just whatever detergent my mom used, and I'll remember that. You know, the good stuff about him."

Finn nods. He can remember but cannot name the exact smell of Franny.

"Look!" she says suddenly, and points to the sky.

"What?"

"That's the Big Dipper," she says. "Or maybe it's the Little Dipper. Do you know?"

He peers at the stars glowing faintly in the dark sky and shrugs.

"It's kind of cold," she says, and puts her arms around his waist. She leans her head against his back. He smells the wet smell of her hair, her shampoo.

"We should get back," he says, his voice breaking in a way he hopes she didn't hear. He can see a light on in the downstairs of the cabin. His mom is back from rehearsals, and he's going to be in deep shit.

"Not yet," she says. "Let's just stay a little bit longer."

The tow truck driver had given Dale the name and address of the shop scrawled on the back of a greasy business card. And Troy offered to give her, and her crap, a ride to the motel. "It's near where I work. It's no Hilton, but they got an outdoor pool and AC. HBO too, I think. And it's dirt cheap. I lived there for a whole month when I first moved to town."

"What do you do?" she had asked as he helped her load her stuff into his truck.

"I'm a tattoo artist," he said. "You got any ink?"

Dale shook her head, thought of Thoreau and wondered what he'd say right now if he knew what had happened to the Bug. Puff the Magic Dragon. Damn.

They got into the truck and he turned on the AC. It felt so good. So cold and good. She trembled.

"You oughta let me do a piece on you. Wouldn't have to be anything big or fancy. Maybe a butterfly? A little rose? A flame?"

Dale shook her head, blushed.

"You got pretty skin," he said. "A nice canvas." He nodded and smiled.

She could suddenly feel every inch of her skin. "Thank you."

The motel was definitely cheap, but it was clean, and the guy at the repair shop promised he'd have the car fixed by the weekend. Troy came by to check on her after she got settled in that night, brought a bucket of chicken. After they were done eating, he started to rub her back, and she knew what was going to happen next. He undressed and she undressed and then they were on the bed kissing and she felt happier than she had felt in a long, long time. He was covered with tattoos, and she imagined the pictures telling a story to her as they made love. And he, unlike Fitz, stayed. He only left when it was time for him to go to the tattoo shop. She spent the entire next day pacing back and forth on the sidewalk in front of the motel, waiting for him to come back.

And he did come back, that night and every night after the tattoo shop closed. They ate dinner together in the motel room: Chinese food, Pizza Hut. They watched HBO and played gin rummy naked. By Wednesday, he'd talked her into it.

"I'm not letting you leave until you get at least a little work done," he said. "Something to remember me by. And it's on the house. My treat."

Now, face down and half naked at the tattoo parlor, she's wondering if she's really got the guts to go through with it.

They'd stayed up late drinking a bottle of Boone's Farm, watching reruns of *I Love Lucy* as she gave him a blow job, and afterward, her tongue prickly and her jaw numb, she'd shown him her idea.

"That is the coolest idea for a tat I've ever heard," he said, grinning. "But you've got to be careful with words. A lot of times people who get words done change their minds after. Like names and stuff."

"I won't change my mind," she said.

"This is going to probably take me a few days. And it's not going to be any sort of picnic for you either," he said. "You sure you don't want something smaller?"

She shook her head. "Let's do it."

Now, inside the parlor, her Boone's Farm bravado is gone.

"I'm gonna go get everything ready," Troy had said. "You're going to need to take off your shirt. Try to relax. I'll be back in five."

She can hear him in the small lobby of the shop, talking to the girl who had taken her ID and had her sign the release. She'd watched to see if he flirted with her, felt a nasty pang of jealousy when he smiled his slow smile at her.

When he comes back in, she shivers.

"Are you cold?" he asks, and walks over to the thermostat on the wall. "Jessica likes it pretty cold in here. I keep telling her I can't tattoo through goose pimples." Troy laughs a hearty laugh and pulls on a pair of latex gloves he gets from a box on the counter.

"Ready?" he asks, bending over so he can look her in the eye.

"I think so," she says, surprised by how frail her voice sounds.

First, he rubs her entire back with rubbing alcohol. The smell makes her nose twitch, makes her remember getting her ears pierced at the Maryvale Mall when she was twelve.

"I'm going to shave your back now," he says, and she grimaces. Does she have *hair* on her back?

"I just have to get all the fine baby hair off. It gets in the way otherwise."

"Okay," she says.

When he's done, he rolls a stick of deodorant across her whole back. "This is to help the transfer stick," he says.

She'd found a used bookstore down the street from the motel. It was pretty small, but they'd had almost all of Sam's books. She'd found a beat-up hardcover copy of *The Hour of Lead* and paid fifty cents for it. Troy had helped her cut out the pages with an X-Acto knife. He'd measured her back with a tape measure he kept in his truck. And he had gone with her at midnight to Kinko's to get them enlarged. At the tattoo parlor, he'd shown her the machine that would turn the design into a stencil of sorts.

Now he lays the design across her back, gently pressing the paper on her skin. He makes his way from the broad expanse between her shoulders all the way down to her waist.

"Does it fit?" she says. "The whole chapter?"

"This is going to fucking rock," he says.

She closes her eyes and hears the crinkle and tear of the paper covering the needles. She opens them again when he turns on the machine, and then there is the first prick and the hum that spreads through her body like a song. *This is the hour of lead. I remember, because I am the one who lived.*

*Hunger (n): hunger, craving, taste, need to eat, de-
sire for food. Lack of food (n): food shortage, starvation, famine, appetite. Desire (n): desire, need, wish,
passion, yearning, longing. Yearn (v): yearn, long for,
desire.*

Sam thumbs through the water-damaged thesaurus, looking for clues. Looking for answers.

*. . . appetence, appetency, appetition, craving, desire,
emptiness, esurience, famine, famishment, gluttony,
greediness, hungriness, longing, ravenousness, starvation, vacancy, voracity, want, yearning . . .*

Sam thinks of the young man from Boston; he considers the
spray of freckles across his nose. He cracks his knuckles
when he's nervous. He misses home. The men, all conscientious
objectors, came from all over the country, unified by their
pacifism, by their idealism, by their youth. He, like the others,
had seen the recruitment brochure: *Will you starve so that others
may be better fed?* He, like the others, had been working without
pay at one of the conservation camps in Maine. When he saw
the brochure, it was as if he'd finally found a way to really help.
A real way to contribute. A way to save lives. This is what he

thought then. But not now, not as he runs his fingers across his ribs, counting their careful ridges, their exact and razor sharp edges. This is not what he will think in the morning as he walks down the long wood-paneled corridor of Shevlin Hall to their dining area with its massive stone fireplace and stained glass. This cathedral of hunger. He will not think of Hitler's victims as he sits down to his plate of pale potatoes, carefully portioned out. This is not what he will think when he presses the plate to his lips and tongue, licking until there is nothing left. Sam closes his eyes and sees him, lying on the narrow bed in the dormitory that night. He can smell the cold seeping in through the windows. It is winter now, and everything aches.

When people are starving, the body begins to break down fat and muscle mass for energy, in order to keep the vital systems functioning (the nervous system, the heart). Catabolysis, the body's attempt to save itself. Irritability. Lethargy. Vitamin deficiency, anemia, beriberi, pellagra, scurvy. Diarrhea, skin rashes, edema. Heart failure.

He closes his eyes, squeezes them until the kaleidoscope stops spinning. *Twist.* Sam remembers Mena lying on the crinkly paper in the doctor's office, the whoosh, whoosh, whoosh as the doctor rolled the Doppler device across her still-flat stomach. He remembers the way the doctor cocked her head and ran the probe across Mena's skin again.

"Is everything okay?" Mena had asked, her eyes and brow creased with concern.

"Do you hear this?" the doctor asked.

"The heartbeat, right?" Mena said.

"Well, that's one of them." She ran the Doppler a few inches lower. "And there's the other one."

"The other one?" Sam asked.

"There are two." The doctor smiled. Whoosh, whoosh, whoosh.

For one surreal moment Sam thought that their baby had two hearts.

"Twins?" Mena asked, her eyes softening and then filling with tears.

"You got it," the doctor said.

Twist.

He remembers going to the twins' room, pressing his ear against their chests, their slumber so deep it was terrifying. He remembers the knock, knock, knock against their flesh and then the crash, crash of his own heart, rushing and flooded with relief.

Twist.

He is running with Franny and Finn down the beach, their bare feet slapping against the wet sand. And then he collapses onto the blanket next to Mena, the kids piling on top of him. He recollects the way his own heart thudded against his chest, the way *their* hearts thudded against his chest. He remembers thinking that they were, for at least a moment, simply parts of one larger, breathing entity.

Twist.

He remembers picking Franny up at the studio once and watching through the window as she danced. She couldn't have been more than ten or eleven years old. She was just starting to dance *en pointe*. He stood at the door for nearly a half hour, watching, amazed by the precision with which every part of her body worked, the fluidity and ease with which her body moved. At the end of class, she saw him and her face lit up. She ran to the door, the wooden blocks of her shoes echoing against the floor. *Daddy!* she squealed, and threw herself at him, hugging him like she used to do when she was little, and he could feel her heart beating hard against his stomach.

Twist.

But he can't do this. He can't look at this pattern, at these fragments.

He clicks the computer monitor on, stares at the luminous pale screen.

When a body is deprived of the proper nutrients, the heart may develop an arrhythmia. Blood pressure lowers. The heart muscle will shrink. Atrophy. And eventually, it will simply stop. It begins and ends with the heart. It begins. And ends. Begins. And ends.

A lice and Finn are in the garden, pulling out the weeds and uprooting all of the male plants. The Web site said that it was important to remove the males before their flowers open. Otherwise, they'll pollinate and you'll wind up with a bud full of seeds. He's got pages and pages of color printouts to help them identify the male plants.

"They all look exactly the same to me," Alice says.

"Me too," Finn says, examining the photos again. "It says the males are taller."

"Just like people," Alice says. Alice is about five feet tall, a whole foot shorter than Finn.

"Here, I think this is one. Can you hand me a plastic bag?" You're supposed to cover the plant before you yank it up so the spores don't go flying everywhere. He covers the plant with the bag and tugs gently.

"What do we do with them?" Alice asks.

"I don't know. Maybe move them somewhere else?"

"Okay." Alice shrugs.

"How many weeks now until your dad's parole meeting?" Finn asks.

"Two."

Alice is examining the top of one of the female plants. "This is pretty," she says. "It smells good too."

For a week now, they have been coming to check on the

plants every day. In San Diego, his mother had a garden. She spent hours out there pruning and weeding and watering. He never understood her fascination with gardening, but now he's starting to. But instead of angel's trumpets and birds-of-paradise and manzanitas as a reward for all that hard work, the way he figured it, he'd have several pounds of kind bud. If he was able to harvest it before they left Vermont, he might have enough to last an entire year. Just long enough to get through his senior year of high school. Not bad.

"Does your mom have like a restraining order or anything?" Finn asks.

"She will, but those things don't mean much to my dad. She had one the last time too."

Alice looks up at him and smiles sort of sadly. She's changed even since he met her; it's funny how teenaged girls do that. Usually Finn didn't get to see the changes until after summer was over, when all the girls came back to school after three months in Europe or Martha's Vineyard or wherever the hell else their parents dragged them off to for the summer. And then BAM! *Boobs. Butts.* Makeup and clothes and all of a sudden Finn started thinking about the same girls he'd teased or picked on in a whole new way. It was weird watching the transformation happen. Alice seems a little taller than she was a month ago, and he thinks she's starting to get real boobs, not the little bug bites that poked out from her T-shirt at the beginning of the summer. He has to concentrate not to notice them sometimes. She's also started wearing her hair down long instead of in braids. Lip gloss and mascara. He can't help but wonder sometimes if she's doing it for him.

He remembers how fast Franny went from being a kid like him to being a real girl. The difference was, she didn't want any part of it. When she started getting boobs, she was pissed off. Dancers aren't supposed to have bodies. "God, I'm gonna wind up like Mom, I just know it," she had said. Their mother was *voluptuous,* at least that was the word he always heard other peo-

ple use when they were describing her. His friends called her a
MILF, which always made him feel kind of queasy. She was
built, Franny said, *like a brick house.* And she wanted no part of
that genetic construction.

"I'm hot," Alice says. "Can we go get something to drink
in your house?"

"Sure," Finn says. "I think we got them all. Oops, here's one
more." This one doesn't come out as easily, the roots are tangled around a rock, and so he grabs his Swiss Army knife from
his pocket and clicks it open. The blood comes before the pain.

"Shit," he says, instinctively thrusting his finger into his mouth.
It tastes salty, warm.

"Oh God, what did you do?" Alice asks. "Here, show me."

He takes his finger out of his mouth, carefully, and the blood
immediately comes to the surface of the wound and spills over.

Alice takes the bandanna she has tied over her head and
quickly wraps it around his finger. "Here, put your hand on my
shoulder. It needs to be above your heart so that the bleeding
will stop."

They make their way back to the house, Finn feeling a little woozy. The bandanna is soaked through, and the blood is
getting all over Alice's T-shirt.

"Sorry," he says. "I'm ruining your shirt."

"Big deal," Alice says.

Finn can feel his heartbeat in his finger now. He hopes he
won't need stitches. He's had stitches before: once when his surfboard cracked him in the chin, and once when he and Franny
got a hold of a rusty pogo stick and a can of WD-40. Something about the pushing and pulling of skin, the thick black
thread makes him feel like he might throw up. He also starts to
panic as he realizes that he's going to need to explain this to his
mother. He tries to think of all of the reasons why he might
have a knife and what he could have been trying to do with it
when he cut himself.

"Okay, so there was this bird trapped in a fishing net? You were using the knife to set him free," Alice says.

"Perfect." He smiles.

Back at the house, Finn's dad is in the barn shooting hoops. His mom is inside, going through a pile of dusty cookbooks.

"Hi, Ma," he says.

She doesn't look up. "Hi, honey."

"Um, I sort of cut my finger," he says.

"What?" she asks, looking up at him, distracted. She's so damn distracted these days.

He sticks the bloody bandanna-wrapped finger closer to her face. "I cut myself."

"Oh, my God," Mena says, suddenly alert again. She quickly and carefully unwraps his finger, examining the wound. "It's deep, but it looks clean," she says. She stands up and leads him over to the kitchen sink. She keeps checking the temperature of the water with her own hand, adjusting it several times before she puts his hand under.

"Ma, this is Alice," he says.

"Alice, I think we've got a first-aid kit in the car. Would you go look in the back of the station wagon?" she says without even looking at her.

"Sure," Alice says, and disappears outside.

"How did this happen?" Mena asks.

"I was trying to get a bird untangled from a fishing net," he stutters.

"Oh, baby," she says. "This is a bad one."

She is turning his finger back and forth under the water, inspecting it. He can smell her breath: teaberry gum and coffee. He realizes he hasn't been this close to her in a long, long time. And for a second, he wants to cry. He wants to howl like he would have even just a few years ago. Whenever he got hurt. He wishes she would pull his head close to her chest and say softly in his ear, *It's okay, baby. It's okay.* The impulse is almost overwhelming. He hasn't felt like this, this terrible need for his mom, for a long, long time.

But then Alice is back. She pulls out some gauze and tape from the kit and hands it to her. "Here's some Neosporin too."

"Thank you," his mom says, still without really looking at Alice. She is on a mission to make his finger stop bleeding. And something about this makes him feel good, *important to her for* the first time practically since he can remember. She makes Finn sit down at the kitchen table and applies the cream to the cut. It burns like a mother, and he bites his lip so he won't cuss. Then she carefully wraps the gauze around his finger, securing it tightly with tape, which she tears off from the roll with her teeth. "There," she says. "All better. If it bleeds through, though, I'm going to take you into town to the walk-in clinic."

Alice plunks herself down in the chair on the other side of the table from Mena. "Hey, is that the *Moosewood Cookbook*? My mom has this. She always makes the cream of broccoli soup." She picks up the cookbook and starts to thumb through it.

His mom looks at Alice like she forgot she was even there. And as soon as she sees her, really sees her, her face goes pale. "Alice," she says too brightly, smiling. "Do you live at the lake year-round?"

"Yeah. With my mom."

Mena is examining Alice the way she was looking at his cut, and it makes Finn's skin crawl. He still feels kind of nauseous.

Finn stands up, suddenly wants to get out of the kitchen, away from his mom.

"You still thirsty?" he asks Alice, going to the fridge and pulling out a couple of cans of Coke with his good hand. They're hard to hold on to with one hand, slippery and cold. He hands one Coke to Alice. His mom doesn't even notice. She hates it when he drinks soda.

"We're gonna go listen to music in my room," Finn says.

"Oh, okay," Mena says, blinking her eyes again, like she's just waking up from a dream.

Finn and Alice are in his room, listening to music. Mena is still stunned, too stunned to make a fuss when Finn closes the bedroom door. Her gut is heavy with a feeling she can't seem to name. Doesn't Finn see it? Can't he see that quality, that something in that girl's face? It nearly took her breath away. And it isn't even that she looks like Franny—she doesn't—but there was something, something when she smiled.

Mena is surpised by the headache. It's been almost two weeks since she last had one, not since rehearsals started. It starts as soon as Finn and Alice disappear into his room. She goes to her own room hoping it will go away in time for rehearsals, but it doesn't disappear. Not even after Alice is gone.

As she gets ready for rehearsals, she tries to ignore the headache, to will it away. The last thing she needs is to have to stay home tonight. At six-thirty, she grabs her purse and kisses Finn on the head; he's at the table still, eating a second helping of dessert. He nods in acknowledgment but doesn't speak.

She goes to the foot of the ladder to the loft and hollers up to Sam, "I'm leaving!"

He leans over the railing. "What time are you home tonight?"

"I don't know," she says. "Not too late." The truth is, in the past week she hasn't been coming home right after rehearsals. She's too wound up, her mind spinning. It takes her at least an hour to get out of May's head, out of May's body and back into her own. The Miss Quimby Diner stays open until midnight every night except for Sundays, and so usually after rehearsals she stops by and has a cup of tea. Reads the paper. She feels guilty not telling Sam. It's innocuous, she knows. Christ, it's just *tea,* but it's a secret. Time stolen away from the cottage, from Sam and Finn.

By the time they get to the second scene, the headache is rippling through her entire body. Still, she tries to push through the pounding, to the other side where there isn't any pain. But as she moves, she can feel the headache in her joints: her knees, her knuckles, her spine. Her words feel thick and round in her mouth, like marbles.

"Mena?" Jake says.

She's standing next to May's bed, bent over at the waist. The headache is pulling her head down. She can barely keep it up.

"Migraine," she says. "I get migraines." It feels like she's forgotten how to talk. She wonders if this is what it feels like to have a stroke.

"Here, sit down," he says. He guides her backward onto the bed. And then Anne is handing her a glass of water. She swallows but it's too cold; it's so cold it almost burns.

"I'm sorry," she says, and tears sting her eyes. "I don't think I can do this tonight."

"Give me your hand," Jake says.

Mena looks up at him, through the blurry pain. The fluorescent lights are hurting her eyes. He is holding his hand out, waiting.

She gives him her hand and he starts to knead the flesh between her thumb and forefinger. His thumb pushes, making heavy circles. She is aware of every muscle, every sinew and bone.

"My ex-wife got migraines. This was the only thing that

helped. It won't make the headache go away, but it should make you feel a little better."

And she does, feel better. As he works that small area of her hand, the currents of pain part, a little, and she's able to lift her head up again.

"I should go home," she says, starting to stand. She squeezes her eyes shut, winces.

"You really shouldn't drive," he says.

"I'm okay. It's not too far."

"Listen, I'll take you, and you can get your car tomorrow." Jake is still holding on to her hand. She feels like a little old lady who needs help crossing the street.

"No . . . we just have the one car. We'll be stranded without it. I'm fine. I'll be fine. I just need to get home and go to bed."

"You sure?" he asks.

She's not sure; she's actually pretty sure she shouldn't be driving, but she's also sure that accepting a ride from Jake is not a good idea.

She gets her purse and sweater from the folding chair where she left it and apologizes to Lisa. "I'll be better by tomorrow. These things pass pretty quickly."

"Just get some rest and let me know if you need to take tomorrow off too," Lisa says, and squeezes Mena's shoulder.

Jake walks her outside and sees her to her car.

"I'm fine," she insists when he offers once again to drive her home. He leans down to her open window. "See you tomorrow?" he asks. His breath smells like cigarettes and coffee.

She smiles, and the effort of it sends shock waves of pain through the right hemisphere of her brain.

She drives slowly, conscious of every bump in the road, every turn. By the time she gets to the dirt road that leads to the pond, she's feeling like she might throw up. She slows the car down even more until she is crawling; she has broken out into a cold sweat and her hands are shaking. She rolls down the window and pushes her face toward the cool night air. And then all of a sudden there are lights flashing, blue and red, and she feels bile rising to her throat.

She pulls the car over, but the embankment is steeper than she thought and the car dips down into the ditch. She bumps her head on the steering wheel. The pain of the bump is a strangely pleasant distraction from what's going on inside her head. She shields her eyes when a blinding light flashes into her face.

"Ma'am, can you step out of the car, please?"

It takes her nearly five minutes and a puff on a Breathalyzer for her to convince the policeman that she's not drunk. He's off duty, not even wearing a uniform. He is shorter than she is, thick neck and wrists. When he makes her walk a straight line she is grateful there is no traffic passing by to see this.

"I've just got a terrible, terrible migraine," she says.

"Well, how far are you from where you're staying?" he asks.

He thinks she's a summer person. No wonder he's giving her such a hard time.

"We just bought the Carsons' old place. About a mile from here."

"Oh!" he says, suddenly softening. "We're *neighbors!* I live just south of you. The red house on the opposite side of the road? I've got firewood for sale out front?"

The dog.

"You've got a dog," she says. The pain feels like a saw now, a dull saw inching its way back and forth behind her eyes.

"Old Joe!" he says. "He chase you yet?"

"A couple of times," she manages. She wants to go home.

"Listen, looks like you shouldn't be driving anymore tonight anyway. Get in and I'll give you a lift home. You can come back for your car tomorrow."

Reluctantly she climbs into the front seat of the cruiser, and he finally turns off the flashing lights. Within a few minutes they pull up at the cottage, and she can see Finn peering out the window at her. This would actually be kind of funny if her head didn't feel like somebody was using it as a snare drum.

"Nice meetin' you, neighbor," he says.

She nods and slams the door to the cruiser behind her, walking sheepishly, like somebody caught, all the way to the front door.

Finn's first thought is that they've found the plants. That he's about to be busted.

He heard the car pull into the driveway and expected to see the station wagon, but it was too early for his mom to be home. When the car triggered the motion sensor his dad installed on the porch, he could see that it wasn't the woody at all but a cop car.

"Shit, shit, shit," he says, standing up and wringing his hands. He has no idea what to do. He paces back and forth across the room, wondering if there's any way he can sneak out to the field and destroy the evidence. It's a ridiculous thought, though. It's too late. *Shit, shit, shit.*

And so he starts to think about how he can get out of it. He's gotten pretty good at lying on the fly. *Plants? Must be somebody's using our backyard to grow weed. I don't even know what a pot plant* looks *like. Sure, I've been in some trouble before, but I'm done with all that. I'm a good kid.* Then he remembers all of the printouts from the *High Times* Web site. They're all crammed into his backpack. With the last of his weed. *Shit.* He's trying to figure out if he can set the papers on fire and get to the bathroom to flush the weed down the toilet when the headlights from the cop car sweep across the room.

His heart is pounding in his throat as he looks out the window again.

But his mother is walking toward the house and the car is pulling away. *Jesus, what the fuck?* he thinks. *Where's her car? What did she do?* His friend Pete got escorted home by the police once. He was Robo tripping; there were three empty bottles of cough syrup in his backseat, but he'd somehow managed to convince the stupid cop he just had a really bad cold. Finn thinks the chances his mom is high on cold medicine are pretty slim, and she was at rehearsals, so she couldn't be drunk. *What the fuck?* He can hear his mother and father talking in the kitchen. Their voices are muffled though. He cracks the door open and strains to hear.

"You okay?" his dad asks.

He can hear his mom crying, and it sends hot liquid down his spine. He hates that sound; it's the worst sound in the whole world. After Franny died, he'd wake up sometimes in the middle of the night and hear it. It would startle him out of sleep and then, even after it stopped, he'd be wide-eyed, awake until morning, waiting to fall back asleep. That's when he started smoking pot.

His whole body aches, and he just wants her to stop. He wants it all to stop. To just go back to normal. He covers his ears to block out the sound, squeezes his eyes shut. He listens to the blood in his ears and tries to think about the ocean, about home. He curls up on his bed and hugs his knees to his chest. Franny would hate this, he thought. She'd be curled up next to him right now, burying her face in his back. *Make it stop,* she'd say. *I hate this.*

Finn wakes just as the sun is starting to come up. He'd been dreaming that he was out surfing with Franny. In the dream, she was telling stupid knock-knock jokes.

"Knock-knock," she says.

"Who's there?"

"Hawaii," she says.

"Hawaii who?"

"I'm fine, Hawaii you?"

"Ha, ha," he says.

"Knock-knock," she says again.

"Who's there?" he asks, rolling his eyes. And then a wave comes. But instead of getting up on her board and riding it in, she's sucked under. Gone, just like that.

D ale pulls into the parking lot at Graceland at ten o'clock on Monday morning.

She'd picked up her Bug ("good as new") as soon as the shop opened and said her good-byes to Troy, who had driven her there.

"Why don't you stay a few more days?" he had said. "Give your back a little more time to heal."

The tattoo had taken nearly four days to complete, and her entire back felt like a tenderized steak. Troy had helped her rub the greasy Neosporin across the places she couldn't reach. Together they'd looked in the mirror, she over her shoulder, at her skin turned into one giant page—at his words, reflected in reverse, covering the entire expanse of her back. They'd screwed in the shower, sitting up, with her straddling him because the sheets stuck to her ravaged skin.

"*Stay,*" Troy had pleaded, holding his hands together in mock prayer, grinning. And a little part of her considered it. What if she just stayed? She tried to picture herself living here, in Little Rock. Answering the phones at the tattoo shop. Working at the Applebee's or the Olive Garden on the weekends for extra cash. Hell, she could probably get a job at the Blockbuster right next to the tattoo shop. She even imagined, for a minute, falling in love with Troy, getting married, having kids.

But it was silly, she knew. Troy was just bored, and she'd been a nice distraction. Besides, she was already a week behind schedule. She needed to get back on the road, and now that the Bug was fixed, there was nothing keeping her from moving forward.

She had thought about driving straight through Memphis, continuing on, but pangs of guilt hit her as she started seeing the billboards advertising Graceland. Elvis's silhouette larger than life. *Elvis Lives.* If there was anything Dale could understand about her mother, it was this.

She remembered being a little girl and watching her mother in the kitchen, shaking her hips to "Jailhouse Rock," the little radio next to the wooden bread bin always set to KOOL FM. That was before her father left, when her mother still danced in the kitchen. Dale remembers thinking her mother was so beautiful when she closed her eyes and her hips swayed to "Blue Christmas," the Christmas lights she'd strung around the windows twinkling. And she remembers curling up in her mother's arms on the couch on Sunday afternoons, watching old Elvis movies on TV. She thinks of her soft lap, the way she stroked Dale's hair as she sang along with all the songs. She remembers thinking that Elvis looked a lot like the old pictures of her dad, the ones in the yearbook he left behind.

The tour takes more than an hour, and her head is spinning from all of the garish displays. She realizes she hasn't eaten yet today and gets a cheeseburger and fries at Rockabilly's Diner, grabbing a *USA Today* and checking the weather in Vermont. In Burlington, it's going to be overcast and seventy-five degrees. In the gift shop she finds an Elvis music box that plays "Are You Lonesome Tonight?" her mother's favorite song. She has the salesgirl wrap it in Bubble Wrap. Before she leaves, she decides to walk around the grounds a bit, take a few pictures to send to her mother with the gift. She follows a wave of people and finds herself standing in the Meditation Garden, looking at the sea of neon flowers and wreaths, at the aquamarine blue fountain, and the circle of stones marking the graves of Elvis and his family members. Her eyes sting.

The tour guide had said that Elvis always considered his mother the most important woman in his life. He bought her a pink Cadillac with his first royalty check. He took care of her and his father. But as Elvis became more and more famous, his mother became more and more anxious. She was taking diet pills, drinking. But even when he was on the road, Elvis would call her every night, whispering baby talk to her to calm her nerves. Then he enlisted in the army, and six months later Gladys Presley died of a heart attack. Some people say she died of a broken heart.

Dale thinks about her own mother at home, imagines her trying to navigate the house, her life, without Dale's help. This is the longest she's ever gone without calling her. She's stopped listening to her voice mail. She knows she should call her soon, to make sure she's okay. But she's so close. She doesn't want that terrible thread that runs between them to pull her back. Not now. Not yet.

She reads the inscriptions on each stone, circling the perimeter of the grave site. There's something strangely moving about the way the stones make a perfect half circle, about the way this family, in death, are all together again. She wipes away tears that are running hot down her cheeks.

A woman in a hot pink pantsuit and plastic sun visor touches her arm. "It's okay to cry, honey," she coos. "He *was* the King."

"We're coming up!" Monty says, and Sam wishes he hadn't answered the phone.

"Up here?" Sam asks.

"Lauren says she needs a retreat. Usually that means a trip to the Hamptons, but I think she's getting adventurous in her old age. The farthest north she's been lately is the Upper West Side." He laughs. "Besides, I want to check on your progress. Snoop around a little bit."

"When?" Sam asks.

"Friday. I think we can get there by dinnertime. We'll stay the weekend. You got room for us?"

Sam tries to think about where they will sleep. Maybe Finn would be willing to camp out for the weekend. He and Franny used to pitch a tent in the yard when they were kids. It seems sort of ridiculous to kick him out of his room though.

"Come on, Sammy. It'll be *fun*. We'll go on nature walks. Watch some birds. Whatever it is you all do up there."

Sam looks out the window at the bird feeder he keeps forgetting to refill. There's a squirrel that's been stealing all of the bird food. He read somewhere that he should put Crisco on the pole so the squirrels can't climb up, but somehow that strikes him as incredibly underhanded.

"Let me talk to Mena. She's doing this play. I'm not sure what her schedule's like," he says.

"A play? She's acting again? That's fantastic. Can we see it?"

"It doesn't open until August. Maybe you should wait and come then."

"Oh, no. Lauren's got her heart set on getting out of the city this weekend. Maybe, if she has a good time, we'll come back."

Sam grimaces. "Let me call you back, Monty. I'm right in the middle of something."

"Work?" Monty asks hopefully.

"Work," he says.

Actually, Sam is right in the middle of heating up some lamb souvlaki Mena left them for dinner last night. They don't have a microwave here, and it's been in the oven for almost a half hour already. He keeps opening the over door and poking at it to see if it's hot. Mena has always accused him of the inability to multitask. At home, she'd catch him staring at the toaster or microwave and shake her head knowingly. What she didn't know was that it was when she thought he was being an imbecile, he was actually almost always thinking about his books. These were the moments when (even if he seemed like he was focused on the toasting of an English muffin or the reheating of leftovers) he was usually caught up in the reverie of whatever book he was working on. As the toaster toasted and the microwave heated, he was imagining. His mother, before she died, would plead with him, "Go do something, Sammy. Play outside." But he *was* doing something; he *was* playing. Even as a little kid, he could look as though he were doing nothing at all for hours. What a relief it was to finally put pen to paper those days, to open up the seams and let the beads of the stories that had been stuck inside spill out.

But today he's simply watching the souvlaki heat up, no creative ponderings to accompany it. Just cold souvlaki in the slowest oven on earth.

When the phone rings again, he answers, irritated, "Monty, give me a few. I said I need to talk to Mena."

"Sam?" It's not Monty; it's a woman.

"Yes?"

"Hi, Sam, it's Hilary Ortiz." One of Mena's friends, a realtor. "Hi, Hill . . . hey, Mena's not here. Can I have her give you a call later?"

"Listen, I was actually calling for you. I know this might be premature; it might even sound a little crazy. But I have a client who is very interested in making an offer on the Sunset Cliffs property."

The Sunset Cliffs property. Their *house.*

"But it's not even on the market," Sam says.

"I know. And the market is hardly what it used to be."

He swallows hard. "How much do they want to offer?"

"We haven't talked numbers yet, but let me just tell you that you should be able to get whatever it is that you decide to ask. They love the place. They're a gay couple from LA, they come down to San Diego a lot, and they actually said they've always loved the house. That they've almost knocked on the door a few times just to see what it's like inside. One of them is a producer; he's got money to burn. You and Mena could retire. Finn's college would be paid for."

Sam thinks about his last visit to the ATM, the dwindling account. The fact that the advance on the book is already gone, and there's still no book.

"And you could start over somewhere. A place without so many memories," Hilary says softly.

"This isn't something I can decide right now. Mena and I will need to discuss this."

"I totally understand, but if you're interested, I wouldn't let it go too long. There's another place up the hill a bit with a killer view, and they've been looking at that property as well."

"Okay. We'll let you know," Sam says, and hangs up the phone.

He opens the oven door, reaches in for the souvlaki.

The house in Ocean Beach was, until he bought this cottage, the only house he'd ever owned. They'd bought it from an old woman who was moving into a nursing home. She took their offer over another couple because she said she liked them, could tell they would take good care of the place. She had no children, and so when she moved, she left almost everything behind.

Mena and Sam had felt like they'd bought a treasure chest instead of a house. They had so little of their own back then, they were grateful for the cupboards full of dishes, the furniture, the TV. For months, they'd discover something new almost every day. Boxes of Christmas ornaments, a steamer trunk of old dresses and suits, stacks of handmade quilts. He remembers Mena going through the drawers in the bedroom and finding a bundle of letters tied together with a hair ribbon. They'd been postmarked from Saigon, the airmail envelopes as thin as air. They found out later that her only child, her son, had died in Vietnam.

Sam had found Mena sitting on the inherited bed, surrounded by the open letters, crying. She was pregnant with the twins then, swollen but, Sam thought, profoundly beautiful. He remembers her being barefoot, her toenails painted bright red.

"I know I shouldn't have," she said, wiping at her eyes. Apologetic. "I'll drop them by the nursing home tomorrow."

"It's okay," Sam said, sitting down next to her and gently laying his head on her belly.

"He was her only child," Mena said, her voice catching in her throat like a burr. "He was nineteen years old."

Sam closed his eyes and concentrated on the sounds of Mena's belly.

The souvlaki is cold in the middle. He eats around it, the hot edges, and then scrapes the rest into the trash.

Mena is in the bedroom getting ready for rehearsals. She's been going for over two weeks now, but she has hardly said a word about it. He asks her, periodically, how it's going and she nods. "Good, good." She almost always gets home long after Sam has fallen asleep.

She comes into the kitchen and grabs her purse from the back of his chair.

"What was the woman's name?" he asks. "The one we bought the house from?"

"Shirley?" she says, digging through her purse for her keys.

"That's right. Shirley O'Connell."

"O'Donnell."

"Right."

"Okay, gotta go." She smiles.

"Come here?" he asks, surprised by how tentative he sounds.

She raises her eyebrow at him suspiciously. She sighs and then comes to him, leans over and kisses his forehead. "Don't wait up for me. It will probably be late."

This is the same feeling he gets every time they go out swimming together in the ocean. They'd always plunge in together, but within moments she'd be swimming away. He liked to stay at the shore, ride the waves. He liked to be where his feet could still touch the ground. She always needed to go beyond the waves, where the water was deeper. Farther. He'd watch her turning into a tiny speck against the horizon, and he hated it. It was excruciating waiting for her to come back.

"Monty and Lauren are coming up this weekend," he says.

"Up here?"

Sam nods.

"Christ, where are we going to put them?"

"I'll talk to Finn about camping out for the weekend. Otherwise, you and I can pitch a tent." He laughs. He thinks about the herbal supplements. He could give them another shot. He remembers a trip to Yosemite when the kids were ten, stolen moments after they'd fallen asleep in the other tent.

She scowls. "I have rehearsal until ten on Friday night. And again on Saturday afternoon."

"Fine," he says, feeling a little angry. "I'll take care of everything. You don't even have to be here." He doesn't want to be like this. "You're the one who suggested they come up."

"I've got to go," she says, glancing at her watch.

When she is gone, he calls Monty back. "We'd love to have you up. Bring your swimsuits."

"That last scene was fabulous," Anne says to Mena during their break. "You and Jake have such a powerful synergy."

Mena feels her cheeks flush with heat. "It's a good play," she says.

"You want coffee?" Anne asks, grabbing a Styrofoam cup from the stack.

"No, makes me too jittery at night. I have a hard enough time sleeping anyway."

Lately, she's not been able to sleep at all. She stopped taking the sleeping pills the doctor prescribed after Franny died because they knocked her out so hard she was afraid the house might burn down around her and she wouldn't wake up. They also made her feel sort of groggy and hungover the next day. She falls asleep okay every night, but around three or so, she wakes up and can't go back to sleep. This is Sam's prime snoring time as well, and so she might have a hard time falling back to sleep even if her mind wasn't racing.

"Me too, but I'm totally addicted," Anne says, pouring the hot coffee into her cup.

Jake is on the stage, talking to Lisa. Mena watches him lean into her. She laughs at what he says and touches his arm. Mena feels her stomach drop.

"You said you're married?" Anne asks.

Mena feels herself blush again, feels caught. "Yes."

"What does your husband do?"

Mena thinks of Sam sitting at the kitchen table, pushing souvlaki around his plate.

"What?"

"What does he do? For a living?"

That expression has always struck her as funny. As if people do whatever it is that they do in order to live. Though, she might once have argued that Sam did write for a living.

"He's a writer. A novelist. *The Hour of Lead,* that movie you saw? It was actually based on his first novel."

"Oh, wow! That's so cool," Anne says. "I had no idea. I'll have to check his books out. Do they have them at the Athenaeum?"

"They should. He just did a book club meeting there last week."

Jake and Lisa are still talking. Lisa keeps flipping her hair back; she is sitting on the bed. *May's bed.*

Anne follows her gaze to the stage.

"I know you're *married* and everything," Anne says, "but God, isn't he just such a tall drink of water? I don't know how you make it through some of those scenes. Seriously."

Mena looks at her feet as Jake jumps down off the stage and comes toward them. "That last scene was good, wasn't it?" he asks Mena. "I think it's starting to come together."

Mena nods and smiles. She grabs a cup from the stack and pours herself some coffee in order to have something to do with her hands. What the hell, she'll be up anyway.

"I've gotta go talk to Lisa," Anne says, pinching Mena's elbow—conspiratorially, Mena thinks.

"Listen, I was thinking of inviting everybody over for a drink after rehearsal on Friday. I figure it might be nice to all get to know each other a bit off the stage as well."

Mena's heart quickens. "That sounds like fun," she says, sipping the coffee, which is both too hot and too strong. "Oh shoot, I can't make it," she says, remembering Monty and Lauren.

"Oh really?" Jake asks. "That's too bad. Maybe next time."
"Sure." She smiles, nodding. Disappointed. "Next time."

The scene they are working on is one of the fight scenes between Eddie and May. It begins with a kiss and ends with a kick in the groin. They rehearse for hours, until her lips feel raw and her arms and legs are tired from fighting. By the time she drives home she is so exhausted she almost believes that she'll be able to sleep tonight.

Up in his loft, Sam turns on his laptop, stares at the scattered words that swim across the page. Letters, disconnected, adrift in that enormous white sea. The words try to stay afloat, but they can't seem to rise up to the surface. They are drowning. All of them. In this terrible, terrible empty white.

He thinks about the man, the one in the experiment. He has a name now: *Billy*. He is no longer a shadow, but the frail sketch of a man. The bones, his rib cage, his long fingers. Today he walks three miles through the snow: part of the mandated exercise during this phase of the experiment. He has lost twenty pounds already.

In the beginning, before the caloric restrictions, before the starvation phase of the experiment, he dreamed of home. He dreamed of *Mary*, of her creamy thighs and the smell of her hair. He'd wake up, his entire body electric and buzzing with desire. He'd have to hide his erections under the covers. He could feel his heart ready to explode with yearning. Every inch of his skin wanted her. But now, he only dreams of food. He dreams of his mother's creamy pea and ham soup, the smell of spiced beef and parsnips and potato bread. If Mary enters the dream at all, she is liquid. No different than the steaming bowls of potato leek soup.

Sam leans back in his chair. Listens to the crickets outside, at the strangely noisy night.

Sometimes, before, when he was working in his office at home, he would stop typing and listen to the sounds of their house at night, and it was like music. In Finn's room, the sound of his stereo, faint but certain, rhythmic: the beating of drums like a metronome. The clinkety-clank of the kitchen, the tinkling of glasses, the rush of water, the cymbal clash of a copper pot. And in Franny's room, the shuffling of feet. There were words for those sounds, whispery words: *tendu, ronde de jambe, degages.* The words come to him again now, the whispers of her slippers on the floor. And *those* whispers turn into the wind howling in Billy's ear as he walks.

The men must walk twenty-two miles every week, even now that their meals have been reduced from three to two a day: watery soup, macaroni and cheese, rutabagas, steamed potatoes, lettuce. The calories going into his body cannot match the ones being spent. Someone in the group is cheating, and in order to find out who it is, the scientists have cut their diets to a thousand calories a day. At night he dreams of oranges, of tearing into the rough bitter flesh of an orange with his teeth only to meet the sweet wet meat inside. He wakes up, gnawing and sucking on his own hand.

The ground beneath his feet is slick with ice; the wind is bitter. He shoves his hands in his pocket and buries his chin inside his scarf. When they were in town earlier that day, he'd caught sight of himself in a storefront and pitied the man he saw. It took several moments before recognition set in. And when it did, it felt like a punch in the stomach, and that pain was indistinguishable from the pain brought on by his hunger.

After leaving Graceland, Dale was only able to make it to Nashville before her eyes started playing tricks on her. She doesn't like to drive at night. All of the lights make her feel like she's playing a video game. Her depth perception is off. She gets dizzy. And so she'd found a Red Roof Inn just off the highway. The room reeked of smoke and something else she couldn't quite identify, and she was too excited to sleep. She had taken her last Ambien the night before, and she knew if she didn't do something, she'd be awake all night in that stinky room.

Next door to the motel was a bar, a small quiet place. She sat down at the bar and ordered a beer and a shot of whiskey. The bartender silently brought her a Bud Light and a shot of Jameson, which she'd thrown back quickly. Energized by the heat traveling down her esophagus, she slammed the shot glass on the bar and took a long pull from the beer. "Another one, please," she said.

The guy sitting next to her was eating a Philly cheese steak, and the smell of onions and peppers filled her nose, tickled her brain.

"That good?" she asked the guy.

He chewed slowly and nodded.

"I'll take one of those too," she said to the bartender, and smiled at the man.

He was older than she was, maybe forty. He was wearing a

cowboy hat and a plaid shirt. The snaps were pearly. Suddenly, she imagined what the sound of them unsnapping would be. She could almost hear the rhythmic pop, pop, pop.

She ate half of the sandwich and drank another couple of beers. By the time she did the next shot, the guy had moved closer to her. Close enough that she could smell Old Spice cologne mixing with Irish Spring on his skin. Close enough that she could imagine what it would feel like to touch the bristly hairs on his chin, those pearly snaps on his chest. She was drunk and leaning into him when he suggested they go back to her motel.

"Whatcha doing in Nashville?" he'd asked.

"I'm a writer," she said as he tore at her clothes. "A biographer. I'm on my way to do a very important interview," as his teeth tore at the strap of her bra.

Afterward, when he was gone, she'd drawn a bath and soaked. Her back stung, he hadn't been as gentle as Troy. She sank into the water and let the heat massage her shoulders. Her skin was still tender; Troy said it could take two weeks or more before the tattoo healed.

She had almost passed out in the bathtub and had to coax her body out of the warm water and into her sweats. When she went to pull the plug in the tub, she gasped. At first she'd thought it was dirt, but while she knew she was probably a little dusty from the road, she certainly wasn't this filthy. Then, as she peered closer at the black flakes swimming in the water, she realized what had looked like dirt was actually hundreds of tiny words. Sam's words. She felt panicked, breathless, wondering if this guy had somehow managed to tear the tattoo right off her back. She yanked off her T-shirt and stood facing away from the mirror, cranking her head around to see her reflection behind her. Her heart was pounding, her hands shaking. But the tattoo was still there. It hadn't gone anywhere.

Scabs. Troy had told her this might happen, the scabbing, but she had no idea it would look like this.

This morning, despite a terrible hangover, she wakes up early, intent on getting to Columbus by dark. No more distractions. No more men. She spreads the map out on the ugly geometric bedspread. Unless something terrible happens with her car, she is pretty sure she'll get to Vermont by Friday. She traces the journey with her finger. Columbus. Then Buffalo. Then Vermont. She is so close.

Outside, it is overcast and muggy. She's ready to go north, to get out of this sticky weather. She puts on a clean T-shirt and balls up her sweatpants. The yellow dress peeks out of the corner of her duffel bag, and she smiles. She touches the soft hem and thinks about what she'll say, what *he'll* say when she finally gets there.

Finn is in the garden, checking on the plants. He and Alice are going to try an experiment; Finn read that sometimes you can force the flowering of the female plants. In nature, they begin to flower when the days start to have twelve hours of light and twelve hours of darkness. He figures that if they cover the plants at exactly twelve hours after sunrise, then uncover them twelve hours later, then they can trick the plants into flowering. And the quicker they flower, the quicker he'll have some bud. He knows it's probably not too smart to call attention to the plants, and a bunch of grocery bags flapping in the wind might be sort of suspicious. So he's not going to do it with all of the plants, but at least a few. He doesn't want to sell the stuff for Christ's sake. He just needs to have enough to help him get to sleep. The stuff from Muppet is gone.

As he examines the plants he thinks about his mother's garden at home, the virtual jungle out beyond their back deck.

Most days after school Finn would go home, change into his wetsuit, and head out to the beach until dinnertime. Because his parents both worked at home, somebody was always at the house. He was the opposite of a latchkey kid. Sometimes he envied his friends whose parents worked all the time, if not their freedom then at least their ability to be alone. The only way he could get any peace and quiet was to go surfing. Except on Fridays.

On Fridays his mother did the grocery shopping, both for their house and for her weekend catering gigs. His father had a weekly chiropractor's appointment on Fridays. And Franny had ballet every day after school, including Fridays.

Finn's dad kept the fridge stocked with beers (and he never counted them), and there was always some really good Greek cheese and olives, something left over from the previous night's dinner. On Fridays before he went out surfing he'd help himself, popping the cap off a Sam Adams and making a plate of cheese and olives, taking everything out to the deck. He'd love to sit there in that wild jungle of plants. The smell of jasmine and hibiscus was so thick it could almost make you high.

After he'd finished the beer and the plate was covered in olive pits, he'd get his board out and lay it across the outdoor table where they ate dinner most nights. He always had a bar of Sex Wax on him—he'd ruined at least two loads of laundry forgetting to take it out of his pocket.

He was methodical about this process. He'd saved for an entire school year to buy the long board. It cost six hundred dollars, custom built by a guy who worked out of his garage down on Newport. He was pretty sure this was kind of Zen, because when he was waxing his board, his head was in such a quiet place. The rhythm of it was like the rhythm of the waves crashing onto the cliffs below. With the plants breathing all around him, it was a sort of nirvana.

But after Franny died, his mom stopped taking care of the garden.

All those plants she'd fussed over for years, she just forgot about. And something about those wilting leaves, about the heady scented flowers curling in on themselves made his stomach roil.

He remembers coming home from school in late November and bringing an entire six-pack out to the deck, not bothering with the cheese or olives. His appetite was shot. And something about that garden gone to shit made him so pissed off he could hardly see.

He'd uncoiled the garden hose from the side of the shed and turned it on full blast, looping the hose under his arm, walking the periphery of the garden. He'd watered every plant, drenched every leaf. But when none of the plants so much as nodded their droopy heads in acknowledgment, he'd taken off down the path to the beach with his board, leaving the water running, the hose spitting and writhing like a snake. By the time he emerged again from the water and made his way back up to the house, the entire garden was flooded. He'd thought he might be able to save the plants, but instead he'd just killed any of them that had even a remote chance of survival.

This wasn't his job, he kept thinking. This was his *mother's* garden, and she'd just let it fucking die.

The recipes in the cookbook swim across the pages. She doesn't want to cook for Lauren. She really wishes Sam had told them not to come. The timing is terrible, and she can't quite figure out Lauren's agenda either. Clearly, Monty wants to see if Sam is making any progress with his book. But Lauren didn't have to come. The idea of her needing fresh air is almost ludicrous. Every time Mena imagines Lauren, she has a dirty martini in one hand and a cigarette in the other. What on earth are they going to *do* with them for two days and nights? Mena is grateful to have the excuse of rehearsals. Sam will have to fend for himself the first night anyway. And the idea of them staying here, in Finn and Franny's room of all places, makes Mena's skin crawl. She had made Sam be the one to ask Finn if he'd be willing to give up his room. She didn't want to be the bad guy. She was always the bad guy with Finn. And amazingly, Finn had been easy. He said he'd pitch a tent and camp out at the far end of the property. Do some exploring.

Finn even seemed excited about it. She hadn't seen him show this much enthusiasm about anything since they got to Vermont. He'd asked her to help him find the sleeping bag and the Coleman lantern. He'd gathered up all of the parts to the tents and ridden his bike into town to get batteries for the radio, which he asked to borrow from her kitchen. She almost wished she was going to get to go on the camping trip instead of being stuck here tomorrow night.

She's looking forward to going to rehearsals tonight. They've been working on the scene when the Old Man reveals that Eddie and May are half brother and sister. When May starts drinking tequila straight out of the bottle, telling Eddie that she doesn't love him anymore. Mena's bruised from the violence of the scene. Lisa keeps telling her she doesn't have to go all out with it during rehearsals, that she's liable to break some bones, puncture a lung for Christ's sake. But there's something so satisfying in the screaming, in the hurling of her body against walls. What Lisa doesn't understand, *can't* understand, is that May acts the way Mena feels. May is her rage. Her sorrow. Simplified.

She decides on *spanakopita* and *xoriatiki,* her mother's Greek salad. It's elegant but easy. And hell, she won't be there to listen to Lauren complain about it anyway. Sam said he'd order out, but the only place to get takeout is the Hi Boy, which serves subs and pizza. She's pretty sure Lauren would have a lot to say about that.

She wonders what Sam is going to show Monty. She wonders if he has anything to show. She's not sure if he's writing while she's at rehearsal. It's a subject she doesn't dare broach.

She knocks on Finn's door quietly and says, "Tell your father I'm headed out to the grocery store. I'll be back in about two hours."

"Yep," he says. Alice is over again, and she can hear her humming along with the music. Her voice is so pure, it makes Mena's knees feel soft.

Alice comes to the door and opens it.

"Hi, Mrs. Mason," she says. And when she smiles, Mena looks hard for that quality, that something, that is Franny.

Dale gets to Buffalo earlier than she had planned on Thursday afternoon and as she checks into the motel, she sees a glossy pamphlet with a picture of Niagara Falls on the front sticking out of a brochure stand by the door.

"Is this close?" she asks the boy working behind the desk. He looks about fifteen with a bad overbite and acne. He's playing solitaire on the computer.

"Fifteen, twenty miles or so," he says without looking away from the screen.

"That's it?" She had no idea that she'd be so close to Niagara Falls. This was where her mother and father went on their honeymoon. Her mother accidentally dropped the camera and broke it when she slipped on a rock, but she was able to salvage the roll of film and the two pictures on it. The first one is of her father looking out one of those coin-operated binoculars at the crashing falls in the distance. The second one is of both of her parents. Her father's arm is draped over her mother's shoulder. She's looking up at him, smiling. He is gazing straight into the camera, looking smug.

She grabs a Mountain Dew from the vending machine outside her motel room and drinks it in a couple of big swigs. She doesn't even bother dumping her stuff in her room. She just gets into the Bug, studies the map on the back of the brochure and heads back out. She rolls the window down and pops the only non-Books on Tape tape she brought into the tape deck. She's feeling so happy, she sings out loud the whole way; she doesn't care who hears her or sees her.

It's incredible. The sound alone makes her feel alive, but the view of the crashing falls, the smell of the wet air . . . it's almost too much.

A woman next to her on the observation tower is tying her son's shoe, struggling to make a double knot as he wriggles and squirms and fusses. There's a toddler in a stroller next to her, and she's carrying a baby in a backpack. The baby has dropped her pacifier. A man Dale assumes to be the father is preoccupied with his video camera battery. Dale picks up the pacifier and hands it to the woman.

"Thank you," the woman says, popping it into her own mouth to clean it off and then plugging up the open mouth of the baby.

Dale peers down below at the crashing water.

"Pretty, isn't it?" the woman asks.

Dale nods, speechless.

"You should take the *Maid of the Mist* tour," the woman says.

"What's that?" Dale asks.

"The boat," she says, pointing to something below them. "It goes along the river and right next to the falls. It's amazing."

"Is it expensive?"

"Twelve dollars or so, I think. But it's worth it." The woman smiles at her. "My husband and I came here on our honeymoon. Three kids later, we still come back every year. Hey, would you mind taking a picture of us?" she asks Dale, and hands her a camera. The family gathers together, smiling, and she shoots.

She tries to imagine her parents returning here. She imagines how her life would be if they'd been that kind of couple. If they'd been this kind of family.

A boat trip under Niagara Falls isn't in her budget. But then again, neither was an entire week in Little Rock. It's only twelve bucks. She checks her watch. It's still early. She considers the alternative: going back to the motel, watching some crappy movie and lying in bed awake, her insides all jumpy. She hasn't slept right since Columbus. She's been like a kid on Christmas Eve ever since she got east of the Mississippi.

She takes the glass elevator down to the landing and is given a blue plastic poncho, which she dutifully puts on with all the other tourists. And then she stands in line. A long, long line. The tour is supposed to be only a half hour long though, so she figures even if she doesn't make the next boat, she'll still be able to get back to the motel before dark.

On the boat, she is overcome by the grandeur of the falls. It's one of those rare moments when the beauty of the world is almost too much to bear. She's only felt this way a few times in her life: the first time she saw the ocean and on the only trip her family ever took to the Grand Canyon. It's the same feeling she got the first time she read a Sam Mason novel. And when Troy finished tattooing the last word, the one near her spine. It's a sort of trilling feeling, a quivering that starts in the pit of her stomach and extends outward. She imagines that this must be what it feels like to be in love. Your heart so full you could cry.

By the time she gets off the boat, her plastic poncho beaded with water, she is completely exhilarated. Exhausted, but exhilarated. Maybe she will sleep well tonight, even without the Ambien. And by tomorrow she will be in Vermont.

She buys an ice-cream cone before she makes her way back to her car. It's peppermint, the kind she would always get at Thrifty when she was a kid. Her footsteps are light, she's humming to herself, and she doesn't care who hears her, who sees her.

She opens the door to the Bug and plops down into the seat, sighing. Happy.

But something's wrong. At first she can't figure it out. It's like looking at those pictures they always have in kids' magazines . . . two seemingly identical photos, and you have to figure out what is different in the second photo. It takes her several moments to figure it out.

The buzz that had been sitting in her stomach like a purring kitten suddenly turns sharp, violent, and she feels like she's going to throw up.

Her backpack. Her backpack, with the aerial maps of Gormlaith, the info about Quimby, the articles she's collected, the Books on Tape and the signed first edition of *The Hour of Lead.* Her laptop. Along with a hundred dollars in emergency cash, her last four tampons, and a king-sized Kit Kat bar. All of it is *gone.*

She leans her head against the steering wheel and starts to cry. She cries so hard, it feels like her throat might explode. A few families walk past, pulling their children close to them, shielding them from her. This only makes her cry harder.

All that joy, all that bliss is suddenly sucked out of her like water down a drain. And then her mind is reeling, putting pieces together, arranging, rearranging, trying to make a clear picture.

Her stomach roils. She is dizzy.

God. It makes sense now. Maybe Sam knows that she's coming. Maybe he's known all along.

She's heard that you can track the IP numbers of people who visit your Web site. Maybe the publisher keeps an eye out for people who visit their authors' pages too often. God, she's probably been on Sam's page fifty thousand times. Her heart is racing, her hands unsteady. Maybe they've been reading the letters she sent to Sam as well. That would explain why he hasn't responded. They've probably confiscated them.

But she only told a few people about where she's going. The hairdresser in Phoenix. The guy who sold her the Bug. The Bug!

She grips the steering wheel, clamps her jaw down until her teeth start to grind. Maybe the Bug catching on fire wasn't an accident at all. Maybe they've been trying to stop her all along. *Troy*. Jesus, was it a coincidence that he was there, in the Walmart parking lot, or was he waiting for her? She should have suspected as soon as he asked to come to the motel the first time. Guys don't want to spend *time* with Dale. And Jesus, Jesus, Jesus . . . he might have told someone about the tattoo. He was the one who kept encouraging her to get one. This way there would be proof. Indelible on her back. Why would he do this to her?

They probably tracked her all the way to Niagara Falls and took her stuff so she couldn't get any farther. She wonders if they'll be waiting for her in Vermont.

Then again, she thinks, maybe Sam doesn't know at all. Why would they tell him? If they did, she knows he would defend her. He'd tell them that she's just writing her thesis. That she's not some crazy stalker. She needs to get to him before they do. He'll explain everything.

She is shaking so hard now she can barely see. And when the acid creeps up her throat she knows it's too late to stop it. She opens up the door of the Bug and vomits pink peppermint ice cream all over the pavement.

Sam knows that Monty is going to want to see something. Anything. He pokes around the documents on the computer, looking to see if there's something he could offer him, a morsel. Monty is demanding and persistent, but also easily satisfied. If Sam can just find a little nugget, some proof that his writing hasn't gone to complete shit, then he'll leave him alone and they can just try to enjoy their weekend. But there's nothing there, and he knows he won't be able to articulate the mess that's inside his head: Billy and the experiment, the cold Minnesota winter, that raw hunger. The bones.

He really wishes Mena were going to be here for dinner tonight. Mena is always so good with Lauren, such a diplomat. She knows exactly the right questions to ask and answers to give when Lauren starts in. Sam's approach is to simply make sure there's enough liquor in the cabin to keep them all drunk, for the entire weekend if necessary.

He comes down out of the loft and finds Mena in the kitchen pulling a fresh loaf of bread out of the oven. He wonders if it's too late to try to convince her to stay home.

"Hi." He walks behind her and leans his head on her shoulder, wrapping his arms around her waist. As if this is perfectly normal. As if he hasn't forgotten how to show her affection.

"Hi," she says.

"It smells good." His cheek is still resting on her back as she busies her hands with the loaf of bread. She smells good. God, has he been so far away from her to forget the smell of her? How could he be feeling nostalgic about his own wife?

"There's spanakopita and salad. I made a cheesecake for dessert. No strawberries. Lauren's allergic, right?"

"How do you remember that?" Sam asks, still holding on to her.

"She reminds us every time we go out for dinner," Mena says, laughing. And then in her best Lauren Harrison voice, "Oh, my *Gawd,* just don't put any strawberries on it. The last time I ate strawberries I wound up at Mount *Sigh*-nye." Then in Lauren's conspiratorial whisper, "Anaphylactic shock. *I almost died.*"

Sam laughs and squeezes her tighter. "Please stay?" he says, pressing his nose into her soft T-shirt.

She stiffens. "It's the last weekend of rehearsals, Sam," Mena says, her voice harder now. She shrinks and disappears out from under his grasp, moving quickly to the refrigerator door.

"It's just one night. I *need* you," he says, and immediately regrets it.

Mena shakes her head and hisses. "*Jesus.*" Her hands are on her hips now; she is in attack mode. If he says the wrong thing, does the wrong thing, she'll strike.

"*What?*" he says, like an ass.

She laughs as if he should know what she's angry about. "*Nothing,* Sam."

"When will you be home?" he tries, sensing this too is the wrong thing to say.

She throws up her hands, exasperated. "I don't know. Maybe late."

She's pulling away, further and further. She's like that white dot when you turn off an old TV. She's going to just get smaller and smaller until she's completely gone.

"Mena, what did I do?" he asks.

She looks at him, shaking her head and chuckling again. He hates this.

"*Seriously,*" he says. "Why are you so pissed at me?"

"I talked to Hillary today," she says. "She told me she had a long talk with you about the house in San Diego."

He nods. He doesn't know where she's going with this.

Mena explodes. "Do you realize you never asked me if I wanted to come here? You never even asked!"

"That's not true," he says. "We talked about it."

"No, we *didn't.* You just made up your mind. You thought that dragging us all the way out here would make everything better. That you could undo everything by leaving that house. Like you can *fix* it. Now. After it's already too late."

It's like he's popped the cork on a bottle of wine and knocked it over. Everything is spilling out, staining, destroying.

"You don't touch me anymore. You can't even look me in the eye. We don't ever, *ever* talk about what happened. Not once have we talked about it. And now here, out in the middle of nowhere, it's not any better! You disappear into your little cave up there and leave me out here in the fucking wild to deal with everything. It's no wonder Finn's such a disaster," Mena screams. Her face is changing. It's like it's not even her anymore. He doesn't recognize her.

"Franny is *dead.* And we could have stopped it. It's our fault, Sam. It's *my* fault." She points at his chest, pushes her finger hard into the place where his heart is. "It's *your* fault."

"Mena," he tries, but she is raging now, swinging her arms at his face. He tries to grab her hands, her arms to stop her, but she is moving too quickly.

Sam has only been punched once. In college, during an innocuous snowball fight on the green in front of Old Mill. He'd accidentally nailed a kid in the temple with a snowball, and the kid came after him. He remembers the pain and then the snow and then the blood that stained the pristine white.

When Mena gets loose and her knuckles make contact with his eye, he stumbles backward and bumps against the table. And then the table collapses.

"Jesus," he says.

The weak leg finally gave out. They both stop and look down at the table. The fruit bowl is broken, and there are oranges rolling across the wooden floor.

"I've got to go," Mena says. Her face is red, and tears are streaming down her cheeks. "You deal with this."

And then she is gone.

Finn comes back from Alice's just as Monty and Lauren are pulling up. He tries to leave as soon as he sees Monty's Mercedes rounding the corner. He likes Monty a lot, but his wife is a train wreck.

He's got everything he needs ready at the door: backpack, tent, sleeping bag. Inside the backpack is the food his mom made (oatmeal raisin cookies, turkey sandwiches on homemade bread, Greek salad). He's also got a whole bunch of plastic grocery bags for the plants. The cottage is pretty quiet. His mom has already left for rehearsals. His father has his tools out all over the place, trying to fix the kitchen table, which finally fell apart. The weak leg finally gave out, his dad said. Just in time for a visit from Monty and Lauren.

He thinks he's got a clear path out the front door, but just as he's hoisting the pack on his back, his dad stops him.

"Five minutes," Sam says. "That's all I ask. Then you can go."

"Shit."

"*Mouth.*" His father is scowling.

"What happened to your eye, Dad?" Finn asks. His father's got an egg over his left eye, and the skin around it is turning purple.

"I bumped it when the table fell. Listen, I want you back by eight o'clock tomorrow morning. And I need to know where you're camping."

"Why?"

"Don't worry, I won't come out there unless you're not back in the morning."

Finn's skin prickles. He doesn't want to tell him where the garden is. He doesn't want him snooping around. Not tonight. Not any time. And so he lies. "You know that path that heads out north? The woods out there. About a hundred yards from here. I'll be able to see the fricking house lights from my tent."

His father nods. "Nice spot," he says. Satisfied, Finn guesses.

"Hey, Dad. Everything okay?" he asks.

"What?"

"Just wondering if everything's okay."

"Sure," his father says. "Everything's fine."

He's pretty sure his dad is lying. And something about the broken table, about that new shiner makes Finn feel sort of sorry for him.

Monty knocks on the door.

"Well, have fun with Monty and the Bride of Frankenstein." Finn thinks that this will make him laugh, but his dad looks distracted.

"Five minutes," he says again. "Just say hi and then you can go."

"Okay, five minutes," Finn grumbles. "But I want to get out there so I can do some hiking first."

He hasn't told his father that Alice is going to meet him there. He's pretty sure his parents wouldn't care that she's coming, but he doesn't want to push his luck. Her mom knows where she's going to be, and it's not like they're boyfriend/girlfriend or anything. But he knows that because of Misty they'd probably worry anyway. Plus, his mom is so weird about Alice. Both times she's come over his mom's acted spooked. He knows Alice reminds her of Franny. But Christ, she's not Franny. She's nothing like Franny.

In order to get to the garden in time to cover the plants, he needs to be there by six o'clock. He told Alice to meet him there. Now it looks like he might not be able to make it on time. He wishes his cell phone worked here. Not that it would make any difference, since she doesn't even have a cell phone herself.

Monty is practically rattling the door off its hinges. "Sammy!"

"Welcome to the wilderness," Sam says, ushering Monty in.

Lauren is standing quietly behind Monty, smiling a huge lipsticky smile. She's wearing blue jeans that are so new they're practically black. High-heeled black boots. A sleeveless sweater that looks like cashmere or something. Expensive. If she weren't such a bitch, she'd be sort of hot, Finn thinks. She's got short black hair and enormous tits. He's never been able to look her in the eyes, not even when he was a kid.

She comes in and sighs. "Well, that was about the longest drive ever. But, soooo glad we're here . . . Sammy!" she says, kissing each of his dad's cheeks, pushing her chest forward and her butt behind her. "Finn!" she squeals, and repeats the process with Finn. She smells good, like a magazine. She pulls away from him and looks him up and down. He starts to feel uncomfortable. Then she releases him dramatically. "Oh, they grow up so fast. Now where exactly is Mena again? Doing a little play with the yocals?"

"*Fool for Love,* the Shepard play. She's got the lead," Sam says.

"How darling. *Fool for Love, Fool for Love.*" She taps her temple with perfectly manicured plum-colored nails. "Is that a musical?"

"It's the one about incest, Lauren," Monty says. *"Shepard."*

"Oh." She grimaces. "Sorry. I'm not a theater person." Her lipstick is also the color of plums. She looks older than the last time Finn saw her.

"Come on in." Sam motions for them to enter the cabin.

Lauren stretches her arms, shoving her chest outward again. Finn stares at his feet.

"What's that smell?" Lauren asks, wrinkling her tiny surgery-perfected nose.

"Mena made dinner before she left. It's *spanikopita,*" Sam says.

"Smells . . . divine," Lauren says, but her face is still twisted up.

Time to go. "I'm out," Finn says, and shakes Monty's hand.

"Sorry to put you out of your room, kid. Where you staying the night? They got a Four Seasons up here? A Ritz-Carlton?"

"They're sending me out to the woods," Finn says, and smiles. "Like *Hansel and Gretel*. I've got some bread crumbs in my pocket."

"But no Gretel!" Lauren laughs.

Silence.

Everyone is horrified.

It takes her a minute. She gasps audibly. Her hand flies to her mouth with her mistake. "Oh, my God. I'm sorry. I'm so sorry."

Train. Wreck.

"See ya," Finn says, and heaves his backpack onto his back. And then he is jogging toward the back way to the garden, through the woods. As he runs, he keeps checking his watch, checking the sky. It's ten until six. He hopes to God Alice is there with some more plastic bags.

When he gets to the garden, Alice is sitting on a rock, staring out at the sea of plants. The air is redolent with the smell of weed. Finn takes a deep breath, inhaling that heady scent.

"Hi!" he says, touching her shoulder. She looks weird. Her eyes are red. Her hair's a mess. "Hey, you okay?" he asks.

"My mom wants to take me away," she says. "Before my dad gets out next week."

"What?" Finn asks.

"We're going to go stay with her aunt in California."

"California?"

"Yeah, isn't that crazy?" Alice shakes her head. "Here you are dying to get back home, and now my mom is buying Greyhound tickets to Barstow. Is that close to San Diego? Where you live?"

Finn sits down next to her. "Not really," he says. His heart is beating hard. He is trying to imagine being stuck here without Alice. The idea of it is incomprehensible.

Alice is playing with her shoelaces, tying and untying them. She looks up at him sadly. "I don't want to go."

"Then don't *go*," Finn says. His chest hurts now.

They're both quiet for a long time. There's a bird making a lot of noise in a tree above them. A woodpecker or something. He never realized how noisy it was out here, almost as noisy as the city. He's racking his brain; suddenly he gets an idea. "No, wait! You can stay with *us*. Your dad doesn't know who the hell we are. He wouldn't come looking for you at our house."

Alice shakes her head. "I've seen your house. You don't have room for us."

"We have room for *you*," Finn says. He's reaching for her now. It feels like she'll vanish if he doesn't hold on to her. "You can stay with me."

She squeezes his hand, looks him in the eyes. "I can't let my mom go by herself," she says. She's starting to cry, and he doesn't know what to do. "I have to take care of her."

Finn can feel his throat growing thick. He concentrates, makes his mind go empty. It's the only way to hold it together.

After a while of just sitting there, holding hands, Finn says, "You're going to miss the harvest."

"I'm going to miss *you*," she says, wiping the tears with the back of her wrist.

M onty starts in right away. "So, when do I get to take a peek at the next Pulitzer-winning novel, Sammy?"

They are both on their second pieces of *spanikopita*. Lauren had pushed hers around her plate several times and then grabbed an orange from the bowl in the middle of the table. Sam had managed to temporarily fix both the broken fruit bowl and the table leg, but he's pretty sure they won't hold out for long. Their dinner, as a matter of fact, might just wind up on the floor. Lauren is sitting next to Monty peeling the orange, scrutinizing a brown patch on the skin. The whole cabin smells like citrus and spinach.

"You know me, Monty. I like to have a good draft before I let it out loose in the world. It's just a bunch of scattered notes right now; it's a mess."

"I've been talking to Frank over at Random House. He says they're thinking about giving him his own imprint. Of course, he may be blowing steam out his ass, but I've heard a few things, and I think it might be true. Anyway, we were just talking about you. Really about *Small Sorrows,* and he was raving about you, asking, *What ever happened to that Sam Mason? He should have gotten a National Book Award for that one.* I did have to remind him about the nomination for *The Art of Hunting,* mind you, but he's a fan. A big one, and I have a feeling he might pay a lot of money to get his grubby paws on the next Sam Mason book. After this one, of course."

Sam cannot even begin to think of a book *after* this book, or whatever the hell it is he's working on.

"I met his wife," Lauren nods. "She's a publicist. So *well-connected;* I bet we could get her on board too. After everything, *you know,* you're probably going to need a good publicist. Put a good spin on things." She's peeled the orange now and has dissected it into segments. He's pretty sure she hasn't eaten a single one of them. There's a pit in his gut, and he imagines it like an orange seed, planting itself in the bile and trash inside his stomach, growing, blooming and blossoming, filling his body.

"Can you give me a hint?" Monty asks.

"Jesus, Monty. Let it alone for five minutes so I can eat?" Sam is trying to be lighthearted about this, but he's getting pissed.

Monty keeps pushing. "Just the *premise.* The main character. Can you give me *something* to chew on?"

Sam sets his fork down hard on the rickety table. He thinks about Mena's fist striking his face. The skin still stings. "*Christ,* Monty, it's about a starvation experiment," he says, and then immediately regrets it.

Lauren's jaw drops. She looks like one of those wooden ventriloquist's mannequins.

"Close your mouth, Laur," Monty says. And then he is nodding, his head bobbing like a bobblehead doll.

Sam rubs his temples. He's gone too far to go back now. "It's not what you think. I mean, it's not some god-awful memoir or anything."

Monty is still bobbing his head; Sam suddenly realizes that he actually looks excited. Eager.

"It's about these men, conscientious objectors during World War II. They volunteered for this experiment, to be starved and then refed. I've only got about ten pages. And to be honest, I'm not sure if it's anything anyone will ever want to read. Monty, you and I have been in this business a long time. I know what it is that publishers want these days. They want the big guns. The heavy hitters. Or, they want some pretty little girl, some Harvard coed protégée. Or some fucking drug addict who rambles on for a thousand pages about how he overcame his addictions. I'm small potatoes, Monty. A relic."

"That's not *true*, Sam," Lauren wines, a mock frown.

"It is *true*, Lauren. Don't tell me you didn't tell all your Colony Club friends that Monty was dragging you up to Butt Fuck Nowhere this weekend to see one of his has-been clients."

"That's enough, Sam. You're just in a slump. You've had some big stuff happen. Some really shitty shit happen," Monty says.

"I may not even want to publish it," Sam says. "Maybe I'm just writing it for me."

"Oh, Jesus Christ," Monty says, laughing. "It's finally happened. That's what this Vermont business is about, isn't it? You came up here to Salinger yourself away. A fucking hermit, writing away, stashing your work in some fucking wall safe somewhere." Monty looks around the room as if he's going to find Sam's hidden treasures behind a picture on the wall.

"*Ten pages*, Monty. And every single one of them is a piece of shit." Sam stands up and rests his hands on the table's edge. He thinks of Mena. *It's our fault,* she said. *It's* your *fault.* He can still feel the place where her finger met his chest. "I didn't come here to *write*. I came here to save my fucking family from falling apart. What's left of it anyway." His voice is booming now; he can feel his face getting red, his ears are hot. He grips the edge of the table, almost willing the whole thing to just fucking collapse.

"Well then," Lauren says quietly to Monty. And then to Sam, "I need to use your restroom."

Sam sighs and gestures down the hall.

After she has closed the bathroom door, Monty says, "I'm sorry about this, buddy. You want us to go?" His voice is full of sympathy. He's been a good friend. Sam feels like shit for disappointing him.

"If you're here for a book, I just don't have it, Monty."

"That's not why I'm here," Monty says.

"If you want to go home, go home," Sam says. "If you leave now, you can get back to the city just past midnight. This was a bad idea. I'm sorry."

"It's not over, Sammy. You just need to get through this rough patch. You're a writer. That's not going to change."

"Monty, I don't even want to write anymore. I just don't even care. I never thought I'd say that, but it's just gone. Everything that drove me to sit down and work every day, that excitement, that passion, has vanished. It's excruciating. It's literally painful to work. I'm spent."

"I believe in you," Monty says. "Just give it time."

"Ten pages in the last six months, Monty. How long am I supposed to wait?"

Lauren emerges from the bathroom, her cheeks flushed pink, a fresh coat of lipstick on her puffy lips. "I saw a motel on our way here," she says, clapping her hands together. "Maybe we can take you and Mena out for breakfast tomorrow or something." And those Botoxed lips pull down into a pity frown. "You look thin."

Lauren gets in the car without saying a word to Sam. Monty shakes his hand and then hugs him at the door.

"Oh shit," he says. "I forgot to give you this. They've been piling up. It's about six months' worth." He reaches into his bag and pulls out a bulging manila envelope. "Fan mail," Monty says. "Don't tell me your career's over. At least the women still love you."

Dale had left Buffalo at 6:00 A.M., but the drive to Quimby took ten hours. She pulled off the interstate and into town at 4:00, exhausted. She'd cried almost the whole way there. Without the printouts, she had no idea how to get to Lake Gormlaith. It wasn't on any of the maps she found at the Vermont Welcome Center. She kept checking the rearview mirror. For about an hour there was a Suburban behind her with tinted windows. Whenever she slowed down, it slowed down. When she sped up, it did as well. She lost it finally when she pulled into a rest area.

She parked the car in the dirt parking lot of a diner and took a deep breath. *Okay, okay. You're almost there. You've come three thousand miles. Just calm down. Eat something. Come up with a plan.* There had to be a place where she could get Internet access here. She'd just print out some new maps. Get up early tomorrow and find the lake. She just needed to get to Sam, and he'd make everything okay.

The bells on the door jingled as she entered the diner, and the smells embraced her. The chalkboard sign said, PLEASE SEAT YOURSELF, and so she chose a two-person booth by the window.

She grabbed a laminated menu from the rack behind the bowl of individual creamers and scanned the breakfast (*Served All Day*) items. The waitress, *Maggie* according to her name tag, took her order—a skillet breakfast (bacon, eggs, hash browns, biscuits and sausage gravy) and a Mountain Dew—and within minutes there was a steaming plate in front of her. She was starving; she had to make herself slow down, take small bites. It was so delicious, she felt her eyes growing wet with each forkful.

When her stomach was full, and the caffeine had kicked in, she felt rejuvenated.

"Excuse me?" she said, motioning for Maggie to come over.

"Can I getcha something else?"

She considered asking her how to get to Gormlaith, but then figured she should be careful. She had no idea who was watching her; maybe this *Maggie* was one of them. "I was actually wondering if you knew of a place where I could get Internet access around here. I need to check my e-mail," she added.

"Library's probably the only place," Maggie said. "I've got a friend who works over there. Do you want me to give her a call and see how late they're open tonight?"

"No, that's okay. I can drive. Where is it exactly? I'm not from here."

Maggie gave her directions to the Athenaeum on a napkin. "My friend's name is Effie," Maggie said. "You tell her I sent you."

Dale got in her car and headed out of the parking lot.

She pulled up in front of the library just as a tiny woman with a long black braid was locking the heavy front doors to the building.

Dale threw open the door of the Bug and raced up the steps. Breathless, she said, "Hi, your friend Maggie at the diner said I might be able to get Internet access here? Are you closed?"

The woman smiled. "Shoot, I'd let you in, but our server's down. We haven't had access all day. This happens about twice a week," she said. "We're open tomorrow at noon though, and the guy who takes care of our computers will have been in by then."

Dale's heart thumped heavily in her chest. Her lip quivered.

"Are you okay?" Effie asked, touching her elbow.

Dale nodded.

"You from out of town?" she asked.

Dale nodded again. "Arizona," she said, motioning to the Bug.

"Oh, I used to have a Bug!" She smiled. "You came all the way cross country in that?"

Then Dale realized she should have lied. Said it was a friend's car. She looked anxiously down the street. All the other parking spots were empty. She worried that the Suburban would pull around the corner any minute. She was shaking so hard she had to grab the railing to keep herself steady.

"Hey, wait!" Effie said. "I don't know where you're staying, but the motel just after you get off the interstate has free Wi-Fi. You have a laptop or anything?"

Dale thought of her laptop, her backpack. All the stolen things. She shook her head.

"Listen, if you come by tomorrow around ten, I'll let you in. I'm coming early to meet the IT guy. He should have it up and running by then."

"Thank you," Dale said, trying to take long, deep breaths. She thought about asking her for directions to the lake as well, but then figured she'd better not call any more attention to herself. She also didn't want to be out driving in an unfamiliar place after dark. "Can you tell me where that motel is?"

Now at the motel, she sits in the dark watching TV. It's still early, but she just wants the night to pass. There's a Clint Eastwood movie on, *Play Misty for Me*. He used to be really, really handsome, she thinks. There's even some quality about him that reminds her of Sam.

Every time a new set of headlights light up the room, she peers out through the drawn curtains. No Suburban.

She'll need to be vigilant. She can't sleep tonight. It's not safe.

After Monty and Lauren drive away, Sam goes up to the loft and opens the laptop. Ten pages. That's it. A file full of printouts, clumsy stacks of books, pages dog-eared and marked with Post-its. The office looks like it belongs to a lunatic. He scrolls to the end of the document where he's been collecting information.

The medieval fasting girls, *Angela of Foligno, Catherine of Siena, Clare of Assisi, Saint Veronica,* lived on herbs, orange seeds, the Eucharist. *Marie of Oignies, Beatrice of Nazareth* professed illness at the sight and smell of meat. Asceticism. Deprivation. *Columba of Rieti.* Self-mutilation. *Practitioners* of hunger, not sufferers. *Anorexia mirabilis.* The miraculous lack of desire for food. They called them *miracle maids,* these holy women who feasted on crumbs, the pus and scabs and lice of the ill. They did not want. They did not desire. They were never hungry.

Sam scrolls through the document, page after page. Girl after girl.

Mollie Fancher, a woman living in Brooklyn in the 1860s. At eighteen years old, she was in an accident in which she fell from a horse car and was dragged for nearly a block before the driver noticed what had happened. After the accident, she was confined to her childhood bed for the rest of her life. She became a celebrity in Brooklyn, falling into trances and exhibiting clairvoyant powers. But most miraculous of all was that she claimed to survive for more than a decade following the accident without nourishment, without food. In a moment, she went from being a normal young woman to a sideshow freak, with hundreds of thousands of visitors traipsing through her bedroom to gawk at her, the girl who did not eat. He wonders if she had any idea that in a single moment she could lose the very essence of what it is to be human.

He thumbs through the Victorian curiosities, these girls and their hunger on display: *Lenora Eaton, Josephine Marie Bedard, Therese Neumann.* These spectacles of starvation. He plucks out the newspaper illustration of *Sarah Jacob,* studies her pencil-sketched face. *The Welsh fasting girl.* She was twelve years old when she stopped eating. At thirteen she died when her parents did not intervene.

He rubs the knot on his head; the flesh is tender. He glances at his reflection in the window beyond his desk. His eye is swollen, purple.

It's your fault.

He rubs his chest. Oranges rolling across the floor.

Mena doesn't know what she's doing here. She has been following behind Jake in his truck for the last fifteen minutes. She can see the silhouette of his shoulders, his head through the window of his truck. Her hands are gripping the steering wheel so hard her palms ache. Jake said that his house was just outside town, but it feels like she's been following him forever. As planned, he'd invited everyone to come over after rehearsals; it was Friday night. Maybe they'd all like to have a couple of drinks. Get to know each other outside rehearsals. And though Mena had said no before, tonight she thought of Sam, of the broken table, of Monty and Lauren and everything she couldn't possibly deal with, and agreed. Besides, it wasn't like she was going alone. Anne had said she'd go for a bit, and she talked Oscar into coming along for the ride. Anne had lent Mena her cell phone to call the cottage, but, thankfully, no one had answered. Mena figured Lauren had insisted they all go out somewhere for dinner, despite her efforts. Maybe they had come into town. She left a message for Sam saying she'd be back later, that they were going to be working late. She doesn't know why she lied. She could have told him that they were all going to Jake's for a drink. But she didn't tell him. And now here she is, at nine o'clock at night, following a guy she barely knows to his house in the woods. She can no longer see Anne's headlights in her rearview mirror, and wonders when she lost her. She and Oscar are nowhere in sight.

Mena feels sort of sick to her stomach. She should turn around, go back to the lake. She should apologize to Sam. She worries that she hurt him. She can't explain what happened to her. It was as though May stepped in. It was May swinging at Sam. God, maybe she's losing her mind. And they have company, for Christ's sake. She can't imagine what Sam is doing with Monty and Lauren. She should go home, but then Jake's blinker starts flashing, he slows down and pulls onto a dirt road on the right. Mena slows behind him and flips her blinker on too.

She sits in her car, leaving it running as Jake cuts his engine and gets out of the truck. He walks toward her car, his hands shoved in his pockets. She rolls down the window.

"You think we lost them?" he asks, looking past her down the road behind them.

"I'm not sure," she says.

"Hopefully, they'll stop somewhere and call. I think my number's on the contact sheet," he says. "You wanna come inside?"

Mena nods. Her throat is too dry to speak. He pulls the handle on her door for her, and she gets out.

"Can almost feel fall coming," he says.

It is sort of chilly; the air has an edge to it. A tightness. She shivers.

"Come on," he says, and motions for her to follow him to the house.

The house is small, set back and surrounded by trees. It's an old farmhouse, with a wide front porch. Two caned seat rocking chairs sit motionless on either side of the front door; an ashtray teeters on the ledge. "Nasty habit," Jake says, and grabs the ashtray, setting it down on the floor away from the door.

He opens his unlocked front door and flicks on the porch light, illuminating everything in a pale yellow light. The house is brown with dark green shutters. There are giant pots with red geraniums, gerbera daisies. She thinks about the garden she used to keep in California.

"Come in," he says, and she follows him inside.

The front door opens up to a kitchen; it's huge, a farmhouse kitchen with an antique wood-burning cook stove, a deep white porcelain country sink. It smells good in here: as if someone has been cooking. It smells strongly of apples and cinnamon, like a homemade pie.

"Do you cook?" she asks.

"A bit," he says. "But it's just me now, so not so much as I used to."

"This is a great kitchen," Mena says, excitedly examining the antique stove, running her hand across the smooth, cold surface. "Did this come with the place?"

Jake nods.

"Everything conveyed, thank God. My ex kept everything we had in DC."

"Is this a pie pantry?" she asks, gesturing to a solid oak piece near the fridge that has punched tin panels.

"I think so. I keep my staples in there. Flour, sugar. Rice and beans."

From the smell, Mena half expected that if she opened the doors, she'd find six steaming apple pies inside.

"It's lovely," she says. "Really. I miss my kitchen in San Diego. What we have at the lake is a little, I don't know, primitive." She laughs nervously and checks her watch.

"What time is it?" Jake asks.

"Just about nine-thirty," she says.

He disappears into the pantry and comes out with a bottle of wine under his arm. He pulls open a drawer by the sink and takes out a corkscrew. "You want some?" he asks.

"No, that's okay," she says, shaking her head. Then she changes her mind. "Actually, maybe just half a glass."

"I'll have the other half," he says and smiles.

"I wonder where they lost us," Mena says, peering out the front window. There is nothing but darkness. The porch light only illuminates the driveway; beyond that everything is pitch black. Something about seeing the station wagon parked behind his truck makes her feel guilty. She's still not sure what she's doing here.

"Listen," he says, handing her the glass of wine, which doesn't look at all like a half glass. "I just wanted to tell you how much fun I'm having doing this play. This is my third or fourth with the Quimby Players, and it's sort of refreshing to work with someone who actually knows how to act. I mean, the others try; they all take this very seriously. But there's a reason why none of them have gone on to bigger and better things, myself included. It feels like a treat to have you."

He is smiling at her, and suddenly she wonders, if she wanted to kiss him, could she? She wonders if she were to press him against that pie pantry, if he would kiss her lips, her neck, her breasts; if she were to make a move toward him, if he would let her fall into his arms. She wonders if he would *want* her. Imagining this makes her feel the worst and most wonderful mix of anxiety and desire. Guilt and the thrill of possibility. She imagines, that with one move forward, she could change her entire life. She takes a deep breath.

"Do you want to see where I work?" he asks.

"Sure." She smiles and sighs. She brings the glass to her lips and takes a mouthful of the very good Chilean wine. Then she touches his hand, just a little. "And thanks, it's so good to be acting again. It really is, and you all are so terrific."

She follows him to the back of the house where he opens the door to his workshop. He flips on the light, and she catches her breath.

Finn pitched the tent and put their sleeping bags inside. There's a half-moon, and it is bright overhead, illuminating all of their hard work.

"Are you hungry?" he asks, unzipping his backpack and pulling out the food his mother made.

"That's okay," Alice says. She's sitting Indian style on the ground by the campfire.

"No, seriously, there's enough here for about five people." He unloads the sandwiches and salad and cookies. He pulls out the beers he stole from the fridge too.

"You sure?" she asks, and he hands her half of a sandwich.

"So when exactly are you guys leaving?" he asks.

"It depends. The parole board is meeting early next week. If they decide to grant parole, he could be out in a couple of weeks. Mom should hear something after the meeting."

"Do you really think they're going to let him go?"

Alice shrugs.

"Are you scared?"

She's picking at the salad in the Tupperware, eating all of the feta and olives but leaving the tomatoes. He should have remembered she said she hates tomatoes. She looks up at him and studies his face. "What is the first thing you remember?" she asks.

"What?"

"Your first memory. What is it?"

Finn closes his eyes. Tries to remember. All of his earliest memories are of the beach. Finding sand dollars, the sting of a jellyfish, the salt in his eyes. He remembers collecting sea glass, hermit crabs, shells. He thinks about learning to swim with Franny. He remembers sunset, his mother sitting on a blanket; it was yellow and orange, paisley, with a satin edge. His mother eating a large peach, watching them. His father taking his hand and then Franny's as they walked down to the water's edge. He remembers the cold sting of the waves as they lapped at their feet, the sound of Franny's squeal. The splash. He remembers the pull of the receding waves; he recollects digging his feet into the sand so he wouldn't get pulled in. He remembers looking back at his mother on the yellow blanket, at the ripe peach in her hand. He remembers her waving, his father holding both of them so tightly. He remembers the sun in Franny's hair. Everything at that moment was golden.

He tells her, "I remember thinking then that there was nothing I loved more in the world than the water. Nothing more than the sun."

Alice smiles. She is quiet for a long time.

"I never told you this, and it's kind of weird, I know, but when I was four years old, I stopped talking. I wouldn't say a single word."

"You're kidding," Finn says. "Why not?"

Alice has put down the sandwich, is playing with the loose strings on her cutoffs. "My first memory is of one night when my father was really hurting my mom," she says. She is looking out toward the trees; Finn wants her to look at him. To turn back. "When I was four, my dad tried to drown my mom in the bathtub. The very first thing I remember is my father's hands holding her under. I remember the way her face looked, distorted under all that water."

"Holy shit," Finn says. He reaches for her hand, holds it in his, like something fragile.

"My whole childhood is like that, Finn. Just one big blur," she says, looking at him. Her eyes are bright. "I don't remember ever *not* being afraid. The way you feel now? All that awful loss and being sad, being afraid; I've felt that way since I can remember." She leans forward, touches Finn's hair, pushes it out of his eyes. "You have a *family,* Finn. I know it's not the same as it used to be. I know there must be nothing in the world that hurts as much as losing your sister. But you still have a mom and a dad who love you. Who want nothing but for you to be safe."

Finn feels like an ass, even though he knows that's not what she meant for him to feel.

"My mom's all I have. All I've ever had."

He thinks about Franny, about that hollow place in his gut. About all the nights he's lain in bed, wide awake, just wishing he could fall asleep. Stay asleep, maybe forever. "I'm sorry, Alice," he says. "I'm so sorry." And he is starting to cry. He can't help it. It's awful.

Alice stands up and comes over to him, puts her arm across his shoulders, and he leans down, putting his head in her lap. She leans over, kisses his closed eyes. He can't stop crying. For the first time since any of this happened. He hasn't shed a single tear in the last year. Not when he came out of the water that day, surfboard under his arm, a pounding headache, and found Franny. Not when his mother moaned. Not when his father cried. Not at the funeral. Not later. Not ever.

"If he gets out, I have to go with my mom, Finn. She needs me, and I need her." Alice forces him to look at her. "And you need your family too."

Finn looks up at Alice, and he realizes that she's the first real friend he's ever had besides Franny. And the first girl he's ever loved.

"Truth or dare," he says.

"Truth."

He touches her hair. It feels like a whisper in his hands.

"I love you," she says, before he even gets to ask the question.

It feels like he's just caught a ten-foot wave. He nods. "Me too."

"More than water?" she asks quietly.

He nods, and nods, and nods. "More than the sun."

In the middle of Jake's workshop is a long wooden table covered with violins in varying states of assembly. Along each wall, instruments are suspended on racks in neat rows. There are tools strewn everywhere. The room smells like chemicals and wood. There is an old apothecary's chest along one wall. She touches the handle to one of the top drawers. "What is this?"

"It's where I store the varnishes."

"How long does it take you to make one of these?" she asks, pointing to a finished violin the color of a red maple leaf.

"Anywhere from eight to twelve weeks," he says. "I'm terribly slow."

"A perfectionist?"

"Just cautious," he says. He runs his hand over the violin. His nails are square, wide, clean. His fingers are long. She imagines them touching her. Her heart stutters in her chest.

"This one took me more than three months to make. She's my favorite."

She wonders, if she were to go to him now, would he unbutton her blouse? Would he slip his hands under the fabric and pull it over her shoulders? Would he press his face against her chest, listen as her heart kept flip-flopping around inside? She wonders, if he touched her, if he'd imagine the contours of her breasts and waist and hips like a violin. Unfinished, rough, and out of tune. Could he bend her, change her, make her perfect again?

She looks at the glass of wine, starts to take a sip, and instead sets it down on the table. She sighs, and smiles. Shakes her head. "I don't think they're coming."

"I don't think they're coming either," he says, stepping closer to her. She instinctively touches the underside of her engagement ring with her thumb, spins it until the small diamond is sharp against her middle finger.

If she wanted him, would he want her?

"Let's get some air," she says. She is dizzy from the smell of the varnish.

Outside on the porch, he lights a cigarette and the smoke disappears into the darkness.

She takes another sip of the wine and feels the heat spreading through her entire body, despite the chill. "Actually, can I have one of those?" she asks, motioning to the pack of cigarettes.

"You sure?"

She nods, and he hands her one. She puts it in her mouth and he leans over to light it for her.

She takes a drag, inhaling deeply. It's been ages since she's smoked. The nicotine goes straight to her knees. She coughs.

"Easy there," he says. "Probably shouldn't take up smoking now."

"I used to smoke when I was in college," she says. "Just cloves though." And for some reason, she remembers the way the clove cigarettes made her lips sweet. She remembers Sam commenting that she tasted like autumn the first time he kissed her.

She wonders, if she were to reach for his hand, if he would take it, kiss her palm, press it against his face. If she were to reach for him, would he put his hand on her waist, his fingers circling her ribs as though they were the spruce ribs of a violin?

He snubs out his cigarette and takes hers from her fingers and snubs it out too. The last of the smoke disappears into the air. He faces her and leans toward her, until his forehead is pressing against hers. She closes her eyes.

And she knows that if she were to open them, he would kiss her. She knows this, and suddenly, that is enough.

When he puts his hands around her waist, she stiffens and pulls away.

"I'm sorry, Jake," she says. And she is. So sorry. "I need to get home. My husband is stuck with his agent and his horrible wife. You have a beautiful house. And this is . . . just amazing." She gestures to everything, to nothing.

He retreats, bowing his head. Graceful, even in defeat.

"Jake," she says, forcing him with her gaze to look at her. "I really am sorry."

He nods, tilts his head at her, as if she might still change her mind.

In the car, she starts to laugh, giddy from the wine. She backs out of the driveway and laughs and laughs so hard that tears begin to roll down her cheeks, and then she is crying, really crying. She has to pull over at one point to get herself together. She finishes, looks in the rearview mirror. Her mascara has run, her eyes are rimmed with red. She takes a deep breath, wipes under each eye with her finger, removing the evidence. And then she drives back down the long driveway, onto the dirt road, toward home.

Sam thinks that he should go get Finn so that he can have his room back. He knows he promised him he wouldn't bother him tonight, but he's pretty sure he'll be happy to know he doesn't have to sleep outside. He looks at the bump on his head in the mirror. It's going to be a bad one.

He pulls on a pair of running shoes and grabs a flashlight. He takes the path that Finn told him about and heads out into the woods. The moon is a half crescent tonight, but it has gotten cloudy, and it is so dark. He can hear the loons calling to each other on the water. There was a time when the loons were endangered here, but now there are signs posted everywhere protecting them. It must be nice to have the world looking out for you, he thinks. For someone to make it their project. To create legislation, organizations all aimed at keeping you and your family safe.

He follows the exact directions Finn gave him, but when he gets to the place in the woods that he thinks is the spot, there's no one there. He looks around, almost positive this is the area Finn was talking about. He finds the fire pit, cold black ash. He turns on his heel, his heart racing. Where the hell is Finn?

He runs back to the house, tries to think about how he might have gotten it wrong. The house is only on about three acres. If he's on the property, it shouldn't be too hard to find him. He sets out in the opposite direction, walking first and then jogging. "Finn?" he calls out. "Finn?" And then the idea strikes him that maybe Finn has run away. Maybe the past couple of months he's just been working on gaining their trust so that he can dash out in the middle of the night. He imagines him standing at the edge of some road, his thumb jutted out into the night, his backpack filled with clothes, stolen money, food from the fridge.

He'd had the same fear that night at home after Finn got in trouble in Tijuana. He was worried that night that he might never find him again. As he drove up and down the coast, from OB up to La Jolla and back down to Imperial Beach, he'd wondered how he would tell Mena that not only was her daughter dead but that her son was gone now too. He thought he'd rather die than go home without him. When he finally found Finn, sitting under the lifeguard tower just blocks from their house, he'd wanted to both kill him and kiss him.

Sam is running now, past the barn, through the woods. It is chilly out, but he is sweating. The flashlight bobs up and down, illuminating the world in wobbly flashes of light. He can feel his pulse in the tender knot on his eyebrow. He is breathing hard, feeling panicked. And then he sees the smoke. At first it could just be fog, filtering through the trees like filmy fingers. But then there is the smell of a campfire, the smell of something burned. When the trees thin out to reveal an open field, he sees the orange glow of the smoldering embers of Finn's campfire. He sees the tent.

He sighs, relieved, and wonders how many times he can go through this. He stops and puts his hands on his hips, bends over to catch his breath. He must have misunderstood Finn's directions. He's here. He's safe.

He starts to trudge toward the tent, just to make sure, the flashlight lighting his way. He's never been this far out on the property. He didn't even know there was anything out here but woods. But this is a big field. A big, open field without trees. He shines the flashlight across the empty expanse, illuminating it in large sweeping beams of yellow light. The light catches on what seems, at first, like glass, but he quickly realizes it is only plastic. A bunch of plastic grocery bags. He walks toward them, curious, and then he sees the plants.

There must be a hundred pot plants out here, about a dozen of them carefully covered with grocery bags, secured with twist ties. *Jesus Christ,* he thinks. This is unbelievable. His first impulse is to unzip the tent and yank Finn out by the scruff of his neck. To shake him until his teeth are rattling. *What the fuck is he going to do?* If he drags Finn out of the tent, he'll run. And out here, there's no way Sam could outrun a seventeen-year-old kid. From the looks of things, Finn is familiar with the area. *Jesus Christ.* So this is where he's been all summer. Out here growing a fucking crop of marijuana.

Furious, he clicks off the flashlight and walks as quietly as he can toward the tent. Finn has left the outer flap unzipped; just the mosquito fly is up. Sam kneels down and peers in. Finn is a heavy sleeper; he's not sure what it will take to wake him up. He may need to shake him back to life. He clicks the flashlight on but doesn't shine it directly on him, and peers into the tent.

Inside:

He sees not one but two figures. Two blond-headed bodies, curled around each other, their bodies (arms, legs, breath) intertwined. Sam stumbles backward, confused. Delirious. For a moment, just for a moment, he thinks *Franny,* and then, as he backs away from the tent, away from the garden of weed, away from the night, he remembers that Franny, unlike Finn, is not coming back.

Dale calls her mother from the motel. She sits on the edge of the queen-size bed, jiggling her legs. "Mama?" she says. It's been almost a week since she called her.

"Where *are* you, honey?" her mother asks softly. Dale can hear the TV in the background. She closes her eyes and pictures the house. She can see the thin fabric of her mother's housedress, the pale pink and blue roses. She can see the blue rivers of knotty veins running down her bare legs. She can feel the hot light of a Phoenix summer sun through the window, smell the Hamburger Helper her mother has made. "When are you coming home?" her mother asks.

Dale can hear her wheezing, worries about her asthma. "Mama, are you okay?"

"Pookie died today," her mother says, her voice catching in her throat.

Dale feels like someone punched her in the chest. "What?"

"I found her this morning. She was curled up underneath the couch. I wouldn't have noticed except her tail was sticking out. I thought she just got under there to scratch and was about to get the spray bottle, but she didn't move. If I hadn't seen her tail, she could have been under there for weeks, and I woulda had no idea."

"How?" Dale asks.

"She was old, honey. We've had her since you were just a little girl."

Dale remembers her father bringing home the kitten in a shoe box. He'd found her on his way home from work. Somebody had dumped her on the side of the road near the freeway entrance. Four lanes of traffic, it was a wonder she was alive at all.

"She wasn't sick though, was she?" Dale asks. Her heart is racing, her mind reeling.

"She wasn't acting sick," her mother says. "She was just old, sweetie."

"What did she eat today?" Dale asks. She's up and pacing now, walking as far as the phone cord will allow before turning on her heel and walking in the opposite direction. Her socks make sparks on the motel carpet.

"Just a Fancy Feast for breakfast. Salmon, I think. Honey, you need to tell me where you are."

"Mama, check her bowl. See if it smells funny."

"Honey, the Fancy Feast was in a can. I just opened it up this morning. She ate it all up. It couldn't have gone bad."

"Mama, just check the bowl."

There are people standing outside her motel room. She can see their silhouettes behind the heavy drapes. Dale walks as close to the window as she can before the cord stops her.

She tries to imagine how somebody could have gotten into the house and poisoned Pookie. Her mother was always forgetting to lock the door to the kitchen from the garage. It would have been easy. If she'd fallen asleep on the couch after breakfast like she often did, somebody could have walked right in.

She hears ice tumbling from the ice machine; two people are still standing there, talking.

"Mama, I've got to go," she says, and hangs up.

She clicks out the lamp that's next to the bed and walks slowly to the window and pulls back the drapes about an inch. It's hard to see, but it looks like a man and a woman. The man has on jeans and a white button-down shirt. The woman's got on a black sweater, jeans, and boots. She's got short black hair, big breasts.

Their voices are muffled. Dale pushes her finger against the window frame and gently slides it open a crack.

"I can't believe we drove all the way up here for *this*," the woman says. She throws up her hands and gestures all around her: at the vending machine, the empty parking lot, the blinking VACANCY sign. "We should have stayed in the city. He's a *mess*. If I were you, I'd just give up."

"Jesus, Laur. Try not to be so fucking sensitive."

"It's not like he's even making any money for you anymore. I'm not sure why you, or the house, are putting so much energy into this. You've got other clients."

Dale sits down in the chair and presses her ear close to the open crack.

"You tried. He doesn't want your help. I'd write this one off, Monty. Call it a day."

"I've know Sammy Mason for twenty years. He's not my fucking client. He's my friend. God, you can be such a bitch."

Dale's eyes widen; she clutches her hand to her chest.

The man pushes the button on the ice machine and a cascade of ice tumbles down; it is so loud, she can't hear what the woman is saying. But it doesn't matter. They've found her. They know where she is.

Mena takes a deep breath and goes into the cabin, and Sam is sitting at the dining room table, which is no longer collapsed and broken on the floor. The bottle of wine she picked up for Monty and Lauren is almost empty, and the pan of spanakopita and three dirty plates are still on the table. The bump on his head is huge, and his eye is completely black and blue, swollen shut. He looks up at her and she can tell he's had at least a good share of the bottle. Her stomach flips. What has she done? What is she doing?

"Where are Monty and Lauren?" she asks. Their car wasn't in the driveway when she pulled up.

"Staying at a motel."

"Why?" she asks.

Sam shakes his head, throws up his hands. He looks defeated.

"Listen," she says. "I'm sorry, about what I said earlier. About what I *did*." She sits down in the chair next to him and touches the bruise softly with her finger. She is overwhelmed, suddenly, with tenderness toward him. As she starts to pull her hand away, he reaches up and covers her hand with his, pressing it to the side of his face. He turns and kisses her palm, squeezing his eyes shut. His lips are warm.

"I didn't mean it," she says. "Any of it. It was cruel. And

God, I shouldn't have hit you. I don't know what happened to me. I snapped."

"Shhh," Sam says, and shakes his head. He stands up and looks at her, framing her face with his hands, contemplating her. *Seeing* her. God, he hasn't even looked at her, *considered* her in so long it feels almost new.

"*I'm* sorry," he says.

"It wasn't your fault," she says, shaking her head.

He steadies her face, forces her to return his gaze. "Look at me," he says. His hands are strong against her jaw, her cheeks.

She does what he says. And she looks into his eyes, the clear one and the one she's damaged. She stares into his eyes, as she has done a thousand times: on those first mornings they spent together back when they were just kids, naked and tangled in sandy sheets. The first time he'd told her he loved her (he'd waited so long, she was almost swollen with love—she thought she might implode). Fourth of July. He'd pulled her under the pier and looked at her, like this (the smell of burnt firecrackers, bonfires and salty air enclosing them). After the twins were born, as she lay breathless and trembling in the hospital bed, he'd sat down next to her and made her look into these eyes. These same eyes that had studied and admired, comforted. The ones that had grown wet with joy and with sorrow. The eyes that had locked with hers with pride the first time they watched Franny dance, and every time after. Those shadowy gray pools that managed to capture any available light in a room and keep it, sparkling. These were the eyes that had told her, *I'm here, I love you, I want you. I know you.*

She is afraid to blink. She doesn't want this moment to be gone; she's afraid that the thread between them has grown so ragged and frail it might snap if she tugs too hard, or holds on too tightly.

"Mena," Sam says, still gazing at her.

She nods, unable to speak.

"I will make this better."

She nods again, believes him. Because in all this time, not once have those eyes lied.

In the morning, Finn wakes up to the sun shining brightly through the open flap of the tent. He is tangled up in the sleeping bag, which has become twisted in the night. His back hurts from sleeping on the hard ground, and he has a trail of bug bites up his left calf. He scratches his ankle and then reaches for Alice, pulling the other sleeping bag back. But Alice isn't inside, and he feels his heart drop. He sits up, rubs his eyes and crawls out of the tent.

It is bright outside already, warm. Everything is green and misty. Alice is bent over in the dew-drenched garden, pulling the plastic bags off the plants.

"Morning!" she says, standing up. The light behind her makes her hair look almost white, a sort of halo.

"Hi," he says. He feels embarrassed now, in the daylight. He rubs his hand across the top of his head, trying to flatten down what he's fairly sure is a big mess.

Her hair is messy too, but she doesn't seem to mind. She yawns. "Are we going to have to do this every morning?"

"Just until the days start to get shorter," he says. "How do they look?"

"Good, I guess."

Finn nods, sits down next to Alice on the ground, reaches for her hand and pulls her down next to him. He puts his arms around her and hugs her.

She kissed him last night. They had kissed for hours. And it wasn't like it was with Misty. For one, they weren't fucked up. No Ecstasy. Not even any weed. Just the two of them. It was nice. And it was enough, just to kiss. They fell asleep kissing each other. It was the first time, in a long time, that he'd been able to fall asleep without getting stoned. And he'd slept so deeply, he was pretty sure he'd had dreams, a lot of them, though he can't remember them now.

"When do you have to be home?" he asks, whispering into her hair, which is so soft. He touches it absentmindedly as he studies her face.

"Doesn't matter. Mom's at work," she says, looking down at their intertwined hands. "What about you?"

"I promised my dad I'd be home by eight," he says. "What time is it?"

"Eight-oh-five," she says, glancing at her watch.

"Shit," he says, grabbing her hand. "I'll have to come back for the tent later."

They run together back to his house, holding hands. He doesn't ever remember feeling like this with anyone before. Certainly not with Misty. Even though he's late, even though his father is going to kick his ass, when they get to the barn, he stops to kiss her again. It's different kissing standing up, in broad daylight. Nice. He touches her face, her hair. He's so much taller than she is, it's sort of awkward. Afterward, she leans into his chest. And then she says, "I'll call you later!" and he watches her as she jogs off toward her house, her hair swinging behind her. She's wearing the same clothes she had on yesterday. He can't stop smiling.

When he gets to the driveway, he sees that Monty's Mercedes is gone. He was hoping they'd be there. His dad can't act too pissed if they still had company. He can't imagine where Monty and Lauren would have gone this early in the morning. Out for breakfast, he guesses. Lauren probably made him drive all the way back to Burlington for some fancy brunch some-where.

Inside the house his mom and dad are both in the kitchen. His dad is sitting at the kitchen table eating an omelet, reading the paper. His plate is a mess of eggs and tomatoes, feta cheese and olives. His mother is at the stove, singing to the radio, her hips swinging. They barely notice him when he opens the door. He lets it slam behind him and stands there, bewildered.

"Want some juice, Finny?" his mom asks, grabbing a glass from the cupboard.

"Sure," he says, waiting for his father to yell.

"Morning," his father says.

"Where's Monty and Mrs. Monty?" Finn asks, taking the glass of juice from his mother.

"They left," his father says.

"When?" Finn asks.

"Last night," his father says, spearing a piece of sausage with his knife, never looking away from the paper.

"Thank God. That woman is wretched," his mother says.

Finn sits down at the table. His mother slides a hot omelet from the pan she's holding onto a plate and sets it down in front of him. She leans over and kisses his head. "Morning, honey. How was camping out?" she asks. "Were you cold?"

"It was fine," Finn says, his ears feeling hot. He tries not to think about the way Alice's lips had felt pressed against his. The way she smelled.

His father won't look up from the paper. He's pissed, he can tell. But why isn't he talking? *What the fuck?*

In the morning, Sam had woken up with a start after sleeping only a couple of hours. He'd tossed and turned all night, trying to figure out what to do about Finn. He knew he needed to confront him about the pot. He also needed to go out there and destroy all of the plants before that stupid cop neighbor with the stupid car-chasing dog alerted the DEA.

But now, in the kitchen, he pretends that nothing is wrong. That he doesn't know what he knows. Mena cannot know that anything is wrong. This would kill her.

"Morning, honey. How was camping out?" Mena asks. "Were you cold?"

Sam can't help but glare at Finn. He wonders what the marijuana laws are in Vermont. He also thinks about the way Finn looked curled up against that other blond girl. Like a little boy again. Like part of something whole. He's clearly been keeping a lot of secrets. Just when they were starting to trust him again. Little shit.

Finn's cheeks are flushed red, and Mena asks him if he is cold. Gives him breakfast, and then all of a sudden, all three of them are sitting together at that wreck of a dining room table. Usually Mena waits and eats after he and Finn have finished. Or she eats at the counter, the scraps of what's left. But today, she joins them. Sits with them as they eat. If someone were to walk into the kitchen, they would look like a normal family, like a happy family.

"What's this?" Finn asks, picking up a manila envelope on the table. Sam had almost forgotten about it.

"Just some letters from readers, I guess," Sam says, dismissing it with a flick of his wrist. "Monty dropped it by last night."

"Any good ones?" Mena asks. A long time ago he had shown her the photos sent by enamored ladies in Dubuque and Detroit. They'd read the missives together in bed. It had aroused Mena to know that there were women all over the country falling in love with her husband. "Anything juicy?"

"I doubt it."

"How about Monty?" she asks softly. "What did you tell him?"

"I told him the truth. I've got shit. Nothing. This next book, if there is a next book, is going to take time."

"Is that why he left?"

"No, he left because Lauren thought I was having a breakdown."

"Were you?" Finn asks, his eyebrows raised.

And Sam snorts. "Maybe a small one." Finn has no idea what kind of breakdown he's about to have if he can't get this problem dealt with fast.

Suddenly, there's a knock on the front door.

For one awful moment Sam thinks it's the police; breakfast turns to stone in his stomach. But then a soft voice comes through the screen. "Finn?"

"Alice?" Finn says, and quickly gets up to answer the door.

Alice, the girl Finn was with in the tent last night, is standing there in the doorway, her eyes streaked with tears.

"What's the matter?" Finn asks. "Alice?"

"They bumped the parole board meeting up. And they never bothered to tell us. He's out. Already," she says, sobbing. "My mom wants to leave for California first thing in the morning. Can I stay here tonight?"

A ll night Dale sat perched at the edge of the bed, waiting for that couple to come back. She dead-bolted the door and locked the door chain. She kept the lights off. She thought about slipping out in the middle of the night, but she was pretty sure they knew what her car looked like, and besides, where would she go? This has to be the only motel in town. She used the pad of motel stationery she found in the night-stand to sketch out her plan, using the glow of the digital alarm clock to see.

In the morning she would put the DO NOT DISTURB sign on her door and walk to the library. It was probably about a mile, but she couldn't risk moving the Bug. At the library she'd pretend she was only checking her e-mail and quickly copy directions from MapQuest (she figured it wouldn't be safe to print them). That woman had said she'd let her in before the library was open, so at least she'd be alone. Then she'd walk back to the motel and check to see if they were gone. It looked like there were only two other vehicles parked at the motel: a beat-up red pickup truck and a shiny black Mercedes. It wasn't too hard to figure out which one they were driving. If the car was still there, then she'd quickly drive to Gormlaith to find Sam. If the car was gone, she'd have to wait. But God, she was so tired of waiting.

She hadn't thought about what she'd say once she actually

got to Sam. She had the manuscript, of course: luckily, it had not been in her backpack at Niagara Falls but stuffed underneath her seat, wrapped in a towel she lifted from the motel in Albuquerque. Now that the laptop was gone, it was the only copy; she'd have to be careful with it. Should she offer it to him like a gift? Maybe she should stop by that drugstore she saw downtown and pick up some wrapping paper. A bow. No, that was cheesy. She needed to be professional about this.

By the time the sun finally crept up and illuminated the room in a filmy glow, she'd contemplated everything she would say to him. How she would plead her case. She'd scratched out a zillion scenarios on the notepad.

It is hot in the motel room now, as the sky and the room fill with light. Sweat is rolling down her sides as she scribbles and crosses out. She looks at the AC/heater unit under the window and realizes it is not on. She gets up and turns the knob. Nothing.

And then there is a knock on her door.

She stiffens, her eyes widening. She peers through the drapes but can't see who's at the door. She stands up slowly, and quietly makes her way to the peephole.

"Maintenance," a voice says.

She is squinting to see if it really is a maintenance worker or not. It does appear to be a man in a blue jumpsuit. Against her better judgment, she unlocks the dead bolt, but not the chain, and opens the door a crack.

She can smell cigarette smoke on his breath. He's too close. "You call 'bout your AC?" he asks.

"Are you here to fix this fucking AC?" a woman's voice says. It's *her*. The woman from the ice machine.

Dale mumbles, *"Wrong room,"* and quickly slams the door shut again. She hears his footsteps moving away from her door and the woman ushering him into the other room. "It's like a goddamn sauna in here," she says.

Dale's sweating so badly now, her neck is starting to itch. The walk to the library is going to be a long one, but she figures she should get out now while they're occupied. She slips on her flip-flops and a pair of shorts and leaves, running as fast as she can toward the main road.

At rehearsals on Saturday morning, Mena is distracted. They are rehearsing a scene where the Old Man is pleading with Eddie and May not to be together. She and Jake have to hold each other. It's excruciating.

"Why don't we break for a few minutes?" Lisa says. Mena is grateful. She can't look Jake in the eyes, never mind *embrace* him.

Anne comes up to her and hands her a cup of coffee. "Hi," she says.

"Hi." Mena smiles. "God, I am just off today."

"Late night last night?" she asks.

"Not really," Mena says, thinking about Sam, about the way he held on to her all night, their bodies pressed together. Then she thinks about what almost happened with Jake. "Where were you guys last night anyway?" she asks.

"Oh God, sorry about that," Anne says. "Oscar and I got turned around. We drove halfway to Canada before we realized we were following the wrong car. My night vision sucks. By the time we figured it out, it was too late so we decided to call it a night. How was it?" Anne asks, smirking a little, Mena thinks.

"How was what?"

"Jake's house," Anne says.

"Nice." Mena nods. "It's a nice house."

"I didn't mean his *house*," Anne says.

"What *did* you mean?"

Anne's face falls. "It's plain as day what's going on between you two," she whispers. "I'm not crazy. Anybody can see."

"Well, maybe you need your prescription changed," Mena says. She hisses, "I'm married."

"Sure." Anne smiles, turning on her heel.

For the next hour, they rehearse the final scene. Mena keeps forgetting her lines. "Line?" she says.

" '*All he could think of was me. Isn't that right, Eddie. We couldn't take a breath without thinking of each other. . . .*' " Lisa recites, exasperated. "Forget it, let's just back it up." She flips through the ragged script. "Martin, start with '*How could it happen?*'"

Jake's voice, gravelly and smooth at the same time, answers: " '*Well, see—our Daddy fell in love twice.*' "

Jake glances at her. Mena cringes.

" '*It was the same love,*' " Oscar, the Old Man, says from the shadows. " '*Just got split in two, that's all.*' "

When they break again, Mena follows Oscar out onto the front porch of the Town Hall. They've got another hour left, but she just wants to get back home. She wants to take a swim, just float.

"So what happened to you and Anne last night?" Mena asks. "Where did you lose us?"

"What do you mean?" Oscar asks.

"*Last night.* You guys never showed up at Jake's house after rehearsals. Anne said you almost got to the Canadian border before you figured out you were headed in the wrong direction." Mena laughs.

"That's funny. I thought Anne called you," he said. "We stopped at the Cumberland Farms, so she could call Jake from the pay phone. When we got in the car, she said she changed her mind, she was getting a headache and wanted to go home. She gets migraines or something. She dropped me at my house. She didn't call?"

Jesus, Mena thinks. What was Anne trying to do to her?

Finn and Alice go to the garden. Finn looks at the plants; the air smells like Christmas. Everything is green. This is pointless. Alice is leaving. *Leaving.*

"I'll go with you," he says. "To Barstow. I've got enough cash for a bus ticket."

"You can't," Alice says. "Your parents would know where you went."

"I'll get on a different bus, take a different route." Finn feels desperate, scared. He doesn't know how he can be here without her. How he can do anything if all of a sudden he's alone again. "I'll meet you there."

"And then what, Finn? My aunt lives in a two-bedroom condo. There isn't enough room."

Finn's eyes sting. "Fuck," he says, reaching for one of the plants and ripping it out of the ground. The air is pungent with the smell of it.

"What are you doing?" Alice says, grabbing his arm.

"What's the point?" he says. "It's not going to flower anyway. I'm not a fucking botanist. I'm just a stoner. I'm just a fucking loser stoner."

"Don't," Alice says. Her eyes are brimming with tears.

He starts to make his way through the garden, yanking the plants out of the ground. His hands are covered with dirt. Everything smells green. He is yanking the plants and hurling them. Ripping them up by their roots. It feels good. He had done the same to his room after Franny died. To the posters, to the giant map on his wall. He had torn down the entire coast of California in one grand tantrum.

"Finn, stop it," Alice says. "You're scaring me."

He turns to look at her and feels terrible. God, she's so sweet. It almost hurts his heart to look at her. He feels *inside-out*. She reaches for him and he stops. This is the last thing she needs, another stupid guy going ballistic.

"You want to know where I was when my sister died?" he asks, looking at the plant, its roots dangling from his hands.

Alice looks at him, her eyes soft with concern.

"I was out on my surfboard, six o'clock in the morning, still fucking loaded from a party the night before." He remembers the party, a bunch of losers hanging out watching *The Endless Summer,* drinking forties. Not a single girl around. Some party. "I must have woken her up when I came home. She tried to stop me from going out in the water. And I was pissed off. As I'm walking out the door with my surfboard, she says, *Don't go out there, you're still wasted.* Here she was worried about *me*." He laughs. "But I went anyway, being the total ass-hole that I am, and by the time I came back she was dead. Just like that.

"And the thing is, my parents think I'm messed up because of her, but the truth is, I was messed up long before. If I hadn't been, then she might still be here."

"How did she die, Finny?" Alice asks, grabbing his arm, pulling him toward her. "What *happened?*"

Finn shakes his head, puts his head in his hands and sits down on the ground, surrounded by the uprooted plants.

By the time Dale gets to the library, she is hot and breathless. The woman, Effie, opens the door for her and lets her in. "Did you walk here, all the way from the motel?" she asks.

The truth is Dale almost ran the whole way, and her heart won't slow down. She bends over at the waist, putting her hands on her knees, and nods.

"Can I get you some water or something?"

Dale nods again.

Effie disappears through a large doorway and comes back with a paper cone filled with lukewarm water. Dale gulps it down. And stands up. She feels dizzy. "Do you mind if I sit down?" she asks.

"Go ahead. Our computer guy's almost done," she says. "There are magazines in there," she says, motioning to a large room with long tables and a fireplace. "Today's paper just arrived too."

Dale goes into the room and sits down. As she catches her breath, she flips through the slim pages of the paper. The headlines are all from the AP. She glances at the classifieds, the movie listings. Near the back, she sees an ad for a play by the Quimby Players.

Mena Mason and Jake Rogers are Eddie and May in Sam Shepard's Fool for Love. *August 6–8, 13–15, 20–22 at the Quimby Town Hall.*

Dale starts to tremble. Mena Mason. His *wife.* They're really here. She didn't dream this. They are really, really here.

Effie comes back and shows her to a computer that is in a private little alcove. Dale can barely type, she's so excited. She grabs one of the mini pencils from a plastic cup and scribbles the directions on an index card. The lake is close, just about ten miles, she figures. And there is a road that circles it. All she needs to do is find the right cabin. She remembers the woody station wagon from the photo on Finn Mason's MySpace page. She couldn't make out the plates, but how many woody wagons could there be? And with California plates, no less. She trembles with anticipation. But then her heart stutters. What if that wasn't their car in the picture? This realization hits her in the gut like a punch. It could belong to the girl. This might not be that easy. She shakes her head, takes a deep breath. She'll just have to take her chances. And worst case, at least she knows where to find Mena.

As she leaves the library, she realizes she hasn't eaten anything since the diner yesterday. She sees a little grocery store across the street and figures she can grab a banana, a Mountain Dew, and then head back to the motel.

She's the only person in the store. It's so nice and cool inside, she lingers in the produce section, pretending to contemplate the baskets of strawberries, the plums. The girl working the register is wearing short shorts and a halter top. She keeps checking her reflection in the store window.

"Excuse me," Dale says, setting the banana and soda down on the counter. Three pints of berries, a half dozen plums and some Windex. The Bug is so dirty. She doesn't want to show up in a filthy car. She has also grabbed a magazine of slow-cooker recipes. The macaroni and cheese on the front looked so good.

The girl looks at her, annoyed.

"Could you tell me where the Town Hall is?"

"The Town Hall?"

"Yeah," Dale says.

"Whatcha want to go there for?"

Dale feels her skin starting to crawl. "Could you just tell me where it is?"

"I think it's that building across from the cemetery. It's just down Main Street there. But, shoot, that might be the town clerk's office."

Frustrated, Dale pays her and grabs the bag without bothering to get her change.

She finds Main Street and starts walking. She's not sure what she's looking for until she sees it.

The woody.

California plates. It's parked right in the dirt lot. Dale feels dizzy again; her ears buzz and hum as she looks around to see if anyone is watching. The Mercedes is nowhere to be found. She takes a deep breath, reaches into her pocket for the little pencil she stole from the library, and grins.

Mena came home from rehearsals earlier than Sam expected. He suggested she go for a swim, said he might join her in a bit. Now, while she floats in the still water of the lake, he tries to figure out how to deal with Finn and the acre of weed growing behind their house. Sam told Finn that Alice could stay there for the night. Apparently her father, some asshole wife beater, is out of jail. Like they didn't have enough problems. And he can't confront Finn with Alice around; he'll have to wait until she's gone. He also figures he shouldn't let on that he knows about the weed until he's got a plan.

His mind is reeling. Finn could go to jail for something like this. *He* could go to jail. Granted, the plants had to have been growing here when they bought the place, but clearly, Finn has been tending to them. Someone has been taking good care of those plants. There must be a hundred of them. And as remote as Gormlaith feels, when it comes to breaking the law, you're never really too far away from an eager cop. *Obviously;* they've got one across the road.

Even though it's nearly four o'clock, he makes another pot of coffee. He hopes that it will help clear his head. While the coffee brews, he sits down at the table and puts his head in his hands. He needs to get rid of the plants. But he's not sure how to even go about doing that. He knows he can pull them up, but then what? Put them in the compost? Can you do that? Goddamn, he wishes he had the Internet here.

The phone rings.

"Hi, Sam? It's Hilary Ortiz. The couple, the ones I told you about, have made an offer. They want the house."

"I'll have to call you back," Sam says. He hangs up the phone and paces.

Outside, he can see Mena swimming in the lake, the robin's egg blue of her bathing suit. Forty-one years old, and she still looks incredible in a bikini. Softer, rounder than she was as a girl, but strong. Graceful.

The library. Maybe the library's still open. He gathers his bag, his keys, and heads outside.

"Mena!" he hollers across the water.

She is floating on her back, her eyes closed. When she hears him, she rolls over and starts to swim toward him.

"I'm running into town," he says. "Do you need anything?"

"Just some eggs," she says. "And Q-tips?"

"Got it!" he says, and watches her swim back away from him. Watches her strong arms, her legs.

Finn. *Christ.*

He gets in the station wagon, adjusts the seat, and turns the key. The car smells like Mena. Like her perfume, Anaïs Anaïs, and coffee. He breathes her in, leaves the windows rolled up, and takes off.

The windows are filthy from the dirt road. He flicks the lever to release the wiper fluid and turns on the wipers. There's a piece of paper stuck under one of the blades.

"Shit," he says. Probably a flyer somebody stuck under there when Mena was in town for rehearsals. A parking ticket? Do they even issue parking tickets in Quimby?

He pulls the car over to the side of the road and yanks the

piece of paper out from under the wiper. He glances at it—maybe it's a coupon for the new pizza place or something. It's damp from the wiper fluid. He starts to crumple it up and then stops when he sees his name: *Samuel Mason.*

He gets in the car with the note in his hands, unfolds it.

Found your little hiding place.

Christ. Somebody's found the weed. Who is it? Jesus, it's probably the fucking cop. He knows this area better than anybody. He imagines him out traipsing around on their property. Trespassing. Jesus.

His hands are trembling. He needs to dispose of the plants right away. But if the cops know, someone's probably staked out, watching. *Jesus.* If they're watching him, he can't exactly go to the library to research how to dispose of marijuana plants.

He is driving faster than he should for this road. He has to concentrate on going slow, watching the speedometer. The last thing he needs is to get pulled over. To have an accident. When he drives past the cop's house, that stupid dog starts barking and running alongside the car. He slams on his brakes and slows to a crawl until he's sure the dog is not underneath his tires. The dog gives one last howl, and Sam watches him disappear in his rearview mirror.

Maybe he should just pretend he doesn't know what's going on. For Christ's sake, they just bought the cabin. They've only been there for a couple of months. He can just warn Finn. Tell him that he's got to stop tending the garden. He wonders what kind of paraphernalia Finn's got in his room. That's it; he's got to just get rid of every shred of evidence in the house. Any connection between Finn and the plants. He gets to a place in the road where he can turn the car around and makes a U-turn in the middle of the road. He creeps past the cop's house again, and the dog has retired underneath a pickup truck in the driveway. He stares Sam down as he passes.

Mena is not in the water when he gets back to the house. She is sitting on a blanket spread out at the water's edge. Effie is with her now, the baby on her lap.

"What are you doing home?" Mena asks.

"Forgot something," Sam says.

"Hi, Sam!" Effie says, waving to him. "Thanks again for coming to the book club. Every one of your books has been checked out ever since. They loved you!"

"Thanks."

Inside, he can see them through the window. He is pretty sure he can do a clean sweep of Finn's room before they come in.

When he goes into Finn's room, he immediately feels like he's trespassing. His own father had told him once that there's nothing as sacred as a person's privacy. He'd never worried about his father coming into his room, going through his things. Of course, he'd had very little to hide back then: *Delta of Venus,* for Christ's sake, maybe some cigarettes. Sam is afraid of what he might find here.

He looks through Finn's drawers. He finds rolling papers, an almost empty Baggie that probably used to have weed in it. He finds a green lighter. A bottle of the sleeping pills Mena's doctor prescribed after Franny died. He throws everything into the trash can he's carrying. He slips his hands between the mattresses, finds a Victoria's Secret catalogue, a *Hustler* magazine. Where the hell did he get that? He leaves those there. He finds some printouts on how to grow and harvest marijuana and he shoves them in the trash. He peers through the window at Mena. She's holding Zu-Zu, laughing. Happy. He opens every drawer, searches through every pocket. He gets down on his hands and knees and peers under the bed.

It's filthy under there. A thick sheet of dust. Dirty socks. Pencils, a pair of sneakers, dryer sheets. There's also a shoe box, way underneath. Sam gets down on his stomach and reaches under, pulling the box toward him with his fingertips. He doesn't know what he's expecting. Drugs. A gun? But when he opens the box, his heart nearly stops. Inside: no drugs, no firearms, no porn. Just Franny's diary, the little blue one embossed with gold they gave her for her fifteenth birthday. It is tethered shut with a flimsy metal clasp. He could pry it open with a paper clip, snap it between his fingers. He imagines her, turning that tiny little key, the one she wore hanging on a gold chain around her neck, locking all of this up, keeping whatever is inside safe from their eyes. Keeping their eyes safe from whatever is inside. And he can't do it. Instead, he takes the journal, as if it were just another piece of contraband, and tucks it into his pocket.

M ena takes Zu-Zu from Effie, putting her on her hip so she can still see her mother. "Take your time," Mena says to Effie. "We'll be just fine."

"God, thank you so much," Effie says.

Effie peels off her clothes and walks into the water. She waves at Zu-Zu. "I'll be right out, sweetie." And then she disappears under the water, resurfacing again about a hundred feet farther out in the lake.

Mena remembers the joy of this: the moments of liberation from the kids. When Sam would take one or both of the twins with him somewhere and she could take a bath. A nap. Read without one or both of them crawling across the pages of her book. What she wouldn't do to have that back, all that chaos. All that need.

"You want to go inside and have some juice?"

Zu-Zu smiles.

Mena carries her back up the hill to the house. Sam has left again; the wagon is not in the driveway. Inside, she goes to the fridge and finds a plastic tumbler in the cupboard, a carton of orange juice. With Zu-Zu still on her hip, she pours the juice into the cup, holds it to her lips. Helps her drink.

"Isn't that good?" she coos. "You're such a sweet baby."

She sits down at the kitchen table, puts Zu-Zu on her lap.

She touches her hair, the tight black coils that spring from her head like little Slinkys.

There's a pile of mail on the table. She needs to go through the stuff that's been forwarded from California, pay the bills. With her free hand, she rifles through the pile. The manila folder that Monty dropped off is still there. Curious, she dumps the letters out onto the table. There are about a dozen inside. Sam hasn't opened any of them yet. He used to love reading the fan mail. They'd read the letters together sometimes. She hesitates and then opens the first one. Sam won't mind. It's postmarked North Conway, New Hampshire. *Dear Mr. Mason, I'm a huge fan. I have read* The Hour of Lead *literally about a hundred times*. Blah, blah, blah. The second one, from Lubbock, Texas: *Dear Samuel Mason, I am senior at Texas Tech, and we are reading* The Art of Hunting *in my Contemporary American Literature class. I was wondering if you might answer some questions I had . . .* She stuffs the letters back into their envelopes. Then there is a bundle of letters, all postmarked Phoenix, Arizona. Mena reads the first one: *Dear Mr. Mason, I just wanted to let you know that despite your request that I look elsewhere for a literary subject, I would like to give you one more opportunity to authorize my biography. I believe that you might reconsider if I were able to talk to you in person. Please call me at your earliest convenience. All my best, Dale Edwards.* She opens the next one as well: *Mr. Mason, I am beginning to think that you are not receiving these letters. I am certain you would have responded by now if you were, indeed, reading them. However, unless you respond, I plan to pursue this project. As I said before, I have a publisher who is ready to publish this with or without your authorization, though we certainly would prefer to receive your stamp of approval.* Mena is confused. Sam hasn't mentioned anything about a biographer. She looks at the envelope again, at the Arizona postmark. She tears open another envelope and shakes its contents out onto the table. It's a printout from a Web site.

A yellow Post-it note stuck to the center says *Last chance!* Mena tears it off.

She gasps, grabbing onto Zu Zu tightly Zu-Zu picks up the Post-it and sticks it to her shirt.

The first photo on the page is taken from the jetty in front of their house. She would recognize this view from anywhere. In the picture, Franny is standing facing the water, alone. She is just a dark sliver of a girl, a frightening silhouette against the setting sun. Just a shadow of Franny. Under the photo, it says, *Fasting is the life of the angels*—Pseudo-Athanasius. *Posted by Ana-Franny.*

The photo below this one makes Mena's stomach turn. It's a young girl, blond curly hair to her waist, wearing nothing but a pale bra and pair of panties. She is standing in front of a mirror, and a camera obscures her face. It is one of those images that is so shocking Mena's mind simply can't accept that it's real. Like looking at a contortionist or some sort of carnival freak. But it *is* real, the girl is real, and in the mirror's reflection Mena sees the antique dresser in Franny's room.

"I'm going with you," Finn says, nodding. "I'll find a place to stay. Nearby."

Alice shakes her head. "You'll be back in California in a month. You can come find me then. I'll come down to San Diego. It'll be fine. I promise."

They are in her purple room. The front and back doors are dead-bolted, and her mother has already left to stay with a friend of a friend in town for the night. Alice is supposed to meet her at the bus station at 6:00 A.M. She is *leaving*.

Finn is lying on the lavender bedspread, playing with the purple fringe on a lavender throw pillow. He stares at the indigo sky above him, at the haphazard constellations.

Alice empties her drawers into a big purple suitcase. He watches her pack her clothes, the careful way she folds the socks and shirts and jeans. He can smell the heady smell of her detergent. It makes his stomach jump. Twist.

"Do you not want me to come?" he asks, sitting up. "You can tell me."

Alice stops packing and sits down next to him. She picks up his hand and holds it in her lap. She is looking at him hard, like she's trying to figure something out. He feels self-conscious; his ears are growing hot. After a long time she says, "Are you sure?"

He nods.

"So what do we do?"

"We'll stay at my house tonight, just like we planned," he says. Already everything is starting to feel real. "And in the morning I'll offer to take you into town. To say good-bye. But then I'll get on the bus too."

"What will we tell my mom?" she asks.

He thinks about it for a minute, looks at the picture of Alice and her mother in the purple fuzzy frame on her dresser.

"I'll get on first, sit in the back. By the time she figures it out, it'll be too late."

Sam throws open the front door of the cottage and finds Mena sitting at the kitchen table. The room smells of tea. The teapot is steaming on the table.

He is still out of breath, panicked. He had taken the paraphernalia he found in Finn's room and driven it to the dump. He thought he might be able to do the same thing with the plants if he could just get to them without being followed.

"Did Effie leave?" he asks.

"Who is Dale Edwards?" Mena asks, lifting up a letter from the table. Her voice is trembling.

"Oh, Christ," he says, taking the envelope from Mena. "Another letter?"

"Why didn't you tell me about this?" Mena asks. Her face looks pained, hurt.

"I didn't want you to worry," he says. "She's just some ridiculous English major. She says she's got an editor who's offered her a book deal to write a biography on me. It's stupid. I told her I wouldn't authorize it, but she keeps insisting. I think she's full of shit."

"Dale Edwards is a woman?"

"A *girl*. A twenty-something-year-old girl."

"Where did *this* come from?" Mena asks, handing him a piece of paper from the envelope.

He takes the paper from her, turns it over in his hands.

He has forgotten. He has managed, somehow, in the last nine months to put images like this out of his mind. When he remembers Franny, it is always the way she was before. Before she became a sliver of a girl, before she wasted away. When he conjures her now, he always remembers her whole.

"Where did she *find* this?" Mena asks. "And what in the hell is she threatening to do with it?"

Sam takes it in his hands and forces himself to study the pictures. He reads the entries, all three of them. "It's like a journal," he says. "A diary." He feels the small blue diary in his back pocket. He thinks of that tiny gold key.

Mena stands up and starts to pace around the small kitchen. She picks things up, examines them as if she's never seen them before: spatula, pot holder, whisk. She stops and turns to Sam. "Why is this woman doing this to us? What does she *want?*"

She takes the printout from his hands and looks at it again. Her hand flies to her mouth. "It's sick, Sam," Mena says, and crumples the paper into her fist.

"I'll contact her. Make her stop. We can get the police involved if we need to. We have rights to privacy."

"I mean *Franny,*" Mena says. "Why didn't we know about this?"

May 22 (101)
Breakfast: one piece toast (no butter!), tea
Lunch: yogurt, carrots
Dinner: two pieces pizza (gross! At least I picked off the pepperoni)

May 23 (103—NO MORE PIZZA!!!!)
Breakfast: one apple
Lunch: yogurt, carrots
Snack: a granola bar from the vending machine
Dinner: nothing!!!

May 24 (100)
Breakfast: oatmeal (weekends are hard)
Lunch: turkey sandwich (scraped off most of the cheese and mayo)
Dinner: pastitsio, my favorite . . . ugh, I hate the weekends!

Page after page after page. May, June, July, August. *There must be a word for this,* for this sense that the proof was here, right here. That a flimsy gold clasp was the only thing between them and the truth. A word to explain regret so deep Sam can feel it in his bowels.

Sunset and a blinking VACANCY sign.

Dale is pacing in the motel room. The Mercedes is gone now, but she keeps checking the window to see if the man and woman have returned. She goes to the bathroom and peels the tissue paper wrapper from a glass. She presses it against the wall and listens. She can only hear muffled sounds, white noise, but maybe she's just not listening closely enough. Even when her arm starts to cramp, she is too afraid to put the glass down in case she might miss something. She switches hands, shaking her arm, and the cramp, loose. She nearly jumps out of her skin when her cell phone rings, dropping the glass, which shatters on the tile floor. She flips the phone open and whispers, "Hello?"

"Baby, it's Momma. Where are you, honey? You need to let me know." Her mother's voice swims to her through the phone.

Dale is sweating so much the phone is slippery in her hand. The AC is still out.

"I gave Dr. Middleton a call today, and he's concerned that maybe you've stopped taking your medication. You didn't stop taking your pills again, honey, did you?"

When Dale thinks of the pills, she thinks of the Tilt-A-Whirl ride at the Arizona State Fair, the swirling, twirling reds and blues as they wound their way down the toilet, their candy-colored trails, swirling, staining the porcelain.

"I'm fine, Momma," Dale says.

"I'm going to send you money for a ticket home. Do they have a Western Union where you are?"

Dale can hear the slur in her mother's voice; she's been drinking, taking her own pills, for a few hours now.

"No, Momma!" Dale says loudly, and suddenly she is thirteen years old again, when all of this started—back after her father first left and she could still hear his voice in her head at night when she closed her eyes, singing the lullabies he'd never sang. She'd press her pillow against her ear to drown it out, but it was still there. And it was there even when she wasn't dreaming, whispering, *Let me take you for ice cream, sweetie,* telling her to meet him at the Thrifty. *You want peppermint, sweetie? With jimmies?* And then she was putting one foot in front of the other, tracing the white lines that separated the lanes of traffic. She could hear the cars honking, but he kept coaxing, insisting. Her sneakers were new, brand-new and white. She dragged them as she walked, scuffing them against the dirty pavement. One foot in front of the other. And then her mother was running across three lanes of traffic to get her, but she kept walking and the horns kept honking. When her mother reached her, putting one heavy arm around her shoulders and trying to steer her toward the median, Dale screamed, "No, Momma!" and sat down in the middle of the road.

There was the hospital after that, the emergency room first for the bump on her head (how did that happen?) and then later all the swirly pills, a flimsy paper cup, lukewarm water and sleep. Until finally, the Tilt-A-Whirl finally slowed down. And she wasn't dizzy anymore; she could finally feel the ground beneath her feet. And she understood that you don't ever walk down the middle of the street in the middle of the summer in Phoenix.

No one knew about those days, and even the memory of all that seemed to belong to someone else. And as long as she kept taking the pills, for years (how many?), she was normal.

She went to school. She stood in line at the cafeteria holding an orange plastic tray. She raised her hand in class. She took tap dancing lessons. She swam in Sarah's piss-warm pool. Her mother gave the pills to her along with a chalky Flintstone vitamin every morning. She went to her appointments at Dr. Middleton's office, sat in his scratchy chair. When one pill stopped working he gave her another. The record kept spinning. She was normal. Normal. She went to high school. College. She wrote papers on Mary Shelley's *Frankenstein*.

She only stopped taking the pills when she was feeling better. When she fell in love with Fitz. And then later when she started to write her book. She had a hard time concentrating at first. The pills made the words too soft. But when she stopped taking them, all of a sudden it was like the clouds lifted. It reminded her of the time when she was ten and she'd had to have her ears irrigated. After the whoosh of warm water, and the earwax came out in ugly brown chunks, she could hear again. *Clarity.* The drugs had stuffed up her head. And now all that junk, that smothering cumulus was gone, leaving only the clear blue sky of her real thoughts.

Dale hears the door to the next motel room over open. She looks out the window, but the Mercedes is still not there. She runs back to the bathroom and then wonders if they are on the other side of the wall with their own glasses, listening.

"Momma?" she whispers into the phone, and then she turns on the water in the tub so whoever is listening won't be able to hear her.

"What is it, honey?"

The water crashes into the tub, Niagara Falls, and Dale sits down on the toilet lid.

"Dale?"

"Love you, Momma," Dale says, flips the phone closed, and tosses it into the water.

Mena makes bread. She watches her hands as they pull the hot loaves from the oven. As they pour olive oil into a pan, as they cut through the yielding rind of a lemon. She listens as the oil crackles and spits, contemplates the way the shrimp curl in on themselves as she tosses them into the heat.

Every night, they came together for dinner. She knew it was a luxury a lot of other families did not have: this ability to convene at the dining room table at the same time each evening. This ritual was a relic of some other time. Her friends, like Hilary and Becca, with their busy lives and busy husbands and busy children, complained that their families were like ships passing in the night. Dinner was something grabbed quickly from the refrigerator or eaten at the desk by the glow of a computer monitor. When their children came over to play with Franny or Finn, they were fascinated by this nightly communion, by the smells in the kitchen and the six o'clock gathering around the table. She was the only mother she knew who planned meals for the family an entire week in advance, who started thinking about what she would feed her family the moment she rolled out of bed in the morning.

The first time Franny missed dinner for ballet class, Mena felt like someone was tearing her heart out. At first it was just on Tuesday evenings. Mena didn't like it, but it wasn't as though she had a choice. That was the only time Intermediate

Pointe was offered. But by her sophomore year there were classes on Tuesdays and Wednesdays. On Fridays. And then there were rehearsals. Sam and Finn and Mena still assembled at dinnertime, but Franny whisked through the kitchen, her ratty ballet bag slung over her shoulder, grabbing a banana or apple from the bowl on the kitchen counter. Mena would fill a plate and save it in the oven for her, but Franny always said she had gotten something after class: grabbed a piece of pizza with friends, a bowl of noodles, a cheeseburger.

Breakfast in the morning was always on the go: hot muffins or thick slices of homemade toast swaddled in napkins and cradled in hands on their way out the door. The lunches Mena packed, stuffed into brown paper sacks.

The doctor warned Franny at her physical earlier that summer that she was too thin, and she'd shrugged it off. He'd smiled when she'd explained her hectic schedule. Mena had sat in the uncomfortable chair and looked at Franny's long, thin legs dangling from the examination table. She was swimming inside the paper gown, her collarbone and elbows razor sharp.

When the doctor sent Franny to the restroom with a plastic cup, he'd said to Mena, "Have you noticed anything different in Franny's eating habits? In her exercising habits? Does she skip meals? Avoid eating around other people? She's lost seven pounds since her visit last year."

Mena had felt like she'd been slapped. She thought of Franny's empty space at the table.

"She's always been thin. She and her brother were preemies. She was always in the bottom tenth percentile." Mena wrung her hands.

"Her BMI is sixteen point five," the doctor said, his brow furrowed.

Mena waited for an explanation.

"Body mass index. She's underweight, not severely, but it is a red flag. Are her periods regular?"

Mena blushed, looked down at her hands in her lap, watched as they twisted and turned.

"Besides her weight, she appears to be a healthy young woman. I've ordered a complete blood workup, and we'll do a urine test. But we need to consider the possibility that there is an underlying psychological problem."

Mena shook her head. "She's *fine*," she says, smiling. "She does well in school. She's just very, very active. I'll make sure she eats. She forgets sometimes."

"I want to make a referral. My wife has a friend who specializes in eating disorders."

Wide-eyed, Mena had taken the doctor's name and stuffed it into her purse.

In the car, she said, "The doctor is worried about your weight."

Franny swatted the air in front of her and laughed.

"He says you need to start eating more. And healthier stuff. No more French fries for dinner. No more vending machine snacks. I'm going to start sending some real food for you to have between school and ballet."

"Okay, Mommy," Franny said, leaning her head against the back of the seat and smiling at Mena. "Don't worry," she said then, and squeezed Mena's hand. Mena felt the bones in her grasp and it made a shiver run down her back.

"Promise," Mena said.

"I promise."

Tonight the room smells so good: lemon and garlic. She crumbles the block of feta in her hands. She rolls her neck, feels the headache in its nape. She closes her eyes and opens them again. Tosses the last of the shrimp into the hot oil. Checks on the soup that simmers in a pot on the stove.

"Dinner!" she hollers.

A lice sits next to Finn, clutching his hand under the table. His mother has made a feast. She does this when she's upset—cooks as though they're having the queen of England over for dinner. He wonders what could be wrong. She'd seemed so happy that morning. He wonders if she suspects anything, if they've figured out his plan to ditch them and head back to California.

Four plates circle the table. Candles glow warmly in the center. They smell like cinnamon. Avgolemono, his favorite soup, in four steaming bowls. Bread, hot from the oven.

Alice smiles nervously and squeezes his hand.

"So you have family in California?" Mena asks Alice, loading her plate with shrimp and rice and handing it to her.

Alice nods, ladling some of the soup with her spoon. "My mom's aunt. She lives in Barstow. We're just going to stay with her for a while, until all this stuff with my dad gets straightened out."

His dad seems distracted. He keeps glancing out the window, like he's expecting somebody.

Finn has stashed his backpack in the barn. He packed some T-shirts and jeans, boxers and a toothbrush. Enough cash for a bus ticket and a credit card he stole from his father's wallet. The plan is that in the morning he'll offer to take Alice on his bike to the bus station. He'll ditch the bike there and get on the bus.

He hasn't thought too far past this. Of course, he'll call them once they've been on the road for a couple of hours. He doesn't want them to worry. A part of his heart snags a little when he thinks of what his mom will do when she figures out he's gone.

The soup is so good. They eat quietly.

"What was the name of that Mexican restaurant in Barstow, Sammy?" Mena asks.

"Hmm?" he says. He's out of it. Totally distracted.

"Remember that time we took the Forty to Flagstaff and drove through Barstow with the kids? They had this burrito, a chile relleno burrito . . . it was so decadent. A chile relleno wrapped up inside a burrito," Mena explains to Alice. "Remember, the kids got the chicken pox? We didn't realize until we got to Barstow, to that *restaurant?*" His mom seems exasperated.

Sam nods. "I don't remember."

"God, Sam. *Remember?* It was that restaurant with the giant fake cactus out front? I took Franny to the bathroom, and her whole stomach was already covered with spots." Finn should have known whatever was going on that morning wouldn't last. They all look at Sam. *Jesus, Dad, just say you remember.*

"I remember the chicken pox, Mena. But I can't remember the name of the restaurant," he says.

Mena shakes her head, as if clearing it. She rubs her temples. Shit, it looks like she's getting one of her headaches again.

"Anyway, *Alice.*" She forces a smile, reaches for Alice's hand. "Look for the place with the big fake saguaro cactus out front. And, oh, the sopapillas and fried ice cream. So good."

Alice nods.

Finn is mortified. His family is a bunch of freaks. He can't wait to get the hell back to California.

"What was that?" Sam asks, standing up, walking across the living room to the window that faces the water.

"What's the matter?" Mena asks. She rubs her temples again.

"I thought I heard something outside."

"It's pretty windy out," Mena says. "The radio says there might be a thunderstorm tonight."

Sam is pacing, looking out the windows.

"You okay, Dad?" Finn asks.

Dale gets in the Bug and starts the engine. A plume of smoke billows out behind her. The lights are out in the motel room next to hers. The Mercedes is still gone. She feels around under the seat to make sure the manuscript is still there. She pops in one of the Books on Tape and takes a deep breath. She looks at her reflection in the rearview mirror and smoothes a crease in the yellow dress. It won't flatten though, no matter how hard she presses. But she keeps pressing and pressing and pressing until her leg hurts, and then she stops.

She drives through town, follows the turn-by-turn directions she printed out. She passes the library, the Town Hall, the cemetery. As she drives past the public pool, she notices the way the air glows green around it. For a minute she thinks about how nice it would be to stop and take a swim. How she and Sarah used to sip Bartles & Jaymes cranberry wine coolers and swim in her pool at night. She slows down at the pool's gated entrance but doesn't stop, even to get out of the car for a second. *No.* She has to remember why she's here, what she's doing. She has to try to quiet her mind, stay focused.

By the time she gets to the turnoff that will lead to the lake, the air feels heavy, buzzing. The sun has set, but the sky is luminous. The stars pulsate in the peacock blue sky. She studies the tops of the trees, which lean eastward. The Bug lists across the road with the steady wind. She's at the mercy of the breeze. It feels almost strong enough to pick the little car up and toss it across the road.

The houses begin to thin out, and soon there are wide expanses of pastures dotted with cows, all lying down. The moon hangs like a marionette in the sky.

Up ahead she sees a gas station, a little convenience store. The neon OPEN sign is on, and there are a few cars parked in the lot. The gas gauge in the Bug is broken, but she's pretty sure she should get some more gas. She pulls into the lot and turns off the engine.

It's one of those places where you have to pay before you pump, so she rifles through her purse. She's almost out of cash, and the credit card is nearly maxed out. It's a good thing she's finally here. She laughs out loud, plucking a forgotten crumpled ten-dollar bill from the depths of her bag.

"Five dollars, please," she says cheerfully, and grabs two Kit Kat bars from the rack below the counter.

She unwraps the first chocolate bar as the tank fills. She cracks one Kit Kat off and pops the whole stick in her mouth. It's so sweet, it almost brings tears to her eyes. She quickly devours the remaining pieces and stuffs the empty wrapper in her pocket. She'll save the other one for later. The wind wraps around her like an embrace, and the pump clicks off.

It would be easy to miss the turnoff. The dirt road is obscured by thick leaves. Someone has hand-painted a sign and nailed it to the trunk of a tree. If she didn't have her high beams on, she would have missed it.

It says: GORMLAITH →

She grips the steering wheel tightly; she's a little dizzy, and this helps ground her. She turns slowly onto the road, and as the gravel and dirt crush under her tires, the air rumbles. There is a flash of lightning in the distance, and it illuminates the whole sky. She feels the shock of it pass through her body.

The road is winding and narrow. She is surrounded on either side by towering trees that bow in deference to the wind. The passenger side window doesn't close all the way, and there is a steady whistle as the wind winds its way in through the crack.

She looks at the map, but it is too dark to see. She knows the road she is on circles the lake, but there is no lake in sight. How long has she been driving on this road? The map had said it was two miles from the turnoff to the lake, but the odometer, like everything else in this stupid car, doesn't work. She's about to pull over to look at the map again when another flash of lightning reveals the glistening surface of water through a thick patch of trees and brush. Her heart thumps wildly in her chest.

Now she just has to slowly circle the lake until she finds the station wagon from the photo, the one she'd seen in town. She'd left Sam a note, though she was too afraid to sign her name. She wanted to surprise him, but she couldn't resist giving him a little hint that she was here.

She passes several cottages. Some of them are lit up inside, their inhabitants' silhouettes moving behind the windows. There is one cottage with a swing out front, stained glass windows splattering color across the dark grass. Thunder cracks like a slap, and her heart jumps to her throat. She creeps slowly forward, studying every driveway. Searching.

The tape in the tape deck is almost over. It is *Small Sorrows*, her least favorite of all of his books. But the end redeems the rest of the novel. And what a coincidence that this is what is playing now: *He wades into the water, looks at the girl floating luminous in the lake. It could be just the moon's reflection in the shape of a girl. What do you do with the remains of a human life? With the perfect geometry of ribs? Build a castle of eyelashes, a fortress of bones, a quilt of flesh sewn together with hair? What do you do with what's left when a life is gone?* Dale's eyes sting. With the next flash of light, she can see the entire lake before her, spread out like a dream.

She wipes her wet eyes with the back of her hand and grips the wheel. She squeezes her eyes shut, and when she opens them again she sees something running in front of the car. She slams on the brakes and yanks the wheel to the left. There is a terrible squeal followed by a series of horrible yelps.

Oh God, it's an animal. She's hit an animal.

The car teeters and then dips down into a ditch, and her head smashes against the steering wheel. *No, no, no,* she says, and opens up the door of the car. Underneath the car, cowering and wailing in the dark, is a dog. Its eyes are glowing, and it is still making that awful sound.

She looks all around her for help. She runs back down the road in the direction from which she came, but the only cabin in sight is pitch black. There are no cars in the driveway except for a truck propped up on concrete blocks. She touches her forehead when she feels something warm. It's blood. *No, no, no.*

She goes back to the Bug and peers under the car again. She's afraid to try to get the dog out; she knows it's probably dangerous to move a wounded animal. She has to get help. She needs to find Sam. She glances around again, looking for someone, anyone to help her figure out what to do next. The dog moans and cries. She covers her ears, shakes her head, and then starts to run.

It's getting stormy outside. No rain, not yet, but the *wind*. Branches keep knocking against the windows; Sam feels as though he might jump out of his skin. He sits back down at the table, and every noise outside makes his pulse quicken. He's waiting for the knock on the door. The one that will send their entire world into yet another tailspin.

His plan is to burn the plants. He'll tear them up and burn them until there's nothing left. No evidence. Nothing to incriminate him, to incriminate Finn. As soon as he can escape the house, he's going to go to the field and tear them all up, put them in Hefty bags and bring them to the barn. When he mowed the lawn that afternoon he saved all of the grass clippings; thank God he hadn't mowed in two weeks, so there was enough to fill three barrels. He'll bury the plants in the clippings, and then tomorrow, he'll incinerate them. Folks burn their grass clipping and leaves around here all the time. He's got three barrels waiting and plenty of lighter fluid.

Mena is talking to Alice about Barstow. About some giant saguaro, some giant burrito. About chicken pox. His mind is spinning. He keeps waiting to see the blue and red lights flashing in the window. He can't eat. He pushes the shrimp back and forth across his plate as the wind howls outside.

Finally, Mena stands and says, "Does anybody want dessert?"

They all shake their heads. Alice says, "There's no room!" grabbing her belly and laughing.

"Okay if Alice and I take a walk?" Finn asks.

"Where you going?" Sam says.

"I don't know. Maybe just around the lake."

"I don't know, it looks like it's going to rain," Mena says. She's getting a headache. Sam can tell by the way her eyelids weigh heavy on her eyes, the way her forehead crimps.

"They'll be fine," Sam says. If he can get them out of the house, he'll have an easier time getting to the field. He figures if he works quickly, he can get all the plants into the barrels within an hour. Though it will likely take more than one trip. "Mena, why don't you go lie down?" He reaches across the table and brushes her hair out of her eyes.

She peers at him and sighs.

"You guys go ahead," he says to Finn and Alice.

After they have left, the screen door slamming with the wind behind them, Sam goes to Mena and touches her hair again. She leans into his hand, looks up at him, her cheeks tear-stained.

"Did you get rid of them?" she asks, and he is startled. How could she know?

"What?"

"The *pictures*. Those awful pictures," Mena says, closing her eyes.

He thinks about the pictures. If they had seen them earlier, read her blog or whatever that was, read that little diary, would it have saved her? God, they'd tried to get her help, but it all happened so quickly. Last September, when the ballet studio called and said that Franny had fainted during practice, they took her to the doctor again the very next day. She'd filled out their questionnaires. The doctor had taken her blood, looked at her teeth, at her skin, at her hair. They had appointments

scheduled for an electrocardiogram, for Franny to see a thera-
pist, a specialist. They'd done exactly what they were supposed
to do. He'd gone to the library and taken out books, which he
and Mena poured over at night in bed, hoping they'd find
something in the pages to explain why she was doing this, if
she was indeed doing this, to herself.

They'd asked Franny to tell them. They pleaded with her
to tell them the truth. But before they even had a chance, before she did, she was gone. It wasn't supposed to happen like
this. None of the books warned them that this could happen
so quickly. All of the books were about the struggle. About the
survivors. They didn't even get a chance to fight.

"Go lie down," Sam says, helping Mena stand up. "I can
take care of this." He motions to the dirty dishes littered with
fleshy shrimp tails and rice, but he means everything. He will
take care of this.

"Come with me?" she asks.

A branch smacks against the kitchen window, and his glance
darts to the door.

"I'm just going to go check on Finn and Alice. You're
right. They shouldn't be out with this storm coming. Go lie
down. Go to sleep. I'll wake you when I come back."

A t first Dale couldn't believe it. It was just like her dream. She found the cottage just up the road from where she hit the dog. The station wagon was parked in the driveway, and there was a warm yellow glow coming from inside. She thought about running up to the front door and knocking, but something told her to savor this moment. To hold on to this anticipation for just a little bit longer. Her entire body was full of electricity. Her fingertips were tingling with it. It felt like there was a current circling through every vein and artery. She could feel every blood cell. Every molecule. And so instead of going to the front door, she crept slowly on her hands and knees to the window at the side of the house.

There were no curtains in the window, nothing to obstruct her view of the kitchen and beyond, into the dining room. At the table, she could see Sam, and it nearly took her breath away. *Her dream.* He was sitting at the head of the table, running his hands through his hair. He looked older than she expected. The hair at his temples was gray, his cheeks and chin shadowed with neglect. His wife, Mena, was sitting on his right side, ladling soup into bowls. The boy, Finn, was there too, a flop of blond curls hanging in his eyes. A faded T-shirt and puka shell choker. And Franny.

Franny. She gasped when she saw the pale-haired girl from the photos.

She was dizzy. The electric current that had been coursing through her suddenly shorted out. Thunder cracked and lightning lit up the whole sky. She dropped to her knees and tried to catch her breath.

How could this be? Franny was *dead*. She'd read about it online. Or had she just dreamed that? If she could have dreamed this table—the soup, the bread, Sam—could she have dreamed his daughter dead too? Or maybe Sam had lied. But why would he lie to her?

Everything was tilty, spinny. Her stomach cramped with the next crack of thunder, and she felt bile rising in her throat, sweet with Kit Kats. She leaned over and threw up in the bushes. She wiped her mouth with the back of her hand. She felt the bump on her head where she'd hit it on the steering wheel, felt the dried blood. He couldn't see her like this. This wasn't at all what she planned.

And then, just as she was trying to figure out what to do next, the screen door slammed open and the boy and the girl came outside. *Franny.* She pressed herself up flat against the side of the house and held her breath. She could smell her vomit, sickly sweet in the air. The wind was getting stronger; it whipped her hair across her face. Stung her eyes. Finn and Franny lingered for a second, whispering seriously, and then ran toward the woods, their voices growing fainter as they disappeared into the trees.

How long did she wait after this? She seems to have lost all sense of time. But now, when she peers through the window again, she sees Sam rummaging through drawers in the kitchen. His wife is not in the room. He pulls out a box of garbage bags and when the wind howls again, he glances toward her. Dale drops to the ground again. Did he see her? God, did he see her like this?

She has to think quickly. What will she do? She needs to get cleaned up. Her dress is dirty. Stained with dirt and puke.

The gash on her head seems to have reopened. This is a nightmare. But before she can figure out what to do next, the screen door swings open again, and it's Sam this time. He looks around as if he's expecting someone to be lurking in the shadows, but he can't know, can he? And then he breaks into a sprint, disappearing down the same path that swallowed Finn and Franny.

Her head is still swimming, spinning. She feels vertiginous. She's come so far. But for what? All of it was a lie. All of her work, her research, her writing, this trip was for nothing. Franny is alive. She's as alive as Dale is. And with Franny here, where does Dale fit in? Lightning flashes again and she leans her back against the side of the house, bangs her head against the wood, softly, softly. Tears stream down her face and she looks up at the sky, feeling the first drops of rain on her face like slivers of shattered glass.

The air still smells like weed; it is heady, pungent, a lingering funk. The wind is vicious, and they are standing in the garden. The moon is full and bright, illuminating everything: the upturned roots, the dying plants.

"Shit," Finn mumbles.

"It was so beautiful," Alice says, picking up one of the decapitated plants.

Finn sits down on the ground and then lies down, flat on his back, staring up at the sky. He knows he is lying in the middle of his ruined garden, but in the dark, he could be anywhere. He could even be home. He looks up at the sky, at the moon hovering, watchful, overhead. There must be a billion stars tonight. A trillion specks of light. And, unlike the ones on Alice's ceiling, these stars make pictures: constellations. They are predictable and certain even in all of this darkness. *Andromeda. Cassiopeia. Orion.*

Alice lies down next to him. She squeezes his hand, and he stares at that pock-marked sky. On the ground the wind isn't so violent, so fierce. The air smells like a memory. Like the remembrance of living things, the pungent tang of something interrupted, cut off before its time.

Before.

He looks at the stars. Each of his memories is like this: one bright, flickering speck, so far away he can't touch it anymore.

Their first trip to the dentist. Finn was afraid, and so their mother made the dentist let Franny sit in the dentist chair with him. As the dentist poked and prodded at his teeth, Franny squeezed his hand. The smell of cherry fluoride, the box of toys they got to choose from when it was over. Finn picked the tiny plastic man with a parachute attached. Franny got a ring, a blazing pink stone, a gold band that pinched her fingers where the metal opened at the back.

The Easter that Finn ate so much chocolate, so many hard-boiled eggs that he threw up half the night. He didn't want to tell their parents because he was afraid they'd never let him have candy again. So, in the middle of the night, as Finn lay doubled up on Franny's bed, Franny changed the sheets. Hid the evidence in the Dumpster outside.

In elementary school, when someone taunted, "Franny, Franny with the big flat fanny," and Finn's fist met his nose. The scuffle on asphalt, the taste of pavement and the metallic blood of his scraped knuckles.

High school, after the dance when he found Franny crying outside in the parking lot by the cafeteria. Another cruelty. And so he'd broken into the back door of the cafeteria and stolen the first thing he could find, a box of frozen Tater Tots, which they'd sucked on. Disgusting, but so funny they laughed until they cried.

A neighbor's trampoline, a bad spring, a broken arm. He couldn't go in the ocean for a whole summer, and so she'd painted the beach on his cast. Waves, sun, sand.

Franny in her room, practicing the positions. *First, Second, Fourth, Fifth.* Hours and hours and hours.

The sound of her feet shuffling across the hardwood floor, the shampoo smell of Franny's hair when she got out of the shower, the way she tilted her head when she listened to anyone speak.

Stars. Flickering, burning out and reappearing again, brighter.

Blinding. And together they form pictures, the pictures of their life. Of his life.

He looks at the pictures the stars make, at the angles of light, and he thinks about bones: the bones of her hands, the bones of her face, her collarbone, her hip bone, her feet. He remembers she wouldn't let him touch her, as if her bones were sharp enough to cut. And he was afraid to anyway, afraid she might crumble in his hands. Why didn't they do anything? Why didn't he do anything? If it had been the other way around, Franny would have saved him. She would never have let him kill himself.

He stares at the moon, at the bright full moon, until the light starts to hurt his eyes. When he squeezes them shut, all he can see are stars.

"I just want to go back," he says.

The three black Hefty bags are stuffed in the pockets of his anorak. He pulls up his hood and turns out the porch light that illuminates the driveway. It is dark, except for the bright white moon. He looks back at the house, at the warm yellow glow of his office. It looks like he's ,home. Like he's working. In case whoever left that note on the windshield is watching him tonight.

He creeps out into the darkness and feels ridiculous: like a teenager sneaking out of his house. He makes his way in the darkness to the path that leads to Finn's garden. It is almost impossible to see. Luckily, the moon is bright, and the portion of the path that runs through the woods is short. The wind beats against the nylon of his jacket as he jogs through the trees. Soon, he is standing in the field, in the wide open. It is beautiful here, and the smell is intoxicating.

"Dad?"

Sam's heart catapults in his chest.

Finn and Alice pop up from the middle of the field, like a couple of jacks-in-the-box. Finn's hair is almost white in the moonlight.

"Finn?"

"Yeah, it's me."

Sam walks toward them, realizing as he walks that all of the plants have already been uprooted.

"What are you doing out here, Dad?" Finn looks panicked. Alice is staring at her feet.

"Alice," Sam says, "why don't you go back to the house. We'll be there in a little bit. I need to talk to Finn."

She nods and looks quickly at Finn before she starts to run back toward the house. It is starting to rain.

Finn is staring at his feet, his hands shoved in his pockets. A little boy about to be scolded.

"Somebody knows about your little project, Finn." Sam gestures to the surrounding crop. "I think it's that guy with the dog who lives down the road. He's a *cop*, Finn. Do you have any clue what kind of trouble we could all be in because of this? I came out here to get rid of the plants before anything terrible happened."

"I already did," Finn says.

"I see." Sam looks at the field; it looks as though it's been hit by a hurricane.

"You're pissed," Finn says without looking up.

"That is an understatement," Sam says, pissed. "What were you *doing?* What were you *thinking?*"

Finn kicks at a rock with his tennis shoe. "Dad, I don't know how to do anything anymore. I don't even know who I am." Finn stares at the ground. He won't look at Sam. "It's like somebody cut off my legs and now wants me to run."

Sam knows this feeling. This severing loss. "But why *this*, Finny? Why would you risk so much for this?"

Finn shrugs. He looks up at Sam then, and his eyes are filled with tears. "I couldn't *sleep*."

It feels like a blow to his chest. He thinks of the way Finn and Franny would curl around each other as toddlers at nap time. As if they were two parts of some larger, breathing thing. And suddenly, remarkably, all the anger he's been feeling toward Finn has dissipated. Fizzled out like an extinguished fire.

Sam wants to reach for him, to hold him in his arms, to let him curl up in his lap like he used to when he was little. He wants to give him the magic kiss with two fingers on the sore places. He wants to fix everything that hurts. But Finn is not a little boy anymore. He's nearly a man, and so instead they stand, facing each other, trying to figure out what to do next.

"What do I do now?" Finn asks.

"Help me bag these up," Sam says, handing him a garbage bag. "Then we'll take them back to the house and burn them with the grass clippings."

It takes nearly an hour to get all of the plants bagged up. The bags are heavy, and the wind is growling now, whipping senselessly, changing directions as they drag the corpses of the marijuana plants along the path back to the cabin. By the time they get back to the barn and start to empty them into the barrels, clouds have moved across the clear sky, and it is really starting to rain.

"Is this all of them? You don't have another crop growing somewhere else, do you?" Sam asks.

Finn shakes his head.

As they come down the path from the barn to the cabin, Finn says, "Hey, where's the car?"

Sam looks at the empty driveway and feels his skin prickle. Mena shouldn't be out driving, not when she's got a migraine. She drove the car into a ditch the last time. The rain is coming down hard now. The roads will be a mess. What the hell was she thinking? Where the hell was she going? And where is Alice? He hopes to God Mena didn't leave her here alone.

Sam throws open the front door and hollers into the empty cabin, "Mena?" He walks briskly down the hall and opens all the doors. "Alice?" Every room is empty. Every room is quiet.

"*Fuck,*" he says, sitting down hard on the couch.

Then Finn leans down and picks something up off the floor. It's a Kit Kat wrapper.

"What?" Sam says, feeling like a percolator about to burst. All hiss and stifled steam.

Finn's eyes are wide and terrified. "Alice's dad always bought her these. They're her favorite. Oh, Dad. This is really bad."

A lice came back as Mena was making some tea. She'd tried to sleep, but she couldn't get comfortable. She was dizzy, her brain cloudy. She'd taken a Valium thinking she might be able to sleep through the migraine, but instead it had just covered the pain with a heavy blanket.

"Where's Finn?" Mena asked.

"With Mr. Mason," Alice said. She looked nervous, fidgeting with a loose string on her cutoffs.

"What are they doing?"

"I think they're taking a walk."

Mena sighed. "Well, would you like some tea? It's chamomile."

"That would be nice," Alice said, and Mena pulled two mugs from the cupboard.

They sat together at the kitchen table, peering into the steam.

"How are you feeling about your trip?" Mena asked. "I know Finn is going to miss you."

Alice smiled at this, her cheeks blushing a pale pink, the tips of her ears turning red. She took a deep breath and said quietly, "I wish I didn't have to leave. It's not fair. This is our *home.*"

Mena thought about that word, *home,* about what that meant. She thought about the empty rooms in their bungalow back in San Diego, about the dusty shelves and unplugged appliances. She remembered watching the house disappear in the side view mirror as they drove away. Like Alice and her mother, they had also run away.

"It won't be for long," Mena said, though she had no idea. "I'm sure you'll be able to come back soon."

Alice looked at her and smiled sadly.

At first Mena thought it was just the wind rapping against the kitchen window. Or it could have been the incessant hammer inside her brain. But when Alice looked toward the door, her eyes wide and terrified, Mena realized that someone was, indeed, knocking.

"It's probably just Finn and Sam," she said, reaching out for Alice's hand. She figured Sam had forgotten his key.

The knocking was louder now, rapid and furious.

"Hold on," she said, rolling her eyes and squeezing Alice's hand. She stood up and went to the door. But when she opened it, she was startled to see it wasn't Finn at all. Not Sam either, but a *girl.*

She was wearing a thin sundress, and there was blood on her face. Dirt on her knees and arms. Her glasses were scratched and sitting crooked and low on the bridge of her nose. "Can you please help me?" she said. "I just hit a dog with my car."

That fucking dog, Mena thought.

"Are you hurt?" she asked the girl, ushering her into the house and helping her sit down at the table.

The girl was visibly shaken, her eyes darting about the room. But she shook her head. "I don't think so. But we have to find the owner. The dog needs to get to a vet," she said.

"It's still *alive?*" Mena said, handing the girl a glass of water.

She drank the water in several gulps and then set the glass down on the table. She wiped her mouth with the back of her hand, like a child. "Can you give me a ride to my car?"

Mena didn't know how to convince the girl that everyone would be better off if the dog was dead.

She was wringing her hands, clearly really, really upset. She kept wiping her face, and she was trembling.

"It's okay," Mena said. "It'll be okay."

Mena didn't want to leave Alice in the house by herself, so they all piled into the station wagon. The girl sat up front to navigate, and Alice sat in the back.

Now, the girl is quiet as they make their way through the rain to where she says she hit the dog. Mena is grateful not to have to make conversation anymore. She is exhausted, and her head is still pounding. She just wants to get home and go to bed. She should have waited for Sam to get back to help her.

The windshield wipers leave muddy streaks on the windshield. The rain is coming down hard now, too fast for the wipers to keep up. They drive about a mile and then she sees a Volkswagen Bug tilted into the same ditch she dumped the wagon into.

"This it?" Mena asks.

"Yeah," the girl says. Her voice is trembling, and she keeps wringing her hands.

"It's going to be okay," Mena says. She lets the wagon idle. "Should we check to see if the dog is still alive?" she asks.

The girl looks nervous. She nods but makes no move to open the door.

"Do you want me to check?" Mena asks.

The girl nods again.

Mena opens the wagon door, and the rain hits her hard. She jogs to the Bug, which is cockeyed in the road. She can't hear anything, no animal sounds, but it's too dark to see underneath the car. She runs back to the wagon and opens the door. Finn had taken their only flashlight to camp out last night. "Do you have a flashlight in your car?"

"In the glove box," the girl says.

Mena goes to the Bug and opens the door. The car smells

terrible. She finds the flashlight in the glove box and clicks it on. The beam illuminates the inside of the car. There are candy wrappers and empty soda cans all over the floor. Dirty clothes and tissues. A banana peel and three empty strawberry baskets. The light sweeps across the mess. She sees what she thinks might be a blanket (good, she'll need a blanket to wrap up the dog if it's still alive), and she reaches under the seat to get it. But it's not a blanket. It's a towel. She yanks on the corner and pulls. Something is wrapped up inside it. She glances behind her to see if the girl is watching, but it's too dark and rainy to see. Inside the towel is a stack of papers. Some sort of manuscript. She pulls the bundle up and puts it on the seat. It's tethered together with about ten rubber bands. She shines the flashlight on the top page. In a huge bold font, it says: **SMALL SORROWS: THE LIFE AND WORK OF SAMUEL MASON, by Dale Edwards.**

Mena gasps. It's the girl. Jesus, it's that insane girl who's been writing Sam letters. It's the girl who sent those awful pictures of Franny. Mena starts to shake, the pain in her head raging. What should she do? What the fuck is this girl going to do to her? Christ, she's got to get Alice back to the house.

She can't let on that she knows who she is. She's fucking *crazy.* Mena is trembling so hard now, she is having a hard time holding on to the flashlight. She shoves the manuscript back under the seat and gets out of the Bug. She takes a deep breath. *Just act normal,* she thinks. *Think, think.*

She shines the light under the car and sees the dog. She grabs a broken tree branch from the side of the road and makes a big show of poking its body. She half expects the thing to come snarling and biting out from under the car. Nothing. It's dead.

"It's dead," Mena says to the girl.

"What?" the girl mouths. The window is up and the wind is whistling like a teakettle now. The rain is pounding the dirt road. Mena feels her clothes soaking through; her whole body is shaking.

Mena motions for the girl to roll down her window. *"It's dead,"* she says again. Then it dawns on her: the dog's owner is a *cop*. Thank God.

"We need to bring him to his owner's house."

If she can just get to the cop's house, then she can tell him what's going on. Who this girl is. She looks harmless but, Christ, she's come all the way from Arizona in this piece of shit car. What could she possibly want from them?

"Help me get him out?" Mena says, and the girl nods.

"Can I help too?" Alice asks, reaching for the door handle.

"No," Mena says, her eyes widening. "Stay in the car."

Alice raises her eyebrows and cocks her head.

"It's okay," Mena says. "I've got it."

Mena starts to suggest that the girl back the Bug up, but then worries she might try to run her over or something. She has no idea what she's capable of.

"Listen," Mena offers. "Give me your key, and I'll back the car up. Then you pull the dog out from under the passenger side tire. You'll have to be quick though, because the car might roll back into the ditch."

"Okay." The girl nods, reaching into her pocket for the key. She hands it to Mena.

Mena gets back into the Bug and turns the key in the ignition.

A male voice speaks out of the tiny speakers in the dash. *"What do you do with what's left when a life is gone? He doesn't know, and so he simply catches her. Cradles her. Carries her home."* Thunder growls angrily, and Mena freezes. This is Sam's novel. One of those Books on Tape her mother always listened to. She sees the hulking figure of the girl crouched in front of the car and thinks for a moment about ending it all here. She can almost imagine the way the tires would feel as they rolled into this girl's soft body. She shakes her head; the headache is making her crazy, illogical. And so she simply, quickly, clicks the stereo off, revs the engine and throws the car into reverse.

They manage to get the dog's body into the back of the wagon, and Mena watches the girl. "I just need to get my bag," she says, and goes to the Bug. Mena considers taking off, leaving her there, but she knows she needs to get her to the cop. Then everything will be okay. Mena watches her stuff the manuscript in a paper grocery bag. Mena doesn't say anything to Alice. She doesn't want to scare her. When the girl gets into the car again, Mena says, forcing a smile, "Ready?"

But when they get to the cop's house, the cruiser is nowhere in sight. All of the lights are out in the house. Mena's chest heaves. What is she supposed to do now?

"Ma'am, are you okay?" the girl asks.

Mena looks at her, at her round face and smudgy glasses. She studies the pale skin of her neck. Her nails are bitten to the quick, cuticles ragged and bloody. She has a pale scar that travels down one cheek and squinty brown eyes.

"What do you *want* with us?" Mena asks quietly.

The girl looks startled, but then she smiles. Her teeth are crooked, a tangled mess of yellowed bone.

Alice reaches across the seat and touches Mena's shoulder. "Mrs. Mason, are you okay? Is everything okay?"

"It's okay. Everything's going to be okay," she says.

The headache tears through her brain like lightning.

The girl looks at Mena blankly, but her eyes start to fill with tears. When she bends over, Mena thinks she's going to retrieve the manuscript she's placed on the floor, maybe insist that she give it to Sam. Demand that he authorize this "biography" or whatever the hell it is.

That's when Mena notices the tattoo. It starts at the base of the girl's neck and seems to cover the entire expanse of her back.

A lot of it is covered by her dress, but it only takes a moment to see what this lunatic has done. *This is the hour of lead . . .*

"What the fuck do you want?" Mena screams, and pounds her fists against the steering wheel.

The girl fumbles around at her feet for a minute, and when she sits up again, she is clutching a hunting knife.

"I want to talk to Sam," she says.

Finn had found the shotgun under his bed when they first got to the cabin and he hid the box with Franny's diary. He didn't think much of it. His dad shot skeet at home on the weekends sometimes. When he brought it to his father, Sam rolled it over and over in his hands. "Just like the one I had when I was a boy," he had said, smiling. Sam used to hunt pheasant with his dad, Finn's grandpa, in the woods near Gormlaith back when he was a kid. Sam had propped it up against his shoulder, peered down the sight, and aimed the gun out toward the trees. "I haven't been hunting in thirty years," he said. Finn thought it was kind of stupid to get so sentimental over a gun, but whatever floated his boat.

Now Finn gets the gun from the closet by the bedroom and runs to the kitchen where his father stashed the shells he'd removed from the gun. *What kind of idiot leaves a loaded gun under the bed?* he'd said. Finn wishes it were loaded now though, because he doesn't know the first thing about how to load the shells.

His father is outside, walking the perimeter of the house, looking for clues as to where his mom and Alice have gone.

"Should we call the police?" Finn had asked.

"Can't," his father said, shaking his head. "Not until we get rid of the plants."

Finn had almost forgotten about the plants lying in stinking piles under grass clippings and leaves. Jesus, what *was* he thinking?

His father comes into the kitchen now, soaking wet and scowling.

"Here, Dad," Finn says, handing him the gun and the shells. He feels like he has to do something, to make up for being such a shit. "I'm sorry," he says. And he is. For everything. If he hadn't been such a screwup, none of this would have happened. For one thing, they wouldn't be here. They'd be back at home in San Diego where they all belong. And if he hadn't been cultivating the garden all summer, if his dad didn't leave the house to destroy all the plants, maybe his mom and Alice wouldn't be gone now. None of this would be happening. He's a total fuckup, and he's so, so sorry.

His dad takes the gun and pulls the hood of his anorak up. "Stay here," he says. "Do not leave the house."

Finn nods.

His father slams the door shut, and Finn watches through the closed curtains as his silhouette disappears into the rain.

He feels helpless and worthless and terrified. He thinks about Franny. What would she do if she were here? She would know exactly what to say, what to do. He listens for her, waits for her to whisper the answers, the promises that everything will be okay this time. But there is nothing but the sound of the wind rattling the windows in their panes. The sound of the rain pounding like fists on the roof. He is completely alone.

He locks the door behind his father, knows he should do what his father says. For once. But if anything happens to his mother, his father will never forgive him. And if anything happens to Alice, he will never forgive himself.

Sam can barely see the road in front of him. The rain is coming down in hard sheets now, watery guillotines. The road is slick, muddy under his feet. It's hard to walk without slipping. He's carrying the shotgun, ready. If Alice's father took them in the car, chances are they're long gone now, but something is propelling him forward. His gut tells him to keep going. He cannot bear the thought that anything has happened to Mena. He cannot lose her. He will not let this happen. He's going to ask Magoo if he can borrow his Cadillac. He'll find them. He has to.

He squints against the wind and the rain, which is pounding against his jacket. He remembers the first time his dad took him hunting. It had rained then too. They'd come here, to Gormlaith, and camped out in the woods. His father had taught him how to hold the gun, how to aim, how to shoot. They'd spent an entire weekend traipsing through the wet forest. He'd shot his first pheasant that weekend. It was exhilarating. His father had patted him on the back, his large hand strong on his shoulder. Proud. Sam had never felt so proud. That night, they slept in their tent and Sam listened to the rain pelting against the canvas. The smell of the pheasant his father had cooked on the campfire, gamey and piquant, lingered in the air. Not even the rain could wash that smell away.

When he gets to Magoo's, all the lights are out, and the

Caddie is not in the driveway. *Shit.* He's probably at his daughter's house in town. Next-door, Devin's truck is not in the driveway either. Not even the Bookmobile Effie drives for the Athenaeum. He starts walking back toward the cabin, trying to figure out what to do.

The cop.

He's going to have to just suck it up and go to the cop's house. Pray he doesn't discover the mountains of grass in the barn. He turns around and starts heading back the way he came. But just as he gets back to their driveway, he sees a pair of headlights coming up the road. He squints, shielding his eyes from the glare. And then he hears the sound of the muffler. He'd know that sound anywhere. His shoulders relax. They're home. Maybe she just went out for something at Hudson's and brought Alice with her. Maybe this was all a big mistake.

Sam walks to the middle of the road in front of the cabin and waits. He peers into the windshield and raises his hand to wave. But then he catches his breath. He can see three figures through the glass. His hand tightens around the shotgun.

When the car stops just short of him, he cocks the gun. Ready. His heart is thumping in his chest, which is swollen. He feels like he might explode.

The driver's side door swings open, and Mena gets out of the car, running toward him. "Sam, do something. Quick."

Sam aims the gun at the passenger side of the woody.

"Get out of the car!" he yells.

He's got one shot. Exactly one shot.

The passenger door swings open, but the guy doesn't get out.

"Get out of the fucking car!" Sam bellows, and peers down the barrel. He releases the safety.

The figure that emerges puts its hands up.

"Jesus Christ," Sam says.

It's a girl. A pudgy girl in a sundress. Her hair is disheveled. She has a gash across her forehead. She is holding a knife in her hand.

He keeps the gun cocked.

"Who the fuck are you?" he asks. "Who the fuck is *she?*" he says to Mena.

"Didn't you get the note I left for you?" the girl says.

"What note?" Sam says.

"On your windshield," she says. "I thought you'd be expecting me."

Mena is leaning into him, but she is speechless.

"Who is she?" Finn asks. He has come out of the house now too.

"I just want to talk to you," the girl says. "To show you my work. I think if we can just talk about it, you'll see."

"What the hell is she talking about?" he asks Mena. "Who the fuck are you?" he says again to the girl.

"It's me, *silly,*" she says, smiling. *"Dale Edwards."* She lowers her arms and steps toward him awkwardly, looking as though she's about to curtsy, still clutching the knife. Her head is bleeding. It looks like she's been dragged through the mud. His grip on the gun tightens. "I'm writing your *biography,*" she says.

Dale. Dale Edwards, the woman who's been sending the letters. The one who sent those awful photos of Franny.

"I need you to leave my family alone," Sam says. Mena clings tightly to his arm.

The girl's face drops, and she scowls. She shakes her head. "I didn't do anything to your family."

"What do you want from us?" Sam asks. "Why don't you just leave us alone?"

Her eyes are wild now, and she is shivering. "Can't we just go inside?" she says.

"Are you fucking nuts?" he says, stepping toward her, aiming. He wants nothing more than to shut her up. To make her disappear.

Her lip starts to quiver and he takes a step closer.

At this, the girl's face snarls in anger. She looks like an animal. She is waving the knife wildly. "I know your secret. I know about Franny."

Hearing Franny's name come out of her mouth turns his stomach.

"You told the newspapers it was a heart attack, something wrong with her heart." When she laughs, it sounds like a gunshot. And then her smile dissolves into a frown. "I believed it. We all believed it. But it was all a bunch of lies. You're a *liar!*" she spits.

"Stop it, stop it, stop it!" Mena screams, covering her ears with her hands.

"See?" Dale says, pointing toward the car. Alice has slowly slid out of the backseat and is standing at the rear of the car. The taillights make an aura of red and gold around her. Her hair is loose around her shoulders, like a blond angel. If you didn't know better, you might think she was Franny.

"*See?*" Dale says again, accusing, crying and pointing wildly. She goes to Alice and yanks her arm, pulling her forward. She points the knife at Alice's chest, sobbing and shaking. "There's nothing wrong with her heart. *Nothing.*"

Sam raises the gun, peers down the sight.

He has one chance. One shot.

Finn is running down the rickety porch steps to the driveway before he has time to think. It feels as though he is watching this from above, with a whirling helicopter view of himself as he runs toward the girl, the one who has Alice.

"Go," he says to Alice as he knocks the girl to the ground. *"Go!"* and Alice slips away.

And then his knees are grinding into the gravel driveway as he wrestles with the girl, grabbing her fleshy wrist, twisting it until she is crying. Her skin smells like rotten strawberries. Her hair is plastered to the sides of her face, and her glasses are cracked. Her eyes dart back and forth behind the muddy lenses, and she's bitten her lip. Blood trickles down her chin.

"Don't hurt me," she says. "Please."

And suddenly, he is ten years old, on the asphalt playground pinning Joey Mendez to the pavement, bending his fingers back, prying the dollar he just stole from Franny out of his dirty hand. He can feel the tendons resisting, hear the joints cracking, and the high-pitched squeal of panic and pain coming out of that little shit Mendez's mouth. It makes him hate him even more; his weakness makes him nauseous. Palm trees swaying above him and salt in his eyes.

The rain makes the girl's skin slippery as he pries the knife out of her hand. She is sitting up now, scooching backward on her ass away from him. She holds her hands in front of her face, as if to protect herself from him. As if he's the crazy one. When he steps back, she smiles at him.

And then Joey Mendez stands up, shaking the pain free from his hand, flipping Finn off with his perfectly undamaged middle finger. Pussy, he says as he starts to walk away, and then Finn is on him again, knocking him to the ground and raising his fist, ready to hit the smile right off his face.

He feels the knife's weight and heft in his fist, and he imagines plunging it right into her heaving chest. He could kill her. He raises the knife now, ready to strike.

But now Franny is saying, Stop, Finny. That's enough.

And Alice is saying, "Stop, Finn. Please."

And then there is a sound louder than thunder, so loud and close, it startles the knife right out of his hand. Gravel and dust fly up into the air, and then the girl is running.

She runs. She hasn't run this hard or fast since she was a little girl. She thinks she could run all the way back home. Her legs are moving so fast. Her heart is pumping blood furiously through her body. She could be an animal out here, she is suddenly so quick and sure-footed. Fast. She feels graceful and light.

The rain has soaked through her dress, and her hair is plastered to her face. Rain runs into her eyes, pools in her open mouth.

None of this is what she expected, what she wanted.

She can hear Sam coming behind her, and part of her hopes he'll just shoot again. The first shot hit the ground next to her. But now, she hopes that he'll aim that awful gun at her heart or head and end this. She thinks of deer, of rabbits. She imagines herself being hunted. And she runs.

It doesn't take long before she loses feeling in her legs, and fears that the earth has fallen out from underneath her. It doesn't take long before Sam catches up to her. She glances over her shoulder at him. He doesn't have the gun anymore. He is alone. And he is calling her name. "Dale?" he says.

Her eyes sting with tears.

"Please stop."

Her legs and feet are completely numb. But when her ankle twists, and the crack rings out like a gunshot, all sensation returns. She screams out, collapses onto the wet ground, and clutches her ankle, which feels like it has gotten caught in a steel trap.

"It's okay," Sam says. "It's okay." He is kneeling down next to her on the ground now. "It's okay. No one is going to hurt you."

And then he is offering her his hand, helping her up. Tears burn in her eyes, and when her wounded foot makes contact with the ground, pain sears through her entire body. She cries out again.

"Here," he says, offering her his shoulder. "Let's get you to the hospital."

His arms are strong, and he smells like pine trees. Like wood smoke and cinnamon. She breathes him in as they hobble back the way they came.

"I only wanted to talk to you," she says, tears streaming down her face. "I just wanted to meet you in person. You have no idea what your work means to me. What your words mean to me."

She leans into him, and he holds her up. Steadies and supports her.

She knows that the police will be waiting there for her. She knows they'll take her away. She knows that there will be doctors again, pills. She knows that soon she'll be back inside that house in Phoenix with her mother, stuck again, working at the Blockbuster and trying to finish the stupid paper on Shelley. But none of it matters now, as Sam holds her up and they walk through the rain toward the warm light of his home. *What do you do with what's left when a life is gone?* Nothing matters but his arm across her shoulder. She in her yellow summer dress. She looks up at him, smiling as he helps her. *Cradles her, carries her home.*

"Thank you," she says. And when he looks down at her, she can see something close to love in his eyes.

Mena is worried about Sam, but she needs to keep it together for the kids. She sends Finn inside to call the police, and Alice stays outside with her on the porch. She is shivering.

"Hold on, sweetie," Mena says to Alice, and goes into the cabin to find a sweater. She grabs a soft gray cardigan from the chair in the kitchen and goes outside again, wrapping the sweater around Alice's shoulders.

"Thank you," Alice says, pulling the long sleeves around her. Mena touches her soft blond hair, brushing it out of her eyes. And that single gesture brings to the surface all of the grief, all of that aching awful loneliness she's been carrying in her bones for the past nine months. She needs to sit down; she worries if she doesn't her spine might simply crumble, one vertebra after another, like dominoes.

They sit together on the steps, knees touching. Mena puts her arm across Alice's shoulder and pulls her in tight. "You okay?" Mena asks.

"You guys saved my *life*," Alice says. "That was crazy."

Mena looks at Alice's eyes, wide and young and hopeful, and thinks about Franny.

That's what it is. It isn't her face, or her mane of blond hair. It isn't her smile, her nose, her hands. It's not even her eyes, but rather something inside them. *Hope.* That's why Alice reminds Mena of Franny. It's the light. The light that was there in Franny's eyes even when she was so sick. If there had been darkness, maybe if that light had gone out, she would have known something was terribly wrong and she could have helped her. But Franny was always so hopeful. Always so *brilliant.*

"The police are on their way," Finn says as he comes out of the house.

Mena looks out at the gravel driveway, at the car with its doors still wide open, the headlights still on. The girl, *Dale,* dropped the manuscript during the scuffle with Finn. Mena leaves Alice on the steps and goes to pick it up. It is wet, the pages bloated and soaked. Mena thumbs through the pages. The ink runs together rendering everything, *The Life and Work of Samuel Mason*, a shivery blur.

"What is that?" Finn asks.

"It's trash," she says.

She knows there are some trash barrels in the barn. She saw Sam filling them with grass clippings earlier. She leaves Finn and Alice and walks to the barn. It is dark in here. Quiet. She looks up at the basketball hoop, down at the dusty floor. She takes the manuscript and tosses it into one of the barrels, which she drags outside. She reaches into the pocket of her sweater and finds the book of matches she remembers putting there. Jake's book of matches. God, what the hell was she thinking?

The rain has stopped. She soaks the clippings with some lighter fluid she found in the barn and strikes a match. There is a whoosh and then hot flames. The manuscript turns black within moments, and then the grass begins to burn.

She can see the lights of the police car twirling in the driveway, illuminating the trees, the cabin, and the sky in flashes of red and blue. The cop from down the road is talking to Sam, jotting something down on a clipboard. And the girl is sitting in the backseat of the cruiser, staring straight ahead. Smiling.

"What's that smoke?" the cop asks Mena. "Something on fire?"

"Just some clippings," she says. "Some trash."

"You know you gotta have a permit to burn," he says, scowling. "From the fire warden. You got a permit?"

"I'll put it out. I didn't know I needed a permit," Sam says. He looks nervous. He's running his hands through his hair over and over again.

"Maybe I better help you. That looks like it's burning real good."

"Don't you think you should get her to the hospital?" Sam says. "I'm pretty sure she's got a broken ankle."

"It can wait. You don't want that barn to go up with it." The cop shuts the door to the cruiser, locks the girl inside.

Suddenly a scratchy voice booms from the radio on the cop's belt. "Eddie? We got a break-in up at Gormlaith. You up there? Got a unit on it already, but they could use some help. Some guy just out of the joint looking for his ex. He tore the place up, tore himself up too."

Alice lets out a small cry. *"My dad."*

The cop speaks into the receiver on his shoulder. "What's the location?"

And then he's jumping into the car. He rolls down the window, and says to Sam, "I'll need you to come down to the station later and give a statement."

Mena goes to Alice, who is still sitting on the steps, her head in her hands. Mena sits down next to her and puts her arm around her shoulder again. And this time, the grief and aching are gone. Now, all that's left is that old familiar tenderness. "It's okay, sweetie. Everything's going to be okay."

"I hope so. I really can't take much more tonight," Alice says, shaking her head and smiling weakly. "I mean, seriously."

Finn sits on the other side of Alice, and they watch as Sam walks to the barn. The air is thick and sweet with smoke. And soon, more smoke billows out from behind the barn. The smell is rich. Earthy and familiar. The smoke curls up into the sky, and only then does Mena recognize the smell of marijuana.

The day that Franny died, wildfires were raging through Southern California. In San Diego, the fires had leapt across the freeways. Runaway flames, blazing and destroying everything in their path, eluded helicopters and firefighters, raged across the mountains in the east and through developments in the west. Million-dollar homes and double-wide trailers were going up in smoke. Indiscriminate destruction. Horses and cattle and lost dogs were dying. Everyone was fleeing.

When Sam woke up that morning, it looked like twilight. The entire sky was filled with an orange haze. Like sunset at 6:00 A.M. When he walked out onto their back deck, and into what looked like snow, it was as though he'd stepped through a looking glass into an upside-down world. Where day was night and sand was snow. He'd never seen anything like it before. It was as though he were dreaming. It was like an apocalypse. Like the end of the world.

He remembers the silence. Outside, the thick marine layer hung suspended in limbo between sand and sky. The ash-covered beach was deserted. Finn was the only one out on the water, a black speck in a sea of white. Living directly under the flight path for almost twenty years, the sounds of the planes had become a part of the orchestra of their lives. But it was early, and the sky was empty save for the helicopters with their whispery hum. He should have known then that it wasn't just their world that was collapsing. It's the quiet he remembers.

It was so early. Even Mena, who usually woke up before dawn, was still asleep. In the kitchen, the old percolator Mena loved wasn't bubbling, and the radio they kept on the counter was silent. Sam was about to start the coffee himself, turn on the radio and find out exactly what was going on, when he saw her.

She was lying on the floor between the kitchen and the living room, curled up in her pajamas as though she were just taking a nap. And everything went numb. Cold.

Shit, shit, shit.

Sam ran to her and picked her up. As he lifted her, he recollected the way she used to feel in his arms when she was a little girl. Light. Small. She felt like a tiny little bundle of bones as he carried her to the living room and gently laid her on the couch. He watched his hands grab her sharp shoulders, shaking her. Felt his mouth moving, even heard the words coming out. And then he was pressing his ear against her chest, the way he had a hundred times, to listen for her heart. *God, her heart.* It's the quiet he remembers.

Sam pulled Franny's body close to him, clutching her in an unanswered embrace. Mena stood in the doorway, bleary eyed and confused.

"Mena, stay with her. I'll call 9-1-1," Sam said.

Finn came into the room then, a wet black seal, dripping salt water onto the floor. "Jesus, goddamn Christ," Finn said. "What's going on?"

And then soundlessly, Mena dropped to her knees, her whole body trembling. She crawled across the floor, like an animal, and climbed onto the couch, curling around Franny's body, making a cocoon of arms and legs and falling hair. Sam opened his mouth to say something, to cry out, but the words, the sounds, would not come.

He went to the kitchen and called 9-1-1, but because of the fires, the woman misunderstood. She kept asking him if Franny was suffering from smoke inhalation. She kept telling him how important it was that they evacuate. Finally, he made her understand that there was no fire. That his daughter, his child's heart had just stopped beating.

When he returned to the living room, Mena was still curled around Franny. Finn sat on the floor next to the couch, holding the unyielding bones of her hand. Afterward, Finn stood up and sat down in the chair facing them. His whole body shuddered, and he put his head in his hands. Sam wanted to go to him, to hold him, but he couldn't move.

It wasn't until later, after the ambulance came, after they went to the hospital, after they left Franny there and returned to the house without her (as if they had simply dropped her off at a friend's, at the mall, or at ballet practice), after somebody finally turned on the radio, that they heard the news that the county was on fire.

There was so much confusion. On TV, it seemed that the entire world was grieving. It was maddening. All of a sudden their devastation was made small, not even a fragment of this much larger catastrophe. But what did those people, covered in ash and embers, have to do with Franny? What did any of this have to do with the infant Sam once carried on his back all the way down into the Grand Canyon, the little girl he taught how to play Chinese checkers and how to swim? What did this have to do with the milky smell of her skin, the small constellation of freckles across her nose, the baby teeth Mena still kept in a jar? These televised images of anguish, this pixilated misery, had nothing to do with their dead child.

Finally, Finn yanked the cord out of the wall and picked up the TV, struggling as he made his way out the French doors to the patio. Mena and Sam stood together, not touching, but both watching as he trudged through the smoky haze and ashy sand down the wooden stairs to the water's edge. Mena leaned into Sam, still trembling, and they watched together as Finn hurled the TV into the waves.

Sam knows it's just a terrible coincidence. But still, Franny was always like that. Modest. Unassuming. She'd be happy to think that their sadness might be obliterated by this history. That they might one day confuse their sorrow with the sorrow of that day. And in a way, she would be right. In the immediate aftermath, Sam started to think that if he could figure out that tragedy he might be able to solve the mystery of their own. If he could figure out how the fire started, how it spread, like an illness, like a virus, then maybe he could understand what had happened to Franny.

It is almost dawn, and the lingering smell of burnt weed hovers in the air like a dream. His mom and dad have gone into town to the police station to give their statements. His mother is pissed about the weed, but she's got bigger shit to deal with. For now anyway.

Alice's mom is on her way to come get her. Her dad is back in jail, and she and her mom suddenly don't have to go anywhere anymore. He and Alice sit on the grassy lawn by the cabin, facing the lake.

"You okay?" Finn asks.

Alice is pale; her eyes look tired. She nods. She turns to him. "You?"

Finn nods and smiles. "That was fucking crazy," he says. And then the absurdity of it strikes him, the insanity of all of this. He laughs. It's one of those laughs you can't control. A laugh so deep inside your gut, it's like it's a living, breathing thing.

Alice snorts, and this makes Finn laugh louder.

Soon, they are both laughing and the loons on the lake are cackling back. Finn's side hurts from the effort, and he grabs at it. She snorts again.

"Stop," he says. "God, you gotta stop."

When they catch their breath, Alice leans into Finn, burying her head in his chest. It makes his knees go soft. His head swimmy. He looks down at her, and she looks up at him. He kisses her, softly on the forehead, on the nose, and on each eyelid. Then he kisses her mouth. Presses his whole body into hers. He kisses her and kisses her and kisses her. He kisses her until the mist over the water has lifted, until the sun is hot and warm on their tangled legs. He kisses her until her mother pulls into the driveway, and then they both scramble up the grassy slope, breathless and holding hands and happy.

"I'll call you later," she says.

"Promise?" he says.

She smiles and jumps up to kiss him on the nose. "Yep."

He watches the car disappear down the road and then he goes into the cabin and crawls into his bed. Within moments he is fast asleep.

They don't press charges against the girl. She's clearly very ill. Deluded. She has no history of violence. Sam felt sorry for her. A tenderness even. It's crazy, he knows. But there was something about her that pulled at his heart. That desperation, that wanting. For something so ridiculously simple. She just wanted to meet him, she said. She just wanted to be able to talk to him about his work. He saved her life, she said. His *words* saved her.

The police called her mother, who explained her history and who would arrange for her to be flown home. There's a restraining order protecting them, but they hardly need it. She's in the hospital, in the psych ward, and besides, her ankle is smashed to smithereens.

As they drive back from the police station at dawn, Mena leans into Sam's shoulder. He kisses the top of her head. The scent of her hair makes his shoulders relax. He can feel her breath growing shallow, her body letting go. How many trips have they taken in this car? How many times have they sat this way: her head resting on his shoulder, the road unwinding in front of them? The kids in the backseat. The windows rolled down. How many miles have they gone?

He is almost looking forward to the drive back to California. Maybe they can take a different route this time: go through Memphis. Maybe they could go even as far south as the Gulf

Coast, let Finn use that damn surfboard he dragged all the way out here. Hell, if they have time, they could see the whole damn country.

There's a weird smell in the car. He can't quite place it. He wonders if one of the windows was left down during the storm. He takes a deep breath. It's a strong, wet smell.

Mena lifts her head up and squints at the sun, which is bright through the windshield.

"What's that smell?" Sam asks.

"Hmm?" Mena asks, her voice like a hum.

"It smells bad," he says. "Almost like a wet dog."

Mena jerks awake. "Oh, *shit*," she says.

"What's the matter?" Sam asks.

"It *is* dog. There's a dead dog in the back of the car."

"*What?*" Sam says, peering into the rearview mirror. He can't see anything except the muddy window behind him.

"That stupid dog. The one that chases cars? The one that belongs to the cop?"

"It's in the back of our car?" Sam asks, incredulous.

Mena covers her mouth with her hand and starts to laugh. "Oh, God, it's not funny." But she is laughing.

And he is laughing too.

"It really stinks," Mena says, trying hard not to erupt into a fit of giggles.

Sam pulls his T-shirt up over his nose and mouth and rolls down the window. Mena rolls hers down too.

They both lean their heads toward the fresh air outside. And their laughter carries on the wind, winding through the trees, rising up into the blue, blue sky of this new morning.

Mena peers out at the audience after the performance, locates Sam and Finn in the middle row. As she and Jake and Oscar all bow, the entire room erupts into applause. Jake squeezes her hand, and she smiles at him. Her chest swells with an old feeling. *Pride.* They did a terrific job. Lisa is in the wings, clapping her hands wildly.

After the lights are on, and she's changed out of May's red dress in the makeshift dressing room, she goes out to find her family in the crowd of people lingering on. Sam is holding a bunch of black-eyed Susans. Her favorite.

He hands them to her and leans into her, whispering, "You were amazing."

"Good job, Mom," Finn says. He's been extra good, extra nice, ever since she found out about the weed, but she senses he means it.

Alice smiles at her and says, "That was awesome."

Effie and Devin are there too, but they have to get back to the sitter.

"We'll call you tomorrow," Effie says, hugging her.

Monty has come up from New York for opening night too, leaving his wife behind this time. He's got a room at the motel in town. He kisses her cheek and says, "Wow, Mena. I had no idea you were so good. Maybe you and Sammy should move to New York so you can get back into acting."

"No thank you," Mena says. "I'm ready to go home."

And she is. So ready. She is actually thinking she might try to do some more acting when she gets there. She's got some friends who run a small theater downtown. Maybe she'll audition for one of their shows. Maybe just a small part.

They turned down the offer on their house. Told Hilary they had no intention of getting rid of the bungalow. Sam said he must have been crazy to even consider it. Already Mena is fantasizing about what she'll be able to cook once she has her own stove back, her own copper pots and pans. Fresh produce from the Farmers' Market on Newport Avenue on Wednesdays. The Greek market. An oven that actually heats up to the correct temperature.

"Are you coming to the cast party?" Oscar asks. His wife is with him, and she is clinging to his arm. Her hair is like a puff of pale yellow cotton candy.

"No," Mena says. "I'm exhausted. Maybe on closing night. But tonight I just want to get home. Have a glass of champagne for me."

"Is it still okay if I go hang out at Alice's for a bit tonight?" Finn asks as they make their way out of the Town Hall.

"Fine," Sam says. "Be back by midnight though, okay?"

"One?"

"Okay, one."

Finn nods and holds his fingers up. "Scout's honor."

"That doesn't mean anything if you were never a Boy Scout," Sam says.

"What time is it now?" Finn asks.

Mena glances at her watch. "It's only nine-thirty. You've got some time."

They drop off Finn at Alice's house. Mena is glad her mother is home tonight. "One o'clock," she warns. "That means you're home by one, not leaving at one."

Sam had sat her down and explained the whole horticultural experiment of Finn's. She was livid at first, but she also thought about the mistakes she'd made. Or almost made. She was tired of pointing fingers. She was just tired of being angry. She also had a feeling she didn't need to worry about him so much anymore.

She *is* worried, however, about what will happen when they have to leave Alice behind next week. This is the first time in so long that she's seen Finn happy. He's head over heels for this girl. He's already asked if they can come back to the lake next summer. He's trying to figure out how Alice can come see him at Christmas.

When they pull up to their cabin, Sam lets the engine idle and turns to her. "I'm proud of you," he says. "I'd forgotten what it's like to watch you on the stage."

Mena brushes the air in front of her face. "Shush."

"You're so beautiful," he says.

She's about to swat this compliment away too, but he grabs her hand before she can. And he kisses her. She stops breathing as their lips touch. This moment is like a million other moments, but completely different. Familiar and entirely strange at the same time.

And then he is helping her out of the car, unlocking the cabin door and guiding her inside.

Inside, he takes the bouquet of flowers from her hands and sets them on the counter. And he pulls her close to him, pressing his whole body into hers, his arms wrapped around her, clinging to her. And then he is kissing her neck, moving his hands along her body's lines, unbuttoning her blouse, his fingers remembering these buttons, nimble and quick. Intent. Her whole body shivers.

He slips the blouse over her head, dropping it to the floor, and presses his head against her chest, listens to her heart, to its frenetic flip-flop. And then he releases the clasp on her bra and she feels the air on her skin, feels his breath on her skin.

"Sammy," she says, and it comes out like a breathy moan.

He shakes his head.

They are alone. And he wants her, wants her.

She pulls his sweater over his head, tears at his buttons, can't get to his skin fast enough. Their clothes fall to the floor. They walk, move, naked together toward the table.

"Wait," she said. "This probably isn't smart."

"What?" he says, breathless.

"This table," she says. "It won't hold us."

He laughs and he lifts her up, cradling her bottom with both hands, her legs wrapped around him as he carries her to the living room. They don't make it to the bedroom. He backs her up to the blue piano, and when her butt comes down on the keys, the noise makes her laugh. He lifts her back up, pulls her toward him with one hand and lowers the lid with his free hand, and then her back is against the piano.

She reaches around him, grabs the strong muscles of his rear end and pulls him toward her. The hard certainty of him startles her.

She opens her eyes and looks into his as if to ask, "You sure?"

It's been so long, it actually hurts. Her eyes sting and she holds on to him, digs into his back as if he were a ball of clay instead of a man.

He whispers into her neck, all those old words. All the best words.

I love you, I loveyou, iloveyou until it is only one word. Until it is the same as breathing.

B efore dawn, Sam leaves Mena in the bed sleeping, naked and beautiful under the covers. He climbs quietly up the ladder into the loft and opens the laptop. And the words are suddenly there again. At his fingertips, spilling, filling the pages. He writes for hours, until his wrists ache with the effort.

When someone has suffered from starvation, bringing them back to health is not as simple as giving them a plate full of food, a fork, a knife. Rehabilitation must come slowly, carefully, so as not to shock the body. Refeeding is an art, the delicate balance of what a body wants and what a body can stand.

Sam closes his eyes, watches as Billy stands in line outside Shevlin Hall. He feels the way his tongue runs over his lips at the smell of bacon that emanates through the closed doors. It is summer, and the sun is warm. He is not the same man who came to this campus last November. He is a shadow of that man, a husk. But he is alive. Still, remarkably, and though he knows that the smells are likely deceiving, that they won't, *can't,* simply allow the volunteers to gorge themselves, he savors the remembrance of other breakfasts. He closes his eyes, feels the warm sun on his eyelids, and dreams the smell of bacon, the sweet acidity of juice, the buttery warmth of fresh biscuits.

Downstairs, Mena is making breakfast. He can hear the shuffle of her feet, the soft hum as she cracks eggs into a bowl, whisks them with sweet buttermilk and cinnamon. As she cooks, he writes, and he watches his fingers in amazement as they tap, tap, tap at the keys.

Finally, Mena calls up to him, "Breakfast!" And he is so hungry.

By the time Finn got home from Alice's house that night, everyone was asleep. His parents hadn't bothered to wait up for him like he expected. No one was there yelling at him about being ten minutes late. He'd even let the door slam shut, waiting for the light to come on. But nothing. He'd crawled into bed and fallen asleep smiling.

Now he wakes up to the sounds of the percolator, the smells of coffee and bacon. To the shuffle, shuffle of his dad's slippers and their hushed voices, quiet so as not to wake him.

When he goes into the kitchen, his mom and dad are already sitting at the table, eating. His mother's face is flushed pink, her hair messy. His father squeezes his mom's hand and they say, together, "Morning."

He plops himself down in a chair and his mother says, "Want some coffee, Finn?"

They never let him drink coffee.

He nods and she gets up, pouring the hot liquid into a chipped mug. "Sugar?" she asks.

He shakes his head and takes a long sip from his cup. The coffee is hot and bitter, and it warms him up from the inside out. And suddenly, he is overwhelmed by everything. By the fractured recollections of that crazy night, by thoughts of Alice, by the sheer stupid nostalgia he's starting to feel about this cabin.

But most of all by the fact that *this* is all he wanted. Really. That simple gesture of pouring him a cup of coffee nearly brings tears to his eyes. All this time, he'd just wanted them both to somehow accept that he isn't the same person anymore. That he isn't their baby. He isn't a kid. He isn't carefree or careless anymore. He isn't *Finny;* he isn't half of a whole. He is just Finn. Almost seventeen years old. More man than boy. Part of this family, but also almost grown.

He holds out his empty cup to his mom, and she fills it again.

"Let's go out to the island this afternoon," his father says to them both. "Just the three of us. Have a picnic. Take a dip."

Finn says, "Yeah. Let's do that. It's going to be like eighty degrees today."

After breakfast, Finn goes to his room and grabs the surfboard, angling it out of the narrow doorway, through the house, and outside. At the water's edge, he strips down to his boxers and steps into the water. And then he is gliding, paddling out across the still water on his board. The air is getting warmer, but the water is still chilly. It is like skimming across glass. He is the only interruption in all this stillness.

When he gets to the center of the lake, he stops paddling and climbs onto his board, straddling it, holding on tight. There are two loons swimming near him. They aren't even afraid of humans, it seems. He wonders what happened to the baby. It's almost the end of summer; he guesses it must be all grown up.

Back at the house, his mom has already started packing. She's ready to go home, she says. Ready. He wonders what it's going to be like to go back to California. But as much as he misses it, part of him wishes they could just stay here. That he could just be here, with Alice, forever. His father has promised that they will come again next summer. And he's got some money saved; maybe he can fly her out to see him during winter break. He tries not to consider the distance between them as he dips his hands into the cool water.

"Tell me a joke," he says to Franny. "Make me laugh."

The ocean is calm today, no swells in sight.

"Knock, knock," she says.

"Who's there?"

"Finn."

"Finn who?" he asks. She is next to him on her board, her hair wet, her eyes sparkling in the light.

"Finn-ish up already and open the door!" she says, throwing her head back, laughing. "Get it?!"

"Ha, ha," he says, rolling his eyes.

They both look behind them toward the endless expanse of water, but the sea is still. No waves. Just calm, calm water.

He lies back down on the board, puts his hands in the water, and starts to paddle back to shore.

Now.

H ere they are now:

Late summer evening: Mena and Alice are in the kitchen of their cottage. Mena is showing Alice how to make bread. Sam watches them through the window from his Adirondack chair in the yard. They are laughing, their voices soft behind the glass. Mena catches him watching her and cocks her head. Smiles shyly. He almost turns away, wondering how long he's been staring, but instead nods back at her, grins.

The air smells like autumn, the smoky musky scent of fall. Already, the air has gotten colder. Today when he and Mena went for a walk around the lake, he saw the first maple yielding to the approaching season: red leaves like a crimson splatter among all that green.

Effie and Devin arrive with Zu-Zu, who runs up to Sam with a plastic container full of cookies. "Tookies," she says to him, thrusting the container into his hands.

"Are these for *me?*" he asks.

She nods her head and squeals, delighted. He takes the cookies from her, and she climbs up into his lap. He opens the container and offers one to her, takes one himself. She leans back against his chest, makes herself at home, and looks out at the water with him, nibbling.

"Don't let her have any more before dinner," Effie says to

Sam. "No more," she coos to Zu-Zu. "Sam, we brought wine too. Is Mena inside?"

"She's in there with Alice," he says, and Effie and Devin disappear into the house.

"Finn?" Zu-Zu asks.

"He's just down there," Sam says, pointing to the shore.

Finn is down at the water's edge, ankle deep in the lake, his naked chest glowing in the half-light. He skips stones across the water, one after the other. He's gotten so tall this summer; he's taller than Sam now. His shoulders have broadened. His hair has grown. His arm is strong, and the stones skim the surface, weightless.

Sam is thinking, of course, about the words that might capture this: the feeling of one child breathing against his chest, while another disappears into the shadows. For the eager moonlight that appears before the sun has even fully set. For summer's quiet acquiescence to fall. For that place between today and tomorrow. The words escape him for now, elusive, but it doesn't matter. Zu-Zu breathes against him. His son walks in and out of light. Summer comes to an end. Tomorrow they go home.

Time to eat, Mena says.

They all sit at the picnic table. Mena lights candles. In the flickering light, Sam watches her. Wants her. He remembers the way her skin felt against his. The warmth of her stomach, her hands, the heat of her breasts.

He pours wine into glasses. Effie lowers Zu-Zu into Devin's lap. Alice and Finn lean into one another. Mena sits down, sighing, smiling. And they eat.

Their voices, tinkling like glass, echo off the still water. It is the end of the summer, dusk, and the lake is theirs. Twilight, and everything is possible.

After dinner, the wine is gone. Finn and Alice disappear into the shadows together. Devin and Effie take Zu-Zu home. They clear the table, and Sam pulls Mena by the hand to the chairs that face the water. He sits down, and she curls up on his lap. It is chilly now that the sun has set. He wraps his arms around her.

The coffee she has made is hot and sweet. The cup sits steaming on the armrest of the chair.

There must be a word for this, he thinks. It is on the tip of his tongue. He struggles, but it still won't come.

"It's not the same," Mena says.

"No," he agrees.

She looks out at the water, at the sun slipping into the horizon.

"I really miss her," she says.

"I miss her too."

Mena leans her head back, into his chest, and he puts his fingers in her hair. She breathes deeply. Soon, their chests rise and fall together, their heartbeats separate but similar. They are somewhere between wakefulness and sleep. Between *then* and *later.* Between *was* and *will be.*

"Tora," Mena whispers as her eyes flutter closed. *Tora, tora, tora,* beats her heart.

Sam closes his eyes too,

tora, tora, tora

concentrates on the steady rhythm, on the contented and certain thrum of

now, now, now.

A Note from the Author

This novel began with Franny. In my mind she appeared first as a six-year-old child, swinging on a tire swing on a late summer evening. She was vivid and bright, as luminous in my mind as if she were real. Over time, she grew into a young woman in my imagination: a daughter, a sister, a talented dancer. And then she disappeared.

Studies have shown that approximately 15 percent of all young women suffer from some form of eating disorder, and that one out of one hundred girls between the ages of ten and twenty suffer from anorexia. According to the American Anorexia/Bulimia Association, one thousand girls in the United States die every year from this disease. In my own life I have watched countless friends, family members and students struggle with their relationship with food and with their bodies. This obsession is pervasive, it seems—even inescapable—in our culture.

I began to think about hunger then, about the most primitive and essential desire we as humans have. I read Sharman Apt Russell's fascinating book, *Hunger: An Unnatural History,* in which she examines the ways in which hunger affects the global population. Hunger is, at the most basic level, the body's reminder that we must eat. It is a physiological alarm clock that tells us our body needs fuel. Hunger is a potent force. It is, perhaps, the most formidable need. For people deprived of necessary sustenance, hunger is suffering. Conversely, for some, it can be a source of power.

I read a lot of books about eating disorders, including the incredibly visceral and honest *Wasted,* by Marya Hornbacher, and the heartbreaking memoir *Andrea's Voice,* by Doris Smeltzer and her daughter Andrea Lynn Smeltzer, who died as a result of her struggle with bulimia. I read the seminal *Fasting Girls: The*

History of Anorexia Nervosa, by Joan Jacobs Brumberg. I also spent hours searching Web sites, including the more subversive (and now often disguised and difficult to find) pro-Ana/Mia (pro-anorexia and pro-bulimia) sites.

What I learned in my research is that this flirtation with hunger has a long history: from the fasting saints in the Middle Ages to the Victorian "Fasting Girls" who achieved celebrity status via their self-denial. From hunger artists whose starvation was a public spectacle to the girls who flaunt their concave bellies and razor-sharp spines on the Web today. I came to understand that this love affair with hunger is irresistible to some, despite its often lethal consequences.

When Franny dies, she leaves behind a family grappling to understand what happened to her. This novel begins with Franny, but it ends with those she left behind. For the Mason family, the end to their hungry season comes only when they are ready to begin nourishing themselves and one another again. My hope is that this story will not only honor those who have lost their lives to this horrific disease, but will also feed the souls of those who love them and those who continue in their struggle to survive.

THE HUNGRY SEASON

T. Greenwood

ABOUT THIS GUIDE

The following questions are intended to
enhance your group's reading of
THE HUNGRY SEASON.

Discussion Questions

1. Discuss the role that hunger plays in this novel. Of what significance is the title? How does it relate to the Mason family and their summer spent on the lake?

2. As Sam struggles to overcome writer's block, he creates Billy, a fictional character involved in Ancel Keys's "Great Starvation Experiment" conducted during World War II, which was designed to study the effects of starvation and the most effective methods of refeeding a starved population. How does Sam relate to Billy? What does this suggest about the creative process?

3. How does Sam's struggle with writer's block relate to his sexual impotence?

4. What is Mena's role in this family, and how does it change with Franny's death? Explore her relationship with Sam and her attraction to Jake. What does she need in order to heal?

5. How does Mena and Sam's marriage compare to the other marriages in the novel? How are they the same as or different from Effie and Devin and Monty and Lauren? What can they learn from both couples?

6. Discuss the role of food in this novel.

7. Saving Finn from self-destruction is the supposed reason that Sam moves his family to Vermont for the summer. Do you think that Finn needs saving? Why or why not? Do you think they could have arrived at the same place if they had stayed in California?

8. Alice is, in many ways, a surrogate for Franny. Do you think that the Masons get a second chance with Alice? Discuss Finn's relationship with both Franny and Alice.

9. Finn claims to smoke pot to help him sleep at night. Do you believe that's the real reason? Is he smoking as a way to deal with Franny's death, or as normal teenage rebellion? If he hadn't turned to marijuana to cope, would Sam have still moved the family to Lake Gormlaith?

10. Dale Edwards is, for all intents and purposes, *stalking* Sam. What is driving her? What does she hope to get from Sam? What is *she* hungry for? Does she get the nourishment she needs?

11. At the center of the novel is Franny, though she has already died by the time the novel opens. What do you know about Franny? How do you explain what happened to her, given her family background? Is her family culpable in her death? And are they able, in the end, to forgive themselves and one another?

12. Do you think that Mena and Sam chose to let Franny pursue her dreams at whatever cost? Were they better or worse parents for not getting in the way of her ambitions? Was there a point where they should have?

13. If you were a member of the Mason family, how would you have dealt with Franny's eating disorder? Do you think you would have noticed it before it was too late? Have you known anyone with an eating disorder? Discuss how it informed your reading of *The Hungry Season*.

14. How do you feel about Dale? How do Sam and Mena feel about her, after everything that happened? What did they learn from her? What was her role in their grieving process and their reunion?

15. Have you read or seen a production of *Fool for Love*, the Sam Shepard play in which Mena stars? Does the onstage relationship between Eddie and May mirror Sam and Mena's? How does Mena's participation in the play influence her marriage?

16. Consider all of the characters separately: Sam, Mena, Finn, Alice, and Dale. With whom do you most identify? Why?